UNREPENTANT LOVER

Just one taste. That's all he wanted. One taste and he could leave the ranch a happy man.

He closed his eyes and his lips touched hers. Ah, she tasted sweet. He could feel her mouth move under his and then she put her arms around his neck. She moaned softly and he pulled her closer. When he felt her press herself still closer to him, he cupped her buttocks and drew her up hard against him.

His lips were moving over her cheeks now, down her neck. God, he wanted her. His body already knew what to do, had done it before with this woman. He had to have her again.

"Oh, Justin!" She broke away from his kiss, gasping for breath.

He closed his eyes and put his head back. She was married. Another man's wife. What he wanted was against God's laws. But his throbbing body cared little about any spiritual concerns.

MONTANA Angel

THERESA SCOTT

LEISURE BOOKS NEW YORK CITY

This book is dedicated with love to Sandy Webster-Worthy and David Worthy and their son, Calum. You've been stalwart friends to us through the good times and the bad times. May there always be far more good times with you!

A LEISURE BOOK®

June 1998

Published by

Dorchester Publishing Co., Inc.
276 Fifth Avenue
New York, NY 10001

Copyright © 1998 by Theresa Scott

ISBN 0-8439-4392-0

The name "Leisure Books" and the stylized "L" with design are trademarks of Dorchester Publishing Co., Inc.

Printed in the United States of America.

With special thanks for technical consulting to:

Gordon Bakken, PhD, Frontier Law, History Department, California State University at Fullerton, CA;

Christopher Johnson, PA/SA, Medical, Olympia, WA;

Sara Steel, Director of Information, Consultant, Office of Archaeology and Historic Preservation, Olympia, WA.

Prologue

Southern Montana Territory
March 9, 1865

How am I going to tell him? wondered Amberson Hawley. She forced her trembling lips to smile as the handsome cavalry officer dismounted from his large bay gelding and strode toward her through the thick, short grass.

Of course, Mama and Papa will be upset when they find out, but I can get Justin to marry me. I know I can!

Justin Harbinger looked more than handsome in Union blue. He looked superb. His broad shoulders filled out his lieutenant's uniform admirably, as did his long legs. She loved the small cleft in his chin, his square jaw, his dark brown hair, and the light in his green eyes whenever he looked at her. Now she knew why some women swooned at the sight of a man. Justin Harbinger could set her swooning at any time. And she loved him.

"Miss Amberson," he said, as he reached her. His deep voice sent shivers down her spine. "I have some news."

Amberson smiled in welcome. She'd pestered her father all morning to allow her to ride over to the field where Justin's company was camped. Finally, after she'd shed many false tears, Papa had consented.

"I was about to ride over to your campsite to see you," she said. "Papa gave his permission for me to say hello."

Justin glanced over to where her parents and friends sat at the campfire, drinking coffee. Ten wagons were pulled in a circle. Horses and oxen munched grass nearby. Amberson's family was wealthy, and it showed in the number of wagons and the fine horseflesh picketed in the field.

"Please, give my regards to your father," he said. "I trust he and your mother are well?"

Though he said all the proper words, there was something different about Justin today. He was edgy, more anxious than she'd seen him.

"My parents are well," she assured him. "My brother, Kingsley, has gone off hunting with two of his friends."

"I have some news," Justin said again.

"So do I," she said softly. She put her hands together, resting them protectively across her belly. She would find out his news before she told him hers—no, not hers, *theirs*.

Amberson's family was moving west and had lingered here for two months, camping beside a river while her father made inquiries about purchasing land in the area.

She'd had two months to learn about Mr. Justin Harbinger. She knew that he was respected by his men and that he'd been in several battles before he and his men had been dispatched to Montana Territory to hunt down renegade rebels.

Though he wore the Northern uniform, his family was from somewhere in the South, which explained his soft Southern drawl. He'd once mentioned that his brothers also were fighting in the war.

But the best thing she knew about Justin Harbinger was that she loved him madly. She had given herself to him, body and soul.

He glanced back at her, and suddenly she was the focus of that steady green gaze. "I must tell you something, Miss Amberson," he said. Taking her hand, he led her a little away so her family could not overhear.

"I must leave," he said, his eyes sad. With gentle fingers he touched her cheek.

"Leave? No!" gasped Amberson.

Justin's green eyes were warm with understanding. He picked up a strand of her chestnut hair and curled it around his finger, his touch reminding her of what they had shared that one moonlit night. "You know I do not want to leave, Miss Amberson, but I must. My orders arrived last night. The men and I are ordered to move out. Immediately."

"But, but—" Her hand went to her throat. "But, Justin—"

He dipped his head and kissed the side of her face. She turned a little to hide the kiss from her parents.

"I will return," he promised. His breath warmed

her cheek. "I will come back to Montana as soon as I can and find you."

She stepped away, a frown on her brow. This was not going the way she'd planned. Not at all.

"My men and I are being sent back to Virginia, Amberson," he told her and there was a seriousness about him now that she barely recognized. "My family has a plantation there. There've been fights, battles near my home. . . ." He clamped his mouth shut, as if afraid to say any more.

"Can't you stay here a little longer?" she begged. "Surely you and your men can find some more rebels to chase?"

"No," he answered, and she heard the firmness in his voice. "I've got my orders, Miss Amberson, and I must obey them."

"But what about us? You and I?" she cried. "Why, I've scarcely begun to know you. . . ." Tears sprang to her eyes, and she didn't wipe them away. Tears always worked with Papa.

Justin brushed away her tears with a gentle finger. "I want to stay here, Miss Amberson," he said. "I want to know more about you, I feel the same . . ."

"Then stay!" she cried. "Stay! Let your men go back, but *you* stay, here, with me!"

He stood a little straighter and she felt him withdraw from her. "I can't do that, angel. These men look to me to lead them. I have military orders. And my orders are to return to Virginia. I am sorry if that does not meet with your approval."

"My approval?" she cried. "I don't want you to go. I want you to stay!"

"I cannot do that, Miss Amberson. Do not ask it of me."

She clutched his sleeve and said, "Justin, you can't

12

leave now. You can't!" She would *make* him stay.

"Miss Amberson," he said patiently, but she could hear in his voice that he wanted to go, needed to go. He wanted to be off to Virginia and the war there. "I must go. I have no choice."

She could feel him gently pulling his sleeve loose from her grip. He was going away. He was leaving her. This couldn't be happening!

"Justin—!" She grabbed for his sleeve again.

"Don't!" he told her. "Don't make it worse than it already is. I have my orders to return. My company and I are pulling out today."

"Today?" she gasped. "No, not today! Why, I—"

"Miss Amberson," he said, and he planted both hands on her arms. His grip was as firm as his voice. "Y'all must understand. I am leaving. I have to go and fight in the war. My orders are clear. I do not want to go, but I must." He regarded her steadily. "I will return as soon as I can."

Then he let go of her arms and pulled out his time-piece. "I have to go. My men are waiting!"

"Justin," she implored. But as she watched him she saw he was already leaving her. His mind was on his men, on what he had to do. . . . He was leaving her to go and fight. He wasn't thinking about her at all. About their love . . . about what they had done to-gether . . .

Lord, what could she do? He said he'd return, but she knew he wouldn't. He'd said the words, made the promise, but anything could happen. He could be killed in battle, he could return to Virginia and de-cide to stay there. He could be assigned somewhere else, meet another woman, Lord knew what else. And who knew how long this war was going to last? She hesitated. There was no man for her but this one. She had to make him stay . . . but how? Maybe Papa could make him stay.

"Please give my regards to your family," Justin said. "I've used every minute of the time my commander allotted me. I must return now." He started to walk over to where his horse waited.

She ran after him. "Don't go, Justin! Stay here, with me. Papa will help you get started in a business of some sort. . . ."

"No." He kissed her on the forehead, then gently set her aside.

Hopelessly, she watched him mount the bay. He couldn't be leaving. He couldn't!

He stared down at her. "What was it you were going to tell me?" he asked, sounding distracted and tired.

He was leaving. If she told him about the baby, would he stay? Or would he do what Eleanor's young man had done, back in Pennsylvania? Her friend Eleanor had told her young man about the baby on the way, and that was the last she'd ever seen of him.

A cold sweat broke out on Amberson's forehead.

"Amberson?"

She shook her head and made one last attempt to catch his interest with a pout. "It was nothing."

He watched her, expressionless. He was already riding off with his men in his mind. *He doesn't want me. He won't want our baby.*

Justin nodded and swung his horse's head to the left. "I have to be going," he said. He gave her a brief salute. "I will return, Amberson."

She nodded, pretending she believed him. But she didn't. It was a vicious war. He could make no promises. No one could. He was leaving her and he wasn't coming back.

She lifted her hand and gave a small wave, her heart constricting in her chest. "Good-bye, Justin Harbinger," she whispered sadly. "I love you."

He gave another salute, then spurred his horse. The big bay galloped off across the field.

She watched Justin go. He would not be back. He would never return to her. She knew it deep in her heart.

She placed her hand across her belly and walked slowly back to where her family was sitting. She would never see him again, she thought numbly. He had said nothing of loving her. . . . There was little reason for him to return once he left.

"That your young man?" asked her father, William Hawley. "Eager one, isn't he?" Her mother, Anne, smiled.

Amberson shrugged. "He came to tell me he and his men have received orders to leave. For Virginia. Today."

Her father paused, his coffee cup halfway to his mouth. Then he took a gulp. Her mother looked disappointed.

"Nice young man, that one," commented her father. "Too bad he had to go."

"Yes," agreed Amberson. "Isn't it?"

Chapter One

Triple R Ranch, Gunpoint, Montana
May 9, 1866

Amberson Hawley Rowan stood at the open door of the big white ranch house and stared miserably down the dusty road. Zig-zag log fences lined the road on either side. Her six-month-old son, Gerald, rode high on her right hip. "Where is Richard, Gerald?" she asked her son. For his sake, she attempted a smile. "Your father should have been home by now."

The baby looked up at her out of big blue eyes and gurgled. He seemed to find her words funny.

Amberson's smile faltered. This son, this sandy-haired, blue-eyed baby, gave her life meaning. Richard Rowan certainly didn't.

After her mother and father had been killed on the trail west, she'd been left alone. Grief had settled over her like a thick gray cloak that muffled everything. Even her thoughts had become muddied and vague. Somehow, in the grayness, she had married Richard, trying to find an anchor to hold her firm through the terrible storm of her grief. To no avail.

In one short year, she'd gone from being the spoiled daughter of a wealthy family to a married woman with a child, solely dependent on her husband. Her life had become sheer drudgery. There were vegetables to grow, men to cook for, a large house to keep clean. . . .

But this baby, this little baby boy had given her something precious. She was his mother, yet she felt as if *he* had given *her* life. Why, now she could even get out of bed in the morning.

"You're so sweet," she whispered in his ear. She caught a faint whiff and wrinkled her nose. "And you smell so bad—"

Her words were interrupted by the faint swirl of dust in the distance. "What is this, Gerald?" she asked. She pointed down the road at the rapidly growing cloud of dust. "Richard is bringing home cattle to start his new herd," she explained to the baby.

The two waited in silence, the woman with the chestnut hair and the child on her hip. Out of the dust cloud galloped a hundred Texas Longhorn cattle: brown, black, red, spotted. They were a sea of colors.

The herd thundered up the road and under the arched wooden sign that read TRIPLE R RANCH. Amberson stepped back onto the porch. Cowboys yelled and swore at the cows; horses whinnied. Gerald waved his arms in excitement. Amberson bit her lip nervously.

Several men rode into the ranch yard, the sides of their lathered mounts heaving.

She squinted through the dust as a cowhand, astride a huge bay gelding, raced over to the corral. He deftly lifted the pole that served as a gate and swung it aside. Expertly, he backed his horse out of the way of the oncoming herd. He wore a distinctive brown-and-white cowhide vest that stretched across his broad shoulders and brown leather chaps on his legs.

He must be new, she thought. She didn't recall seeing him with Richard's men before.

The hundred head of bawling cattle bumped and snorted their way into the corral. When they were all inside, he replaced the pole and whipped off his brown slouch hat, revealing his shaggy dark brown hair. He wiped his forehead with the dirt-covered sleeve of his once pale shirt. His every movement spoke of coiled strength.

For a moment Amberson's eyes followed the man— there was something vaguely unsettling about him— before she swung around to look for Richard.

She caught sight of him, tall in the saddle, his black hair and dark blue coat setting him apart from the other men, who all wore the patched, dull-colored clothing of Montana cowboys.

She took a breath, dreading to speak with Richard, yet knowing that she must, eventually.

Without waiting to talk to him, she hurried into the house and began setting up the meal for the sixteen hungry men who would soon descend on her kitchen. She set out the food she had spent hours preparing.

The kitchen was the biggest room in the two-story house. She'd tried to make it look homey, with red-

and-white checked curtains at the windows and a vase of purple wild flowers on each of the two long tables lined with benches.

The men straggled into the ranch house, talking and laughing now that their work was done and the cattle were safely corralled. They crowded into the big kitchen where she'd set the tables with beef stew, potatoes, and homemade bread. She smiled to herself as she heard their happy exclamations at the sight of their first homecooked food in two months.

Richard was one of the last men to walk up the porch steps and enter the ranch house. Someone slouched in behind Richard, but it was Richard that Amberson watched warily.

"You're back," she said, at a loss for polite words, here, in front of the men.

Richard grunted and reached for Gerald. He lifted the child and nuzzled him. "How you been, my boy? You been good? Papa brought you some cows." His soft murmurings to the baby were distinctly unlike the way he usually spoke to Amberson and she stiffened, tamping down an unwelcome feeling. Jealousy—of her own son.

Richard handed the baby back to her with a snort of contempt. "Baby stinks. Change him. You know better 'n to bring him to me stinkin'."

Amberson clutched Gerald to her, her cheeks heated in humiliation. He found fault with everything she did.

A cowhand pushed past Richard and she flushed anew, realizing he had overheard Richard's unkind words. She caught a glimpse of the surprise in the cowhand's green eyes as he moved past.

Suddenly her heart pounded and she stared. It was—She swallowed. No, it couldn't be—!

Richard clapped the large man on the shoulder. The two men were of a height, but the stranger's shoulders were broader and he was more strongly built than Richard. "Go ahead, Justin," said Richard, playing the role of genial host. "Help yourself. Plenty of food."

Justin.

Numb, Amberson watched as Richard and the cowhand sauntered over to a table. She blinked, unable to believe her eyes. It couldn't be he. It couldn't!

A sudden surge of anger rose in her breast, an uprising of the righteous rage that she knew he so richly deserved. She took a step toward him, wanting to claw at Justin's face. Her heart thudded so loudly she was surprised no one at the table turned at the sound.

But no one noticed. No one knew.

The baby squirmed on her hip then, and she was reminded of Richard's petty remark about changing him. "Come, Gerald," she said softly, realizing she could not reveal that she knew Justin, not this way, not here in front of all the cowhands. She knew suddenly that she did not want to see him, or Richard, or anyone. She needed some time—alone—to think.

She fled the room; the laughter and joking of the men rang in her ears.

From upstairs in her bedroom, she looked out through white lacy curtains at the vast grasslands of the Triple R. Richard's ranch stretched for eighteen hundred acres, a huge spread.

Only Amberson and Baby Gerald slept in this room now. Richard had moved into his study before Gerald's birth. It was right around that time that he'd begun his regular visits to Gunpoint.

Dropping Richard from her mind, Amberson set

20

about working on her new problem: Justin.

Placing the baby on the bed, she went about the motions of changing him, all the while her mind working furiously. *What is he doing here? How did this happen?*

Finally, she realized she was worrying herself into a panic, and for what? Justin was a stranger to them all. None of the hands, or Richard, knew him. None of them could possibly know him. And he will be leaving soon, she assured herself firmly. He is a cow-hand, hired for one job, and when it is finished, he will be leaving.

The thought calmed her, and she picked up Gerald and cooed to him. The little one smiled and waved his arms at her. "Oh, you are so precious," she murmured. "Mama loves you." She hugged him to her. What she would do without Gerald she did not know, nor did she ever want to know. He was her life.

Heartened by the press of his solid little body, she kissed him on the top of his bald head and placed him back on her hip. "Come along, Gerald," she said aloud. "Mama will not be frightened out of her own kitchen by that nasty man. Mama is brave. And you will be too!" Inside, her heart quavered and made a lie of her words.

She reached the bottom of the stairs and steeled herself for what lay ahead. Taking a deep breath, she sauntered into the kitchen. Men sat at the two long tables, benches on either side. Bowls of food passed up and down the table and everyone ate in studious silence.

No one noticed her, and she had time to gain some semblance of calm. She smoothed her blue print dress with one hand, trying to reassure herself. Then one of the men caught sight of the baby. "That baby

21

is so big, he's gonna tip you over on one side, Missus Rowan," joked Beau, one of the men. There were several good-natured guffaws and chuckles and she smiled politely.

Richard sat at the end of a table and ladled stew onto his plate, ignoring her.

Justin reached for a chunk of homemade bread.

She would not look at either of them, she would not!

Making her way to a corner of the closest table, she reached blindly for a chair. She sat down, and congratulated herself on a job well done.

When the men finished eating they began shoving the benches back. In all the pushing and shoving and leaving, she found herself glancing at the next table in the direction of Justin.

And met his narrowed eyes staring right back at her.

Anger flared in his green eyes. Anger and accusation. For a moment they stared hard at one another; then the noises of the men intruded and she glanced away.

What does he have to accuse me of? she demanded of herself. Nothing! She tightened her lips and reached for a serving bowl still half-filled with stew. She slopped a ladleful on her plate, not seeing the food, conscious only of the broad-shouldered man at the next table.

She took a bite of meat and Gerald reached for her mouth. "No, little one," she murmured. "You get to eat later."

She did not look up as the rest of the men left, but kept her eyes on her plate. One by one, she heard them tramp out to the bunkhouse on the far side of the yard.

"Amberson."

It was a command. Richard's.

"Yes?" Dread mingled with the food in her stomach.

"This is one of my new men, Justin Harbinger," said Richard.

She heard the thick sound of their boots and spurs on the wooden floor as the two walked over to where she was sitting. "This is my wife, Mrs. Richard Rowan," said Richard. Amberson could hear the sneer in his voice.

She dragged her eyes up from her plate. "How do you do, Mr. Harbinger?" she said politely.

"I'm doin' fine, Mrs. Rowan. Just fine," Justin said in his soft drawl. His green eyes were cool, revealing nothing.

Her own narrowed. She clenched her jaw and forced herself to stare at him. *I have nothing to hide,* she told herself defiantly. *You are the one who has the explaining to do.*

But she said nothing aloud.

"Harbinger is my new ranch foreman," announced Richard. "He'll be staying on at the bunkhouse."

Justin turned away, as if bored with the topic. Amberson managed to snap her jaw shut.

The two men walked out of her kitchen, the sound of their boots echoing in the emptiness. Alone, she let go of her false, polite face. Her shoulders slumped. She bowed her head and squeezed her eyes closed as helplessness crawled over her. She'd thought she'd seen the last of Justin Harbinger fourteen months before.

Dang, but she looked even better than she had the last time he'd seen her, thought Justin angrily. Even with her long brown hair done up in a homely bun, she was still the prettiest woman he'd ever set eyes on. Obviously marriage and motherhood agreed with her.

He ignored the pain in the region of his heart.

No sooner had he left than she had taken up with another man. He had *told* her he would return!

He frowned. He was better off without her. It was obvious she'd hooked up with the first man she could find. And a rich one at that. And she'd *known* he was coming back for her. The heartless witch.

He pounded his fist into the tight straw mattress on the bunkhouse bed and drew it back. Again and again he hit the mattress, until his anger receded and he had a throbbing hand. How could she do this to him? How could she forget him so easily? How could she marry—marry, for God's sake!—another man?

His jaw clenched and he surveyed the tiny little room, looking for something else to punch. Nothing caught his eye and he settled for smashing the mattress again.

"Hey! What you doin' in there?" came a voice through the wall. "Keep it down. I wanna get some sleep."

He gritted his teeth. Dang! How had this happened?

His hand still hurting, he threw himself on the bunk. Sleep wouldn't come; he tossed and turned. Finally he gave up and thought about what he had been trying not to: Amberson Hawley. He corrected himself—Mrs. Richard Rowan, as she was now known.

He rolled over onto his back and stared up at the rough wooden beams of the bunkhouse ceiling. That first time he'd seen her, ah, but she'd been an eye-ful. . . .

He'd been in Montana Territory for a month or so—he and his Federal troops. He and his men had fought skirmishes with the Rebs, following some of them even as far west as Montana Territory. That day, the summer sun had burned overhead and he had been dog-tired from chasing down some ma-rauders wearing ragtag uniforms of gray. The ma-rauders escaped, and Justin and his men had hobbled their horses in preparation for an overnight camp in a grassy field.

Then he'd heard pounding hoofs, heard her before he spotted her. She came riding toward him, gallop-ing fearlessly on a big chestnut mare, her thick brown hair flying behind her, sitting that horse as sure as any seasoned cavalry soldier. The mare was spirited, too, but the girl had held that mare, and she brooked no sass from the horse, he could see that.

"Sir!" she called. She sounded breathless, as though she had just made love, or so his fantasy told him, but he knew it was from the quick gallop across the fields. "My father, Mr. William Hawley, late of Pennsylvania, conveys his most cordial invitation to you and your men. He invites you all to a fine dinner this very evening, given in your honor as brave fight-ing men of the Union."

Reminded of the war, Justin had glanced down at his blue lieutenant's uniform, his buttons no longer as shiny as they'd been when he'd headed out from Virginia a lifetime ago. His soul was no longer as shiny either, truth be told. Fighting and killing had taken the shine from those buttons. As for his soul— well, there wasn't much hope there. Not when the

Good Book said "Thou shalt not kill," and Justin had done so, many times over.

Then he glanced back up and looked into the most beautiful hazel eyes he'd ever seen in his life. Thick brown lashes framed her green-brown eyes. Her cheeks were bright with the excitement of the ride. An angel.

There was an innocence, a cleanness that sparkled in those hazel eyes. She had no doubts about *her* soul, he could tell.

He swallowed. His men were tired, and the last thing they needed was to be the entertainment at some rich man's dinner, but he wanted to see her again. "Miss Hawley, please thank your father for the invitation. We will be proud to visit."

"Seven sharp," she'd said then. "Our camp is across the field." She'd pointed to several covered wagons in the distance, near a stand of cottonwoods by the river. Then she wheeled the mare around. He was still watching her, as though struck dumb. She gave him a happy little wave of her hand before she dug her heels into the mare's sides and raced off back across the field.

His men had been treated to a fine dinner that night, though what they ate he could not remember, so besotted was he with the beautiful daughter of their host. Justin had been unable to take his eyes off her. She was a feast for his eyes, and for his tired, sick soul.

Thoughts of her had sustained him through the remainder of the war and its aftermath. After he'd sold the plantation, he'd returned to Montana Territory determined to find her. . . .

Well, he'd found her, all right. The sick knot in his stomach told him he wished to God he hadn't.

Chapter Two

Amberson bent over the hot wood stove, stirring a pan of thick cornbread. While the baby napped upstairs, she had come downstairs to the kitchen to prepare the main meal of the day for the ranch hands. She wiped at her forehead. Cooking for sixteen men was a huge task.

She heard the clump of boots on the porch and recognized Richard's step. He had kept to himself in the four days since his return. She, in turn, had said little to him. The strain between them could be tolerated, she thought, if they did not speak to one another.

Richard walked in, followed by some of his men.

"When you going back to the freight line, boss?" asked Whiskers, a grizzled, bewhiskered, weathered man who'd worked for Richard for ten years. For a lark, Whiskers had ridden on the cattle run up from

27

Texas. Usually, he worked on the freight lines as a mule skinner.

Richard owned several freight hauling lines, manned by tough men who cursed the mules and oxen to make them run faster and pull the big loads. His men drove wagonloads of goods to the army outposts. Sometimes his mule skinners hauled loads to the mining towns between Gunpoint and Bozeman or Butte.

"Tomorrow," answered Richard with a yawn. "I've got to put a new crew on the run to the fort. Got another military contract. Want to go?"

Whiskers shrugged. "Sure."

There were several grunts of approval at Richard's news. It meant the men would have something better to do than ride herd on Richard's new cattle.

For Amberson, it meant relief that Richard would not be around. Their marriage, she thought, wiping at her sticky forehead, seemed as thick and unmoving as this cornbread she was trying to stir.

But what could she do? She had the baby; how else would she take care of him? If her parents were still alive, she would go to them. And if Kingsley, her brother, was here, she would go to him. But he was gone too. Not dead, of course, but headed west. The very day her parents were killed, he ran off. He'd said something about going to a town in California, but she'd seen the fear in his eyes. He was running scared.

She paused, straining to remember the name of the town he'd said he was going to. Bodie. That was it. She shook her head sadly. She'd heard somewhere that Bodie was a rough town. She hoped her brother could take care of himself, impulsive as he was.

Her thoughts were interrupted by the sound of

men laughing as they sat down. She reached for a cup to pour hot coffee for Whiskers.

Richard's voice boomed out behind her. "Did you know that Harbinger here is getting married? He's come to Montana to fetch his bride."

Amberson jerked, and scalding coffee spilled over her hand. She winced in pain.

"You all right, Missus Rowan?" asked Whiskers in concern.

Amberson tightened her lips and bit back a cry. She shook her head, trying to tell him she was fine. She ran over to the sink and plunged her hand into a pot of cold water.

"Should warn you, though, Harbinger," continued Richard, "that marriage is a highly overrated institution. Isn't it, dear?" he sneered nastily at Amberson.

She colored and brought her stinging red hand to her mouth, turning away, not bothering to dignify his rude comment with an answer. A baby's cry came from upstairs.

She handed the soup ladle to Whiskers. "See that the men get their food," she ordered, and hurried from the room.

She refused to look at Richard as she went past. Her way was momentarily barred by Justin Harbinger; his cool green eyes bored into hers. They held neither shame nor explanation. She snapped at him without thinking, "I'm sure Mr. Harbinger will have a very fine marriage!"

Mortified at how bitter she sounded, she raced from the room and up the stairs. What was the matter with her? Who cared if he was getting married? She certainly did not!

She picked up Baby Gerald and hugged him to her.

He was crying and waving his arms. Tears slipped from her eyes as she calmed the baby and her own wildly beating heart.

Married! He couldn't be getting married. Why, she'd thought, wanted . . . No! She buried her face in her son's little chest. She had been a fool to think she'd wanted to marry Justin Harbinger.

The baby sobbed. "There, there," she soothed him. "Baby is awake. Mama will take care of you."

Would she? Could she? How would she take care of him, in a crumbling marriage, thousands of miles from anyone she knew? How would she?

Amberson ignored the insistent questions pounding in her head and laid the baby on the bed to change him. When she was done, she picked him up again. She held him close and breathed in his warm baby scent. Oh, he smelled good. Thank God she had Gerald.

Feeling calmer now, she carried Gerald down the stairs.

The men were eating at the tables, the talk going back and forth. Richard and Justin Harbinger sat at one table and appeared to be engaged in serious conversation.

She glanced at the two of them, their heads together, talking, and a sense of uneasiness assailed her. It did not bode well for her that they appeared to be such good friends.

Amberson walked over to a table and set her bowl down beside Whiskers and Beau.

"How did you happen to meet Mr. Harbinger?" she asked as casually as she could. Whiskers kept on eating his beef sausage and beans, slurping out of a big spoon. Amberson wondered if anyone was going to answer her question.

Beau, a dwarf who had been with Richard for two years, said hesitantly, "Mr. Harbinger saved Mr. Rowan's life."

"He did?" said Amberson in surprise.

The dwarf nodded as he continued to eat, with better manners than his bewhiskered neighbor exhibited.

Whiskers lifted his head, wiped his mouth with the back of a hand, and said, "Yup. Mr. Rowan was down on all fours, the cattle was stampedin' at him, and out of nowhere this fella comes and swoops him up, just seconds before them cattle tromped him. Thought he was a goner, f' sure."

"A goner," confirmed Beau.

"Oh." Amberson pondered this for awhile. No wonder Richard was being so kind to Justin. He'd saved his life.

Whiskers let out a resounding burp. "Beggin' your pardon, Missus Rowan," he said sheepishly when she jumped at the noise, "but I sure do like the sausage."

She smiled faintly. "I'm so glad."

The baby gurgled a little and watched her out of big blue eyes.

"That kid is gonna be in the saddle next week," said Sandy, one of the younger cowhands who was named after his hair color. "Your boy's growin' that much!"

She nodded, pleased at the exaggerated compliment. She glanced up just as Justin leaned forward to cut up a chunk of sausage, using a strange black knife. His big hands moved easily and she flushed as she recalled just how easily those hands had moved on her body. And oh, how easily she had given herself to him!

Her lips tightened. Never again, she told herself

ominously. Never, ever again! To distract herself, she asked Whiskers sharply, "What is that odd knife that Mr. Harbinger uses?"

Unfortunately for her, there happened to be a lull in the conversation at that very moment and her words sounded unnaturally loud in the silence. Several men turned to look at her, including Richard and Justin.

Amberson clutched the baby tightly and wanted to slide under the table to avoid all the eyes looking at her. However, she lifted her chin and waited, her heart pounding.

"This odd knife," said Justin, in an even voice, "has a deer antler handle and a blade made of black obsidian, a glasslike, sharp rock. I received the knife from a Union soldier who told me it could only be used for protection, for good works, or for healing. I reckon cutting up sausage fits somewhere in there, don't you, Mrs. Rowan?"

There was amused laughter among the men, and she flushed anew. Did anyone else besides herself hear the contempt in his voice as he said her name?

"That Union soldier," she retorted, "another man whose life you saved, I presume?" Her voice was as cold as she could make it.

"Unfortunately, no, ma'am," Justin answered, his voice like the wind off a glacier. "He died."

Words choked in her throat. She could feel the men staring at her. "I—I'm sorry to hear that, sir."

"Are you?"

She wanted to dump a bowl of beans and sausage over his head. She was not the cruel-hearted woman he implied.

The men went back to eating.

Amberson snapped her mouth shut, thinking frantically of how she could skewer Justin. "I'm sure your new bride is eager to see you—and your knife, Mr. Harbinger. What a truly lovely present it will make for her!" She hoped he heard the heavy sarcasm in her voice.

He straightened, and any trace of amiability in his manner was gone. "I killed a man with this knife, Mrs. Rowan. In the war," he said soberly. "I won't be giving it to my bride."

His bride. Hard to believe how the words could hurt. Amberson swallowed. So, he *was* getting married. She could not believe it. Could not accept it. Yet it was true.

Why do you have such a difficult time seeing the man for what he truly is? she demanded of herself. *He is a conniving, double-dealing seducer of women!* She wanted none of him. None!

"Let us hope your bride can appreciate what a truly *honorable* man you are," she sneered.

Richard was looking at her rather strangely. So were the other men.

Justin Harbinger regarded her silently, his eyes glittering green stones.

Beau cleared his throat. "Uh, Missus Rowan? More coffee?"

She looked at him blankly. "Coffee?" She glanced around at the watching men and met fifteen pairs of inquisitive eyes. Oh, heavens! She had made a perfect spectacle of herself!

"Yes, more coffee, please," she said quietly to Beau and found herself inordinately grateful to the dwarf when he poured her a fresh cup. She brought it to her lips and drank, and only returned the cup to the table when she again heard the deep murmurings of male conversation.

As soon as she could, she took the baby and fled upstairs.

Chapter Three

"If it wasn't for the dang money, I wouldn't stay," muttered Justin Harbinger as he swung the ax. The sharp blade bit into the fence post wood. "Hell, I should leave. To hell with the money. He can't pay me enough to look at that woman every day."

But he had accepted the job, and Richard Rowan was paying Justin a good wage. Most cowhands barely eked out a living.

It was decent of Rowan to hire him and decent of him to pay him a fair wage, and he should dang well take his eyes off Rowan's wife, Justin told himself.

He went back to working on the fence post. Several of the cowhands chopped at fence posts nearby. Richard Rowan couldn't fence in all the land his cattle roamed, but he had insisted on fencing the acres he *did* own, and who was Justin to tell him any different?

He swung the ax again and again, feeling the

stretch of his muscles with each blow. As long as he was chopping the fence post wood he didn't have to look at Mrs. Richard Rowan. Or her baby. Who were right now sitting in the shade under the spreading branches of a lodgepole pine at the side of the house. Amberson played with the baby, bouncing him on her long, outstretched legs. She sang to him too.

Justin sweated, and it wasn't from the heat of the sun or the work of chopping. No, it was much worse. It was from the ordeal of looking at the woman, and especially at the baby, a constant reminder of how she had betrayed him. What he really wanted to do, Justin decided, was to throw down the ax, jump on Samson, his horse, and ride off. What was he here for, anyway? There wasn't enough money on earth to pay him for the misery he was going through.

Now she was putting the baby in the wicker basket he slept in.

Justin threw down his ax and reached for his canteen. He popped the cork off the top, brought the canteen to his lips, threw back his head, and drank great, cooling draughts of water. Just as he was shoving the cork back in, Richard Rowan came charging out of the house.

Justin watched in surprise as Rowan stormed down the porch steps and marched over to where Amberson sat. Yanking her by the arm, he propelled her to her feet. Evidently the baby was fast asleep in his basket because he did not cry out. Rowan dragged Amberson back into the house and slammed the door.

Frowning, Justin went back to chopping fence posts. Loud shouts issued forth from the house. Rowan's deep voice and Amberson's higher, screaming voice were in terrible counterpoint to one another. The words were not civil, nor was the tone. Justin wondered if they did this all the time.

"I told you to stop spending so freightin' much money on yourself!" he heard Rowan yell.

Justin kept chopping through Amberson's shrill answer. Grimly, he told himself she deserved it. She deserved to be in such a marriage for the way she had treated him.

They continued yelling. What is Rowan's problem? wondered Justin. She has wealthy parents. She can afford to buy whatever clothes she wants for herself—and the baby. What's Rowan's complaint? Not every man is fortunate enough to marry a rich woman.

Justin glanced around at the other ranch hands. They chopped wood steadily, ignoring the sounds from the ranch house. More yelling, and still the ranch hands worked, giving no sign they'd heard anything louder than the occasional bird call.

Uneasily, Justin returned to his chopping. Suddenly he noticed there was silence. No yells, no screams, nothing.

The door opened and Amberson tottered down the stairs, smoothing her hair and rubbing one cheek. She scurried over to the tree and peeked in the basket. She sat back, surreptitiously wiping at her eyes.

Justin set his jaw grimly. Crying, was she? He tamped down his rising concern. Amberson Hawley Rowan deserved to be in a miserable marriage. He would not feel sorry for her—no matter how much her husband yelled at her. Or she at him, for that matter.

The door opened again and this time Rowan barged out. He stomped down the steps and threw himself on his big buckskin horse, already saddled and waiting, idly swatting flies with its black tail. Rowan yanked the horse's head around, dug in his heels, and galloped down the dusty road as if pursued by a stampeding bull.

Justin paused in his chopping and watched the dust spiral up. Rowan made a turn at the end of the long fence and headed toward the town of Gunpoint.

Justin glanced around. The other men continued chopping; no one looked up, no one paused. It was as if nothing had happened. And very little had happened, Justin assured himself. The boss had had a fight with his wife. No big deal. Justin went back to chopping. She deserved a miserable marriage. No doubt about that.

Looked like that was what she had, all right. A miserable marriage. Too bad for the kid, though. Shame for a baby to be trapped between fighting parents.

Justin glanced over at the tree once more. She was sitting by the basket, staring into it, one hand resting on her cheek. The sad look on her face wrenched his heart. Stop it, he warned himself. She deserves it. And that's that!

Soon the chopping of wood was the only sound.

Chapter Four

The ranch hands sat at the kitchen tables eating the evening meal of potato cakes, ham, and vegetables that Amberson had prepared. She'd picked the potatoes and carrots from her own garden at the back of the house.

Richard was leaving tomorrow and she would be glad to see him go.

But this evening, he was in the town of Gunpoint. And she knew what he was doing there. Everyone else on the ranch knew, too. Everyone but Justin Harbinger, and she would die before she would tell him what Richard was up to.

She was just glad none of the men had seen her crying beside the baby's basket after that fight with Richard. She felt so ashamed now, just thinking about it. She had screamed back at him, trying to defend herself against his baseless accusation that she spent too much money. She spent very little. She and the baby had to have clothes. Why did Richard begrudge her the few dollars it took for her to clothe herself?

But she knew why, had known for some time. When he had first married her, he'd thought he was marrying a wealthy heiress. She had tried to tell him, tried to warn him that she was penniless, but he'd already heard the rumors about her father's great wealth. Heard that her father had made a pile of money back in Pennsylvania, before the family had headed west. Richard preferred to believe the rumors over anything his new bride said.

But there was no money. Everything her family had owned had been invested in that ill-fated wagon train. Bad luck had dogged her father's wagon train from the very start. Some of their wagons had been swept away at river crossings; some had been accidentally burned, their contents destroyed. The last, most terrible thing to happen was when their wagon train had been attacked by rampaging Indians. Everything was burned and what little was left was stolen.

Amberson and her brother, Kingsley, had barely escaped in a mad, wild ride across the prairie. When they'd returned, after the Indians rode away, the burned wagons and the dead bodies of her parents sent Amberson into shock and grief.

So now she had nothing. Nothing. She'd told Richard that, even before they married, but he hadn't believed her. He didn't think women knew about business or how to count. He didn't believe her until the Pinkerton man he'd hired and sent back to Pennsylvania returned to Montana to confirm that, yes indeed, the Hawley family was penniless.

Well, *now* Richard believed her, she thought

grimly. And he took every occasion to throw her poverty in her face. He could stay in Gunpoint for all she cared.

"Some rustlers took Mr. Ridley's cattle, I heard," said one of the men. Standing at the wood stove, Amberson restlessly flipped some potato cakes, the men's talk interrupting her thoughts.

"That's the second time this month," said another ranch hand. "Them rustlers are gettin' bold. Last time they rustled some cattle off the Double M Ranch. Old Man McManus was right sore when he came back and found his cows missin'."

"You'd be, too, if they was your cattle," commented Beau.

Some of the men laughed, but Whiskers said soberly, "Mr. Rowan better watch out. This here's a big spread and he's got the most head of cattle of any ranch around. Heck, Old Man McManus and Ridley had a piddlin' amount of cows. One sweep through their places and those rustlers will have cleaned 'em out."

"Mr. Rowan is gone a good part of the time, too. The rustlers might find easy pickings here," commented Beau.

No one said anything to that, but a chill ran down Amberson's spine. She quickly straightened. She would not let rustlers frighten her.

"Mr. Rowan has left me in charge of the ranch," came a deep voice. "He left me a few hands to keep watch for rustlers. Y'all want to join us, Whiskers?"

Amberson flushed at the sound of Justin's voice. It was from the heat of the stove, she told herself.

"Naw." Whiskers shook his head. "I'd rather be a mule skinner any day than follow around a bunch of cows."

Justin shrugged. "Suit yourself."

The men's talk faded as they went out the door. Amberson heard footsteps approach her at the stove and then stop. She knew who waited behind her.

"Where's your husband, Mrs. Rowan?" came a sneering whisper. "I notice he doesn't spend much time with you, does he?"

She tightened her lips and turned. No one was paying her any attention and she would not allow Justin to speak to her this way.

"It's none of your business where Richard is," she hissed.

He smiled down at her, but his green eyes were angry. "You married a man who doesn't stick around. What did you marry him for?"

"That is none of your business, either!" She wanted to screech at him but didn't dare for fear of drawing the other ranch hands' attention to them.

"His money? Was that it? A big spread like this. A freight line operation. He makes money, all right. What's the matter? Wasn't your daddy's money enough for you? How much money do you need, anyway?"

The contempt in his green eyes almost undid her resolve not to explain anything to him. But she couldn't. It was he who owed *her* an explanation!

"You ask an awful lot of questions for a man who is about to be married," she sneered back, marveling that she'd found the strength to return his attack. "And just who is the unfortunate woman who is your bride-to-be? I *do* pity her."

Justin looked taken aback and she felt a little blaze of triumph. "Does she know she's getting a shiftless saddle bum for a husband?" needled Amberson.

Justin's eyes widened at her words and she wanted

to hug herself in joy for the blow she'd dealt him.

"She's no one you know," he said, his voice low and strong. "No one you'd know at all."

"Not fit for my company, is she?" asked Amberson sweetly, wondering where this witchiness in her had come from. Amazed that she was capable of dealing a blow to a man she had once loved—no, not loved—*thought* she loved.

His narrowed eyes assessed her. "As a woman who married the first rich man who came along, you are in no position to insult people."

"Get out of my way," she said through gritted teeth, pushing past him to the counter.

She stared at the water bucket, trying to gather her wits. A minute later, when she glanced behind her, Justin was gone. The nerve of the man! How dare he speak to her like that? How dare he!

Trembling from their encounter, she headed upstairs to see the baby. Gerald had taken a late nap and she must wake him or he'd be so well rested he'd be awake until midnight.

She stared down at the baby in the crib until her trembling stopped. She took a deep breath. "Gerald," she said gently, her heart softening as it always did when she looked at his sparse sandy hair and plump little cheeks. "Gerald, time to wake up." She leaned down and kissed his warm cheek as he stirred. She smiled. "Time to get up, big boy," she cooed.

He awoke and looked at her, slowly blinking his big blue eyes. She swept him up into her arms. Lord, how she loved this child. He was the only good thing in her life and she loved him dearly.

She nursed Gerald, changed him, and took him back downstairs. Mercifully, the kitchen was empty.

The men had left to do their chores before turning in for the night.

She set about cleaning the kitchen, leaving Gerald in a corner on a blanket. She talked to him as she washed the dishes. She didn't pay any attention to the footsteps she heard on the porch until the door opened. She swung around, expecting to see Richard.

It was Justin.

"One more thing," he growled, walking up to her. He stood in front of her and she resisted the impulse to shrink away from him. "Does your father approve of your marriage?"

She gaped at him. "What are you talking about?"

"Your father. Does Mr. Hawley approve of your marrying a man who never spends time around you?" He grasped her arm.

He didn't know. She wished suddenly that she was able to tell him in a better way, a better place. "My father," she stated dully, "is dead. So is my mother."

She saw the stricken look in Justin's eyes, the bloodless color of his face.

It was better this way, she told herself. Sympathy between them would be deadly. To her.

He whirled and left the kitchen.

She stared after him, wanting to call him back . . . to explain. But in the end, all she could do was croak, "Dead. They've been dead for over a year."

Why, suddenly, did she feel even more alone?

Chapter Five

Two weeks later

Amberson stood in her bedroom and stared through the white lace curtains at the ranch yard below. But she did not see the ranch yard. Instead, she saw that long-ago moonlit night . . .

She remembered looking into Justin's green eyes, then glancing swiftly away. It took greater courage than she had to look into those green eyes that challenged her, eyes that wanted her.

Justin lifted her chin. "Are you afraid of me?" he asked in a low, warm voice.

She shook her head. And, in truth, she wasn't afraid of him. She trusted him. He'd always been kind to her. He spoke often with her father, with her mother. . . . No, she wasn't afraid of him.

"What then?" he pressed, his voice sending a shiver through her.

She was afraid of . . . what? Herself? Of how much she wanted him? Of what to do?

When she didn't say anything, he waited. Then he reached for her hand. She felt his warm fingers on hers. Felt the strength of him.

"I—I must get back," she said, brushing her hair out of her eyes with her other hand. "My—my parents will be asking for me. . . ."

"Hush," he whispered. "Just stay a little longer. . . ."

He was lonely. She could hear it in his voice. A matching loneliness rose in her. Was this what it was like when you found the man you loved? When you found the man who would love you and stay with you forever? She didn't know. Some part of her sensed that she was too young to even know herself, never mind what another human being might think. But she thought maybe, just maybe, this was what it was like when you found *him.* That he was the one.

She let him lead her over to a log. He took off his jacket and laid it down on the grass so that they could sit and rest their backs against the log.

In the weak moonlight, she could see the outline of his broad shoulders in his pale shirt. His military uniform fit him well, she thought. When they sat down she could still feel the warmth of him emanating from his jacket.

"It's a beautiful night," he said.

"Yes," she whispered. She stared up at the round white globe of moon. He put an arm around her shoulders and she relaxed against him.

He plucked her hand up from where it rested on his jacket and raised her fingers to his lips. As he kissed them, she leaned toward him, yearning . . . yearning, for what she did not know. . . . The scent of him filled her nose. It was a heady smell of man, exciting . . .

Crickets serenaded them. He pulled her closer to him and his hands wandered over her body, caressing her, making her his own.

She gasped when she felt him cup her breasts, the touch unexpected. His mouth moved over hers, silencing the next gasp. She began to relax more, and let his hands weave their magic.

How it was that her long white dress came off, she didn't know, but it was off her, and his shirt was gone too. They lay together, and she shivered slightly in the warm breeze.

"I'll hold you," he promised her. "You won't even feel the cold with me." And he leaned over her, his warm chest pressing against her naked breasts. She gave herself up to his kiss. Then his mouth moved lower, took one breast, played with the nipple, and she felt a strange stirring in her stomach. Her hips moved of their own accord and she strained toward him.

"I'm here," he murmured, and she heard the eagerness in his voice, an eagerness she found herself responding to. How warm his touch felt. How snug she felt in his arms. She wished he could hold her like this always, just the two of them, together. . . .

She felt his hands moving down her sides, now on her hips, now on her stomach. Now lower, lower, lower still, until she pushed at his hand to stop him. He halted, but kept on kissing her. She got lost in the kiss and didn't notice his hand moving ever closer, closer to the center of her womanhood.

Not until he touched her there did she become aware. And then the awareness was of a warm, swirling feeling. She murmured and he swallowed that small sound with a kiss.

His fingers were doing wonderful things to her, things that had never been done before, his touch gen-

tle. She parted her legs for him, to let him do more of the wonderful touching. But then something heavy, thicker, was moving in the way. Coming inside her. She cried out, tried to push him away, but he kissed her again, murmuring soothingly, the murmurs changing to groans as his mouth sought hers, and it was as if he would devour her.

Her head thrown back, she felt she was being feasted upon. But he was already inside her, and they were moving. That is, he was moving, and she was following. He gave several thrusts and cried out in a low voice. She felt his big body clench, everything about him went still . . . and she waited. Then he reached down and gently touched her again. There.

A warm, swirling, rising feeling began to take hold of her center. Her hips strained upward. She wanted . . . she wanted . . . Oh, Lord, she wanted . . . something. . . . She wanted it to fill, to happen, whatever it was, she wanted it! Then suddenly a gigantic cresting feeling rippled sweetly through her body and it was she who was stiff, she who was groaning. She held on to him, held on to the sweet feeling and prayed it would last forever.

When she finally sank back to earth she was in his arms. He kissed her on the top of her head and his arms tightened around her. "You're mine," he whispered. "Mine . . ."

The sound of yelling and clapping broke her reverie. Beau led a fractious, high-stepping bay mare to the corral. Some of the other hands were perched on the fence, and it was their loud yells and claps she heard. Richard rode up on his buckskin and dismounted. The men fell silent. She turned away from the window. It was foolish to spend her time daydreaming of Justin Harbinger. Resolutely, she squared her shoulders. She had other, more immediate problems.

Richard had been back from his freight line for a day and already she could hardly wait for him to leave again. What was wrong with the man? He was sullen and rude to her. To everyone, except Gerald. Baby Gerald he would hold and speak kindly to. She shook her head. There was no understanding the man she'd married, and she'd given up trying. It was best if they just spent as much time apart as possible.

Since Richard showed no sign of leaving the Triple R on this hot day, she must be the one to do so. She woke the baby and dressed him, then went downstairs.

Beau sauntered past the front porch and she ordered him to hitch her chestnut mare up to the buggy. She was going into town!

Once there, she would go to Hinckley's General Store and buy herself a cool bottle of her favorite drink, sarsaparilla. The Triple R, and Richard, were more than she could endure and she had to get away. Had to.

Stomping boots told her Richard had entered the kitchen. She took a breath and went to meet him, the baby riding on one hip.

"I would like to take Gerald to town, Richard," she said evenly, holding the baby as she pulled on her gloves awkwardly, one at a time. That done, she patted her hat more firmly on her head while she awaited Richard's reply.

"To spend more of my money, I suppose," he said.

She tightened her lips and did not deign to answer. She wondered if Richard would forbid her to go to town. He had not done so before, but he had been in a black mood since his return from the freight lines.

She heard the buggy pull up and saw Beau waiting beside it on his pinto pony. "I will return around dinnertime," she informed Richard.

Let him refuse her, just let him!

"Who'll make dinner for the men?" he demanded.

"There's ham left over from last night's meal. I'm sure the men will be happy to eat it."

At his frown she added pointedly, "They seemed to survive well enough on beans and bacon when you were on the cattle drive. Leftover ham is a good sight better than beans."

"Make sure you have a rider with you," growled Richard. "I don't want Gerald in danger. There've been rustlers. . . ."

She paused. She'd forgotten about the rustlers. "Very well," she mused. "Beau can come with me."

"No. Not Beau. Take Harbinger with you."

She turned to look at Richard. "Mr. Harbinger? I don't—" She almost said, "I don't want him," but she knew she could never explain anything to Richard, so she said instead, "I don't believe he's nearby. Beau will do just fine." Not Justin, she thought. Anybody but Justin.

Richard turned to Beau. "Get Harbinger," he ordered. Beau took off at a gallop.

Amberson and Richard waited for five strained minutes. She stared out the parlor window, her stomach in knots. Finally Beau returned, and behind him rode Justin Harbinger on his big bay gelding.

Amberson went carefully down the steps, carrying the baby and refusing to look at Justin. Let Richard explain what he wanted. She did not need to talk to the man. She did not want to talk to him ever again.

"I want you to accompany Mrs. Rowan to Gunpoint, Harbinger. Keep a look out for rustlers."

Dismay crossed Justin's face. Amberson's eyes narrowed when she saw it. So he didn't want to come with her? Well, she didn't want him with her, either!

Justin touched his brown slouch hat reluctantly. "Will do," he finally said to Richard. He said nothing to Amberson, didn't even look at her.

Beau held the baby's basket. Amberson took it from him and lifted it onto the buggy seat and then she climbed up. She tied the basket securely behind the seat. When it was firmly anchored, she picked up the reins and slapped the broad back of her mare. Amberson kept her eyes averted from Justin. "Giddap, Jessie."

Jessie moved forward and the black, covered buggy rolled after her. Richard stepped off the porch and mounted his buckskin. He galloped off down the lane without a farewell. Amberson refused to look at Justin, who rode a little ahead of the buggy.

They went down the long drive, passed under the Triple R sign, and turned onto the dusty road that led to Gunpoint.

Amberson watched Justin's broad, unrelenting back in the brown and white vest. She sighed. It was going to be a long trip to town.

She had the hour-long ride to Gunpoint in which to contemplate how she did *not* love Justin. He had abandoned her. He'd said he'd return, but he hadn't, not until now, when it was far too late. She'd already married someone else. And, she thought with a sick feeling, she would have to live in that marriage for the rest of her life. She'd made a vow.

She was roused from her somber thoughts when they reached Gunpoint. The town was a collection of shacks, houses, buildings, stores, and even tents set at the foot of a hill. The small community had been thriving for two years, long enough to cultivate a sheriff's office, a newspaper, an assayer's office, a telegraph office, a church, two mercantile stores, two hotels, three undertakers, five lawyers' offices, and eight saloons.

Amberson pulled her buggy up in front of one of the mercantiles, a brown building with a sign reading HINCKLEY'S GENERAL STORE. HINCKLEY PARKER, PROPRIETOR. ESTABLISHED 1864.

Amberson tied Jessie to the rail, all the while avoiding Justin Harbinger's narrowed gaze. She carried the sleeping baby in his basket into the store, heedless of whether Justin followed her or not. While she might need him to ride guard for her between the Triple R and Gunpoint, she did not need him while she was in town, thank you very much!

She passed a handmade poster nailed to the outside wall of Hinckley's store. The poster advertised the Gunpoint Ladies' Culture Club's newest inspiration: a Shakespearean production of *A Midsummer Night's Dream* with the lovely Mrs. Annabelle Parker Simmons, who happened to be Hinckley Parker's married sister, playing the role of the fairy queen, Titania.

Amberson walked into the dark interior of the building. The vinegary smell of pickles from a nearby barrel assaulted her nostrils and caused her to reel back for a moment. Eyes watering, she sneezed.

It was considerably cooler inside the store, and she was glad she'd brought little Gerald in with her. Hinckley Parker, eldest son and scion of the Gunpoint Parkers, owner of the general store, sat behind the counter sucking on a pipe and reading last week's edition of the *Gunpoint Gazette*. Coils of blue smoke enveloped his head.

Amberson coughed from the pungent tobacco smell.

Rolls of cotton fabrics in reds, browns, blues, pinks, greens, and yellows lined the shelves against one wall. In the middle of the store, dry goods were stacked neatly on shelves set as high as a man's head. The remaining half of the room was devoted to large bags of flour and sugar, pottery jars of blackstrap molasses, chunks of bacon, and sacks of coffee beans, all the staples of frontier life.

In a corner two well-dressed matrons spoke with one another. They were members of the Gunpoint Culture Club and Amberson nodded politely to them. "Good day, Mrs. Stanton. Good day, Mrs. Reedy."

In response to Amberson's greeting, Mrs. Hyacinth Stanton and Mrs. Dorothy Reedy tittered behind their hands. Amberson reddened and turned away, bemused by their actions. A vague uneasiness spread through her, and she wondered if she would be the topic of discussion at the next Ladies' Culture Club meeting.

Annabelle Simmons, president of the Gunpoint Ladies' Culture Club, had once invited Amberson to join the club. Curious, Amberson had gone along to a meeting. The ladies, all the wives or daughters of the town's finer—wealthier—citizens, were planning a tree-planting-in-pots party to decorate the main thoroughfare of town, Gold Fever Street. Such a project would undoubtedly improve Gunpoint, and Amberson was most interested. However, the ladies talked more of the latest dress, fresh from St. Louis, that Estelle of the House of Beautiful Ladies wore the last time she paraded down the street, and of how Joe Parker, the proprietor of the Plugged Nickel Saloon, shamelessly chased after her when what he should have been doing was looking for a decent, law-abiding woman to marry.

Once, Amberson got up her courage to comment on how lovely larch trees would look planted in the pots. Heads turned her away, there was a long silence, and then Mrs. Stanton wondered aloud if anyone had heard that Fred Knox, the town's most dashing attorney, had been seen going into one of the local opium dens late last night.

Shortly thereafter, Amberson had politely taken her leave. When pressed by Mrs. Simmons, Amberson had cordially declined to join the Ladies' Culture Club. After that, Mrs. Simmons and some of the other ladies of the town had been noticeably cooler to her.

Hinckley Parker lowered his paper and glanced at her. He closed the paper and set it down methodically. Then he laid down his pipe next to a little tin. He cleared his throat. "How do you do, Mrs. Rowan?" he said. "Can I get you something on this fine day?"

"A sarsaparilla, please," she answered. Her throat felt dry. Suddenly she heard someone come into the store and walk up behind her. She turned around to see Mr. Fred Knox, one of the town's five attorneys, eyeing her speculatively. And standing next to him was a blond woman with eyes of ice blue that would have frozen a side of beef at twenty paces in the middle of a heat wave. She was the incredibly lovely Miss Madeline Mueler.

Mr. Knox tipped his hat to Amberson, and she thought she saw admiration in his dark eyes. Miss Mueler, on the other hand, lifted her perfectly dimpled chin and said, "Let's not associate with poor white trash."

At Amberson's gasp she sailed out the door.

Amberson gritted her teeth. There was nothing, absolutely nothing, she had to say to Miss Madeline Mueler.

Mrs. Stanton and Mrs. Reedy tittered some more behind their hands and Amberson's sharp ears distinctly heard the word "mistress."

Feeling suddenly dispirited, Amberson wandered among the shelves, acting as though she was fascinated by the sacks of flour and containers of molasses. She thought she saw pity in Mr. Knox's eyes the one time she glanced his way. She would not, she vowed, let Miss Madeline Mueler's very existence annoy her.

Justin leaned against the outside wall and looked through the window into Hinckley's General Store. A blond woman marched out the door and he perfunctorily touched the rim of his hat to her. She paused and glanced at him, interested.

He noted her fierce blue eyes. Someone to reckon with, he decided.

She sailed past him up the street, lifting her skirts as she glided along the boardwalk. He watched her go, admiring the fine sashay of her hips.

Two older women came out of the store just then, nudging one another. "Did you see her face?" demanded one.

"Oh, positively red!" assured the other.

"And Miss Mueler! That woman! The nerve! She strolled past the very woman whose husband she's sleeping with! Ha ha! Did you see it, Hyacinth?"

"Oh," answered Hyacinth gleefully, "I'm terribly surprised that Mrs. Rowan would dare to show her red face in town, aren't you, Dorothy? Whatever must she be thinking?"

"I know *I* would be squirming inside," emphasized Dorothy, "if it were *me* and if *my* husband had that little tart on the side. His mistress! Can you imagine? If my Henry even looked at another woman, why, I'd poke him in the eye with a hat pin! How can Mrs. Rowan dare to come to town and show her face?"

They hurried past Justin, shaking their heads and clucking like brooding hens.

Justin frowned. So that was the way of it, was it? The woman with the fierce blue eyes must be Richard Rowan's mistress. That explained Rowan's numerous trips into Gunpoint.

Justin quashed down the vague sadness he felt on Amberson's behalf. Dang it, she was the one who had betrayed him, to marry Rowan. Let *her* be betrayed. She deserved it. Fair enough.

Angry at his softness, he pushed himself away from the building and headed across the street to the Plugged Nickel Saloon. He'd have a whisky while she was shopping or doing whatever she was doing in there. He would not feel sorry for her!

Inside the Plugged Nickel, a party was in progress. Three brothers, Sean, Paddy, and Joseph Coyle, identical triplets with red hair, blue eyes, and freckles, sat at one of the round tables, laughing heartily. Justin had ridden with them on the Rowan cattle drive from Texas. Once they'd been paid for the drive, the rowdy Irishmen had promptly quit, preferring town life in Gunpoint.

Sean told stories that would charm a leprechaun and Paddy had a voice that made a cowboy weep just to hear him sing, he was that good. Joseph was the quiet one, except when he drank. Then he was apt to do odd things like jump up and lasso a heifer, toss her on her back, and pour a beer over her head.

"Harbinger," called Sean. "Come on over."

"Yeah," chortled Paddy. "Ye'll want to hear this. We're going to take us some wives!"

Shaking his head, wondering what the Irish cowboys were up to, Justin ordered his whisky, straight, at the counter. The bartender was a balding old man in a white shirt and black suspenders. His thin frame reminded Justin of a stick, but he poured a decent enough drink. At one end of the bar sat an old woman wearing a dirty blue gingham dress and nursing a whisky. She stared into space. Now and then she'd give a rough cackle and wipe at the highly polished mahogany counter with a gray rag.

A warped mirror and a row of glasses ran the length of the bar. Several high stools were pulled up for those customers who wanted to chat with the bartender while they took liquid refreshment. The floor was sawdust. Tables and chairs filled the rest of the room.

"Nice place you've got here," said Justin. At least it would keep his mind off a certain brown-haired, hazel-eyed termagant for a while.

"It's my son's," said the thin man proudly, mopping at the counter with another gray rag. "My son Joe owns this saloon." At Justin's nod, the man held out his hand. "Name's Pyrite Parker, but you can call me 'Pa.' Everyone else in town does." He pointed to the old woman nodding drowsily at the end of the counter. "That's Tildy, my wife. You can call her 'Ma.' 'Course she's not much of a 'ma' to anyone now." He lowered his voice. "Too old. An' ornery."

Inebriated, too, Justin noticed. He took a sip of the whisky. Expensive, it burned its way straight to the pit of his stomach. He took another sip. "You been here long?"

"Long enough," said Pa. "My family started this fine township two years ago. Me and my boys. And the old lady. My son Joe owns this saloon. My other son, Hinkley, owns the general store. They're my two successful boys," he bragged.

Justin nodded.

" 'Course I got some other sons, too." Pa lowered his voice conspiratorially. "But they didn't turn out so good. Took after their ma's side of the family, if you get my drift."

Justin raised an eyebrow in mild curiosity.

"Well, now, my son Hank, he owns a hotel and he's an engineer, too. He's workin' on a machine that will separate gold from gravel. 'Sposed to do the work of three men." Pa's forehead wrinkled with worry. "But it's taken him a good long while, it has. Don't know if he'll ever get the damn machine made."

Justin took another sip. He wiped his mouth with the back of his hand.

"Got another son. Larry. 'Loser Larry,' he's knowed as. Maybe you heerd o' him?"

Justin shook his head. "Can't recall having heard the name."

"Loser Larry. He had a mine, a good, producing gold mine. Lost it in a damn, rigged card game." Pa's disgust was evident from his downturned mouth. "Lost it to an important lawyer about town whose name I won't mention for fear he'll sue me for blackening his already black name." Pa's mouth turned down even more.

Justin swallowed another sip of whisky.

"Then there's Clive, my mule-skinnin' son. Works for that big, expensive outfit run by Mr. Rowan. Mr.

Rowan owns the Triple R Ranch." Pa peered at Justin to see if he was impressed.

Justin said, "I work for Mr. Rowan, too."

"You do? You knowed my son?"

"Can't say I've had the pleasure, sir," murmured Justin, staring into the shallow depths of his drink.

"Well, if you met him, you'd remember him. Got a mouth on him would blister a mule's ass. Not a curse word that boy don't know. Knows some I never even heerd of, and that's sayin' somethin'. Me and his mother raised him to be a good boy, too," Pa said morosely. "Don't know what went wrong with the boy."

Justin raised his glass in silent toast to good fathers who raised bad sons. He'd had a little experience with that himself. The bad son part, anyway.

"Got another boy, too," whispered Pa, leaning closer confidentially. "But I don't talk much about him."

"Oh?"

"Naw." Pa industriously wiped at the counter with the dirty rag. "Nothin' much to say."

Justin nodded. He lifted the glass to his lips and swallowed a mouthful of whisky.

Pa lowered his voice. "My last boy, Harry, he was his ma's baby. He fell down a well when he was fifteen. Hit his haid. Never been right since. Talks about hell and goin' to hell and fire and damnation, and how we all are headed straight for the hot place. Hee hee!" Pa wiped his forehead with the counter rag. "We call him 'Holy Harry.' But he ain't a great deal of fun to be around, if you get my drift."

Justin nodded.

"Got us a daughter too," sighed Pa. "Annabelle. Married the banker." Pa Parker brightened a little.

"Mr. J. V. Simmons. Don't suppose you heerd of him yet, newcomer like you?"

Justin shook his head. "No."

"Well, she married him. Right after Ma and I caught her sneakin' out the winder. They was tryin' to run away. Without," said Pa, raising a bushy gray brow, "the benefit of the state of matrimony, if you get my drift. Ma and me, we put a stop to that, right quick. Made him marry her. I got out my rifle, Bessie . . ." He reached reflexively under the counter and Justin saw the butt of a rifle.

Pa saw him eyeing it. "Bessie and me keep control of this place," he explained. "Some of the boys come in, a little fight breaks out. I'm pree-pared."

"I see that, sir," agreed Justin cautiously.

Pa shook his head. "That Annabelle. More trouble than all my boys put together, she was. I was right relieved to marry her off, I can tell you that. All them cowboys hangin' around her all the time . . . All them miners . . . All them mule skinners . . . All them soldiers . . . I sure was glad when that banker hit town, I'll tell you, though he took a little convincin'." Pa shuddered and took a drink of beer, trying to shake off obviously unhappy memories. "Ma!" he yelled at the woman sitting at the far end of the counter. "Didn't we fix Annabelle, Ma?"

Both the woman and Justin jumped.

"Wh-what?" said the woman.

Pa shook his head in disgust. "Her hearin's goin' too. Brain's goin'. Eyes goin'. Everythin's goin' on that woman. Used to be an armful of fun, if you get my drift." He shook his head mournfully. "Not no more. Not no more. Pretty soon won't be nothin' left of the old bat." He raised his voice. "I said, we put a quick stop to that, didn't we, Ma? When Annabelle was sneakin' around?"

The woman looked at him and blinked several times. She half rose from her stool, then settled back down and reached for her beer. She took a swig.

Pa waited in silent disgust. "Well, I see she ain't gonna answer me. She's a cocky one, that's for sure."

'Cocky'? Justin studied the old woman. She looked tired and drunk.

He placed his empty glass on the counter.

"Never did know what to do with Annabelle," confided Pa. "She bein' a girl and all. They're different."

"They sure are," agreed Justin fervently.

"Say, want another drink?" Pa was obviously eager for a kindred soul to talk to.

Justin stared at the mirror. He wondered if Amberson would be ready to leave by now.

"My family and I," boasted Pa expansively, "we built this town. We're the backbone of this here goddamn town!"

Justin slithered off the stool. Time to get back to the general store.

More laughter came from the triplets' table. Justin walked past them.

"Join us, Harbinger," urged Sean. He swung his beer mug back and forth.

"Come on, Harbinger," shouted Paddy. "You be needin' a drink."

Pa materialized at his elbow and handed Justin a fresh glass of whisky.

Justin paused, shrugged, went over, and sat down. "What are you boys up to?" he asked in idle amusement. He should get back to the general store; he could still see Amberson's face, pale and sickly looking, when that blond woman marched past her. But he wasn't ready, not yet.

He smiled absently at the young men. Maybe they'd amuse him for a while and he could forget about that danged Mrs. Rowan.

"We've got a plan," snorted Sean.

"A wonderful plan!" added Paddy.

"We're going to find us a bevy of wives," hooted Sean, waving his beer glass.

Justin took a judicious sip of his whisky. "So what's your plan?" he asked.

Sean leaned forward confidentially. "We're going to invite a preacher of the Mormon faith to Gunpoint. A bishop. And he'll teach us how to be Mormons, and then we'll get some wives. Three or four each!" he crowed. His good-natured face beamed.

Justin stared at them, feeling considerably older than his thirty-two years. "Now why would you want more than one wife? Most men I know can't seem to handle even one." He was surprised at the bitterness in his own voice.

"Ha ha," laughed Paddy, obviously thinking Justin was trying to amuse.

Sean and Joseph Coyle hooted.

Justin didn't think the remark was that funny.

"You can come and listen to the bishop too," said Sean kindly.

"Yes. Add to your collection of wives," added Paddy.

"What collection?" Justin asked in puzzlement.

Sean snorted. "Don't play the fool with us, Harbinger. We rode with you. We're friends. We heard about it."

Mystified, Justin stared at their expectant faces.

"You'll be getting married soon, remember?" prodded Sean. "One of the Triple R boys was in here a few nights ago. Told us so himself."

Justin shook his head. "No."

The three young men stared at him in surprise, then resumed their drinking. Sean eyed him narrowly. "Ye be tellin' us the truth?"

When Justin merely nodded and didn't say anything more, Paddy said, "We're sendin' for the Mormon bishop tomorrow. We're about to con-vert." He sounded serious. Then he winked at Justin.

"Yep. Con-vert," echoed Sean with a grin.

Justin got to his feet. All this talk of women and marriage was putting him in a sour frame of mind. "Got to be going," he explained. "I'm riding herd on Mrs. Rowan for the boss."

Sean grimaced. The others chortled and Paddy waved his beer glass in a wide circle. "Stay and have another drink," they chorused. Joseph added slyly, "Sean's buying."

Sean chortled so hard Justin knew it was a joke.

He shook his head and put on his hat. He headed for the door. Time to find Amberson and get her back to the ranch. Then his job would be done and he could get on with some real work; no more of this danged baby-sitting.

By the time he was on the road back to the Triple R, he wished he'd stayed for that drink the boys had offered him.

He glanced at Amberson's hunched shoulders for the tenth time. He sighed. She'd said not a single word to him since he'd found her sitting in the buggy, waiting for him outside Hinckley's General Store.

Well, Justin had nothing to say to her, either. He'd

mounted his horse and they'd ridden out of town, neither one speaking.

But her shoulders continued to slump, and her head drooped. She looked generally miserable. When he got back to the Triple R ranch, he was going to tell Richard Rowan that he, Justin, was done. Finished. He'd take his pay and his saddle and leave tomorrow morning. No more hanging around the gloomy Mrs. Rowan for him. No sir.

Come on, Harbinger, he scoffed, *be honest with yourself. It's not that the lovely Mrs. Rowan is gloomy. It's that her baby is a constant reminder of her betrayal, and you can't stand seeing her every day without wanting her for yourself. That's what the problem is!*

"Indeed, you're right," he muttered aloud to himself. Hell, if she wasn't going to talk to him, he might as well talk to himself. "And no amount of money Rowan pays me is worth this," he reminded himself. He had hoped to put away some cash for the ranch he wanted to build. But it wasn't worth going through this kind of torture. No sir.

Amberson looked up. "Did you say something?" she inquired.

He was surprised she'd even heard him, so despondent had she seemed. "I said we'll be at the ranch soon," he improvised.

She nodded and slumped back into herself.

He turned away. So Rowan's betrayal with the blonde was sapping the life out of her, was it? He frowned. The Amberson he saw here was nothing like the high-spirited, happy girl he'd seen at her father's wagon train that first evening so long ago. Nothing at all like her.

Troubled, he spurred Samson, and galloped ahead

of the buggy. He glanced around now and then, as was his duty.

He slowed Samson until the buggy came abreast of the horse.

Determined not to back out of what he knew he must do, he finally said to her, "I'm taking you back to the ranch. I'm leaving tomorrow. Quitting. It's better this way for both of us."

He saw surprise flare in her hazel eyes, then relief.

She nodded, and he was glad she didn't ask for an explanation. He'd have found it difficult to put into words what he was feeling. This way he didn't have to tell her that he couldn't stand the thought of Rowan's hands upon her. Nor did he have to tell her of his fury at her for marrying the rancher. Or that he couldn't stand the sight of her baby. . . . She'd betrayed him. . . .

No, it was better this way—for both of them. Nothing more to say.

They rode in silence. Justin dropped to the rear of the buggy as they plodded on.

They rounded a hill. Several shouts from behind made Justin turn in the saddle. Behind them galloped four men, red bandannas covering the lower halves of their faces.

"Rustlers! Ride!" Justin cried to Amberson. He saw the startled look on her face when he hit her mare in the flank. "Run!"

The mare raced off with the buggy bumping along behind. The reins were wrapped around Amberson's fists. She had to keep the buggy on the road while he dealt with the rustlers.

Justin pulled his rifle out of its case and lifted it.

Two shots rent the air. They were already shooting at him!

He'd be a fool to stick around. Firing off several shots in rapid succession, he spurred his horse and raced after the buggy.

Samson gained on the buggy, and Justin could hear the yells behind him as his pursuers chased him. A bullet whizzed past his ear.

He spurred the horse faster. Not too far away there was a huge tree. If he could make it to that, he could shoot at them and have protection for himself and Samson. He hoped to delay them so that Amberson and the baby could get to the ranch—and safety.

He raced along just behind the buggy. There was still a goodly distance between the buggy and the rustlers. Amberson's face was pale, but her grip on the reins held firm. The wild eyes and flaring nostrils of the chestnut mare told him it was a marvel Amberson had the horse under control at all.

They reached the tree. He veered off to the left and stopped under the wide branches while the buggy barreled on down the road. Before his horse even halted, Justin slid off and ran for the cover of the tree. He took careful aim and let off two shots.

He winged one of the rustlers, who now half leaned in the saddle. Another outlaw galloped back for the wounded man. Justin fired off two more shots, both close to the oncoming riders.

It seemed they didn't care for his brand of fighting. They wheeled their lathered mounts and raced off, back up the hill, leading the wounded man's horse. Justin fired one last shot. It kicked up dirt behind the fleeing horse's heels.

"That ought to give them something to think about," he told Samson. "They won't be back." He reloaded his rifle, then jumped on the horse. Ahead of him, the buggy was a small dot in the distance.

He spurred the gelding and they raced down the road after the fleeing buggy.

Chapter Six

Amberson held Gerald in the crook of her arm as she poured the morning coffee for Sandy, one of the cowhands. She caught sight of Justin Harbinger walking up the porch steps and deliberately turned her back. He was the last man she wanted to see.

Richard's heavy footfalls told her he'd left his study and was headed for the kitchen. Richard was the second-to-last man she wanted to see. Why was it, she wondered as she set more water to heat for coffee, that she must endure these awful men? What had she done to deserve this fate? One, a husband who betrayed her, and secondly, a so-called lover who had betrayed her as well. Whatever was the matter with her?

She kept her back to Richard and Justin, a difficult feat, since both men moved easily around the room, greeting men here and there and stopping to speak now and then. She expected any minute to hear Jus-

tin announce he was quitting. And, she thought gleefully, I can't wait to hear those words!

But breakfast was almost done, the last of the grid-
dle cakes cold on her plate, and Justin had yet to
announce his intention to leave. She'd been peeking
at him now and then. Each time she discovered Justin watching her in a kind of odd, almost thoughtful
way.

If he expected her to go up and thank him for her
and Gerald's safe return to the ranch after those rustlers chased them yesterday, he had another think
coming. She would *die* before she thanked him for
anything. *Anything.*

The men soon cleared out and breakfast was offi-
cially over.

The baby slept in Amberson's arms as she moved
about the kitchen. She set more water on the stove
to heat, poured herself one more cup of strong coffee, and sat down. She'd take a minute to calm herself before she launched into washing the dishes.

She was sitting there, sipping coffee and idly wondering how Richard would take the news of Justin's
leaving, when the very person she was thinking of
presented himself to her view again. Justin Harbinger. Rightfully named, she thought resentfully. He
was an omen, a warning actually. And unlike another meaning of his name, there would be no safe
harbor for her with this man, ever. That was certain.

"You still here?" she asked, pleased at her rude-
ness.

From the grin on his face, she wished she'd not
said a single word to him. Who could tell the way a
man's mind worked, especially this man's?

"Yes, ma'am. I'm here." He reached for the coffee-pot. "The boys are all working fence posts today. Guess I will too."

Dismay filled her. "But—but you said you were leaving. You told me so yesterday!"

He shrugged and took a sip of the steaming brew. "Mr. Rowan's a hard one to catch. I haven't had the chance to tell him yet."

Hope raised its ragged sails in her heart. Her eyes narrowed. "I expect you to be gone by noon."

He shrugged again, obviously uncaring what she hoped for or planned. "Good coffee," he complimented.

She turned away. "The sooner you're gone, the better," she muttered.

"Do you think I like being here, ma'am?" he demanded. "Do you think I like looking at you day after day, knowing you share a bed with Rowan? Do you?"

"Who I share a bed with is none of your concern," she told him icily. She was not about to tell him that he was getting his shirt in a knot for no good reason. She had not shared a bed with Richard for the better part of a year.

She swung around to face Justin and saw he was glaring down at the baby. She moved so that she blocked his view of the child with her body.

A look of disgust crossed Justin's handsome face, and for a moment she cringed inside at the contempt he held for her.

"Tell him," she ordered. "Tell Richard now."

"Tell him what?" demanded Justin. "Tell him I *know* you? In the biblical sense? Shall I tell him that?"

She felt the blood drain from her face. "I mean nothing of the sort. Tell him you're leaving and then get out!" She wanted to scream at him.

He came up to her then, and she could smell the coffee on his breath. His green eyes glittered like shards of emerald. "I'm leaving, all right, and I'll be glad to see the last of you, *Mrs. Rowan*. You and your husband deserve one another." He gave a low, cruel laugh.

She flushed. She was afraid to ask what he meant. Feeling cowardly, she whirled to leave the room.

But he blocked her way. "Oh no, you don't. Not until we have this out."

"I have nothing to discuss with you," she said stiffly, backing up a pace.

"That may be, but I sure as hell have something to discuss with you." He took a step forward menacingly.

"And what might that be?" She tilted her head up to look at him, genuinely curious.

"Tell me this," he said, and his voice was low and held a desperate note. "Tell me why you married him." He grabbed her arm.

"Let go of me!" When he released his grip, she said, "I married him for the usual reasons."

" 'The usual reasons,' " he mimicked. "Money, in other words." When she didn't answer, he demanded, "Do you love him?"

She shrugged. "Think what you want." She turned away from him, her face feeling frozen in a perpetual grimace. What was it about this man that gave him the ability to rile her so? "I think you'd better leave."

There was no sound and she peeked over her shoulder to see if he'd tiptoed out.

He glared at her. "I'll leave," he said heavily. "And I won't be back."

"Good," she said. "Get out and never come back to this ranch again!"

"Oh, you're safe from me, ma'am. Don't worry about that. I won't set foot again on this sorry piece of Montana sod, not as long as I know you're here!"

She wanted to throw a pot at him. "Get out!"

"I'm going." He headed for the door. His footsteps stopped at the threshold. "I hope you're happy with Richard," he said, his voice dripping insincerity. "I hope he does to you everything you did to me."

The vileness of his curse stunned her at first, until she realized he did not know what Richard was already doing to her. Nor did he know that she had been alone and desperate, and Richard had been the only one she could turn to in her time of grief.

"Get out," she seethed, her voice low with hate. "Get out!"

He drew back his lips in a fake grin that was more of a snarl. "Enjoy your life, *Mrs. Rowan*," he said with a false jauntiness that grated on her. He walked down the porch steps, and even his broad back seemed insolent to her.

She closed her eyes and took several breaths. She knew now what it felt like to want to kill a man.

What the hell had gotten into him? he demanded of himself as he stomped down the porch steps. It was as if he couldn't look at the woman without wanting to chew nails. And her life wasn't going to be easy; Rowan would see to that. So why this desire to punish her? To inflict more pain?

And why hadn't he gone to Rowan first thing this morning? Why this uncharacteristic lingering? To see if she'd ask him to stay? He snorted in disgust.

She'd betrayed him, the witch. Because instead of waiting for him to return to Montana as he'd expected, she'd upped and married the first rich man she could find. And had his baby.

Justin wanted to kill something, so angry did he feel. It was a good thing he was leaving the Triple R this morning. He couldn't guarantee that he'd keep his temper if he stayed any longer.

Over at the corral, Rowan shouted orders at Beau and Sandy and some of the other men. Justin veered in the direction of the corral, intent on telling Rowan he was through.

But the men with Rowan were getting on their horses now and Richard was mounting his big buckskin.

Justin quickened his pace. "Mr. Rowan," he called.

Rowan waved. "Got to get these men down to my freight house. Then I'm goin' into town. Be gone a couple of days. See to it that no rustlers bother my ranch." He gave another wave and spurred the buckskin. The horse reared on its hind hooves, then bolted down the dirt wagon track leading from the ranch.

"Son-of-a—!" How the hell was Justin supposed to quit when Rowan wouldn't even hear him out? Justin ran after the disappearing Rowan until he felt like a fool. He tore off his brown slouch hat and slammed it on the ground. Dang it! Now he was stuck another two days. With *her*. And the baby.

Just ride off and leave her here, baby and all, he told himself. A small internal voice quickly countered, "Yeah? And let the rustlers attack a defenseless woman?"

Everything Justin had ever been taught or believed in went against the notion of just walking away. No, he was stuck here. For the next two days. He'd better get used to it.

He stomped back up the dirt road, to the bunk-house. By the time he reached the cowhands' quarters, he'd worked up a sweat, but his temper had cooled some. What the hell do I do now? he wondered. He shaded his eyes from the hot sun as he glanced over at the ranch house.

She was in there. Her and the dang baby.

He pulled out the sack of tobacco he kept in his pocket and rolled himself a smoke. How had he gotten into this mess? More importantly, how the hell was he going to get out?

The cigarette tasted like cow dung and he tossed it aside half-smoked. He ground the glowing butt under his boot heel and glanced over at the ranch house, then up at the sun.

Noon. She'd given him until noon to leave the ranch. His lips curled in a humorless half-twist.

Gee. She'd just be tickled pink to see him again.

Chapter Seven

He'd put in a good day's work. No rustlers around, but he'd yet to set foot in Mrs. Amberson Hawley Rowan's kitchen since the set-to they'd had this morning. He figured dark was about as long as he could be expected to stay away, and it was dark now.

He was tired, hungry, thirsty, and, yes, ornery enough to go in and demand some supper.

He stomped up the porch stairs, his muscles aching from a day spent working on the fences within sight of the house. He paused on the porch. Everything seemed quiet inside. Perhaps he should just head back to the bunkhouse. But his growling stomach objected to that idea.

And then the door opened and Amberson was standing there, her slim figure silhouetted in the lamplight. He curled his fingers to prevent himself from reaching for her. God, he couldn't still want her.

"Well, are you coming in?" Her taut voice held no welcome.

He took off his slouch hat and looked at her. Really looked at her. What he saw was a tired, listless woman. There were dark circles under her eyes and her chestnut-colored hair had worked its way out of the neat bun she'd worn it in this morning. Wisps of hair framed her pale face. Sadly, he realized that this woman would grow old before her time if she stayed with Richard Rowan.

"Yeah." He stepped inside the warmly lit kitchen. The fragrant aroma of roast beef made his mouth water.

"I saw Richard ride off," she said, and he could hear the trembling in her voice. "I don't suppose he said where he was going."

He looked at her in astonishment. "You're married to him. Don't you know?"

She shook her head as she closed the door behind him. "He doesn't tell me much," she said wearily.

Where was the fiery woman he'd argued with this morning? wondered Justin. "He said he'd be gone for a couple of days." Justin watched her slowly cross the kitchen. "Said he was heading into town."

Unbidden thoughts of what Richard was going to do in town entered Justin's mind. From the weary slump of her shoulders, he guessed she, too, knew that Richard visited the blond woman in Gunpoint.

He suddenly remembered his own words from the morning. Richard was doing to her just what she had done to him.

He should be glad. Then why did he feel like a horse had just kicked him in the belly?

Amberson gestured vaguely at the stove. "Help yourself. I'm going upstairs to get the baby."

He nodded and took the roast out of the oven. He sliced off some meat, spooned some potatoes onto his plate, and grabbed three hot biscuits from the pan. He sat down at the closest table and wolfed down the meal, glad he didn't have to eat it in her presence. He was drinking a cup of coffee when she came downstairs, the baby in her arms.

The baby's cornflower blue eyes fastened on him. Justin turned away and stared at his cup. "Look, it was not my idea to stay," he said. "I was ready to go. But if I left there would be no one to keep an eye on things here."

"To watch out for rustlers, you mean," she said in that tart voice of hers.

"Woman, you sound like you just drank a barrelful of vinegar."

"What is that supposed to mean?"

He shrugged. "You aren't exactly sweetness itself."

He stirred his coffee, wondering what had happened to the lovely chestnut-haired girl he'd first met. That angel had somehow been replaced by this vinegar-tongued harpy.

She set the baby in his basket and stood, arms akimbo. "Sweetness? You want sweetness?" She looked angry.

He straightened. "It'd be a nice change."

"Hunh!" she snarled. "What do you know?"

Somehow Amberson must have got her second wind while she was upstairs doing whatever it was she did for the baby. Her tiredness had fled and she leaned forward, spoiling for a fight.

"You want sweetness?" she cried. "Sweetness wouldn't give me a roof over my head! Sweetness wouldn't put food on my table! Sweetness wouldn't take care of my baby!"

"No need for you to scream at me, woman! I get the point. You married the man for his money. You weren't the first woman to think of it; you won't be the last." He finished his coffee and stood up. "I got to be going. A fight ain't exactly my cup of tea after a long day mendin' fences."

He must have taken the wind out of her sails with that one for she plopped down on the bench and looked visibly wilted.

"Well, you certainly weren't here when I needed you," she said in a calmer voice. "Where were you? Running off after your regiment. And the war ended a month later!" A look of suspicion crossed her face. "I never did believe that regiment story anyway."

He frowned. "What do you mean? I had to take those men back to Virginia. I had orders—"

"Orders?" She lifted one brow wryly. "How convenient that you had to return just as—" But she didn't continue.

"Just as what?" he prompted.

"Nothing." Her voice was sullen as she glared at the floor.

"I don't see why you're so concerned about a roof over your head and food on the table. Your daddy must have left you a goodly sum." He waved a hand, taking in the kitchen. "Wasn't what he left you enough? Some women are just plain greedy, I guess."

She raised her eyes to him then, and he saw fire gleam in their hazel depths. He stopped himself from taking a step back.

"You know nothing," she hissed.

He shrugged. "I know enough. I know what it feels like when a woman swears she'll wait for a man and then she goes off and marries the first fellow she finds. I know what that feels like."

There was a throbbing silence in the kitchen. Only the ticking of the clock gave a semblance of normalcy to the room.

"How about," she said, in a honey sweet voice, "when a man says he's coming back and never shows up?"

"Then I'd think the woman would wait. If she loved the man, like she said she did, she'd wait. A good woman would. A *faithful* woman."

She gasped and looked stricken suddenly at his words. He'd struck deep.

"Well, a good man means what he says," she countered, when she'd gotten her breath back. "An *honest* man. But then, we're not talking about an honest man, are we? We're talking about a man who seduces a woman by moonlight, says sweet words to her, then leaves with his regiment at the first opportunity."

"There was a *war* going on, for God's sake! I had *orders!* There were men being killed. I had to return to Virginia. I had no choice!"

"Neither did I!"

Her words made no sense to him.

"And," she added triumphantly, "said dishonest man returns to Montana to marry another woman!"

He glared at her. He wasn't about to tell her that the woman he'd thought he was going to marry was her. Not when she'd upped and married Rowan already. No. That secret he'd take to his grave. She wasn't going to make a fool of him twice.

"I'm sure you sweet-talked her into giving her body to you too."

The words fell heavily between them.

He couldn't deny he'd enjoyed making love to Amberson. She'd been so sweet, so trusting. . . .

When he didn't answer, she said cynically, "Probably in the moonlight too."

He flinched and hoped she didn't see.

"Tell me," she continued, too sweetly, "does she sneak away from her family to meet you too? Do you pretend to be good friends with her papa and her brother too?"

"That's a low blow, Amberson," he said unsteadily. "I respected your father. I regret his death. As for your brother—"

"Hah! You didn't respect my father! You only pretended to. So you could sneak away with his daughter and do unspeakable things to her!"

"Unspeakable?" He glared at her. "What are you talking about? What we did was normal for a man and woman—"

"For a *married* man and woman," she cried. "Not for a young girl and a grown man."

"You were twenty! That's full grown."

"Nineteen."

"You told me twenty."

She was silent.

"You lied to me then." He stuck out his jaw stubbornly.

"Not as much as you lied to me!" She was breathing fire.

"I didn't lie to you."

"You're lying to me now!"

"I am not!"

"Are!"

"Am not!"

There was a lengthy silence as they both realized they did not sound like the full-grown man and woman they each claimed to be.

"Where is your brother anyway?" tossed out Justin.

"Kingsley is—away."

"Away? Away where?"

"None of your concern."

He shrugged. "How come your brother isn't here to help you?"

"Help me? I—I don't need help."

"Oh?"

Her hazel eyes dared him to say anything further. He decided not to mention the blonde in Gunpoint.

"And I see you're using the same worming tactics to make yourself indispensable to Richard!"

"What are you talking about?" he asked grimly.

"Richard. You convinced him he needed to hire you."

Justin gave a rough laugh. "He didn't need convincing. He thought it up himself."

"Oh, I know how sly you can be."

He crossed his arms over his chest, wondering what was coming next.

"Making him think you saved his life . . ."

Justin snorted. "It is unfortunate that it had to be me who saved Rowan's life, isn't it?" he needled. "But, as the cattle were stampeding, and Rowan was thrown from his horse into their path, and as there was no one else around to do the job, I figured it was up to me to save him." He bared his teeth in a grimace of a smile. "I thought I might as well rescue him before the cattle stomped him flat."

"Humph," she snorted back.

He glanced around the kitchen. " 'Course I didn't know then what a cozy situation you were in. I guess I could have let the cattle stomp him—" He rubbed the back of his neck, as if considering such an outrageous thing.

"You wouldn't dare!"

"Of course not. I saved the man's life. Hell, I didn't know who he was. Or what he was. If he was rich or poor, beggarman or thief! All I knew was, his life was in danger and if I didn't do something, he'd be pushing up weeds next week."

She was silent at that. Finally she said, "I can tell when a man is telling the truth."

"Yeah?"

"And that day you left me, kissing me good-bye oh so sweetly, I knew then you weren't coming back."

"Huh?"

"I knew you had no intention of returning."

"That so?"

"Yes." She walked across the kitchen as though in a daze. "I watched you. You couldn't wait to get on your horse. Your eyes were on your men, telling them to saddle up, to head out. You weren't thinking of me, didn't even know you were talking to me—"

"I had orders—!"

She turned her fiery gaze on him. "I knew then that you weren't coming back. Not to me."

She sat down on a bench with a heavy, disheartened thump. Her bright gaze dared him to say anything.

"Is that why you married Rowan?"

"Yes. I knew you weren't coming back."

So. She'd had no faith in him. It seemed he had none in her either. They were doomed from the start, he thought gloomily.

He headed for the door. They'd said enough. He stepped onto the porch and looked up at the shining stars. "Nothin' left to say," he said quietly.

"Nothing," she agreed from the kitchen.

"I'll be goin' back to the bunkhouse, then. Thanks for supper."

He stepped off the porch and the door slammed behind him. He jumped at the loud sound. Her final words came through the door. "Next time get your own damned supper!"

Chapter Eight

Justin peeled off his shirt. It was hot as hell. The sun blazed down on him as he chopped at the poles to make more fence posts. He'd be glad when this fence post chore was done. If it was up to him, he'd never come within ten feet of another fence post the rest of his life.

He glanced at the ranch house. It was some distance away, but the land was flat, covered with knee-high grass, and he could see anyone who approached the house. Except from the creek side, of course.

The creek ran through the Triple R Ranch about a quarter mile from the house. There was a point of land where the creek jutted away from the dwelling. Several acres of aspens, cottonwoods, and willows grew in thick profusion on that point.

He thought about swimming in the creek to cool off, but finally decided he'd better stay close to his horse in case he had to ride to the house. After all, guarding Mrs. Amberson Hawley Rowan and her dang baby was his job.

Just the thought of the wretched woman made him grit his teeth. He should have hotfooted it a little faster after Rowan yesterday morning. Should have told him he was quitting. Right then. Wouldn't have taken no for an answer, either. No sir.

Justin swung the ax a little harder. The shiny steel blade bit into the wood, and he felt some satisfaction at that. He needed the hard work just to keep himself sane after being around Amberson.

After much chopping, he paused and wiped the sweat from the back of his neck. He heard a loud snort from his horse. Samson was tied to an upright fence post and had spent most of his time with his eyes half-closed and his black tail flicking flies off his back.

"What is it, boy?"

The animal's ears were back and he shifted around to look in the direction of the creek. He tried to pull away from the pole; the whites of his eyes showed.

Justin stared at the clump of aspens near the creek. "You hear somethin', Samson?" Justin stood stock-still, listening.

"I hear it too." He reached for his shirt. As he did, four men suddenly broke from the aspens and galloped directly for the ranch house. All four wore red bandannas across their faces. One had his arm in a white sling.

Justin threw his shirt aside and raced for his horse. Swiftly, he untied Samson from the post, mounted the animal, and wheeled the gelding's head around. "Let's go!" he shouted, spurring the horse.

Samson leaped forward. As he galloped, Justin pulled out his rifle from its case on his saddle.

Meanwhile the rustlers had headed for the corral, where a small herd of twenty or so cows stood. Rowan had corralled them there days before with the intention of branding them when he returned.

Either the rustlers didn't give a damn about Justin or they had yet to see him, for they were taking their time rounding up the heifers.

Which was fine with Justin. He lifted his rifle to his shoulder and fired, deliberately aiming high above one of the men's heads.

Startled, the man glanced his way; then he began yelling. The others tried to hurry the cows out of the pen. It was obvious they wanted the herd and were willing to take a risk to get it.

"Time to fire a little closer," grated Justin to Samson. He squeezed off another shot, this time a little closer to the leader's head.

The frightened man called to his comrades and they turned as one and raced for the beckoning safety of the aspens.

Justin veered toward the creek and fired one more shot. The men disappeared into the trees.

Justin raced up to the point of land where the trees started. He had a choice: cross the creek, go into the trees, and take his chances with the four desperadoes, or he could return to the ranch house and hold them off if they decided to have another try at the cattle.

The second alternative seemed the wisest, so Justin wheeled Samson around and galloped for the house. No one shot at him or chased after him. Maybe he had frightened them away, after all.

"It's a good thing Rowan is paying me so well," he told Samson. "I'm doing more guard duty on this ranch than anything else."

He tied the horse to the porch post and ran up the steps. He didn't wait to knock, just opened the door and barged in.

"Mrs.—?"

Before he could call her name, Amberson came racing down the stairs and barreled into his arms. "Did you see them? It's them, the ones who chased us!"

He looked down into her wide, frightened hazel eyes, more green than brown in her fear. "Yeah. It's them," he agreed. "I recognized two of the horses. A bay with a blaze and a white forefoot. A chestnut with a white, half-moon scar on one flank. And the man with the sling—I wounded him the other day. It's them all right!" His body tightened. Holding her like this, feeling the curves of her waist, smelling the scent of her—

Her loosened hair tumbled over his hand. He could feel her trembling and he tightened his arms around her. God, she felt good in his arms again. He'd forgotten how good. He closed his eyes and inhaled her lavender fragrance.

"Oh, Justin," she moaned. "They could have taken the baby!"

"Not likely," he corrected her gently. "They were after the heifers, not babies." Slowly he ran his hands up and down her back. It had been so long, God, so long since he'd held her. . . .

She looked up at him then, leaning into him. "You drove them away. I'm so glad! I don't know what I would have done—!" She started to tremble again.

"Ssh, you're safe," he whispered, his lips lowering to hers. Just one taste. That's all he wanted. One taste and he could leave the ranch a happy man.

He closed his eyes and his lips touched hers. Ah,

she tasted sweet. He could feel her mouth move under his and then she put her arms around his neck. She moaned softly and he pulled her closer. When he felt her press herself still closer to him, he cupped her buttocks and drew her up hard against him.

His lips were moving over her cheeks now, down her neck. God, he wanted her. His body already knew what to do, had done it before with this woman. He had to have her again.

"Oh, Justin!" She broke away from his kiss, gasping for breath.

He closed his eyes and put his head back. She was married. Another man's wife. What he wanted was against God's laws. But his throbbing body cared little about any spiritual concerns.

She pushed on his shoulders. "We mustn't, Justin. I can't—!"

The sound of rapid hoofbeats outside the house froze them both. She pulled out of his embrace, jumped back, and ran to the window. "It's Richard!"

He saw panic in her eyes. More panic than when the rustlers had struck.

He wanted to pull her back into his arms. "Richard?" he repeated, to buy time. He fought to make sense of what she was telling him. "Can't be. He's supposed to be in town."

The door opened and Rowan charged through. "Harbinger," he cried. "I saw it all!"

Justin braced himself for the attack. Amberson's fist flew to her mouth in a guilty start.

Rowan marched up to Justin, seized his hand, and began pumping his arm up and down. "I saw you chase those rustlers, Harbinger! You protected my son!"

Justin flushed. "That's what you hired me for," he answered gravely.

Rowan beamed. "I saw it all! I saw them run! Saw you shoot at them!"

Justin nodded shortly, guilt eating at him. What you didn't see, he thought, was me holding your wife.

Rowan said to Amberson, "Get the boy. I want to make sure he's all right."

"He's asleep, Richard," she implored. "Let him nap."

"Get the boy!"

She turned and walked up the stairs. Rowan watched her go, then turned to Justin. "You get more pay, Harbinger, starting today." He clapped Justin on the back. "Why, I'm paying you double, more than any two of my men." He grinned. "But you're worth it. That was fine work you made of those rustlers. I know my boy's safe around you."

But not your wife, thought Justin with another stab of guilt.

Amberson came down the stairs, her sleepy son whimpering in her arms. "He's tired, Richard," she pleaded. "He needs his sleep."

But Rowan drew the boy out of her arms and peered at him. "Looks all right to me," he pronounced. Satisfied, he handed the boy back to her. "Take him back upstairs if it's so damn important."

Amberson snatched the child to her breast and hugged him.

Rowan shook his head at Justin and said, "Women! Who needs 'em?"

Amberson spun on her heel and carried Baby Gerald back upstairs, her ears and face burning. Richard treated her as though she was nothing to him, nothing! Which, she realized, was exactly what he thought of her. Nothing.

And as for Justin . . . she fumed as she laid Gerald back in his basket, hoping he'd fall asleep once more . . . with Justin her response had been nothing short of humiliating. The man had only to touch her, kiss her, and she threw herself into his arms. Well, it would not happen again. She would make certain of that. She had said vows of marriage to Richard before God and man. She would abide by those vows. She would!

She would not go near Justin. She'd given herself to him, once, long ago, and she would never do so again. She had learned the hard way about Mr. Justin Harbinger. And she would never trust him with her heart again!

Chapter Nine

There was no one else at the ranch besides Justin, Amberson, and Richard Rowan. And the dang baby. The two men sat at one kitchen table and ate the evening meal of beefsteaks. Amberson sat at the other table and nibbled at her food, now and then warily lifting her head to watch the two men.

Dinner was a mite awkward, noted Justin, as he drank his evening coffee and wondered when to tell Rowan he was leaving the ranch. The reminder of how much Rowan was paying him might have had something to do with Justin's reluctance to say anything. With what the man was paying him, he could start his own ranch months earlier than he'd planned.

Amberson and Rowan had barely spoken two words to one another through the entire meal and Justin was tired of trying to start a reasonable dinner conversation. So he'd let them ignore one another and all three had lapsed into silence. But now the baby started crying.

Justin wanted to plug his ears. Even Amberson looked a little piqued at the loud cries of her child.

"Time to get back to the bunkhouse," Justin said as he hastily finished his coffee. He rose to his feet.

Amberson and Rowan seemed to take his imminent departure as a signal to attack each other. Rowan snarled at Amberson, "I know you've been spending my money again!"

"I have no idea what you're talking about," she retaliated, her eyes flashing. The baby wailed.

"Shut that baby up, for crying out loud!"

"I can't! He just cries."

"Then make him stop."

"I don't know how! He'll stop soon!"

Justin had frozen halfway to the door. Now, trying to pretend he wasn't there to hear their argument, he slunk another step toward the door.

The baby let out more cries and Amberson started walking back and forth across the kitchen floor with him, bouncing him in her arms to try to calm him.

The baby wailed louder.

"Oh, for God's sake," cried Rowan in disgust, getting to his feet.

Justin had almost reached the door by now, and was wishing he was invisible.

"Why the hell did I marry you?" snarled Rowan. "You're one hell of a poor mother, you're a limp rag in bed, and you can't even shut up a baby!"

Amberson whirled. "Don't start in on me," she cried. "You won't like what you get, I assure you!"

"And what might that be? More of the same? Spending my money like it was water? Marrying you was one sorry proposition, I'll tell you that. If you hadn't told me your old man was so rich—"

"I didn't tell you!" screeched Amberson. "You thought that up all by yourself. I told you my father was poor! He was impoverished by all those wagon accidents!"

"Hell, you didn't tell me that until my Pinkerton man walked through the door, just returned from Pennsylvania! You tried to beat him to it. Only the news was old, real old, and you'd known a long time that your old pa didn't have a pot to piss in!"

"That's a lie!" Amberson sounded livid.

Justin made it to the front door, slipped through, and closed the door quietly behind him. Then he hightailed it to the bunkhouse. The last words he heard were Rowan's: "I don't care what the hell you think! I'm going where a woman understands a man! I'm going to Gunpoint!"

Justin reached the bunkhouse just before he heard the front door of the ranch house slam. He glanced back in time to see Rowan stomp down the steps and whistle for his buckskin. The animal whinnied in the corral and Rowan marched over, threw the bridle on his horse, tossed the saddle on, climbed on the big animal, and galloped off in the direction of Gunpoint.

"Whew!" exclaimed Justin to himself. "Those two were as mad as wet roosters!"

No, he did not envy Rowan his marital life. Watching Rowan and Amberson in action gave a man the idea that the marital state was to be avoided at all costs. It was the first time Justin had heard, however, that Amberson wasn't the rich woman he'd thought her to be. She'd shouted something about her father being impoverished by wagon accidents.

Justin frowned. If that was true, he could see why

she'd stuck around the ranch. She had no money, except for what Rowan gave her. He supposed she had no place else to go.

Where the hell was Kingsley, her brother? he wondered. From what Justin knew of the man, surely he would be concerned about his sister.

Justin spent a fitful night, his sleep disturbed by dreams of Amberson calling out to him for help. When dawn finally arrived, he watched pale light streak through the cracks in the bunkhouse and wondered if he should even go to the kitchen for a cup of coffee. He decided he would, then he'd go to work on the dang fence again.

When he reached the ranch house, all was silent. There was no sign of Rowan's buckskin gelding in the corral. That meant he must have spent the night in Gunpoint, mused Justin. He wondered what Amberson thought of that.

Justin paused at the top of the front steps, but he could hear no sound of movement on the other side of the heavy door. She's not awake yet, he decided. He'd light the fire in the huge stove, make his coffee, cook some bacon, and be on his way to the fence posts before she rose.

His plan went well until he sat down to eat his breakfast. Then he heard her soft footfalls in the stairwell.

His stomach did a somersault as Amberson walked into the kitchen wearing a blue-checked cotton dress and with her chestnut hair done up in a neat bun at the back of her head. Just the sight of her made his senses sharpen. What was it about the woman?

There was a desperate gleam in her eyes and a shaky smile on her strained face. She carried the dang baby propped upright against one shoulder. This morning, Justin noted morosely, the baby slept quietly.

Amberson shuffled over to the pot of coffee he'd made and, with one hand, poured herself a steaming cup.

After she'd been in the kitchen a full three minutes and had yet to say a word to him, he asked, "How's the baby doing?"

He didn't really want to know how the dang baby was doing, but anything was better than watching her with his tongue hanging out.

She stared at her cup. "Baby's fine," she answered slowly, shifting a little so that he couldn't see the boy.

She tottered over to the table, to the farthest spot away from Justin, and sat down. She stroked the baby's back and murmured soft words, then pulled up a white blanket and covered the baby's head with it, shielding the child from Justin's gaze. Justin had the sudden irrational thought that she was protecting the baby from him, of all people.

Well, hell. If she was going to be unfriendly, he might as well go and work at fence posts. While he finished up his bacon and bread, he waited for her to say something else, but she didn't.

He heaved himself to his feet. "Got to get to work," he said, for the sake of saying something.

She looked up then, and he saw her flush. She nodded her agreement and he wondered why she didn't remind him that he had said he was going to quit. The old Amberson, the one he'd known first, would have. "Watch out for Richard," she said instead. Her voice quavered.

He paused at the door and turned. "Beg your pardon?"

"Richard. Watch out for him. He's not a man to cross."

"I don't plan on crossing your husband, ma'am," he answered. "I just plan on working for him."

She looked at him then and he saw the trapped look in her eyes. She clutched the baby to her. "Of course," she said softly. "Don't mind me, Mr. Harbinger. I didn't mean to say that." She forced a faltering smile.

He crossed the floor to her and stared down at her. How had the bright, laughing Amberson Hawley he'd known come to this?

After a moment he asked quietly, "Why didn't you remind me that I said I'd leave?" Somehow, if he could just get her mettle up, maybe he'd see the Amberson he once knew.

"Leave?" She closed her eyes. "W-Why, I know you won't. Not now. Richard is paying you too much. You'll stay. Any man would." She opened her eyes and glanced away, refusing to meet his gaze.

"You think Richard Rowan has bought me?" he asked, incredulous.

She shrugged. "He buys anybody he wants. Why should you be any different?"

Anger rose in him. "What about you?" he observed nastily. "I'd say Rowan bought you—with this big house and his freight-line business."

She refused to answer, but he saw a vein at her temple throb. He felt a grim satisfaction. "Why do you stay?" he asked, enjoying her discomfort. "Do you love him? Does he love you? Why, right now, he's off with another wo—uh, off in Gunpoint." Somehow throwing Rowan's mistress at her was too low a blow—even for him.

"The baby," she said simply. She ducked her head

and he saw that her cheeks were flushed. She nuzzled the top of the white-blanketed head.

He sucked in his breath and glanced down at the sleeping child. He'd suspected the baby was the reason she stayed, but somehow he was not prepared for her to admit it.

She shifted on the bench and moved a corner of the blanket again so that it covered the baby's head, blocking Justin's view. Sure was protective of that child.

"I'm not going to hurt your baby," he said softly, wondering why he bothered to reassure her. Nothing, nothing had gone right between them since he'd first set foot on this ranch.

"No, you won't," she confirmed. "Because I won't let you." She sat up a little straighter.

He shook his head, baffled. He forced himself to walk to the front door. He opened it, wondering why he'd ever bothered to try to talk with the woman.

He paused at the open door and asked, "Does Rowan go into Gunpoint often?"

Amberson's head jerked up at his words and her huge hazel eyes fastened on him. She looked suddenly ill, as though he'd betrayed her in a terrible way. He couldn't look at her any more once he saw tears well up, in her eyes.

"Rowan's a fool," added Justin; then he stepped onto the porch and closed the door behind him. Indeed, Rowan was a fool. He had a beautiful wife, a child that was healthy—that is, Justin supposed the child was healthy. He'd found himself ignoring the child as often as possible—but still, Rowan had a family, for God's sake. Why was he trotting off after the blonde in Gunpoint?

Some men, Justin thought to himself as he

plunked his slouch hat on his head, didn't know when they had it good.

He took a breath. It wouldn't do for him to get caught up in Amberson Hawley Rowan's problems. He reminded himself that he'd seen people in worse situations. Far worse. Like dying on the battlefield during the war. No, Amberson didn't need his pity. She'd married the son of a bitch, now let her live with him.

His angry feelings roiling inside him, Justin stepped off the porch and headed for the line of fence posts. Maybe a whole day of digging fence-post holes would clear his head of the softness he seemed to exhibit whenever he was around Mrs. Amberson Hawley Rowan.

Chapter Ten

Richard returned to the Triple R Ranch the next day, and Amberson wished he'd stayed in Gunpoint. She didn't want to see him, to look at his smug face and see the all-too-apparent signs of his betrayal. She knew what he did in Gunpoint, and with whom. Indeed, the whole town knew. Even Justin knew. Now.

The question he'd put to her yesterday, asking if Richard went to Gunpoint often, had startled and humiliated her. She didn't want his pity, didn't want anything from him. But to have him know that Richard thought so little of her . . . Lord, she'd wanted to drop through the floor! Odd, though, now that she thought about it, how she'd felt a tingle of warmth when she'd caught Justin's words: "Rowan's a fool." Somehow, that one statement made her feel a little less alone.

At this moment, the house was quiet. Richard was in his study, working on the accounts for his freight-line business. He'd be in there most of the day. Baby Gerald was asleep upstairs, taking his afternoon nap. The whole house was silent.

Beau and some of the other ranch hands had returned earlier in the morning from working the freight line. To her surprise, Beau had volunteered to stay in the house and call her the moment he heard the baby cry. That left her free to do what she really wanted to do, which was to ride her chestnut mare, Jessie. It had been so long since she'd ridden astride that she feared she'd forgotten how. A ride along the lane and over the hills would give her a chance to forget the misery of her life with Richard. And it would take her thoughts off Justin Harbinger.

She took one last peek at the baby. Gerald still slept. Yes, she would use this time to go for a ride.

She reached the barn and found that Jessie was as anxious as she to get out. Stroking the white blaze on her horse's forehead, she whispered, "You're such a good girl, Jessie. We're going to go for a nice ride today, aren't we?" Jessie's ears twitched forward as she moved closer to Amberson to hear the kind words.

Jessie was the only possession Amberson still owned from the time before tragedy struck her family. Her father had given her the mare for her sixteenth birthday. Everything else her family owned had been lost in unfortunate mishaps as they traveled west. Amberson was thankful that she and Kingsley and Jessie had been spared. They'd escaped by riding double off across the grassy plains. When they'd returned, it was to find the smoking remains of her father's wagon train.

Even now, there were days when Amberson could scarcely believe that her father and mother were gone. She sighed. But they *were* gone. Fortunately, she still had Jessie. And Baby Gerald. And she supposed she had Kingsley, her brother, but he was so far away.

Telling herself firmly not to dwell on her unhappy past, Amberson fed two carrots to the horse and cooed love words to her. Jessie's Arab bloodlines showed in her small head and arched tail and her love of running. She would give lovely foals one day.

Amberson put the bridle on the mare. Jessie was frisky, knowing she was going to be ridden, and Amberson had to speak calmly to her several times to get the horse to settle down. She put the saddle across Jessie's broad back and was just tightening the girth when someone said, "Who said you could go riding?"

Her heart fell. "Is there a reason you don't want me to go riding, Richard?" Or is it plain old animosity? she wanted to add, but didn't.

Richard said nothing, just reached for the mare's bridle. His sudden action caused the mare to rear her head back. A waft of whisky drifted past Amberson's nose. He'd been drinking. Fear skittered down her spine.

"I don't want you riding this horse. You might fall."

Now why would that bother you? wondered Amberson. She tightened her lips to hide her frustration and to keep from riling him. "Is the baby still asleep?"

"Far as I know." Richard turned to face her. "Look, Amberson, let's not fight."

She rubbed her cheek thoughtfully and took her time, answering carefully. "*I* don't want to fight, Richard."

"Good. Neither do I." He patted the horse's nose

and Jessie sidled away from his touch. Jessie doesn't like him either, thought Amberson.

"You're the mother of my child," said Richard earnestly. "Let's try and get along. For Gerald's sake."

She glanced at him out of the corner of her eye. She'd heard Richard speak like this before, usually after a romping good time in Gunpoint. Guilt did strange things to the man.

She tightened the girth and turned to face him. "Fine. Let's. For a start, how about you stop seeing Madeline Mueler?"

Richard's smile was bland. "Miss Mueler? What do you mean?"

"Do I have to say it outright, Richard? We both know what—"

He put up his hand. "Now, Amberson, don't go getting me angry. I don't like to hear you talk this way. Miss Mueler is a fine woman. Leave her out of this."

Amberson turned back to the girth and checked it. A needless action, but something to do besides watch Richard stand there and lie to her. She took several breaths.

"I respect Miss Mueler, as I do many of the citizens of Gunpoint," continued Richard in that smooth, bland voice. "I don't know what's the matter with you. I truly don't. I'm a good husband. I provide for you and the baby. A roof over your head, food on the table . . . You've got no reason to complain. But that's all you do. Whine and complain."

Amberson gave the saddle girth another needless jerk. Jessie grunted.

"Oh, sure," Richard added, "so I go into town now and then and have a few drinks with the boys. Where's the harm in that?" His voice started to rise.

"It's a wonder I don't chase after other women, the way you treat me—"

"Richard," she interrupted, before he could launch into a tirade against her, a tirade she'd heard too many times before, "I really don't want to discuss this—"

"I really don't want to discuss this," he mimicked in a falsetto, his blue eyes spitting fire.

She turned to him. "You said you didn't want to fight."

"That was before I tried to talk some sense into you. Now I see it can't be done."

She glanced down and saw his fists clench. She knew what was coming next.

"Richard," she said, as calmly and as soothingly as she'd spoken to Jessie earlier, "I want to go for a ride. Please step aside so I may do so."

He set his jaw and glared at her.

"Please." God, she hated the pleading in her voice, but she had to placate him.

He stepped in closer. "You damn witch. What right do *you* have to tell me to step aside?"

"None, Richard," she said meekly, casting her eyes down. If only he'd stop . . . he was working himself up . . .

"I wish to God I'd never married you," he snarled.

Why did you then? she wanted to ask, but did not dare.

"Madeline Mueler is ten times the woman you are!"

She kept silent, kept her eyes on the stable floor. Maybe he'd—

Crack! The blow caught her by surprise. She spun to the side and fell against the hard floor. Moaning, she tried to get up.

Richard stood over her. "You witch! You think because I married you, you can talk to me any damn way you want to!"

She shook her head and tried to rise.

He kicked her; she buckled to the floor again, holding her stomach. Oh Lord, it hurt. She closed her eyes, trying to blot out the angry vision of his face.

"I don't want to hear a single word out of you, you horse turd! That's all you are. You hear me?" He gave her another kick. "A horse turd, that's what!"

She moaned again and tried to protect her stomach. "Richard," she whispered, "please stop."

"Ah, what's the use?" he demanded. He turned on his heel and stormed out of the stable. She relished the silence after he'd gone. Maybe she'd just stay here on the floor; things were hazy, after all. And her stomach hurt. Lord, it hurt. And her head. He must have hit her really hard this time; she couldn't remember it hurting like this before. . . .

Sometime later she awoke on the stable floor. How Jessie had avoided stepping on her, she didn't know.

Stiff, sore, Amberson slowly sat up. She looked at herself. Horse manure on her hand . . . straw in her hair . . . what had happened to her?

Fuzzily, it came to her. Richard. He had come to the barn. He'd hit her. . . .

She groaned and got slowly to her feet. How long had she been unconscious? There would be no ride for her today. . . . Gerald, she had to see Gerald, make sure her baby was all right. How long had she been gone from the house?

"Sorry, Jessie," she murmured, staggering as she lifted off the saddle. Oh, her stomach. It hurt so much.

She managed to get off the bridle and let the horse

out into the paddock at the back of the barn. I've got to get some rest, she thought.

She staggered to the house. Beau looked at her strangely when she came in. "You all right, Missus Rowan?"

She nodded. "Just tired, is all," she said, smiling weakly. Wouldn't do to tell Beau what had happened. What could a dwarf do against Richard? Nothing.

But she was unprepared for Justin. She hadn't known he was in the ranch house. He came out of Richard's study just as Amberson reached the foot of the stairs.

"Miss Amberson?" There was surprise on his face. And something else . . . pity? Horror?

She glanced away from him so he wouldn't see her bruised face and staggered up the stairs. She washed herself at the water pitcher, pulled some straw out of her hair. She peered in the mirror. Lord, she looked a mess. No wonder Beau had looked so concerned. Gerald was still asleep, thank God. What Justin thought, she didn't want to know. She could never face him again, she *did* know that.

Amberson fell across the bed and slept for the rest of the afternoon. She awoke to Gerald's cries and the late afternoon sun slanting through her bedroom window.

She felt her face. It was puffy where Richard had hit her. Maybe if she wore her hair down, she could hide it.

She heard footsteps on the stairs. Richard's. She couldn't help herself; she curled up into a ball on the bed.

"Amberson?" He didn't sound so confident now. His words were slurred. He lurched into the room.

"You gonna make dinner for the boys? They're all waitin'."

Nothing said about what he'd done to her.

"Whassa matter with you? Get off'n that bed. It's way past time for you to make dinner."

He swayed in the doorway. He looked out of place next to her lace-draped windows. She had banished him from her bedroom as soon as she'd found out about the Mueler woman. He had not set foot in her room, her domain, since that first time she'd accused him of sleeping with Madeline. Which he'd denied, of course.

He stepped closer. Swaying. "Whassa matter? Get up!"

Did he remember nothing?

Stiffly, she sat up, straightening her hair. She got to her feet. She wished her head didn't throb so.

Richard staggered over and peered at her. "You all right, Amberson?"

He didn't remember, then. She sighed and nodded. "Yes."

He blinked slowly at her. She wondered if he even knew where he was.

"Richard," she said slowly and carefully, "I want you to do something for me."

"You make dinner, then I'll do something for you."

"Very well," she agreed cautiously. "As long as you do this one thing for me."

"Whass zat?"

"Fire Justin Harbinger for me."

Richard blinked again and started to laugh. "Hell no, Amberson. Why would I do a thing like that? He saved little Gerald. He saved me. Hell, I'm not gonna fire him. You're a fool to ask."

She straightened her hair around her face a little more, then reached for the baby.

"Go make dinner," Richard ordered.

She picked up Gerald and buried her nose in his soft neck. She inhaled his fragrance. "I love you, Gerald," she whispered.

"Get goin'! Men're waitin'! Don't have all night . . ."

Amberson clutched the baby to her and headed for the stairs. She took a breath and, bruised and aching, started down the stairs to the kitchen to face her complete humiliation in front of the men and, most especially, in the eyes of Justin Harbinger.

Chapter Eleven

Amberson hunched over the stove and kept her back to the men, but Justin wasn't fooled. Something was wrong. He'd seen it on her face earlier in the day when he'd walked out of Rowan's study. The boss-man had wanted to drink whisky and talk about the ranch and Justin had humored him—for a while—until Rowan started repeating himself for the third time.

Justin had been very surprised when he'd seen Amberson stagger into the house. At first glance, he'd thought she was injured. But when one of the men, Beau, asked her about it, she'd answered that she was all right. Justin had wanted to believe her, but now, seeing her again, fear curled deep in his belly and he had his doubts. Dinner had been late; she was moving slowly. The baby's fretting didn't help matters either.

Justin watched her closely through the evening

and what he saw disturbed him. Amberson kept to herself, but then, there was nothing new in that. She was often quiet around the men. But tonight, she wore her hair down, not in its customary bun, and it hid most of her face. And she carried herself carefully, as if she was afraid she might fall and break.

Occasionally Justin found himself glancing at Rowan, wondering if he had anything to do with Amberson's new state of fragility. But Rowan had been nowhere near her when she'd entered the house this afternoon. He'd been in his study. Drinking.

Justin brooded over his evening cup of coffee. This ranch and the people on it were getting to him. He'd be better off quitting and finding a job on another ranch—one far away from Rowan and Mrs. Amberson Hawley Rowan.

He tossed back the bitter dregs in his cup. The problem was, he was feeling less and less like approaching Rowan about quitting. He had a gut feeling that whatever was going on with Amberson would suddenly get worse if he left.

He snorted to himself. Where did you get that big head from, Harbinger? he asked himself. Suddenly the woman can't live her life without help from you? Shaking his head, he rose from the table and headed out into the night.

The stars winked overhead and he found himself staring up at them. They were like pinpricks of light shining in the black velvet sky. He contemplated Amberson.

No, he decided. Mrs. Amberson Hawley Rowan could live her life without his help. She'd managed to find and marry Richard Rowan without Justin's help. And have a baby without his help. In fact, she'd managed to live her whole life without his help. So he'd be danged if he was going to stay around and play nursemaid to her. If she had problems, she could solve them—without his help.

He should be thinking about the ranch he wanted. Truth to tell, he hadn't been thinking much about what he wanted or what he was going to do. His whole reason for coming west had been to find Amberson again and marry her. The war had convinced him that he needed a woman, and a family. . . .

When he'd returned to Polk, Virginia, he'd gone home to his parent's plantation. To his horror, he'd found that everyone in his family was dead: his father, his mother, and his two brothers. Both his brothers had been killed fighting for the South.

One of the townsfolk, Mr. Catter, had told Justin that his mother had died of a broken heart when she'd found out Justin had left to fight for the North. Mr. Catter's eyes had shone with hatred when he'd delivered this malicious bit of gossip, but Justin didn't believe him. His mother had died, but he did not think it was from a broken heart. She'd been a tough plantation woman and nothing her youngest son did could have destroyed her. Or so Justin told himself.

Mr. Catter also seemed to take great delight in telling Justin how his father had died of a heart attack shortly after burying Justin's mother.

The whole town hated Justin; he could see it in men's eyes when he rode Samson past the white magnolias blooming in the town square. He guessed that was to be expected when a good Southern boy chose to fight for President Lincoln.

He shouldn't have been surprised. He kept his face impassive, but it hurt, seeing the men's and women's contempt, men and women he'd grown up with. And it hurt when the older men, friends of his father, turned their backs to him as he rode by.

He'd finally decided to leave and head west, back to the Montana hills and mountains. There was a freedom there, a freedom that no longer existed for Justin in Polk. As far as the townfolk were concerned, Justin Harbinger was worse than dead—he was a traitor.

Justin managed to sell the cotton plantation to one of the carpetbaggers descending from the North. No resident of Polk made him an offer on the land. And while he didn't get the price he wanted, still, it was better than nothing. He knew he couldn't stay in Polk, not now. So he'd ridden out, headed for a new life away from the scarred land of his family's plantation.

He'd been riding along, just on the outskirts of Polk, when he'd seen a black man dive into a weed-filled ditch. He was being careful to stay out of Justin's way. When Justin rode abreast of the man, he recognized him. It was Luther, a slave whose owner had occasionally hired him out for a day's labor to Justin's father.

Luther was a free man now, and Justin wondered if he wore his new freedom as awkwardly as Justin wore his.

He nodded at the black man and prepared to ride on by. Luther scrambled out of the ditch and up to the side of the road. He waited, poised to run, but he kept looking at Justin. Finding his behavior unusual, but not threatening, Justin halted Samson. "You want something?" he asked the man.

Luther took off his battered hat and shook his head. "No, suh."

Justin nodded and eased up on Samson's reins. Before he could ride farther, the black man took a step forward. "Suh?"

"Yes?" Justin waited, puzzled.

"Suh, are you the Harbinger son who fought for Mr. Lincoln?"

Justin nodded. "I am. I was with Colonel Hayes of the Twenty-third Ohio Volunteers."

Luther crumpled his hat nervously with both hands.

Whatever was wrong with him?

The black man took a step closer. "Ah fought for the North too. Suh."

Justin started. He hadn't expected that.

"Ah fought in the United States Colored Troops, suh. Ah was in the Battle of Spotsylvania Court House."

Justin pondered. He'd heard of black soldiers who'd fought for the Federal government, men who'd fled North and joined up with all-black regiments to fight against their owners in the South. There were even some Indians in the United States Colored Troops, and Justin had heard stories of how the colored men fought extremely bravely in battle.

Justin smiled and reached down to shake Luther's hand. "I'm pleased to see you again, sir. I heard about that battle. You fought the good fight."

The black man shook hands and smiled for the first time. He seemed to relax and, to Justin's eye, stand a little straighter. Justin guessed Luther had had an even uglier reception in Polk than he had—if anyone even knew Luther had fought in the war. "You visiting family?"

"I am, suh. Trying to get my wife to go North with me. We're gonna leave soon. It's better up North, Chicago-way." But there was a bleak look in Luther's eye. "My wife, she don't want to leave the children. Some of them grown now."

Justin nodded slowly. It would be hell living in Polk for a man with Luther's history. Chicago was indeed a better place. He hoped the man could convince his family to go north with him. "Best of luck to you, sir."

"Name's Luther Strong."

Justin nodded. "Mr. Strong." A thought struck him. He reached into his pocket and pulled out the money he'd received from the sale of the plantation. He peeled off some bills, one-fifth of the money he'd received for his family's land. He handed the money to Luther.

The black man, eyes wide, backed away. "Oh, no, suh. Can't take that."

"Take it, Mr. Strong," Justin said. "You and I went through something bigger than both of us. Take it. Help start a new life with your family."

The man was eyeing the money, wanting it, Justin could tell. Colored soldiers were paid seven dollars per month, while the white privates received thirteen, so Justin knew the man probably had very little money. And he also had no land to sell, as Justin had.

"Take it," Justin urged.

Slowly Luther Strong reached for the money. His brown fingers wrapped around the bills. "Why you givin' this to me, suh?"

Justin couldn't explain it, not even to himself. He shrugged. "We fought on the same side."

Luther Strong nodded. He seemed to accept Justin's explanation, and something about it felt right to Justin.

The two men parted and Justin rode away from Polk, feeling hopeful for the first time. A new order had come to the land—an order where men were equal, regardless of color. . . .

Justin stared up at the sky. The Civil War had marked his life. It had marked most every man and woman of his generation. He was glad it was over.

He sauntered down the steps. Behind him the door opened and Rowan stepped out onto the porch. He pulled the door closed behind him.

Justin turned in surprise. "Mr. Rowan?"

"That you, Harbinger?" Richard Rowan's words sounded slurred.

"It is."

"I'm goin' into town, gonna see a friend. A good friend." Rowan chuckled as he swayed on the top step. He gave a sharp whistle for his buckskin horse, then staggered down the steps.

"Maybe you should stay home tonight," suggested Justin. "It's gettin' late."

Rowan whirled. "Don't you tell me what to do!" he snarled. "Nobody tells me what to do! I said I'm going to town!"

Justin said nothing.

"Help me saddle up my buckskin," ordered Rowan.

Justin thought that if he left the man to his own devices the horse would never be saddled. Or, if he did manage to saddle it, Rowan would probably fall off the horse on the way to Gunpoint.

Justin worked silently, putting the bridle on the horse and tightening the girth. After the buckskin was saddled, he said, "I'll go saddle my horse and accompany you." That way, he could at least make certain that Rowan reached town.

"To hell with that," snapped Rowan. "I don't have

time to wait for some cowboy to find his damn horse."

He kicked the buckskin, hard, and the horse half-reared, but Rowan managed to keep his seat. He galloped off down the road and into the night.

Justin watched him go. He glanced up at the white stars and took a deep breath. The sooner he got off this ranch, the better.

Chapter Twelve

Amberson pushed a string of lank brown hair out of her eyes. Lord, but she was tired. Would the baby never stop crying? Wearily, she patted his back and rocked him gently, murmuring to him. While he perched on her shoulder, she rose from the bed and walked back and forth across the cool wooden floor, trying to settle him down. Oh, if only he'd go to sleep.

But Baby Gerald showed no signs of wanting to sleep. In fact, he hadn't slept all day. She glanced at the clock. The face showed six in the evening. And still Gerald cried.

She sat down on the bed and took out her breast, nudging at the baby to drink. But he turned his head away, still crying. "What is the matter, little one?" she cooed. It was unlike him not to eat.

She tried to feed him once more and again he turned away. She watched him, worry forming. He hadn't eaten all afternoon. Surely he should be hungry by now. What was the matter?

His crying was getting weaker, she noted. Not surprising, since he'd cried all afternoon. But the weakness of his cries seemed to stem from exhaustion more than anything else. He should have eaten and fallen asleep long before this.

Uneasily, she rubbed his back. His bowel movements had been loose, and that was also unlike him. She pulled back his white nightgown and examined his little stomach. There was a lump near his navel. He'd had that bulge ever since he was born. She knew it would go away if she pushed on it. Of course it would pop up again days, sometimes weeks later, but all she had to do then was to push on it and it would go away again.

She eyed the bulge uneasily. It had never looked quite like this, blackish blue mixed with a bright, angry red.

She gently touched the bulge, intending to push it back inside. Gerald screamed. His screams frightened her. Finally his harsh cries died down into sobs. What was wrong with him?

She stared at him. "Gerald. What is wrong, sweetheart?"

He kept sobbing. What was wrong with him? He hadn't eaten, hadn't slept, his umbilical bulge looked bruised . . . If Richard were here, she would have asked him what to do. Perhaps he knew about babies and their illnesses. Unfortunately for her, Richard was gone—to Gunpoint.

And the rest of the men were either in town or mule-skinning on the freight line. The only adult at the ranch besides herself was Justin Harbinger, who had taken it upon himself to remain. He was in the bunkhouse, and she wondered if she should call him. She grimaced; she was that desperate.

She put Gerald back on her shoulder. No, she wouldn't call Justin. She would take care of her baby herself, as she had always done.

The bulge felt hard, she thought, unlike the way it normally felt. Something was wrong with her baby and she strongly suspected it had something to do with the umbilical bulge.

Gerald whimpered. She placed him on the bed and lay down beside him. Maybe he'd sleep. She was exhausted, even if he wasn't. He'd started fretting early in the morning, before dawn, and she'd not slept since then. She would just close her eyes for a few moments' rest. . . .

She woke to the sound of Gerald's pitiful moans. She sat up, alarmed. "Gerald! What's the matter, Gerald?"

She picked him up. "Why, you are burning up!" Indeed, his skin was hot to her touch.

How long had she been sleeping? A glance at the clock told her it was eight o'clock. Two hours!

"Oh, Gerald," she murmured, unbuttoning the front of her dress. "Mama forgot to feed you, you poor little thing."

She put her breast to his mouth, but he showed no interest. He moaned, and seemed lethargic.

"Gerald, you have to eat!" she told him frantically. Surely a baby could not go a full day without eating. Frissons of fear crept up her spine. "Gerald?"

But he showed no interest in eating. She picked him up and held him to her, inhaling his baby scent. She loved him. She loved him beyond anything, anyone on earth. Gerald was the one good thing in her life. If anything happened to him . . . Oh, Lord, it didn't bear thinking upon!

"Gerald?"

But his head lolled back, and he whimpered. A cold lump of fear knotted in her belly. She had to do something. Her baby was ill. Very ill.

She thought frantically. "I've got to get you to the doctor," she told him. She set him on the bed while she quickly gathered his diapers and blankets. "We have to go to town, Gerald. I'll take you to Dr. Cooper," she informed him. "He'll know what to do."

She hoped she spoke the truth. She didn't know the doctor well, had seen him but a few times when she'd been in Gunpoint. She'd never been to see him about an ailment, and he had not delivered her baby. A midwife, Mrs. Winslow, had. However, Amberson had heard excellent reports of Dr. Cooper's skill from Annabelle Simmons. Mrs. Simmons swore up and down that Dr. Cooper had cured her mother of the shingles.

In a frenzy, Amberson scooped up a few more things. They had to get to Gunpoint! A quick glance at Gerald assured her she could spare these few minutes to get ready.

Wrapping him in a white blanket, she set him carefully in his basket. She fled downstairs, lugging the basket. Panting, she clomped across the porch, down the steps, and hurried across the yard to the barn.

She must have made some noise in her hasty attempts to get Jessie hitched to the black buggy because before she knew it, Justin Harbinger appeared.

"Miss Amberson?"

She whirled. "The baby—" she gasped. "He—he's sick. . . . I'm taking him to town. To Dr. Cooper!"

She looked into his eyes and saw concern flare in

those green depths. She wanted to cry out her fear to him. She wanted to throw herself into his strong arms and never let go. Instead, she choked out, "Gerald's got a fever, and his stomach hurts."

She saw Justin glance toward the baby's basket set on the straw. But she knew Justin couldn't see anything. The white blanket covered Gerald, who was quiet in his basket.

"I'll finish hitching up the mare," Justin said calmly. "You put the baby in the buggy."

Glad of his help, Amberson ran to the basket. Baby Gerald was asleep, but he moaned several times in his sleep. He looked pale and exhausted.

She placed the baby behind the front seat of the buggy, careful to wedge the basket securely. Then she climbed up and took the reins.

"Wait by the corral," Justin told her. "I'll saddle up Samson."

She nodded and urged Jessie to move. It was growing dark and it would be pitch black by the time they reached Gunpoint. "The lantern—" she began.

He waved her on. "I'll get it." He ducked into the bunkhouse.

When she reached the corral, he joined her and placed the lantern beside her. Then he saddled up his horse. He wasted no time and they were soon on their way down the road that led to Gunpoint. Somewhere deep in her heart she felt an odd gratitude that Justin was with her.

Now and then Baby Gerald whimpered. Each time he did so, Amberson shook the reins. "Giddap, Jessie!"

Jessie traveled at a swift trot and they made good time, but to Amberson the hour's ride seemed to take a week. Justin rode ahead of her and she took some comfort in watching his broad back in the waning light. They stopped once and lit the lantern when it became too dark to see. Jessie's pace slackened after dark, but they finally reached Gunpoint.

Amberson noticed nervously that the baby now slept, moaning now and then in his sleep.

She guided the buggy along the dark streets of the town. Raucous laughter and singing came from the saloons lining Gold Fever Street.

She halted the buggy in front of Dr. Cooper's modest woodframe house. A lamp shone in the window and she prayed he was home and not out delivering a baby or tending to a wounded patient at a saloon.

She stepped down from the buggy, tied Jessie to the hitching post, then ran back and grabbed up Gerald's basket. She raced up the stairs to Dr. Cooper's front porch.

Justin was right beside her. He pounded on the door.

"Dr. Cooper!" they cried in unison. Amberson could hear the trembling in her own voice. He had to be home! He had to be!

She heard movement behind the door. Slowly it opened. Mrs. Cooper stood there, a tall, thin woman with her gray hair done up in a bun. She wore thick glasses and a gray dress. A gray knitted shawl draped her shoulders.

"Is Dr. Cooper in?" demanded Amberson. Fear made her voice a hoarse whisper.

Mrs. Cooper blinked several times. The glasses made her eyes—also gray—look huge. "Dr. Cooper is in," she confirmed. Her voice still held traces of her native England. "However, he has retired for the evening."

She looked as though she meant to bar the way to

her husband and Amberson stiffened. "It's my baby—he's terribly ill. I—I—"

The woman glanced at the basket. When she met Amberson's eyes again, her own gray ones had softened. "Come in," she said, her voice warming.

Gratefully Amberson entered the house, with Justin right behind her. The yellow kitchen was neat and tidy, with a table, two chairs, and a wood stove against the center wall. A parlor room off to the left held a crowded array of brown velvet couches, ornate chairs, and polished wooden tables. Various bric-a-brac covered every inch of the surfaces of the tables. More knickknacks were set on shelves fastened to the walls in the parlor and the kitchen. There was a spicy, nutmeg smell in the kitchen.

Mrs. Cooper said, "I will tell the doctor you are here." She disappeared behind a door in the back.

She returned a few moments later and said, "He will be here shortly."

Amberson nodded. She pulled off the blanket and took Baby Gerald out of his basket. His little body felt so hot!

"He has a fever," she told Justin. "I fear he is very sick." She wanted to say more, to tell him of her fears, but he only nodded, looking uncomfortable and out of place. She shouldn't have brought him with her, thought Amberson with sudden regret. But she was so afraid for Gerald . . . she'd accepted Justin's help without thinking clearly. And he'd been so comforting. Just having him along had given her hope for Gerald.

"Mrs. Rowan . . ." Justin cleared his throat. "Mrs. Rowan, I'd better go and get Mr. Rowan. He should be here . . . helping you. His child . . . I can find him . . ." Justin shifted his brown slouch hat awkwardly. They both knew where Richard was.

Dr. Cooper walked into the room. He took one look at Amberson and said, "Let me see the baby." She cradled him first, then reluctantly handed him to Dr. Cooper. Mrs. Cooper cleared a space on the kitchen table and placed a blanket on it. The doctor laid the fretting baby on it. He began a thorough search of the child.

Amberson relaxed a little when she saw his efficient manner with her son. "Is he—? Will he—?"

Dr. Cooper glanced at her thoughtfully. His dark brown eyes were set in a wrinkled face. His nose dominated his face, but she cared little about appearances. What she needed was competent help for her baby.

"I must ask you some questions before I can tell you anything." The steadiness in his voice was momentarily reassuring.

He shot a series of quick questions at her while he continued to examine Gerald. He fell silent when he saw the distended black bulge of the baby's navel.

"Mrs. Rowan?" It was Justin. She'd forgotten all about him.

"Mrs. Rowan, I'm going to go and find Mr. Rowan. He's the one who should be here."

The doctor looked at him curiously, and Amberson flushed. Before she could say anything, the doctor said gravely, "I assure you, sir, the baby's father should be here, if at all possible. This is a very serious matter."

"My baby!" cried Amberson. "What's wrong with my baby?"

"I'm afraid, Mrs. Rowan, that your child suffers from a strangulated hernia."

She looked at him blankly, fear rising inside her.

She might not know what the words meant, but she could easily read the somber tone of his voice.

"It means," he explained, appearing to choose his words carefully, "that your child has dead tissue inside him. It may poison him, causing gangrene."

"Gangrene!" Everyone had heard of gangrene. During the Civil War, countless men had lost limbs to gangrene infections. Many men had died.

"Oh, Gerald! Oh, my God!" Panic rose in her.

She felt a warm hand grip her arm. "Easy, Mrs. Rowan," said Justin. "Take it easy."

"My baby! My baby! My God, I can't lose my baby! He's everything to me! Everything!"

Justin eyed her, and she closed her eyes to his pity.

"Fetch the father," said Dr. Cooper.

Justin turned to leave. Rowan should be here. His son's life was in danger.

"Wait!" Amberson's hand on Justin's arm stopped him.

"Don't get Richard," she whispered. He raised an inquiring brow. "Not just yet," she pleaded.

"Mrs. Rowan," said the doctor, "the child's father should be here. This is a very serious time. I have grave doubts about your child's health."

Amberson's face whitened. "Will he die?" She mashed her fist against her mouth, as though trying to push back the dreaded words.

"It is possible," answered the doctor. His dark eyes were sad.

Amberson's moan tore at Justin's heart. "Please, doctor," she said, her eyes huge and frightened. "Do everything you can to save him. Please!"

"Of course I will, Mrs. Rowan. I fear I must operate

to do so." To Justin he repeated gently, "Fetch the husband."

Amberson wrung her hands. Unaccountably, given the imminent danger to her son, she followed Justin onto the porch.

"Justin," she said, her voice hoarse, "wait a moment."

Puzzled, he said, "I must hurry, Miss Amberson, if I am to find Mr. Rowan."

She swallowed, and a guilty look crossed her face. "It will do no good to have Richard here."

"What do you mean?"

She took a breath, her hands clasping one another so tightly, the knuckles were white. When she still said nothing, Justin said gently, "Miss Amberson, I know this isn't easy for you. I've seen men die." He hesitated. "But not children. I know you love your son," he added gruffly. He swallowed. Damn, this wasn't going well. Whatever her shortcomings, Amberson's love for her son was genuine. If he died, it would surely devastate her.

She stared down at the porch; she was not listening to him.

"I think Mr. Rowan has a right to be here, Miss Amberson," he continued. "Regardless of how you two get along . . ." He stopped, debating how far to continue. Amberson and Rowan fought like cats and dogs, but now, when his son was critically ill, Rowan should be here. Not off somewhere in town, doing God knows what to an icy, blue-eyed blonde.

Justin tried again. "It's his son," he explained gently. "He would want to be here."

She looked up at Justin then, and, by the light of the half-open door behind them, he saw tears well in her eyes. God, he could stand anything but her tears.

"I'll get him now," he said hastily and fled down the steps.

"Justin," she called softly into the night. Something in her voice made him stop and turn.

He took a step back to her. She stood on the porch and held out her arms to him. When he stayed stubbornly rooted where he was, she dropped her arms. "Richard is not Gerald's father." Her voice sounded leaden.

Stunned, Justin stood there. Had he heard her aright? "Miss Amberson?"

She hesitated, then set her jaw. "Richard is not Gerald's father, Justin. Richard has no right to be here."

A feeling of dread stole over Justin. "Who is his father?" he asked hoarsely.

"You are."

Chapter Thirteen

Justin's jaw dropped and he stared at her. Then he leaped for her.

"You said what?" he roared. "Gerald is my son?"

His fingers closed around her shoulders before he could stop himself.

"Justin!" Eyes squeezed closed, she reached for his fingers and fought with him. The pain of her sharp nails gouging grooves in his skin awoke him to the strength of his grip.

He quickly dropped his scratched hands and held them rigid at his sides. Fury surged through his body. His jaw worked as he sputtered, "Amberson, what in hell's name do you mean, he's my son?" He wanted to yell his outrage to the heavens. His son!

A quiet voice said from the doorway, "Mrs. Rowan, Dr. Cooper needs your help."

"She'll be there in a minute, Mrs. Cooper," said Justin gruffly. He closed the door firmly in the woman's face. He had to have this out with Amberson. Now. Here. "And just when," he snarled, "were you going to tell me?"

"I wasn't," she replied simply.

He wanted to shake her. "I can see that," he shouted. "You were going to keep him. My son! You were going to keep him from me. Son-of-a-bitch!" he howled. Hitting the side of the house did not assuage his anger, but it damn sure hurt his fist.

She watched him out of tired eyes. "I was never going to tell you. I didn't want anything to do with you after you left me."

"He is my son," snarled Justin. "I had a right to know!"

"You had no right," she answered. "You left me."

"I intended to return."

She was silent. He knew she did not believe him.

"Does Richard know?" he demanded.

She shook her head. "He thinks the baby's his. He loves Gerald."

Justin had seen that with his own eyes. For all his poor treatment of Amberson, Richard Rowan had always shown love for his son. No, not his son. Justin's son.

My son, he marveled. My son. I have a son!

A son who is about to die, he remembered bleakly. "Let's go inside," he ordered heavily. "I want my son to live!"

He heard her sigh wearily, but he was beyond caring about what Amberson Rowan wanted or felt. To hell with her. She'd kept his son from him all these months. Never even intended to tell him about Gerald. The witch. He'd deal with her later. The most important thing now was Gerald. He had to live! Justin hadn't just discovered him only to lose him to death.

He marched into the doctor's kitchen; Justin's whole attention was focused on the baby. Gerald slept on his blanket on top of the table. Occasionally he moaned or twitched in his sleep.

"How bad is it, Doctor?" Justin knew he should let Amberson ask about the boy, for appearances' sake, but appearances be damned. He'd been denied his own son, and he wasn't about to make things easy for the woman who had done this to him.

"The father?" asked Dr. Cooper.

"I'm the father, sir," answered Justin brusquely. He ignored Mrs. Cooper's small gasp and the doctor's look of surprise. "I want to know exactly what the problem is."

The doctor cleared his throat. "Very well," he answered. "The baby is in grave danger of dying from infection. I must operate to take out the infected flesh near his navel. The sooner I do it, the better."

Justin had seen medical operations performed on the battlefields, sickening maneuvers made by men who sometimes had little training and few medical implements. And even well-trained doctors had nothing to prevent infection after the operations, unless someone commandeered whisky or distilled spirits. Both sides of the Civil War had lost many lives to infections.

It seemed to Justin that Dr. Cooper was holding back. "And?" prodded Justin.

"Your son is tiny. I'm used to operating on larger people, of course. I hope he will survive the operation, but I cannot guarantee success."

He eyed both Justin and Amberson. "I do know that if we do nothing, your son will die."

Amberson pressed herself against Justin's back and he heard her sob. He felt a fleeting moment of softness, followed by hate. He hated her intensely at this moment. But hating her would not save Gerald's life.

"Very well, you need to operate. I have whisky in my saddlebag. That will disinfect the wound," said Justin.

The doctor held up a hand. "I have disinfectant. What I do not have is a blade fine enough to operate on such a small person."

Justin reached into his boot for his black obsidian knife. He pulled it from its scabbard and handed it to the doctor. "Use this knife," he said. "It cuts very clean, very fine."

The doctor solemnly examined the knife. "I'll use it," he decided at last.

Justin let out his breath. "I had some experience in the war. Helped with wounds and operations on legs and arms. I'm willing to do whatever I can to help you."

The doctor eyed him assessingly. "Very well. Wash your hands—use that soap by the sink. You and I will do what we can to save your son." He noticed Amberson's white face, her wringing hands. "Mrs. Cooper," he ordered his wife, "take Mrs. Rowan into the parlor. She needs to rest."

"No!" replied Amberson sharply. Her eyes were focused only on Gerald.

"Mrs. Rowan," said Dr. Cooper gently, "I will do a better job on your son if I don't have to worry about his mother."

Slowly Amberson moved toward her son and

kissed his forehead. Then, as though in a dream, she let herself be led to the parlor by the older woman.

Justin was relieved when she was gone.

"Let's get to work," said Dr. Cooper.

Chapter Fourteen

Sweat dripped down Justin's face and blurred his vision. He straightened, every muscle in his body protesting. He'd been leaning over the baby for a long time, while he and Dr. Cooper did all they could to clear away the dead flesh from the baby's intestines.

But now the surgery was over. And, thank God, it looked like Baby Gerald had survived the operation.

"He's sleeping well," commented Dr. Cooper.

Justin sank into a kitchen chair, his weary eyes fastened on his son. His son.

"I'm tired," muttered Justin. The doctor handed him back his obsidian blade, newly cleaned. "That knife made a difference," the doctor observed. "I wouldn't mind having a scalpel blade made of that stuff. What is it?"

"Obsidian," answered Justin wearily. "Got it from a dying soldier."

Dr. Cooper didn't ask anything further. He looked

to Justin as though he could use a good night's sleep too.

"What time is it?" muttered Justin. It felt as if he and the good doctor had been standing over the baby and cutting through flesh for a long, long time.

"Three A.M.," came Mrs. Cooper's low voice behind him.

Justin glanced into the parlor. He could see Amberson's pale face watching him. He had expected her to fall asleep, but he saw she'd kept a vigil—of worry.

Tough. He hardened his heart. He couldn't bear to look at her, after what she'd done to him, first betraying him, then keeping his own child from him, so he turned to watch Gerald instead.

After a few minutes of rest, Justin heaved himself to his feet. "Time to take the boy home," he said.

Dr. Cooper nodded. "He should sleep for the next couple of days. An operation tires a body out."

"Right," answered Justin. He picked up the baby's basket off the floor. Amberson appeared at his elbow. Dr. Cooper helped her lift the sleeping child into the basket.

"Thank you so much, Dr. Cooper," murmured Amberson. Justin was unmoved as she thanked the doctor, her huge eyes full of gratitude. He turned away when she clasped the doctor's hand and kissed it.

"Let's go," Justin said gruffly. "And thank you, sir," he added.

Mrs. Cooper, a gray shadow, moved to stand beside her husband. "Thank you for the help," said Dr. Cooper. Justin nodded and they left. The older couple stood watching in the doorway.

Justin had nothing to say to Amberson right now. Later, when he wasn't so dang tired, he'd have plenty to say. But right now he was exhausted, from worry and from straining to concentrate on every part of the operation so that he was of some help to the doctor. Justin would deal with Amberson Hawley Rowan another day.

"Justin?" she asked after she'd secured the baby behind the buggy seat.

He shook his head, unwilling even to speak to her. He mounted Samson and turned the horse's head down Gold Fever Street.

He heard the buggy roll after him and slumped in the saddle. He pulled his rifle out of its case and kept it propped on one arm as he rode.

It was a quiet ride back to the Triple R. Justin kept an eye out for rustlers. Grimly, he'd decided that if the rustlers chased the buggy tonight, they'd get a dang rude surprise. Justin did not intend to fight fair tonight. If they crossed him, he'd kill one of them, as surely as he sat atop his horse.

They finally reached the ranch. At the stable, Justin helped unbridle the mare and put away the buggy. Together, he and Amberson carried the baby between them toward the house. Justin's jaw was set. There was nothing kind he wanted to say to her. Rather than begin yelling at her again, which was what he really wanted to do, he kept silent. She must have sensed his anger bubbling just below the surface, for she said nothing either.

They reached the porch and he released the baby's basket handle. "Good night," he said gruffly to Amberson. But his eyes were not on her pale face. Instead, he watched the sleeping baby. The curve of the little one's cheek almost unmanned him. His son. When he finally looked at Amberson, it was all he could do not to sneer at her. "I'll talk with you in the morning."

"Yes," she said reluctantly, and he knew she did not relish the coming interview. Well, hell. She'd kept his child from him, his own child! What did she expect? That he'd say, "Oh, everything's fine, let's have tea"?

He waited until she'd closed the door; then he stepped off the porch. He glanced over to the corral to see if Rowan's buckskin horse was there. No buckskin. Rowan must have stayed in Gunpoint, happily committing adultery the whole time Justin and Dr. Cooper were operating on Baby Gerald. Well, hell again. A fine mess this is, thought Justin as he stomped back to the bunkhouse.

He slid between cold blankets and lay there, his heart pounding as he thought of his son. Gerald. His own child. He put his arms behind his head and thought about what this meant. He needed a plan. But the idea of his son was so new, left him so stunned, he felt as if he'd been kicked by a horse. He sighed deeply. He'd figure it all out in the morning.

She shouldn't have told him. God help her, she shouldn't have told him. Regardless of whatever momentary fear or insanity had possessed her, she should have just let it pass. How *could* she have told Justin about Gerald? How could she?

Because you loved him and needed him, said a tiny voice in her mind. And you were desperate.

Seeing a sullen and moody Justin drinking coffee across the table from her did not help matters. It was noon by the time she'd awakened and heard him moving around downstairs. She'd managed to feed the baby and dress him before he fell back asleep.

She carried him downstairs in his basket. She was prepared to be pleasant. But did Justin Harbinger cooperate? No. Fool she was to expect it.

He was mean-looking this morning, with two days' growth of beard and as nasty a snarl on his sculpted lips as she'd ever seen on a man. He looked even angrier than he had last night, when he'd found out the baby was his.

Lord, she wished she'd kept her mouth shut. She should have lied. Told him to fetch Richard. But dealing with Richard when she thought Gerald would die was more than Amberson could have handled, and she was honest enough to admit it.

Justin hadn't taken his eyes off the baby all morning. Watching him watch the baby made her uneasy. What was he planning? Knowing Justin, there was something going on behind those green eyes. Something that did not bode well for her.

"Good morning," she said. At least *she* would try to keep things on a pleasant level, even if he didn't.

He ignored her and sipped his coffee, keeping his eyes on Gerald the whole while.

She let a few minutes go by, and when he showed no inclination to speak, she tried again. "It's really not such an important matter," she said, watching him closely. "Why, men father children every day. It doesn't mean they have to stay around and raise them." There, she'd give him every opportunity to get out of her life. She bared her teeth in what she hoped was an understanding smile. "Feel free to leave the ranch anytime."

Was that rage she saw banked in those green eyes? Hastily, she added, "Richard doesn't need to know. Let's just keep this little matter between ourselves."

He raised one dark eyebrow at that.

If Richard found out the baby was not his, he'd kick her off the ranch. Where would she go? How would she and the baby survive? She needed time, time to work out a plan, time to get some money so she wasn't dependent on Richard. But she had to get rid of Justin Harbinger first. If only he'd leave the Triple R.

The sneer on Justin's handsome face deepened, if such a thing was possible. Still he sipped his coffee and said nothing.

"There is no point in being rude about it," she said archly. She glanced at Gerald.

"The baby looks a little better this morning," she said brightly. When she saw a softening on Justin's hard face, she knew she should not have mentioned the baby. The less said about Gerald, the better.

"Look, Justin," she pleaded, "we have to talk."

To his silence, she coaxed, "Even you said so, last night."

Silence.

"You can't stay here now," she pointed out reasonably. "Tell Richard you have another job offer, somewhere else. He'll believe you."

He watched her out of green eyes and she thought she saw disgust in them. Well, let him think anything he wanted of her. She was fighting for her baby's life in a different way than Justin had last night. But she was fighting just the same, and she would say anything, do anything, to keep Gerald.

"I'll tell Richard you were called away," she offered. "He'll understand. He'll find someone else to do the fence posts. It can't be that difficult to chop fence posts."

Yes, that was definitely anger in his eyes. She'd overdone it, mentioning the fence posts. Better try a different tack. Last thing she needed was a furious Justin Harbinger on her hands. "And to guard the ranch, of course." There, he should like the sound of that. Important. She peeked over at him. No response.

She glanced out the window. Richard could be returning at any time from Gunpoint. And he didn't even know about Baby Gerald's operation. She sighed. How had her life suddenly become so complicated?

Well, she didn't have much time and she was in a particularly bad situation; she admitted that. But she couldn't let Richard find out and she couldn't let Justin take the baby. So that left getting rid of Justin and keeping silent with Richard.

"I—I'll pay you to leave," she said at last. "I don't have much money. . . ." Lord, she didn't have *any* money. All she had was the little bit that Richard allowed her to charge at Hinckley's General Store. But she could make up a story to tell Hinckley, something about needing the cash, and thus get the money to pay Justin. He had to leave, he had to. And he'd leave sooner if she gave him money.

"I can get it for you this afternoon," she promised. She would ride into town, tell Hinckley her story— she'd think one up during the buggy ride to town— and she'd give the money to Justin. Then he'd leave. Forever.

He looked interested.

"How much?"

She should have known. The only two words out of the man this morning and they were *how much*. Not "How's the baby?" or "How are you?" or "Gee, what a nice baby we made," but "How much?" She smiled. She was glad he was so damn shallow.

She'd start a little low, because she guessed he'd try to talk her up. "Ten dollars," she answered as confidently as she could. Ten dollars would buy five acres of land somewhere up in northern Montana Territory. He could go there. Far away from her.

"Ten dollars," he repeated slowly.

He appeared to be mulling it over. Good.

"Of course, if you leave this afternoon, I could make it fifteen." She smiled and bit her lip. God, she hated bargaining like this for her baby, but if it would get Justin out of her life, she'd do it.

He was frowning. Fifteen was a little low. Maybe she should go a bit higher. But she didn't want to appear too eager.

"I need six hundred for the ranch I want to buy."

"Six hundred," she gasped. "I don't have six hundred!"

Lord, why did he have to ask so much? Six hundred!

He was watching her, and she felt like a helpless bird being held by the sheer intensity of a snake's gaze. "I—I could never—" She snapped her mouth shut. He didn't need to know she couldn't get that kind of money. Maybe she could convince him to leave, that she'd get him the rest of the money later. Yes, that might work. "Six hundred," she repeated slowly as her brain raced. "Where is the ranch?"

"Up north."

"Near Helena?"

He nodded.

That was good. Richard was unlikely to find him there. And Justin would be far enough away that he wouldn't bother her and the baby.

She smiled. "I think you and I can do a deal," she

answered confidently. She'd be rid of him, rid of him at last!

He leaned closer, his green eyes veiled. But she knew he was interested. She could read it in the tension of his body as he leaned forward. Six hundred dollars.

She, too, leaned forward, and an observer would assume the two to be lovers, the way they almost touched one another. That is, until they spoke. "Let's make this clear," she said. "You'll leave this ranch forever for six hundred dollars."

He didn't say yes, but he didn't say no, either. She took encouragement from the impassive look he gave her.

She continued. "What I'll do is this: I'll give you fifteen dollars now. You leave and I'll send the rest to you in Helena."

When he didn't say anything, she added casually, "By the way, that's five hundred and eighty-five dollars. I'll have Beau take it to you. To Helena." She smiled expansively. "You'll be a rich man. You'll be able to buy your ranch." She paused expectantly.

"When?"

"When what?"

"When will you send the five hundred and eighty-five?"

She watched him warily. He was probably impatient for the money. Better not make it too long a time from now. "Next month," she answered blithely. She wouldn't worry about where she'd find that much money between now and next month. The important thing was to get rid of him immediately. ·

He sat back. "So let me get this straight," he said.

She smiled, waiting.

"You'll pay me six hundred dollars to leave and

140

stay away from you, the baby, and Rowan."

She nodded. "That's right."

He smiled, baring his white teeth. "Forget it."

The smile disappeared from her face. So he wanted more, did he? "Twelve hundred." It was a wild sum, one she would have a difficult time getting, but she'd rob J. V. Simmons' bank in Gunpoint if she had to!

Justin was grinning at her now. Playing with her. "No."

"Fifteen. Fifteen hundred dollars." She enunciated every word slowly, so he'd understand the huge amount of money it was.

"No."

"Sixteen."

"No."

"Seventeen."

"No."

She paused, her mind working frantically. "Two thousand," she whispered at last, her voice hoarse. "Two thousand dollars and I never see your hateful face again!"

"Oh, so now I find out what you really think of me," he scoffed.

She was in no mood for joking. "Two thousand dollars. That's my final offer." She knew she would have a terrible time coming up with the money. She'd have to find her brother, Kingsley, have to beg him—

"No."

"No?" Her hand flew to her chest to still her wildly beating heart. "No?" She got to her feet, enraged now. She placed her hands on the table and leaned over him. "How much?" she snarled. "How much will it take to get you out of my life?"

He sat back and laughed. He laughed so long she began to think he'd become hysterical, if a man could do such a thing.

"What's so funny?" she demanded.

"You." He kept laughing. Tears ran down his face. "I wish you could have seen yourself. Fifteen, sixteen," he mimicked, and he was off into another gale of laughter.

"I do not see," she said in a frigid voice, "what is so damn funny."

He sat up then, straightening at the tone in her voice and the fact that she had cursed.

"Would *you* take two thousand dollars to leave Gerald?" he asked her, suddenly as sober as a preacher. If she didn't know better, she'd think he was making her a real offer.

"No!" she snapped.

He eyed her steadily and she knew he wasn't joking now. "How about four thousand?"

"Four thousand? Dollars?" she gasped.

"Think about it," he said in a silky voice. "You get the money. I get the baby."

Some part of her mind registered shock that he wanted the baby that badly. And for a moment she did think about his offer. She could take the four thousand, steal the baby back, and run away. She'd have enough money to start a good life, far from here. No Richard, no Justin Harbinger. Just her and the baby—and the money.

She smiled. Let him think she would go for the deal. "Four thousand," she repeated, playing with him, the way he'd played with her. "And where would you get this four thousand? You don't even have six hundred. For your ranch," she reminded him.

He grinned. "Don't worry about where I'd get it. Do we have a deal?"

He'd probably rob J. V. Simmons' bank too, she thought.

She hesitated. He was watching her closely. She'd be living life on the run, moving now and then so Justin wouldn't find her and the boy. He'd probably give up after a while. Maybe she should . . .

At last she shook her head. It was nothing but a fantasy. "No." She slumped in her seat.

He leaned back. His eyes nailed her. "Then know this: Neither will I take payment. My son is not for sale!"

He said each word distinctly, like pebbles dropped into a well. He glared at her.

She sank back down on the bench. "Not for sale? Why, I thought—"

"Gerald is not for sale. I'm not leaving him."

As the full implication of his words sank in, she felt despair enter her heart. She was stuck with Richard and Justin knew about Gerald. Only God knew what he'd do now.

Wilted from their battle of wits, she laid her head on her arms, face downward so she didn't have to look at Justin.

"You've just destroyed my life," she sobbed.

"What about *my* life?" he answered pitilessly. "What about Gerald's life?"

She couldn't answer him, only turned her face to the wall and sobbed harder.

Chapter Fifteen

A day later, Richard walked in the door. Justin and Amberson were eating their evening meal, sitting at separate tables.

Richard nodded briefly to Justin, then walked over to Amberson. He pulled the baby out of her arms. "How's my boy?" he murmured, nosing the baby.

Amberson could not look at Justin. Somehow, the last six months of deceiving Richard, of not telling him the truth about Gerald, she'd not thought too much about it. Now that Justin knew the truth, it was as if she had awakened to what it would be like for Richard to learn the truth. She did not feel very good.

Richard grinned at the baby and cooed to him. He hugged the baby.

Seeing his big face next to Gerald's small one, Amberson felt a debilitating stroke of guilt. She'd told herself for so long that she kept silent to protect herself and the baby. Richard's behavior to her was so mean that she couldn't trust him with the truth. She knew this, yet the guilt still gnawed at her.

"There was a Celestial killed in Gunpoint," announced Richard.

Amberson's eyes widened. "What do you mean?"

"Last night. One of the Chinamen was murdered. His body was found in his bed. Dead."

"How do you know it was murder?" asked Justin.

"Not many people slit their own throats with a knife, now do they?" joked Richard.

"The sheriff find who did it?" asked Justin.

Richard snorted in disgust. "Sheriff Logan? That blundering fool? Not likely." Richard grinned at the baby. "My guess is he won't find out who did it either. Those Chinamen opium fiends stick pretty close together. They're not going to tell a white man like Logan who the killer is."

Justin nodded.

Amberson was surprised at the news. There were occasional murders in the town, though so far no one she knew had died. Still, it was unsettling. "How do you know he was an opium fiend?" she asked.

"Aren't they all?" answered Richard. "Every Celestial I ever saw liked the pipe. Some whites do too." He chucked the baby under the chin.

Justin watched Richard and Gerald carefully.

Amberson wondered if Richard had ever smoked opium. She had read recently in the *Gunpoint Gazette* that there were a hundred opium fiends living in the thriving town of Gunpoint. They couldn't all be Celestials, could they? She wanted to ask him about it, but Richard was so unpredictable, she thought better of it.

Richard lowered his head and peered at the baby's stomach.

"What's this?" he asked Amberson, pointing to the bandages on the baby's stomach.

"Gerald had an operation." She swallowed. "I—I took him in to Dr. Cooper."

"An operation?" Richard looked up, stunned. "Just like that? My son has an operation and I don't know anything about it?" He looked angry.

Amberson got up off the bench and went to fill her cup with more coffee. She kept her back to Richard. Lord, but guilt felt miserable. Now that Justin knew that Gerald was his son, and not Richard's, it made her feel low, as if she had irreparably injured Richard in some way. Which was silly. She hadn't hurt Richard.

She glanced at Justin's narrowed green eyes. She hadn't hurt Justin either. She was just trying to survive.

She decided to distract Richard. "You'd have known about the operation if you weren't so busy chasing after Madeline Mueler," she answered coolly.

There was a throbbing silence in the room. Justin, she noticed, still watched Richard and the baby warily.

"I've told you before," said Richard, thrusting the baby at her. "I'm not chasing after Madeline Mueler." He looked at Justin and shrugged. A manly shrug. A man-to-man, what-does-she-know shrug. A lie.

Amberson tightened her lips as she received Baby Gerald. If Richard wanted to pretend he was not visiting that woman, when the whole town knew he was, it was his choice.

Justin got to his feet. "Time to get back to the

bunkhouse," he said heartily. Too heartily.

"Fine, Harbinger." Richard dismissed Justin with a wave. To Amberson he said, "Just what kind of operation did Gerald have?"

"His stomach was infected. That lump, near his navel—" she answered. "I took him into town. Dr. Cooper operated on him." She wouldn't mention that Justin had accompanied her.

Richard rubbed a hand wearily across his face. "Is he all right now?"

She nodded. "He's recuperating very well. The operation helped him." Saved his life, she wanted to add. But there was no telling whether Richard would become enraged if he knew how close to death Gerald had come. She did not want to court disaster.

Richard beamed at the baby. "Sounds like he's doing fine," he said hopefully. He glanced at her with his blue eyes sly. "You were in town, then."

He's wondering if I went looking for him at Madeline's. She shrugged casually. "Yes, I was in town. I was at Dr. Cooper's. I stayed with the baby the whole time."

He regarded her closely for a full minute.

"Gerald needed me, Richard," she added.

He relaxed then. "Good, good," he said and patted her shoulder awkwardly. Her reward for not searching him out in town, she supposed.

He stepped away from her, as if embarrassed by the little display of approval he'd shown her. "I'll be in my room if you need me," he said gruffly. The study door closed behind him.

The kitchen was quiet. It was just her and the baby. And the guilt . . . oh, Lord, the guilt.

* * *

The next afternoon, Amberson woke from a nap to hear running footsteps pounding on the front porch. Someone knocked loudly on the front door. "Open up!" Blinking, she lay there, trying to understand what was going on. It sounded like one of the ranch hands.

She hastily threw a shawl around her shoulders—the late afternoon air was cooler now—and hurried down the stairs.

She opened the front door and came face-to-face with one of the younger cowhands, Sandy. "What ever is the matter?" she demanded. She could hear the baby crying upstairs. "You woke Gerald."

"Sorry, Missus Rowan, but it's awful important."

Behind her the study door opened and she heard Richard shuffle toward them.

"Whasssit you wan'?" Richard demanded of Sandy.

Oh, Lord, he's been drinking again, she thought.

"Mr. Rowan," said Sandy earnestly, "rustlers raided the ranch."

Richard blinked, his stance unsteady. "What d'ya mean?"

"Rustlers, boss. They've raided the ranch. Took some cattle."

"Where?" interposed Amberson hastily before Richard could say anything. "How many cows were taken?"

"About twenty cows, ma'am."

"Why, that's almost a quarter of the herd," she exclaimed. "When did this happen? Who did it?"

"I think it happened this afternoon, ma'am. Can't say for sure, though. Me and Beau and the boys just found the tracks now."

This afternoon. While she was napping.

"I think they mighta taken some horses, too," volunteered the cowhand.

"Horses missing?" she clutched her throat. "Oh, Richard, this is serious."

Richard, swaying, appeared to be trying to make sense of what Sandy and Amberson were talking about. "Get the men," he said at last. He waved a hand vaguely. "Follow 'em. Bring those cows back."

"Yes, sir," agreed Sandy at once. He whirled and ran for the bunkhouse. For her part, Amberson was just glad that Richard was able to make a decision despite his alcoholic haze.

She saw him stagger unsteadily toward the corral, where his buckskin stood. She followed him to the corral fence.

"Richard," she called, "don't go. Let the men take care of it." If he rode in this condition, he might fall off his horse and be killed. "Please, Richard."

"Quit yer damn whining, woman." He staggered over to the buckskin and grabbed the bridle. The big horse whinnied and shied away. Richard tightened his grip on the bridle and smacked the horse across the face. The animal half-reared, trying to pull away from the angry man. Richard yanked savagely on the reins to pull the horse back down. "Stop it, you four-legged piece of cow dung!"

"Richard!" she cried. "Don't hurt that horse!"

Justin Harbinger ran into the corral and grabbed Richard from behind, wrapping both arms around him and pulling him away from the horse. He carried Richard outside the corral and freed him.

"You can't treat a horse like that!" said Justin, panting from carrying the heavy man.

"It's my horse," said Richard, like a sullen child. "I'll treat him any damn way I want!"

Justin wiped his forehead. "You treat him like that, and he'll kick you in the head. You want to be kicked?"

"Keep out of my business, Harbinger," snarled Richard.

Sandy came riding up, along with Beau and three other ranch hands. "We're goin' to find those rustlers, Mr. Rowan. Me and the boys."

Richard glanced at them and waved a hand, his buckskin horse forgotten. "Yeah. You do that." He tottered off toward the house.

Amberson watched him go. She shook her head, despairing of ever understanding the man.

Sandy touched his hat. "We'll find them, ma'am. I promise."

She nodded. "Try and get the cattle back if you can." She glanced at Richard and then risked an order she knew he would never give. "But don't risk the men."

Sandy nodded and they headed out.

"I'm going with them," Justin told her.

"Amberson!" It was Richard, yelling at her from the porch.

She shrugged. "Suit yourself, Mr. Harbinger." She turned wearily toward the house.

"Damn baby's crying. Do something!" yelled Richard.

"He's going to find out sooner or later," said Justin ominously.

She turned on him. "Not from me, he won't." She eyed him firmly. "And he'd better not find out from you, either."

"You threatening me, Mrs. Rowan?"

She could see a muscle flicker in Justin's clenched jaw. "Warning you," she explained. "If Richard finds out that Gerald is not his, there will be hell to pay." She added wearily, "And I'll be the one to pay it."

She hurried back to the house, to the crying baby and the yelling man.

Chapter Sixteen

Justin rode off after the other ranch hands. He caught up to them just as they reached the main trail that led to Gunpoint. The cowboys turned the other way, however, and took the trail away from Gunpoint, toward the hills.

He galloped along behind them, content to let Sandy take the lead.

Justin had enough on his mind, namely one Mrs. Amberson Hawley Rowan. This chase after rustlers was merely a distraction for him; he had to keep his mind off her. He felt as if his life had suddenly been thrust into the careless, lily-white hands of a hazel-eyed harridan who was twisting him in knots. How could he have let this happen?

He was a father now. A man with a son. No wife, but he did have a son. And his son belonged to Richard Rowan, a man he was beginning to suspect had a whole general store list of problems.

As Justin rode, he fumed. Amberson had no right to keep his son from him. No right whatsoever. She could have told him about the baby when he first showed up at the Triple R. She had had plenty of opportunity to tell him about Gerald then. But had she? No, she had not!

She never gave him a chance. Not one. When she'd first learned she was pregnant, she could have written to him then. Told him what had happened. Despite the war, he would have gotten back here to marry her. Somehow. Just how, he wasn't sure. He had men to lead and a war to fight, but—but he would have found a way. But did she tell him? No. Instead she'd found the richest man she could and married him.

Then she'd given Justin's son to Rowan; that was what it amounted to. Oh, she might not have said, "Richard, here is Justin Harbinger's precious son. Let's see what you can make of him," but that was surely what she had done by marrying another man. "Here, Richard, take Justin's son, raise him so that Justin will never know about him."

Justin swallowed the acrid taste of bile as he thought about what Amberson had done. And the worst part was, she had never intended to tell him! Never. She'd admitted as much that night at Dr. Cooper's.

She'd have been happy to let Justin go on believing the boy belonged to Rowan. And to think, Justin remembered irritably, he'd ignored and even taken a dislike to Gerald—his own son!—because he'd seemed to be a constant reminder of her betrayal with Rowan.

And another thing—what about Richard Rowan? She was tying that man in little tiny knots too, lying to him too, not letting him know that the child he loved was not his own flesh-and-blood son.

Yes, Mrs. Amberson Hawley Rowan had much to answer for. She'd made fools of them both.

However, thought Justin, he did not particularly want to be the one to tell Rowan what had happened. Richard Rowan in a rage would not be a pretty sight.

On the other hand, Justin thought with a sigh, Rowan would find out fairly soon, because Justin did not intend to leave matters as they currently were. No sir. He intended to retrieve his son.

He continued to ponder as he rode along. And though the chase for the rustlers turned out to be futile, it gave him time to decide one thing: Gerald was his. He, Justin Harbinger, would be the man to raise the boy, not Rowan. Too bad that Amberson wouldn't like it. Neither would Rowan. But Gerald was Justin's and Justin was not about to let something as precious as his own son slip away from him.

Chapter Seventeen

It was the middle of the afternoon. Two ranch hands worked farther down the line on fence posts. The rest had gone into town with Richard.

Justin took one last chop at a fence post, neatly splitting the wood off to form a point. That done, he set aside the ax. He wiped his sweating forehead and glanced around.

It was a warm, sunny day. The two cowhands some distance away from him chopped steadily.

A slight breeze blew, cooling his heated skin. He shrugged into his blue shirt and walked toward the ranch house.

It was time to talk to Mrs. Amberson Hawley Rowan, the bane of his existence. As he tramped toward the house, he thought about what he was going to say to her.

The way he saw it, if he was a philosophical man and inclined to compare running his life to running a ranch, he would have to compare Mrs. Rowan to a fence post—the biggest, most difficult fence post on the ranch, and the one in which no amount of chopping made a single dent. That was Mrs. Amberson Hawley Rowan, as sure as he was Justin Harbinger kicking rocks out of his path.

He reached the ranch house, coming by the back way in case Amberson was working in her garden. She was not there. He rounded the house and stepped up onto the porch. He stood in front of the door and stared at it, summoning the courage to knock.

When he finally did knock the door flew open, almost beneath the first touch of knuckles to wood.

"It's you!" Amberson made no effort to hide the annoyance in her big hazel eyes.

He leaned against the doorjamb. Her hair was down and the sun caught the highlights, turning them to bronze. "Who were you expecting?" he asked.

"Not you," she snapped.

"Can I come in?"

"What for?"

"I need a drink."

"Don't we all?" she sneered.

"Of water."

She glared at him, then reluctantly stepped aside. "Very well. The water bucket's on the counter. Help yourself."

He pushed himself away from the doorjamb, keeping his eyes on her warily. Mustn't forget she's my enemy, he warned himself. Ignore the way the light reflects on her hair, and the liveliness you see in her eyes. She's got something you want—your son—and don't you forget it.

Justin walked across the wood floor, marshaling his thoughts. He poured himself a crystal-clear glass of water and raised it to his lips, keeping his back to her as she waited by the door. He needed to buy time for himself. Too much rested on this one encounter. They had to talk about Gerald.

He drank the water, feeling her eyes boring into his back the whole time. He set the glass on the counter, wiped his mouth with the back of his hand, then slowly turned to face her. He crossed his arms and leaned back against the counter.

"Let's talk."

"Hah! A drink of water, you said."

"I lied."

"You're good at that!"

"So are you," he shot back.

"I've never lied to you."

He raised a brow. "You kept my son from me."

"Oh. That." She didn't look the least bit contrite, the witch. "I had to."

"He's *my* son."

"I know. And I wish I'd never told you."

"Too damn late for that, isn't it?"

Silence.

"Say what you're going to say and get out." Her voice was cold.

"I want my son."

She laughed, a sharp sound. "He happens to be living with me. He's mine."

"He's mine too."

She prowled across the kitchen floor; her eyes met his. "Look, Justin," she said, suddenly cajoling, suddenly sweet.

Mistrust rose in him.

157

"Let's take our time about this," she crooned. "After all, this is a big decision."

"What is?"

"Well, what to do with Gerald. I presume that's what we're speaking about."

He uncrossed his arms, irritated with her. "Where is he?"

"Upstairs."

"Get him."

"He's napping."

"I don't care. I want to see him."

A baby's cry could be heard.

"He's awake," said Justin triumphantly. "Get him."

With a sour look, she fled upstairs.

Some of the tension went out of him now that she was out of the room. He wouldn't want to be in Amberson Hawley Rowan's high-button boots right now, but it couldn't be helped. Richard was not the father; he, Justin, was.

She brought the baby down the stairs and he walked over, removing the corner of blanket that covered the sleepy child's face. The baby looked at him and blinked.

Justin couldn't help smiling at the boy. He was sweet. There was a family resemblance, around Gerald's eyes. "He has eyes like my mother," mused Justin. "The boy's mine, all right."

Amberson drew the baby away, a frown on her face. "He's mine!"

"Look, Miss Amberson," he said reasonably, "we have to come to terms here."

"Do we?" she answered coolly.

"Yes," he said sharply. "Otherwise—"

"Otherwise, what? You'll tell Richard?"

"No. I wasn't going to say that."

"But you'll do it."

"If I have to."

Silence.

Finally, her head bowed and her shoulders slumped. "Don't tell him."

"I will if it's the only way you'll let me have my son."

"Don't tell him." She was shaking. "Please." Her voice was a whisper.

He shook his head, irritated with this sham of fear. Didn't the woman have any backbone? What was she going to do next? Try tears?

"What do you want me to do?" he sneered. "Tiptoe around Rowan for the next twenty years, waiting for Gerald to grow up?"

She didn't answer, just kept her head bowed.

"Because you're too damn chicken to tell Richard," he added for good measure.

She lifted her head at that. Sure enough, there was a glistening of tears in her hazel eyes. Dang the woman!

"Please, Justin. We can find some other way. Just don't tell Richard. Not yet. I need time."

"Time? How much time?" He wanted to yell at her that she'd had enough time. More than enough. A year of time that she'd known the truth.

She shrugged and he smelled a faint whiff of lavender. His body tightened with desire. He wanted to curse himself. How could he be attracted to this lying witch?

"Surely we can find some way to work this out," she said unhappily.

"Can we?" he taunted. "Doesn't seem to be any way that I can see."

She was staring at the floor now, looking cowed

and surprisingly un-Ambersonlike. He remembered the feisty girl she'd once been.

He sighed. "What will Richard do if he knows?" Justin felt as though he was walking on a nest of rattlesnake eggs in his stocking feet. If she tried tears again, he would walk out that door.

She shook her head. "Nothing." Her shoulders slumped dejectedly.

That sounded odd. Rowan would surely have something to say or do about the matter. "Are you sure?" he asked.

She shrugged listlessly.

"Then what's the problem?" he asked as patiently as he could. This woman must have been sent to try men's souls. He knew it. And she was certainly doing a good job on his.

"I—I don't want him to know."

Justin snorted with exasperation. "Well, he's sure as hell going to know soon. How long do you think you can keep it from him? He's not Gerald's father. I am!"

She was silent, that same hangdog expression on her face. She sighed. "Don't you tell him. I'll tell him."

He didn't like the sound of that. He wondered if she'd run from the ranch rather than tell Richard Rowan the child he loved wasn't his. He suspected she would.

"When?"

She was silent a long time.

"When?" he prodded again. What the hell was the matter with her? Under his demanding question, she turned away from him. He stared at her, the curve of her back, at her naked nape, where her hair parted on either side of her neck. He softened toward her.

"Miss Amberson," he said gently, "Rowan has to

be told sometime. The man deserves to know the truth." *Something you've kept from him for a long time. From me too.* But he didn't say the words aloud, fearing to destroy the gentle moment between them. Truth could do that.

She looked up at him then and he saw a tear streak down her cheek. Dang her! His gentle intentions fled under her manipulation. He hated seeing a woman cry.

"Amberson, listen to me," he said roughly. "Rowan has got to know. Sooner or later, he's got to know."

She shook her head. "I don't want him to know."

Exasperated with her stubbornness, Justin could only glare at her. His eyes fell to the baby, the source of their contention. Gerald's face was calm, his blue eyes peaceful. Damn! How had all this happened?

She saw him staring at Gerald and moved the boy, partially blocking Justin's view of his son.

"The sooner he knows, the better," said Justin.

"For you," she bit out.

"For you too," he shot back.

She gave him a withering glare and for a moment he saw the younger, feistier Amberson he'd once known.

"I need time," she snarled. "You come barging into my home, telling me that I have to tell Richard . . ." Her jaw worked, but she couldn't say the words, not even to Justin, who already knew the truth.

"I don't care what you need," answered Justin, getting angry himself. "You never thought about what I needed."

"Hah!" she sneered. "I don't care what you need either! You're the one who started all this!"

"How?" he demanded.

"You're the one who seduced me!"

"I did not!"

"In the moonlight," she accused him, as if it were some grave offense.

"You were willing!" he defended himself.

"You—you—!" she shrieked. "I was *not* willing."

He glared at her. "You could have fooled me. Why, you were hot for it."

"How dare you!" she screamed. The baby started to cry, but she ignored his whimpers.

"It's too damn late to pretend we didn't make love," he snarled.

"Ooooh!" she cried, so furious that her cheeks were red blotches.

He grinned at her suddenly, remembering that night, how she'd looked. Her dress, a frothy white creation with a blue ribbon at the waist, a girlish dress, really. He'd been hungry for her. He'd taken her with the ease of a man cajoling a young, inexperienced woman for her first time.

Guilt, and regret, stirred a little in his conscience. She *had* been young. And beautiful. And he'd needed her so badly. . . . In the middle of an ugly war, she was the one good thing he'd had. . . .

"Get out!" she screamed at him, clutching the crying baby to her breast. "Get out!"

"Not without my son!" he cried, reaching for the baby. Gerald cried louder and Amberson held on to him.

Justin found himself trying to pull the child from her arms. "This is ridiculous!" he roared. "Give me my son!"

The door flew open behind them. "What the hell is going on?" demanded Rowan.

Chapter Eighteen

Richard, chest heaving, swung around to face Justin. "And what the hell do you mean, your son?"

There was a silence in the ranch house, a terrible silence that throbbed between the two men. Why, oh why, did Richard have to come home now? Amberson wondered.

She didn't know what to say to him, but holding Gerald tightly to her bosom comforted her. Nothing Richard or Justin could ever say would make her release this child. Gerald was hers; he would always be hers!

Justin didn't answer Richard either. Amberson saw the muscle in his jaw twitch, and she knew he was angry.

Richard moved a step forward. "What do you mean, Gerald is your son?"

"Richard, I—" began Amberson.

Justin held up a hand to cut her off. "Gerald *is* my son, sir," he answered quietly.

Richard looked bewildered. "How—how is this possible? You did not know one another, had never met before I brought you home. . . . You saved my life. . . ."

Amberson swallowed and looked at the baby. Strange, how after all Richard had said and done to her, the pain and confusion on his face could hurt her. Foolish woman, she actually felt pity for the man.

Justin answered shortly, "We knew one another. During the war."

Richard prowled closer. "Is this true, Amberson?"

She couldn't meet his gaze, only nodded mutely.

She felt his glare but did not look up. She couldn't.

"Gerald? Not my son?"

Amberson wanted to cry at the trembling bewilderment in his voice. She closed her eyes. She hadn't thought to hurt him this way, hadn't planned it. . . .

"Answer me, you lying, scheming sidewinder!" he snarled at her.

Finally, she raised her eyes. "I didn't plan it this way, Richard," she said quietly.

"You snake!" he cried. "You . . ." Words failed him and his mouth worked in fury.

Amberson swallowed.

"Goddamn it all!" erupted Richard. He lunged for Justin. Justin, of a size with Richard, pushed at the other man, but Richard was in a fury and he hit out at Justin wildly. Blows and punches landed on Justin's shoulders and back.

Amberson caught a last glimpse of him ducking to miss Richard's fist before she raced up the stairs with the wailing baby.

Gerald cried all the harder from the short run and Amberson kicked the bedroom door shut behind her.

Downstairs she could hear thumping and pounding as the men fought. From the hollow thuds resounding through the house, she guessed they were throwing one another against the walls.

She clutched Gerald to her and cooed to him over and over, "We're safe up here, Gerald. We're safe up here."

But Gerald would not be comforted. He cried even louder and waved his little fists. She feared he might pop open the stitches Dr. Cooper had sewn to close his stomach. Finally, she was able to coax the baby to nurse, and blessed silence settled over the room.

Downstairs she could still hear thumps and bangs. Finally there was silence down there too. She bowed her head. Oh, God, now what would become of her and her son?

Chapter Nineteen

Amberson tiptoed downstairs while the baby slept. The house was quiet and dark except for a single oil lamp glowing on one of the kitchen tables. A clock on the wall said ten. The door to Richard's study was closed. That meant only one thing: He was drinking again.

She peeked out a back window and saw the shining lights of the bunkhouse. Justin was probably there. She wondered how he'd fared in the fight. She swallowed past the lump of fear in her throat. He could take care of himself.

She glanced around uncertainly, not knowing quite what to do. One thing was certain; she would stay away from Richard's study.

She padded into the kitchen and poured herself a cool glass of water from the bucket.

Suddenly the study door was flung open and Richard staggered out. She whirled. He stared at her, weaving back and forth on unsteady feet. He waved an empty whisky bottle in an attempt to keep his balance.

"Richard!" She gasped and took a step backward, feeling the counter bite into her spine.

He looked awful. Both eyes were blackened and he had a cut across his forehead.

He tottered toward her, rage in his eyes. "Get out," he snarled. "Leave this ranch and don't come back!"

Suddenly his arm arched and he threw the bottle at her. It whistled past her head and shattered against the wall. Shards of glass slid down the wall, leaving a dark trail.

"And take your bastard with you!"

He swung around and headed for the study. He paused for a moment and she could see him draw himself up. She wondered at that small, telltale movement; had it cost him anything, anything at all to speak of Gerald like that?

Richard marched into the study and slammed the door.

Amberson headed bleakly upstairs. She and the baby would leave at dawn.

Amberson took a last halting step and glanced around the darkened kitchen. The oil lamp shed a dull light in the room, adding nothing to the glum dawn breaking through the red-checkered curtains.

This morning she wore her hat and her green go-to-town dress, and she carried Gerald in one arm and her blue satchel over the other. Everything she owned was crammed into that satchel. The baby whimpered.

"Shush, Gerald," she reprimanded softly. "Richard must not hear us."

She tiptoed toward the door. She opened it and walked straight into Justin's broad chest. "Oh!"

He did not look handsome this morning. Not at all. One eye was puffy and a purple bruise darkened one cheek. It had been quite a fight.

"Goin' somewhere?" Justin asked innocently, as if ignoring the fact that it was the break of day and she was dressed in her go-to-town clothes with a warmly wrapped Gerald in her arms.

"What are you doing on my porch?" she demanded.

"Waitin'," was his calm reply.

"Well, get out of my way," she huffed. She prepared to step around him, but he moved with her.

"You're not taking my son," he said.

"He's my son too," she snapped. "Now let me pass!"

"You can pass. My son cannot."

"Huh!" she sniffed. "How will you feed him? How will you care for him?"

"Wet nurse," he replied laconically. "He'll live."

"I will not give him to you!" she yelled. The next moment the study door opened and Richard swayed in the doorway. He looked groggy in his rumpled clothes. Obviously he'd slept in them.

"Oh, no," she moaned. "Not you too!"

"I told you you were fired!" yelled Richard at Justin.

"I know. I'm leaving," answered Justin coolly. "And I'm taking my son with me!"

"No, you're not!" Amberson was so angry she was shaking. She dropped the satchel and wrapped both arms around Gerald. The baby started to cry.

"Get out of here, you shhhnake," Richard yelled at Amberson. "And get that kid out of here! Damn crying! Always crying!" He lurched over to where Justin and Amberson faced each other. "Whore!" he spat.

"She is not a whore," answered Justin evenly.

"Shesshh a whore," slurred Richard.

Justin punched him in the nose and Richard reeled against the wall. He lurched away from the wall, unsuccessfully trying to staunch his bleeding nose with his fingers.

"What the hell? You wanna go at it again?" Richard took up a boxing stance, but his shaking legs buckled and he fell to the floor. He struggled to get up. "Get out of my house!"

The baby wailed louder. Richard glared at Amberson. "Get that kid out of here. I never want to see him again! Get out!" Amberson's heart contracted. Richard had loved Gerald.

"I'll take the baby," said Justin.

"No, you won't," answered Amberson swiftly.

"I don't care who takes the baby," shouted Richard. "Both of you get the hell out! And take that crying kid with you!"

Justin reached for Gerald. Amberson's arms locked tightly around her son. Gerald cried all the while.

"Let go," cried Amberson. "He's mine."

"He's mine." Justin's lips were set in a firm line, his grip strong on the child. "I'm not leaving without him."

Richard watched the struggle with a bleary-eyed, dazed look on his face. Finally he staggered over to where the two tussled for the child. "I don't give a damn what you do, you shhhnake," he told Amberson.

He glared at Justin. "But I sure want you the hell outta here!"

"Tell him to go!" Amberson encouraged Richard through gritted teeth.

Richard glared at her, looking frighteningly sober for a moment. "Huh! What the hell makes you think I'd do anything for you, you cheating, lying snake?" To Justin he said, "You want the kid? Take him," and he grabbed one of Amberson's arms prying loose her death grip on the baby.

"No!" she cried. "No!"

"Shoulda thought of that when you were lying to me, shouldn't you, witch?"

"You just want revenge!" screamed Amberson.

"Damn right I do." Seeing that Justin had a better grip on Gerald, Richard pried Amberson's other arm away from the baby. "Take the damn kid!" he yelled.

"Stop it! You fool!" she shrieked, struggling to free her hands from Richard's viselike grip.

The baby wailed.

Justin held the child. He swung around and strode down the porch steps, heading toward his fully saddled horse. Saddlebags bulged on the bay gelding.

"You planned this!" shrieked Amberson accusingly at Justin. He ignored her, mounting the horse while holding the baby tightly.

"Let me go!" she cried at Richard.

"I'll let you go when I'm damn good and ready." A blast of Richard's whisky-laden breath hit her and she looked away, gagging.

But now was not the time to be weak.

"Richard, let me go! My baby!" she cried frantically.

"Too damn bad," he snarled. "Shoulda thought about that when you lied to me."

"I didn't lie. He *was* your son. I did everything I could to make him your son. . . ."

"Yeah? Then how come that saddle bum claims him?"

Amberson glanced at Justin. "Noo!" she cried. She twisted in Richard's drunken embrace. "Let me go! My baby!" She had to get to Gerald, she had to!

She struggled hard, but drunk as he was, Richard was still stronger than she.

She heard Justin's horse's hooves pounding the ground as he and the baby galloped away. Fighting fiercely, she finally managed to get Richard to release one hand. She clawed at him, not caring that she drew blood. She must get to Gerald. She must!

He held her other hand so tightly, she squeezed her eyes shut in pain. "Let me go," she pleaded. "I'll do anything . . ." She started to cry in frustration, frantic to get to Gerald. "Let me go, I tell you!"

"Anything?" taunted Richard, dragging her closer and breathing his foul breath on her. When she was an inch from his face he roared, "Too damn late! I don't want you. I can't stand you!"

"Go to your damn Madeline Mueler then!" she cried.

"I will!" He cast her from him and she fell against the rough wood of a porch post and slid to the wooden floor. She sprang up, running down the steps and after Justin.

"Justin!" she screamed, panting as she ran. "Bring back my baby!"

She heard the scrunch of footsteps behind her and didn't care that Richard followed her.

"Justin!"

She kept running, lifting her green skirts so she could run faster. "Justiiiinnn!" she screamed. "Come back!"

She raced as fast as she could, but Justin was easily increasing the distance between them.

She held out her arms as she ran, imploring . . . "My baby! Oh God, my baby! Don't take my baby!"

Coughing at the swirling dust from his horse's hooves, she kept running. The hot sun beat at her, and her high-button shoes, never made for running, pinched her feet. All the while, Justin grew smaller and smaller the farther away he rode. He never once glanced back.

"Justin!" she cried hoarsely. "Oh, God, please, Justin! Don't take Gerald! He's all I've got!"

She didn't hear Richard behind her any more, but she couldn't waste time glancing back. She had to keep watching the little speck that was Justin . . . and her child. "Oh, Gerald," she moaned. "Come back, please come back."

She must have run a mile before she started to slow down. She wasn't going to catch him, she knew that now. Her baby was gone, taken from her. She could keep running, but it would do no good. All she knew was that he was heading in the direction of Gunpoint. If she turned around, got her horse, she could ride after them, get Gerald. . . .

Exhausted, she tripped and fell. Too tired to rise from the dirt, she lay there. "Gerald," she moaned feebly.

"Oh, my baby. Come back . . . please . . ." Tears ran down her cheeks and dripped into the dust, forming little balls of salt water.

She heard hoofbeats behind her. Self-preservation dictated that she at least roll out of the road. She pulled herself to her knees and crawled to the side of the road, uncaring of the dust all over her once green dress.

A thundering buckskin bore down on her, the rider

wearing a dark blue coat, its tails flying. "Richard," she groaned helplessly. "Go away!"

He reined in his buckskin as he drew abreast of her. The big animal reared on his hind legs. "Didn't get too far, did you?" jeered Richard. "Why I reckon that saddle bum and your baby will be long gone once you get to Gunpoint, don't you agree?" He laughed.

"Richard," she pleaded desperately, "help me. For the love of God, help me. I'm on my knees to you. Justin took my baby. Help me get him back! Please!" Richard was her only chance. With his help she could get Gerald back . . . she just knew it.

"Why the hell should I?" Richard shot back. "You lied to me. Passed off that brat as my own. Whyever the hell should I help you, snake?"

"Richard," she pleaded, crawling closer. Some part of her registered the pathetic figure she must make, groveling in the dirt, trying to convince Richard to help her, but she didn't care. She was desperate. There was no other way. "I know we haven't had the best marriage—"

He snorted. "You didn't do much to help it, did you?" he accused.

"—but surely to God you can help me, Richard. You love Gerald!"

"Hell, no," he corrected. "Not anymore. All he is to me now is some bastard kid passed off on me. I don't give a damn about him and I sure as hell don't give a damn about you!"

"Richard!" She recoiled from the coldness in him. She staggered up, her feet catching in her dress, making her stumble once more. He sat there atop his horse and watched her with a look of black contempt.

"Have you always been like this or do *I* bring it out in you?" she demanded.

"Any man married to you would be driven to other women!" he yelled at her. "It's all your fault our marriage is nothing. *All* your fault!"

"But you did some of it too," she cried. "What about Madeline Mueler?"

He turned away with an exasperated glower. "You insist on bringing her into this, do you?"

"Yes! She's the reason you turned away from me."

Disgust crossed his face. "I don't know what the hell you're talking about. You're crazy, you know that? You should be committed to a sanitarium. You know that? You're stark, raving nuts!"

"Me?" she cried. "Living with you would drive any woman crazy!"

"See, you admit it!" he cried.

"I admit nothing!" she vowed hoarsely. "You're the one who hits me, betrays me . . ."

"Shut up, you whore," he cried. "You're a fine one to talk about betrayal. You, who had a baby by another man!" His face reddened in fury. "I thought Gerald was mine!"

"He still could be," she cajoled. Somehow, in all the arguing, she'd forgotten the most important thing: to get Gerald back. "Richard—" she held out her hands beseechingly—"if you help me get Gerald, I'll bring him back here. We can live like we always did. I'll stay here at the ranch with Gerald, and you can be his father. You can even visit Madeline—"

Hah!" he barked. "And what the hell do I get out of that? A dishrag for a wife and a saddle bum's bastard!" He spat at her, narrowly missing her face.

"Don't talk like that. You know you love Gerald!"

Richard's face was grim. The buckskin reared up

on his hind legs once more, so tightly did Richard grip the reins. "Get this through your head, snake," he growled. "Once and for all." He leaned down so his face was level with hers. "I ain't gonna help you. Not to get your bastard back, not in any way! Got that?"

She glared at him, misery and hopelessness warring in her heart. "I've got it," she answered sullenly.

"Good. I'm going to town," he told her. "You be gone by the time I get back." He spurred the big buckskin and galloped off down the lane.

She watched him go.

She was alone. Richard wouldn't help her. Justin had stolen her son from her. There was no one willing to help her get Gerald back. There was no one to help her right the terrible injustice that had occurred. Her son was gone and she was alone. She threw herself on the road, uncaring of the hard rocks under her arms and stomach, uncaring of the brown dust.

Her tears dripped into the road and her whole body shook with the force of her sobs. Gerald was gone. Her son, the only person she loved in the whole world, was gone. Lost to her as much as if he'd died.

She wished she could die.

Chapter Twenty

"Ma'am?"

For a few moments, the soft voice didn't register with Amberson. Somehow, in all her misery, she was unaware of her surroundings.

"Ma'am?"

She blinked, trying to rouse herself. Her back felt hot from the sun beating down on her. Her face was red and puffy from crying. She peeked out over her elbow.

Beau.

She lifted her face and peered at him.

He gasped.

"What do you want?" she demanded belligerently. Who cared what she looked like? Who cared what he thought? Who cared about anything anymore? She didn't.

He backed gingerly away toward his pony, as if expecting her to bite.

"Can I help you, ma'am?"

When she remained silent he gingerly stepped forward again. Then he squatted down beside her. She wanted to cry all over again at the compassion she saw on his sun-browned face. There was no one in the world to help her, no one. Could her life get any worse?

She tried to sit up, but she must have been lying in the roadway for so long that her muscles had stiffened. He reached under her elbow and helped her sit up.

"I know the boss has gone to town," he said apologetically.

"It's not your fault," she said.

"No. But I know he don't treat you too good."

"No one does," she answered listlessly.

He pondered that. "True," he agreed at last. "But I'll help you, Missus Rowan."

She looked at him. What could he do? "Thank you," she answered politely.

He scrambled to his feet and tugged on her elbow, trying to pull her up.

"Wait," she said. "I'll do it."

He nodded, dignified, and suddenly she gave a bitter laugh. Here she was, sitting in the middle of a dusty road, a woman alone, her child gone, no family in the world to help her, not a penny to her name, and she was being helped to her feet by a dwarf. Had the world gone crazy?

When she finally staggered to her feet, he said, "What are you going to do, Missus Rowan?"

She glanced at the ranch house. "I'm going to go back and get my satchel," she said with determination. "Then I'm leaving for Gunpoint. I'm going to get my baby back."

"Ma'am?"

She heard the cautious note in his question.

"What is it?"

"I don't mean to tell you what to do, ma'am. It's just that . . ." He hesitated, fiddling with his battered black slouch hat.

"Out with it," she snapped, and then wished she could have taken back the impatient words when she saw his mouth droop.

"I think you need a plan, ma'am," he said slowly, "before rushin' off to Gunpoint. You're up against two determined men. One's used to gettin' his own way, and the other . . . the other one I don't rightly know much about. He seems like a good man. . . ."

"Justin Harbinger is decidedly *not* a good man," she informed him through gritted teeth. "He is a saddle bum."

Beau said thoughtfully, "He may be a saddle bum, but he's a smart saddle bum, and he's got your baby."

Amberson frowned uneasily. She slapped off some of the dust on her green skirt while she thought about his words.

"I want my son," she said at last. "And you are right, I do need a plan."

She started walking back to the ranch house. Beau followed, leading his pony.

Some time later, they reached the porch. Amberson's feet hurt and she was limping, but the walk had given her time to think.

"There's one more thing I'm going to do," announced Amberson crisply as she marched up the steps.

Beau nodded. "Ma'am?"

From the top of the steps, Amberson drew herself

up regally. "Yes," she answered at last. "There is one more little thing."

He cocked his large head to the side, inquisitive, waiting.

"I'm not going to lie to myself or anyone else ever again. It gets me into too damn much trouble."

Chapter Twenty-one

By the time Justin got to Gunpoint, the baby's wet diaper had soaked half his shirt. Gerald had also cried himself to sleep. Justin was glad about the last part.

He rode past the fancy Two Star Hotel with its two stories of well-appointed rooms. Men who'd made a lucky gold strike stayed there—also, some of the town's richer attorneys were known to keep suites there. As for Justin, the town's second-rate hotel would have to do. He carefully dismounted in front of the Hank Parker Hotel, keeping the sleeping baby balanced carefully in his arms. With one hand he tied Samson to the hitching post.

Hank Parker had stretched the truth a little, calling the place a *hotel*, Justin decided. It looked more like a wood and tar-paper shack, with more tar-paper shacks added on.

Entering the hotel, Justin glanced around. The

lobby had a counter on one side of the small room and four varicolored, overstuffed chairs grouped together in the middle of the room. In one corner of the room was propped the mummified body of a miner. Draped around his wrinkled, dried neck was a sign advertising EDDIE'S EMBALMING EMPORIUM.

Presiding over the counter was Pa Parker.

"Greetings, sir," he said to Justin. "Would you like a room?" He peered at Justin through the dim light. "Oh, it's you, sir. Howdy. Been over having a quick one at my son Joe's Plugged Nickel Saloon?"

"No, sir," answered Justin. "I need a room."

"Well—" Pa Parker smacked his lips in satisfaction—"I'm just helpin' out my son Hank. You knowed him?"

"Can't say I've had the pleasure, sir," answered Justin.

"Oh. Well, I've got three rooms to rent. Big, middle, and little. Which one you want?"

Justin glanced around. He didn't want to stay long at this "hotel," but there was no other place to go for the time being with a baby.

"I want one that's got a bed and a bath," he said.

"Oh, all of 'em's got beds and none of 'em's got baths," answered Pa cheerfully. "Hank only did one room with a bath, and it's out back. He's puttin' in a commode."

Justin lifted his eyebrows hopefully.

"All our customers share the bathtub, and the commode will be ready next week," chortled Pa. "Hank's still workin' on his mining invention and he ain't quite got enough time to do the commode. Yessir." Pa Parker coughed and cleared his throat. "Say, is that a baby you got there?"

Justin nodded. "Looking for a wet nurse, sir. You know of one?"

Pa stroked his thin gray beard. "I'll have to ask the missus. That's her department."

A thin young man wandered in. "Larry!" barked Pa. "Go find your ma. She's at the Plugged Nickel."

Pa leaned forward and confided to Justin, "She's probably havin' her lunch. You know and I know it's a beer, but we don't want the other customers hearin' that."

Justin glanced around, looking for the other customers. There was only he, Gerald, Larry, and Pa. The mummified miner didn't count. "If you say so, sir," Justin acknowledged.

Pa nodded happily. "Tell your ma to git herself over here quick," he said to the young man hurrying out the door.

"That's Loser Larry," said Pa conversationally. "He's my son that lost the gold mine."

"The gold mine?"

"I tole you about it. Loser Larry gambled with a certain lawyer about town whose name I won't mention for fear of adding slander to his already sullied reputation." Pa's bushy eyebrows waggled up and down in agitation.

"Anyhow, Larry lost his gold mine. Now he's tryin' to find another one. In the meantime he works here and at the Plugged Nickel for his brothers." Pa shook his head mournfully. "It's a shame. Young man like that. Fetchin' for others. He has been gravely reduced in his social circumstances, if you get my drift."

Justin nodded. "I've been reduced in my social circumstances a time or two myself."

"Nice baby," said Pa, leaning over the counter to get a better look at Gerald.

Justin moved the baby away from Pa. All of a sudden he felt protective. "I'll take that room you were going to show me," he said.

"You want the big one, then," said Pa, eyeing the baby. "Baby like that needs lots of room."

Justin thought Gerald didn't care about the size of the room, but he knew Pa was trying to make money for Hank.

"The middle room will do," he told Pa.

Pa took a key off the back wall and walked over to a closed door. He unlocked it. "Here you go, sir. Make yourself right at home."

Justin peered into the darkness. Pa sauntered past him into the room and lit an oil lamp. He smiled cheerily as he left.

The room was small, rather than middle-sized, barely big enough for a bed and a chest of drawers with a cracked pitcher and a basin on top. One tiny window let in light.

A faded blue-and-yellow patchwork quilt graced the top of the bed and dingy gray curtains covered the windows. The curtains reminded Justin of the counter rags he'd seen Pa using at the Plugged Nickel Saloon.

"Pretty nice, isn't it?" asked Pa eagerly. " 'Course, I know it's a mite small. You'd probably like the bigger room."

The old rascal wanted his sale.

"It's fine," answered Justin. He was only going to stay one night. He'd find a wet nurse and then look for a ranch in the area. While he didn't have the six hundred dollars he'd hoped to save for a ranch, he did have five hundred, courtesy of the plantation sale and past wages from Rowan. Rowan still owed him back wages, but Justin doubted Rowan would pay him now. Not after the fight and the way he'd carried on about the baby. Well, five hundred dollars was enough to buy a ranch if someone was desperate to sell.

He walked back to the counter. "You know of any ranches for sale?"

Pa considered. "A couple of boys, customers of Joe's over at the Plugged Nickel, might want to sell." He frowned, thinking. "Seems I heard Old Man McManus wants to sell since them rustlers wiped out his herd. His ranch ain't too bad, either. Loser Larry was over there the other day, prospectin'. Lookin' for another mine."

Pa leaned forward. "I sure would like it if Larry found another mine. That boy gotta watch his gamblin', though. He tole me he's got true gamblin' instincts. I tole him he ain't got sh—" Pa glanced at the baby. "Uh, got anything." Pa winked at Justin. "No swearin' in front of a baby. Them's hotel rules."

Justin went back to his room. He closed the door and laid the baby down on the bed. Luckily, the baby didn't wake up.

Justin peered out the window. It gave an expansive view of one weathered gray wall of Hinkley's General Store.

Turning back to the baby, Justin watched in dismay as a huge puddle formed under Gerald and soaked through the faded patchwork quilt. He groaned. "I've got to get you some diapers, Gerald," he muttered.

Back at the counter, he said to Pa, "Do you know of any woman around here with a baby? I need to get some milk, some diapers."

"For the kid?"

Justin nodded.

Pa scratched his thinning hair. "Gee, don't know what to tell you."

Just then Loser Larry walked in the front door, pulling an old woman after him.

Pa brightened. "But my missus ought to be able to help you. She knows about babies. Birthed six of them," he proclaimed proudly, reminding Justin of a bantam rooster.

The bantam hen, however, stumbled as she staggered across the threshold of the hotel. Larry pushed her along from behind until they reached Pa at the counter.

Pa frowned. "Ma, you know anyone in town with a baby?"

She swayed. "Baby?"

"Yeah."

"Annabelle?" said Ma.

Pa turned to Justin. "Ma says Annabelle will be happy to help you out with your baby."

Justin stared at the old woman, then at the bright-eyed old man watching him. "She didn't say anything of the sort."

Pa nodded his head vigorously. "I knowed her for years. That's what she said." He turned to his son for confirmation. "Didn't she, Loser Larry?"

Larry looked bewildered at being brought into the conversation. "Huh?"

"I said," growled Pa, "that your ma recommends your sister Annabelle to look after the baby."

"She does?" Larry looked as surprised as Justin felt.

"She does," confirmed Pa. "Go on now, boy. You

got another gold mine to find." Pa ushered a confused Larry out the door.

"Now," said Pa, rubbing his hands as he turned to Justin. "Let my wife take your baby over to Annabelle's. She'll take good care of him. 'Course, it will cost you a little. Ain't nothing free in this town."

"No thanks," answered Justin. "I'm going to look around for a wet nurse."

"Suit yourself," shrugged Pa. "I'm just trying to help, is all." He glanced over. "Ma, get outta that room. That's for customers." He hurried over and dragged her out of one of the hotel rooms and led her to a red overstuffed chair. "Foolish ol' woman," he muttered under his breath.

Justin picked up Gerald and headed for the door. He had to find some diapers for Gerald and a wet nurse—without Pa Parker's help.

Late that evening, Justin was back at the hotel. He'd searched the town and his choice of a woman to look after the baby was clear: it came down to Miss Susie, a recently retired lady of the night from Estelle's House of Beautiful Ladies, or Mrs. Parker and her daughter, Miss Annabelle.

Justin sighed as he tore up a sheet and wrapped a piece of cloth around Gerald's lower anatomy. He'd better find a ranch—fast. Leaving the baby with Mrs. Parker was impossible. The woman could not even stay on her bar stool.

He hoped her daughter, Miss Annabelle, would be a better choice. He sighed. He'd find out in the morning. What he and Gerald needed now was a good night's sleep.

The baby fell asleep, crying softly for only a short time.

It was fortunate Justin had found that miner who owned a cow. Now he could get milk for Gerald every day.

Justin lay down beside the baby and stared at the tar paper–lined ceiling.

Pounding feet running up and down the boardwalk in front of the hotel kept him awake until the early hours of the morning. Raucous shouts coming from the two saloons at this end of Gold Fever Street competed with exuberant yells coming from the three saloons at that end of Gold Fever Street.

It was some time before Justin finally dozed off.

Several times he blinked awake groggily to the sound of slamming doors and men's shouts coming from the direction of Estelle's House of Beautiful Ladies.

Morning came when a rooster crowed loudly somewhere behind Justin's tiny window. Staggering from bed, he managed to splash cold water from the pitcher onto his face. The stinging coolness of the water woke him up, sputtering.

Today he'd find Miss Annabelle and leave Gerald with her, just for the day. Then he'd go looking for a ranch. Talks last night with several men at the Plugged Nickel Saloon had revealed that there were at least three ranches for sale in the area.

He had to find a ranch right quick. The Hank Parker Hotel was no place to bring up a baby.

Chapter Twenty-two

Hinckley Parker set aside the *Gunpoint Gazette* on the counter and took the pipe out of his mouth. He peered at Amberson from behind round-rimmed glasses. "You look a mite peaked, ma'am," he had the nerve to say. "Can I fetch you a sarsaparilla?"

Amberson blinked. She glanced down at her green dress. It looked bedraggled from the dusty treatment of yesterday, but she'd thought she'd managed to beat most of the dirt out of it. Then she realized he hadn't been talking about the dress.

Her hands flew to her cheeks. Did she really look so awful? Did her night of crying for her son show on her face?

Beside her, Beau said, "I'll wait outside for you, Missus Rowan."

"Thank you," she told the cowboy. She watched him leave the store. Her only friend in the world.

She turned back to Hinckley. "Yes, please," she

said as brightly as she could. "I would like a sarsa-parilla."

He went to the back room, where he kept the drinks cool in a barrel. He returned and handed her a bottle.

"How've you been?" he asked conversationally.

She wasn't about to tell him she'd lost her son and been kicked off the Triple R Ranch and had nowhere to turn, so she smiled and lied through her teeth. "Fine."

He picked up his newspaper and perused it. "There's a meeting of the Ladies' Culture Club this afternoon, ma'am. At my sister Annabelle's house. You might like to attend."

"Thank you, Hinckley," Amberson answered politely, turning away as if to examine some bolts of yellow-, blue-, and red-checked cloth. The last thing she wanted to do was spend time with that set of gossips!

She wandered around the store, sipping the sweet drink. The bolts of material failed to hold her interest and she began to wonder again how she would find Gerald. Where would Justin take him?

Finishing the last sip of sarsaparilla, she frowned. She and Beau had talked about what she could do to get her baby back and he'd suggested that she find out what her legal rights were. She set down the glass on the counter. "Thank you, Mr. Parker," she said softly.

He nodded and kept reading his paper.

She walked out of the store and squared her shoulders. She marched down the boardwalk until she came to Mr. Fred Knox's office. ATTORNEY AT LAW was painted in big black letters on the upper half of the door. She opened the door and went in.

Mr. Fred Knox glanced up from where he was seated at a large desk. Papers were piled neatly at all four corners. Painted pictures of swans and ducks lined the four walls of his office. Upon seeing Amberson, he closed the ledger he'd been writing in, set down his quill pen, and rose from his big leather chair.

"How do you do, Mrs. Rowan?" he asked politely. There was a knowing look in his brown eyes, and for a moment she wondered if he'd heard what had happened to her. But then she decided she was making things up. He didn't know. He couldn't.

"I am well," she lied as she smiled at him.

"Glad to hear it, ma'am," he answered heartily. Too heartily.

Oh, Lord, he knew. Her smile faltered. "I—I've come to ask you about something." She hesitated. Should she ask him about Gerald? Oh, why this hesitation? She'd come to his office to find out her rights. She must do so.

"Please," he said, indicating the chair in front of the desk. "Won't you sit down?"

She sat down. He was watching her in a kindly, if detached manner. She took a breath. She must find out her legal rights, for Gerald's sake. Lifting her chin, she began, "My son has been taken from me. I wish to get him back."

Mr. Knox sat down in his big leather chair. He leaned back, his brown eyes narrowing on her. "Hmmm. Who took him?"

"His father."

Mr. Knox lifted a brow at that. "There's not much you can do then, ma'am. Son belongs to his father."

"But he's *my* baby!"

Fred Knox shrugged. "That's the law."

Amberson's mouth drooped. This had certainly been a fruitless visit. "Isn't there anything I can do? He's my son. I must have him back!"

The attorney studied her, pursing his lips. "As I said, Mrs. Rowan, the son is considered the father's, in all legal respects. That doesn't leave much of anything for you, does it?"

"No," answered Amberson shortly. "Can my brother get him back for me?"

"Your brother?"

"Yes. If my brother were to represent me, could he get my child back?"

Fred Knox toyed with the quill pen on his desk. "Afraid not, Mrs. Rowan. Mr. Rowan is still the father."

"Mr. Rowan?"

"Yes. He *is* the father we are speaking of, I presume."

Amberson's lips tightened. She should get up and walk out. Now. Before she went any further with this. If she told Fred Knox that Justin Harbinger was Gerald's father . . . well, this was a small town. Word would get around. She could just forget about showing her face in town.

"Is something the matter, Mrs. Rowan?" Fred Knox looked sympathetic, she had to admit. His brown eyes had a kindly light in them.

She took a deep breath. She had promised herself, and Beau, that she would tell herself and others the truth. Already, at Hinckley's General Store, she had lied once. Then she'd lied once already to this man. She was not "well." Did she want to continue lying? Hadn't she learned the destructiveness of lies? How important was this little town to her, anyway? If she told the truth and the people snubbed her, she could always move. Nothing bound her to Gunpoint except Gerald.

"Actually, Mr. Knox, Mr. Rowan is not the father. Another man is."

There was a flicker in the warm brown eyes. "Oh." A long pause, then, "I see."

Amberson could see that he did not see. He stood up. "As you can see, Mrs. Rowan, I am a busy man. I have a lot to do today. . . ." He nodded politely at her.

Flushed with mortification, Amberson rose to her feet too. "I thank you for your time, then," she said softly. He thought her a loose woman. A woman of terrible moral character. She could tell by his eyes. They were cooler now, and the warm brown was gone as if it had never been there. Get used to it, girl, she told herself harshly. This is what it's like if you tell the truth. To yourself and others. No one said it would be easy.

She straightened. "Good day to you, sir," she said and marched to the door.

As she was opening it, he said, "Mrs. Rowan?"

She turned. "Yes?"

"Mrs. Rowan, I always have need of a good-looking woman to dance in my Hurdy Gurdy Palace. You would make a fine dancer. And I pay my dancers well, ma'am." He smiled. "Very well."

She colored. He really thought her very low. "No thank you, Mr. Knox," she said crisply, flinging open the door. "I will find my own way to perdition!"

Outside, on the boardwalk, she was so angry she was shaking. How dare he! How dare he think that she would want to dance at his horrible Hurdy Gurdy Palace! Women who worked there wore fancy, tight costumes, costumes no lady would ever wear. They danced with men, many men. For money. She shuddered. She was not that far gone. Not yet.

As she marched down the street she vowed she would find Gerald, with or without legal help, thank you!

She walked along the boardwalk. The more she thought about Fred Knox's crude offer, the angrier she got, so it took several marches up and down Gold Fever Street before she was able to calm herself. Hurdy Gurdy Palace indeed!

She was passing by Mrs. Annabelle Simmons's white house for the fifth time when she saw several ladies gathered at the front door and filing into the house.

Mrs. Simmons's house was built of white-washed wood. In a city back east one would never notice such a modest home, but here, in Gunpoint, the house was lavish; indeed, it was considered a veritable mansion by the awed townsfolk of Gunpoint.

"Hello, Mrs. Rowan!" called Mrs. Reedy, waving her hand in Amberson's direction.

Too late, Amberson realized she could not just slink away, not with several of the Culture Club ladies looking at her.

"Come and join us," called the wretched Mrs. Reedy. Why was she being so friendly when the last time Amberson had seen her, she'd been giggling behind her hand with Mrs. Hyacinth Stanton?

Amberson shuffled over to the white picket gate, her mind desperately searching for excuses as to how she could avoid the Gunpoint Ladies' Culture Club. But her encounter with Mr. Fred Knox and her subsequent marching and anger seemed to have taken up all creative thought, leaving her brain devoid of excuses. "Hello," she answered weakly.

"Do join us," urged Mrs. Annabelle Simmons herself, stepping onto the porch. The tall, bouncy blond woman wore two long, floppy bug antennae on her head and a green, filmy, form-fitting dress. She sported two large white wings on her back.

"Mrs. Simmons?" Amberson gasped, staring at the strange apparition. "Annabelle Simmons?"

Annabelle laughed, a tinkling little laugh. "Oh, please do not look so surprised," she giggled. "I am trying on my costume for my role as fairie queen."

"The Shakespeare play," prodded Mrs. Reedy. "*A Midsummer Night's Dream.* You know the one, I'm sure," she said simperingly to Amberson.

As Annabelle Simmons danced across the porch she quoted,

> " *'Come my lord and in our flight*
> *Tell me how it came this night*
> *That I sleeping here was found*
> *With these mortals on the ground.'* "

Then she gave a low bow and made a grand flourish with her arm.

"Titania." Amberson remembered vaguely seeing a poster about the play.

"Yes," agreed Mrs. Reedy happily.

"How very nice," Amberson said. It must be wonderful, she thought wistfully, to have nothing to do all day but put on fairie costumes and prance around and practice plays. To not have to worry about where your son was, or how you would get him back. . . .

"There now, dear." Mrs. Reedy was leading Amberson along the path through the garden. Now they were walking up the steps to the wide porch. "We need you to help us with the play."

The next thing Amberson knew, she was inside Mrs. Simmons's house, seated on a lovely yellow couch imported all the way from St. Louis, balancing a flowered teacup on her knee and telling the ladies about ranch life. She couldn't quite bring herself to tell them the part where Richard had kicked her off the ranch and Justin had taken her child. She wondered just how honest she had to be to start a new life.

Around her, also drinking tea from dainty cups carried by wagons from the east, sat the flower of Gunpoint womanhood. Besides Mrs. Hyacinth Stanton and Mrs. Dorothy Reedy, whom Amberson was relieved to see were not giggling behind their hands at her, there was the buxom Mrs. Hortense Fuller, spouse of the largest mine owner this side of Bozeman. The voluble Mrs. Fuller bossed Mr. Fuller from morning until night. He never listened.

Across from Amberson sat Mrs. Bea Schwartz and Mrs. Cleo Throgmorton on a green velvet couch. The combined weight of the two ladies threatened to tip over the couch.

Mrs. Schwartz was the plump, smiling wife of the town's second-most successful attorney. There were people in this town who considered Mr. Fred Knox the town's most successful attorney, but Amberson no longer did. If she had any more legal business, she would take it to Mr. Schwartz.

As for Mrs. Cleo Throgmorton, it was rumored that the dark-haired beauty was heartless. She'd started out her career in Gunpoint as the town laundress and had once been engaged to marry the town's assayer. When her fiancé had let slip that a high grade of gold was recorded as coming from a certain Clarence Throgmorton's mine, lo and behold, Cleo had hastily broken the engagement to the assayer and gone to wash Mr. Throgmorton's clothes exclusively. By the end of the month she was married to the mine owner.

The only other lady Amberson recognized among the several women present was Mrs. Bertha Pippin, the preacher's wife. Mrs. Pippin reminded Amberson of a busy robin, pecking here and there for worms, though Amberson had to admit Mrs. Pippin preferred gossip to worms.

"I am so curious about that new Mormon preacher," spoke up Mrs. Pippin. "The preacher—I hear he's a bishop!—arrived in Gunpoint the other day." Her voice throbbed in excitement. "He had five wives in tow!"

"Five!" exclaimed several women.

"Does he bed all five of them at once?" asked Cleo Throgmorton lazily. Mrs. Pippin flushed in embarrassment as silence descended on the houseful of women.

Mrs. Reedy coughed. "He must be very busy."

"No doubt," agreed Mrs. Pippin. She cocked her head.

"I hear that some of the young cowboys asked him to come to town. Seems they want to have five wives each."

"Oh, no!" exclaimed several women, happily aghast.

"Harold could take a second wife and I wouldn't mind," announced Mrs. Stanton. "She can have bed duty!"

Several of the ladies gasped, but Amberson heard a distinct twitter or two.

Amberson sipped at her tea, wondering how soon she could make her escape. She had to find Gerald.

"I am so tired," muttered an older woman at the far end of the yellow couch.

"Let me introduce you to Miss Henny Penderson, dear," Mrs. Reedy said to Amberson. "She is Mr. Fred Knox's secretary."

Amberson nodded sympathetically at the tired, gray-haired woman. She could just imagine the difficulty of working for such a man.

Henny looked older than most of the women; her hair was iron gray. "I swear," said Miss Henny in a distinct southern drawl, "that Mr. Knox is trying to wear me out."

"Miss Henny!" gasped Mrs. Reedy, shocked.

"Whatever do you mean?" asked Mrs. Stanton, leaning forward eagerly.

"Oh, you naughty girls. It's not what you think."

Mrs. Reedy and Mrs. Stanton leaned back in their chairs, no longer so attentive.

"Mr. Knox," explained Miss Henny, "is forever having me write these boring letters to the governor." She leaned over and whispered to Amberson, "He is such good friends with the governor."

Amberson nodded politely and sipped her tea.

"Mr. Knox wants to rid our fair town of the Celestial opium fiends," said Miss Henny.

Several of the ladies sat up straighter.

"I wish," said Mrs. Fuller, "that he would rid our town of Estelle's House of Beautiful Ladies. Now *that* would be doing every honest woman in Gunpoint a great service!"

Several women nodded and exclaimed agreement at this pronouncement. Mrs. Fuller looked quite satisfied with herself, as well she should, for her husband spent a pound of gold dust every week at Estelle's.

"Did you see what she was wearing?" demanded Mrs. Bea Schwartz, the attorney's wife. "Why, that Estelle woman was wearing the latest St. Louis fashion. I saw it myself, in the broad light of day! The gown dragged the ground and it was made of that shiny stuff."

"Satin," said Mrs. Stanton helpfully.

"Yes, satin it was, blue satin. And she was wearing a white shawl to cover up her you-know-whats," said Mrs. Schwartz, hitting a definitely flattened portion of her own anatomy.

"I'm surprised you didn't see Joe Parker hotfooting it after her," giggled Mrs. Pippin. "Anytime I ever see him, he's chasing after that woman!"

Mrs. Pippin had to keep her voice lowered because Joe was Mrs. Annabelle Simmons's brother. But Annabelle's bug antennae had slipped off her head and she was trying to put them back in place, so fortunately she didn't hear what Mrs. Pippin was saying.

"As I said," Miss Henny went on severely, dragging the ladies' attention back to the task at hand, "Mr. Knox wants to rid the town of opium fiends. To do that, he has demanded that the governor close down the opium dens."

"Where are they, dear?" asked Mrs. Reedy. She stood up and went over to straighten Titania's antennae.

"Oh, here and there, about town," answered Henny airily. "I'm sure it's up to the governor's men to find them, not me."

"Perhaps our Ladies' Culture Club could help," suggested Mrs. Hyacinth Stanton hopefully. "I'm sure Harold would be happy to help close down those dens of iniquity."

"So would Mr. Schwartz," piped up Mrs. Schwartz.

"Humph," whispered the pastor's wife to Amberson. "That Harold Stanton is probably one of the opium fiends."

"Well, I think," said Titania, interrupting them all, "that it is not the business of our club to chase opium fiends. That is for the governor to do. Our job is to bring the Arts to Gunpoint, which is sorely in need of them. To that end, I suggest we begin to collect books."

"Books?"

"Whatever for?"

Amberson felt a splitting headache coming on. She had to get out of this house.

"Books!" Titania nodded firmly. "What this town needs is a library!"

While the women considered that, Amberson stood up. "I really must be going. . . ."

"Oh, do sit down, dear," said Mrs. Reedy, tugging on her skirt firmly. "You haven't had a second cup of tea yet."

"I—I—"

Titania waved her wand. "Do sit down," she said, "and let me tell all of you what my mother did to me today."

"Oh, no," came the chorus.

Amberson sat down in surprise. Annabelle seldom mentioned her mother—out of embarrassment no doubt, for the whole town had seen old Mrs. Parker staggering along the boardwalk more than once.

"My mother," announced Titania with a huge flourish of her wand, "brought me a baby!"

"A baby!" gasped Mrs. Reedy in surprise.

"A baby?" echoed Amberson. Her knees suddenly went weak. Oh, no . . .

"A baby, can you believe it?" shrieked Titania. "It was all baby: dirty diapers, crying, spitting up, doing all those terrible baby kinds of things." Titania shrugged delicately.

"Oooohh," groaned some of the ladies sympathetically.

"Poor girl," said Henny.

"What—" began Amberson cautiously, "what did this baby look like?"

Titania rolled her eyes. "Like a baby. Somebody lift the train of my gown," she directed. "How can I practice prancing when I'm tripping over my own feet?"

"Oh, here, dear, let me help you," said Mrs. Reedy. She bent down and picked up the trailing green material of Titania's lovely dress. "There, now it's not in the way."

"You look like Estelle," chortled Mrs. Cleo Throgmorton. "All that dress and more material to spare." She giggled.

Some of the women laughed at the remark.

"Please," begged Amberson, "the baby. What did the baby look like?"

Titania shrugged. "The usual. Blue eyes. Fat. Dirty."

"Boy or girl?"

"Boy. Dirty little boy, ugh." Titania shuddered, picked up the train of her green gown, and twirled around so that the ladies could admire her wings.

"What—where is the baby now?" Amberson's heart pounded with fright. They were speaking of Gerald: she knew it.

"I think you need a cape," decided Mrs. Stanton, observing the twirling Titania. "A lovely green cape to match your dress."

"Won't it cover my wings?" objected Titania.

"No, dear, we can make it so it will be just perfect," said Mrs. Reedy, clapping her hands together happily.

"The baby?" Amberson ran up and grabbed hold of Titania's arms. She wanted to shake the woman until her wings fell off.

"My bug antennae!" cried Titania, trying to grab for her head. "What are you doing? They'll fall off!"

"I want to know what happened to the baby!" screeched Amberson.

"Let go, let go! Ouch." Titania winced. "Let go of my arms and I'll tell you!"

Amberson, lips so tight they were pale, released her grasp on Annabelle's graceful white arms.

"Where is he?" Amberson gasped. "Where's the baby?"

"I gave him back to my mother. Why? What's the matter?" Titania's lovely face looked puzzled.

"Where is your mother?" cried a frantic Amberson.

Titania frowned. "The usual place. At my brother's saloon, Joe's Plugged Nickel."

Amberson whirled and darted out the door, not caring that she left behind buzzing, bewildered female voices.

"Don't forget the play!" called Mrs. Reedy after her. "It starts tomorrow night!"

Amberson ran down the street as fast as she could. She ran past the Hurdy Gurdy Palace and Hinckley's General Store, past the Hank Parker Hotel until she came to Joe's Plugged Nickel.

It took her eyes a few minutes to adjust to the darkness inside. Then she saw an old woman sitting at one end of the counter.

Amberson ran up to her. "Where is he? Where's my baby?" she screamed.

The woman looked at her and blinked. A voice from behind the counter said, "Hey! Don't you scream at my mother like that!"

Amberson whirled. Behind the counter was a wide-shouldered, droopy-mustached man with dark hair.

"My baby," Amberson yelled. "This woman has my baby!"

Joe Parker regarded her for a moment. With a shrug, he threw the gray counter rag over his shoulder and said to the woman, "Ma, you got a baby with you?"

When the old woman didn't answer, he scratched his head and said to Amberson, "All I can say is, ma'am, you've been sadly misinformed. As you can see, ain't no baby here."

"My baby!" cried Amberson glaring around the bar. "He's got to be here!"

She ran to the end of the counter where the woman sat and peered under her tall stool. No Gerald. She dashed to a nearby table, yanked aside chairs, searched under and all around the chairs for her son. No Gerald. She darted to the next table. No Gerald. She ran to each of the ten tables until at last, in a far corner, she found a little blanket-wrapped bundle. Inside the faded quilt lay Baby Gerald, unmoving.

"Gerald!" She hoped he was asleep—and not dead. She grabbed him to her, clutching him for dear life. "Oh, Gerald!" she moaned. Blinking, she saw the tiny rise and fall of his chest. He breathed!

"Oh, God, dear Gerald," she moaned. "What has he done to you?"

Chapter Twenty-three

Justin rode into Gunpoint at sunset, tired and worn from his search of the ranches in the area around Gunpoint. It had taken the entire day to look at the three ranches that were for sale, but it had been worth it.

Though exhausted and hungry, he felt a strong satisfaction. He'd found a ranch he liked and he'd made a deal. Old Man McManus had agreed to sell his ranch at four hundred and fifty dollars, accepting four hundred dollars from Justin now and agreeing to wait for the remaining fifty as long as it was paid within three months. Justin would have liked to conclude the deal at four hundred dollars, but Old Man McManus had stubbornly held out for the larger sum.

Well, Justin thought as he wiped his brow, the ranch would make a good home for himself and the baby. In addition to some grassland on it, there was a log ranch house, solid, well made, and, most valuable of all, a spring-fed creek that cut across the land.

The old man had sold the ranch to Justin because he wanted to get out of the ranching business. Said a man couldn't make a go of ranching in Gunpoint. If the weather didn't get him, the rustlers would. It had already taken five years of his life and he was damned if it would take another day. He was moving to San Francisco where his daughter lived. Couldn't wait to leave.

Justin wished him well. He'd bring Gerald to the ranch and they could start a new, better life.

He bit his lip. He had only a hundred dollars left to buy cattle and supplies for the ranch . . . and the other fifty he'd have to come up with soon. Ah, well, he'd make it somehow.

He rode up to the white house where Mrs. Annabelle Simmons lived. It had been a stroke of luck that the woman had agreed to take care of Gerald for the day. Justin much preferred her to her mother.

He dismounted and whistled a happy tune as he walked up the front stairs. He knocked on the door.

A man in a blue suit opened it. "Yes?" he asked. A banker, or some town businessman, thought Justin, taking in the stiff suit. He glanced at his own dusty canvas jeans. "I've come for my son, sir," he told the man cheerfully.

"Who are you?" demanded the man. His nose looked large for his face, and his eyes reminded Justin of a hawk.

"My name's Justin Harbinger, sir. I've come for my son. Your wife kindly consented to look after him today."

"Annabelle?" The man frowned. "That's not like

her." He shrugged. "She's not here right now. She's visiting friends. There's no baby here." He closed the door.

Odd, thought Justin. He knocked on the door again. It opened again and the pale, austere face peered at him.

"Where is she visiting her friends, sir? I do hate to trouble you, but I want my son."

"She's at the Schwartz home. Second house from the end of Gold Fever Street." The door closed with a thump of finality.

Still whistling, Justin walked along the boardwalk, passing hotels and saloons along the way. The tinkling sound of a piano caught his attention and he paused at the open door where a painted sign read HURDY GURDY PALACE. A woman dressed in a frilly yellow and black costume danced, showing off her long legs to the two lounging miners who sat at a table. Justin watched for a few minutes, then walked on.

He reached a squat brown house with frilly white curtains at the windows and sauntered up to the door. Knocking, he waited impatiently. He had to get some milk for Gerald before he put the baby to bed.

The door opened. Justin touched the tip of his slouch hat politely to the stout woman who answered.

"I've come to speak to Mrs. Annabelle Simmons, ma'am," he said.

"Oh." The woman's eyes shone with curiosity. "I'll get her." She turned away, leaving the door ajar. He could see a table with a lamp and two books on it. A man sat at a rocking chair reading a large tome.

A few minutes later, Miss Annabelle came to the door. "What do you want?"

He frowned. She didn't seem like the cheerful woman she'd been this morning when he'd left Gerald off at her house. He hoped things had gone well for Gerald.

"Hello, Mrs. Simmons. I've come for my son."

The tall blond woman waved a hand airily. "Oh, he's not here."

Justin straightened. "What do you mean, he's not here? I left him with you. You were supposed to take care of him." Alarm raced through him. "Where the hell is Gerald?"

"No need to swear at me," she scolded him. "I've heard enough of that to last me a lifetime, what with five brothers."

"Look," he said through gritted teeth, "I don't care about your brothers. Where is my son?"

He kept his hands at his sides, his fists opening and closing. "What have you done with him?"

"I gave him back to Ma." She started to close the door. He stuck his foot in it.

"Remove your foot," she ordered imperiously.

"Not until you tell me where my son is."

She looked at him out of narrowed green cat's eyes. "Try the Plugged Nickel Saloon. End of the counter." She shoved his foot aside with her own and slammed the door.

He stomped down the steps and out to the road. Then he ran down the street until he reached the Plugged Nickel. He pushed open the doors and looked inside. Several men sat at tables, lifting mugs. A young, burly man with a long black mustache tended the bar. Justin marched up to the man he guessed to be Joe. "Barkeep, where's your mother?"

The bartender eyed him, but Justin was bigger than he and in no mood to be threatened by some half-soused bartender. "I said, where is your mother?"

Joe studied him. "You lookin' for a baby?"

"Yeah. Where is he?"

Joe shrugged. "Don't know," he answered. "Woman took him out of here a while ago."

Justin wrapped one hand around the top buttons of Joe's shirt and jerked. "When?"

The bartender grabbed his hand and pushed it away. He shrugged. "Two, three hours or so. What's your problem, mister?"

"What did she look like?"

"The woman?"

"Yeah."

He twirled one end of his black mustache. "Tall. Good-looking. Had all this brown hair flyin' out of her hair bun. She was kinda upset, though."

Justin frowned. It had to be Amberson.

He turned on his heel and left the saloon. She couldn't have gone far.

Chapter Twenty-four

Now that Amberson had Gerald back, everything was going to get better. That was what she told herself. Never, ever again would she let him out of her sight. The baby would stay with her for the rest of his life.

She'd spent the last several hours just holding him and cuddling him. She cooed to him, she kissed him. He gurgled back and touched her nose now and then, smiling. Lord, how she loved him!

She hugged him to her once again. Suddenly it dawned on her that he smelled bad. Oh, what was she going to do? She had no place to take him to clean him up, and no money.

That wasn't quite true, she cautioned herself. She did have some money—credit—actually. At Hinckley's General Store.

It was getting late in the day as she made her way along the boardwalk. There were more men crowding into the saloons at this hour. From an open door across the way she could hear the tinny sound of a piano. The Hurdy Gurdy Palace.

Ignoring that dreaded place of infamy, she walked faster. She had to get Gerald cleaned and fed. Oh, what should she do?

Suddenly she spotted Beau, sitting in the wagon in front of Fred Knox's office. Tied behind the wagon was her mare, Jessie. She'd forgotten all about Beau and his offer of help. He must have returned to the ranch to check on things. She hurried over.

"Evenin', Missus Rowan," he said, tipping his hat. He handed her the blue satchel.

"Good evening, Beau," she returned. "And thank you." She took her satchel from him. "Take Jessie over to the stables. Tell them I'll—I'll pay for her hay later in the week."

"I see you found the baby." He smiled and hopped down from the wagon.

"Yes, I found him, but now I've got to clean him. And feed him." She knew she had no mother's milk left to offer the baby. Her milk had all dried up because of the fear and worry of losing the baby, and the day and a half separation.

Beau eyed the whimpering child in her arms. "Tell you what, Missus Rowan," he said, "you take care of the cleanin' part, and I'll go take care of the eatin' part."

"That would be very helpful," she answered. He was walking away. "Uh, Beau?

"The baby needs to drink milk," she explained, not sure how much he knew about babies. "Goat's milk, cow's milk . . . any kind of milk you can find."

He touched the worn brim of his hat again. "Yes, ma'am. Don't you worry none. I won't bring him no whisky." He chuckled and headed down the board-walk.

She wondered what Beau would find in this town that the baby could eat, then shrugged off her worry. It was his problem, for now. Hers was to get Gerald cleaned up. Whoever had looked after her baby had done a very poor job. His diaper stunk. And Justin Harbinger should be hanged for treating his own child so carelessly.

Her feet made a hollow sound on the wooden boardwalk as she hurried along, worrying about her plight. Finally, she found herself in front of Hinck-ley's General Store. Not knowing what else to do, she entered.

Hinckley was sitting, staring at the wall, his smok-ing pipe on the counter before him. No one else was in the store. "Hinckley?"

He gazed at her, a vacant look on his face.

"Mr. Hinckley Parker?"

He started. "Yes? Can I help you?"

My, but his manner seemed slow this evening. She wrinkled her nose. She didn't like the smell of what-ever he was cooking for dinner, either.

"I was wondering," she hesitated, "that is, my son, Gerald, is dirty, you see." This was not coming out well. Perhaps it was Hinckley's distant, glazed look that was interfering with her thoughts.

She tried once more. "I need somewhere to wash my child."

He blinked. "You can use the buckets of water in my living quarters, ma'am." He stood up, and now he looked more like the Hinckley she knew and was accustomed to ordering a sarsaparilla from.

"Oh, thank you," she said. "I truly do thank you."

He nodded and reached for his pipe.

Heading for his living quarters, she spied a pile of empty flour sacks and scooped them up. His living quarters were simple and neat, quite unlike what she would have expected from a bachelor. She'd been mistaken about him cooking dinner. There was nothing cooking on the stove to give off the peculiar, sweetish odor she was smelling. She found a full bucket of water and a basin on the counter and began to clean Gerald up.

Later, with Gerald cleaned and wearing a fresh flour-sack diaper, she carried him back into the store. Never would she have expected that it would be Hinckley Parker, of all people in Gunpoint, who would be the one to let her clean up her baby in the back of his general store, but he had. She felt a warm rush of gratitude to him, for he hardly knew her.

"Thank you," she said quietly. During the times she'd visited his store, she'd thought he'd hardly noticed her. That just went to show one, she told herself. He was a kind man.

His eyes still had that glazed look, but he nodded politely to her as she left.

She carried Gerald out of the store and stood on the boardwalk, peering down the street for Beau. He was another person she had not appreciated fully. And with Beau's help, her next step would be to find her brother. She'd finally decided to contact Kingsley in Bodie, California. She was desperate and needed his help. Perhaps if she telegraphed him, he would send her some money. Perhaps she could move to Bodie. . . .

Not seeing Beau, she swung her head in the opposite direction. Coming toward her, walking like a lumbering bear who'd just seen a ripe berry patch, was Justin Harbinger. Well, if he thought he was getting Gerald back, he could think again.

She stood her ground, keeping a firm grip on her son. Nothing Justin could say or do would ever, *ever* convince her to let her baby out of her sight again.

"You found him!" said Justin, rushing up. His hands were outstretched toward Gerald and she knew he intended to pluck the baby from her arms.

"No! He's mine!" She whirled from his grasp at the last second.

Justin dropped his arms and regarded her soberly. There was a full day's growth of beard on his square jaw and she shrugged off how handsome he looked. When she looked into his green eyes, she saw confusion there.

"I found Gerald," she yelled, "lying on the floor of the Plugged Nickel Saloon! Where were *you?*"

"I was busy."

"That's all you have to say? You were busy?" She screamed in frustration and anger. "Aaaaaaah you, you—!" Words failed her. There was nothing she could say to tell him of the horror, the fear she'd had about Gerald. "Gerald could have died!"

"I know." At least he had the grace to look contrite, the blackguard. Even contrite, he was handsome. Damn the man!

"What, *what* can possibly be your explanation?"

He shrugged his broad shoulders. "I have none, ma'am."

"None?"

"Would you believe me if I said I tried?"

"Tried what?"

"Tried to get care for Gerald before I went looking for a ranch to buy."

"He could have died! No one took care of him—not Annabelle! Not her mother!"

"Believe me," he said, his voice rough, "I regret this more than you do."

"No, you don't!" she yelled. "He's my child! He could have died!"

Justin was silent. He crossed his arms and thrust out his jaw, and she knew he was angry too. Well, too bad. It was his fault Gerald had been left in such a poor situation.

"You steal my child from me and then you lose him!"

He frowned and gritted his teeth. A nerve in his clenched jaw twitched.

All the fright she'd felt in the last twenty-four hours suddenly overwhelmed her. "Don't you see?" she cried. "I can't let you have him. You don't take care of him! He's not safe with you!"

Justin uncrossed his arms and they hung at his sides. "Miss Amberson," he pleaded, "it wasn't like that—"

"No! I won't listen to your talk. You can't have Gerald, not ever again!"

Gerald started to cry.

Amberson glanced down at the baby. She looked up in time to see Justin's eyes rove over her and the child, almost like a physical caress. He loved Gerald. The thought softened her a little. "Why did you leave Gerald with Annabelle Simmons?" she asked, trying to calm herself. "Annabelle didn't look after him. She gave him back to her mother at the saloon."

"I didn't know she'd do that." He looked as though he sorely regretted the whole ordeal. Well, too bad. She was still angry at him.

"I'm going to find my brother," she told him. "He'll help me."

"Kingsley?" The disbelieving look Justin gave her irritated her.

"Kingsley will send me some money. The moment I send for him, he'll come here to Gunpoint and help me."

Justin raised one dark brow at that. He patently didn't believe her. She tossed her head. "Beau and I will take care of the baby."

"Miss Amberson," said Justin slowly, "where are you staying?"

"None of your business." She wasn't going to let him know she had nowhere to go.

He regarded her silently, as if willing her to tell him. She raised her chin mutinously.

He shrugged. "Very well, ma'am. It's getting late. The baby needs rest. Let's talk further in the morning."

"We have nothing to talk about."

"Don't be too sure," he said. He started walking away. "I'm staying at the Hank Parker Hotel if you need me."

"I don't! I'll never need you, Justin Harbinger!"

He touched the brim of his hat briefly. The action reminded her of a mock military salute more than a polite gesture. She was reminded of how handsome he'd looked in his uniform when they'd first met. She turned away, fuming.

Beau was walking toward her. He reached her and looked up at her and the baby. "I found some milk for the baby," he said, holding up a glass jar of white liquid.

"Milk!" she exclaimed. "Where did you find it?"

"Old miner has a milk cow. We can get more milk

tomorrow," Beau assured her. He held up a boat-shaped glass bottle with a nipple on it. "Found a new-fangled baby bottle for him too. From one of the mercantile stores."

"Why, thank you, Beau. How very resourceful of you." She glanced around, not knowing what to do, or how to feed Gerald here in the middle of the street.

Loud voices were coming from the saloons, and up the street she could hear the distinct sound of someone singing off-key.

"I'm going back to the ranch," Beau told her. "Got chores to do." He glanced around, a worried look on his face. "Do you have anywhere to stay tonight?"

She refused to give him another thing to worry about. "I do," she said brightly, a plan forming. "I have just the place."

"Glad to hear it, Missus Rowan," he said, looking relieved, and she was glad she hadn't burdened him further with her own plight.

He waved to her and headed toward the wagon parked in front of Fred Knox's office. She turned away, clutching her blue satchel and holding Gerald tightly to her bosom as she made her way slowly up the street. She stopped in front of a small, modest house with a lamplight shining in the window.

She hurried up the walk, Gerald asleep in her arms.

She knocked on the door. A gray-shawled woman answered the door. "Mrs. Rowan?" said Mrs. Cooper, the doctor's wife. "How very nice to see you."

"I hope so," said Amberson, embarrassed. "Mrs. Cooper, I have a problem. . . ."

"Come in, come in," said Mrs. Cooper. "Do tell me about it."

Amberson smiled and kissed the top of Gerald's head. Then she entered the cozy, well-lit kitchen that smelled of spice cake.

Chapter Twenty-five

Next morning, Mrs. Cooper finished washing the breakfast dishes and Amberson helped by drying them. They'd just put the dishes away in the cupboard when there was a knock at the door.

While Mrs. Cooper went to answer the door, Amberson went into the back bedroom to check on Gerald. He still slept and she smiled to herself to see his rosy lips and plump little cheeks. At least he seemed to have recovered from his ordeal of yesterday. That rat, Justin Harbinger, had better never dare ask for his son again after this!

"Mr. Harbinger!" exclaimed Mrs. Cooper, as if Amberson's very thoughts had conjured him up.

Prepared for the worst, Amberson went back into the kitchen.

Justin stood there, his bulk filling the kitchen and threatening the delicate porcelain knickknacks on the kitchen walls. Her traitorous heart beat faster at the sight of him.

"What do you want?" Amberson asked rudely.

"And a good morning to you, too, ma'am," he answered. "I wanted to walk with you. We need to talk."

She heard the firm note in his voice and glanced helplessly at Mrs. Cooper, who was busy trimming the oil lamp. "Go ahead, dear," said Mrs. Cooper, the traitor. "I'll watch the baby."

Outmaneuvered, Amberson opened the door and walked out, uncaring of whether he followed. She marched down the steps and stomped along the garden path until she reached the street. Then she crossed her arms and tapped her toe in the dirt as she waited for Justin to reach her.

"I suppose," she said, glaring into his emerald eyes, "you want to talk about Gerald."

"I do, yes."

"Well, the only thing I have to say is, you'd better not ask to look after him ever again, because while he was under *your* care, I found him on the floor of Joe's Plugged Nickel Saloon!"

Justin crossed his arms and clenched his square jaw. "I've already apologized for that. But I am still his father and I have my legal rights."

She fumed, wondering what she could say to that.

Before she could come up with anything, he said, "What are your plans?"

The question caught her off guard. Her eyes narrowed. "What do you care?" she tossed off.

"I care because I assume your plans involve my son."

She took his words to mean that he recognized she had at least some claim to Gerald. Things were improving. "Do you mean you actually would accept me in your son's future?" she needled.

He frowned. "Not if I didn't have to."

"What's making you?"

He uncrossed his arms and let them drop to his sides. "I love Gerald. I didn't like finding out he'd been left in that saloon either."

His admission shocked her into speechlessness. Was he actually admitting something?

"I was glad you found him when you did," he added. "I didn't get to the saloon until a couple of hours after you found him."

Her jaw dropped and she stared at him. Big, bad Justin Harbinger actually telling her that he was pleased with something she'd done?

"Well," she answered cautiously, "Gerald seems to be all right this morning."

"Good. I'm glad to hear it."

She studied him. He kept his face impassive, but his green eyes watched her warily.

"Your plans?" he prodded.

"I am going to telegraph my brother and get his help."

"Where is he?"

"Bodie, California. I plan to telegraph him today."

"I see." The disapproval he'd expressed last night about her contacting Kingsley seemed to have disappeared.

"Kingsley will help me," she assured him. "He's a good brother." A little irresponsible, she could have added, but didn't. She couldn't help thinking that if Kingsley had remained in Gunpoint when her parents had died, she wouldn't have had to marry Richard Rowan, despite her pregnancy. Ah well, that was old news now. "Kingsley will come and help me."

"It'll take him some time to get here. How long can you stay with the Coopers?"

"I don't know," she conceded honestly. "I only asked to stay for last night."

"Will Rowan let you go back to the ranch?"

She shook her head. "No, and I don't want to go back. I've decided to leave Richard. Our marriage is over." Where had that decision come from? But in saying the words aloud, she realized they made sense. "I am leaving Richard," she stated, mostly to hear the words again. She stood a little straighter.

"Does Richard know?"

"He can guess. After all, he told me to leave the ranch and I did." She drew herself up bravely. "I think a—a divorce is for the best. We—we did not get along all that well." Divorce. Maybe she'd better think this through. Divorced, she'd be run out of town, treated worse than a dance-hall floozy.

Justin didn't say anything to that, just continued to frown at her. "I want to know where you and Gerald plan to live—while you're waiting for your brother to arrive here."

"I don't know," she said in a small voice.

"Do you have any money?"

"No."

"Does Kingsley?"

"I don't know."

Justin's frown deepened. "How do you plan to take care of my son?"

"I'll manage," she squeaked.

He sighed and fiddled with the rim of his slouch hat. "You have no place to go, no money, and your brother, *if* he gets your message, and *if* he decides to come to your aid, won't arrive here for at least two weeks. . . ." He scratched his head. "I'd say you were in a pickle, Mrs. Rowan."

"A pickle?"

"Yes. Decidedly a pickle."

She smiled sadly. "Perhaps you're right," she admitted. Lord, but she hated to admit it, to him of all people. "But I do have a friend."

To her disbelieving eyes, he smiled. His teeth were so white against his tanned skin. "And who might that be?" he asked.

"Beau."

"Beau?" His smile disappeared. Had he thought she'd meant him? As a friend? Justin? The man was daft.

"Beau will help me." Though truly, she didn't know what the dwarf cowboy could do. Still, she couldn't let Justin think she had nothing and no one to help her.

"Well," he answered doubtfully, "I am glad to hear that, ma'am. Beau was always one of Rowan's better cowhands."

"In fact," she said in relief, "here he comes now."

The small cowboy was walking his paint pony along Gold Fever Street toward them. With one hand he held the reins; in the other hand he carried a glass jar.

He approached them and held out the jar to Amberson. " 'Morning, Missus Rowan. I brought the baby's milk."

"Good morning, Beau," she said brightly, gratefully taking the jar from him. She turned to say dismissively to Justin, "I think that will be all, don't you?"

"Oh, yes, Mrs. Rowan," he said sarcastically. "I see that everything is going along just swimmingly."

He shoved his hat back on his head and marched off down the street.

Despite the seriousness of her situation, Amberson had to giggle. Justin had looked so peeved that she had a friend to help her. She felt a twinge of satisfaction at having bested him, if only in this tiny way. "He looks like he's just eaten a pickle, doesn't he?" she observed to Beau.

"Huh, ma'am?"

"Kind of a sour look on his face, wouldn't you say?" The dwarf looked at her blankly.

She laughed. "Thank you for the milk, Beau. Now, tell me, who shall I talk to about getting a divorce? And please, don't tell me Fred Knox. He was absolutely no help at all."

The short cowboy scratched his chin. "I hear Mr. Schwartz ain't too bad on the law, Missus Rowan. You might try him."

"Yes, I do believe I will." She sauntered back to Dr. Cooper's house, the jar of milk in her hand, a smile on her lips. The day was growing brighter by the minute.

Dang Amberson, thought Justin grimly. Why didn't she just come out and ask him for his help? Why couldn't she see that he'd help her? She had nowhere else to turn, but would she ask him for help? No! She'd ask a cowboy she barely knew for help rather than him, Justin Harbinger, her own child's father!

No money, no place to stay, yet not once did the word *help* cross her full lips. What the hell was the matter with her?

As for her brother, Kingsley . . . Justin snorted. Some help that boy would be. From Justin's memories of Kingsley Hawley, he was someone who did exactly as he pleased and answered to nobody. In fact, it would surprise Justin if Kingsley bothered to answer his sister's telegram.

Justin stomped down the street. He had to make sure Amberson and Gerald were taken care of. There had to be something he could do. Had to be.

Chapter Twenty-six

Late that afternoon, Amberson plopped down in a chair in Mrs. Cooper's kitchen. She was exhausted. She'd spent the day walking around the town looking for work. In that time, she'd collected ten indecent offers from ten drunk miners, three proposals of marriage from three sober ones, and a lurid suggestion from a saloonkeeper that she apply to Estelle's House of Beautiful Ladies because she "had the body for it." She refused to count the one young, red-haired, freckled cowboy who'd asked her to be his second wife—while his first wife was standing there! Gunpoint was getting worse than it used to be, in Amberson's opinion.

And to top the day off, she'd had the misfortune to run into Fred Knox who'd looked at her out of those hawklike brown eyes and told her he still had an opening for a dancer at his Hurdy Gurdy Palace.

Outraged, she'd kicked him in the shin and stomped off.

"How was your day, dear?" asked kindly Mrs. Cooper.

Amberson sighed. "Not too bad if you ignore the fact that Fred Knox threatened to sue me."

"Mr. Knox? Sue you?"

"For bodily injury."

Mrs. Cooper sat down across from her, fascinated. "Why, Mr. Knox is one of Gunpoint's leading citizens. Why ever did he threaten to sue you?"

Amberson shook her head. "I don't want to talk about it."

Mrs. Cooper looked taken aback, as if all of a sudden she'd learned she was harboring, in her very own kitchen, a dangerous criminal.

"How is Gerald?" Amberson asked to cheer herself up.

"Sleeping, dear. He's slept most of the afternoon."

Amberson nodded. At least Gerald wasn't troublesome for the older woman. But what was Amberson going to do? She'd had no success in finding a job in town, and even when she did find one, what was she going to do with Gerald? She couldn't impose on the kindly Mrs. Cooper much longer.

Amberson put her hands to her temples, feeling a splitting headache coming on.

"What are you going to do?" asked Mrs. Cooper, echoing her thoughts. Amberson glanced at her and saw that she no longer seemed to think she was harboring a dangerous criminal.

"I am going to take in washing."

"Be a laundress?" mused Mrs. Cooper.

"If I have to. I have to do something to support Gerald and myself until my brother gets here."

"Did you hear from Kingsley?"

"Not yet. But I will hear from him soon," replied Amberson confidently. "I telegraphed to Bodie this morning."

"Very good. I'm sure he'll answer you just as soon as he can," said the good woman.

Amberson squashed the tiny doubts that rose at her hostess's words. Kingsley would contact her. He would.

"Laundresses seem to do well in Gunpoint," said Mrs. Cooper thoughtfully.

"Cleo Throgmorton did very well."

"But not at laundering," reminded Mrs. Cooper. "She did well by marrying Clarence Throgmorton and his mine."

"True, but until she married Mr. Throgmorton, I hear Cleo had enough laundry business to keep her washing from dawn 'til dusk."

"Long hours."

"I'll do it," said Amberson stubbornly. "I have to. For Gerald's sake."

There was silence at the kitchen table, each woman occupied with her own thoughts.

"I need a tub," observed Amberson. "And a scrub board, a place to build the fire to heat the water, some wood for the fire, some soap, a line to hang the clothes on . . ."

"And some customers . . ." Mrs. Cooper pointed out gently.

"I'll have those," said Amberson. "This town is full of men with dirty clothes. Miners, cowboys, freight haulers, soldiers . . ."

"You'll have no lack of customers," agreed Mrs. Cooper.

"I know just who to start with," said Amberson.

"Who?"

Amberson smiled. "The three miners who proposed to me today."

"Only three?" asked Mrs. Cooper in surprise. "What's the matter with the others? Are they blind?"

Amberson chuckled. "Well," she reminded the older woman, "I *am* already married. That probably stopped a few proposals right there."

"Oh. Yes, probably, dear."

"What the hell are you doing?" asked Justin.

Amberson's red face was coated in sweat and big wet half-moons darkened the underarms of her blue dress as she stirred something in a steaming tub. Her hair was askew, half-pulled out of its usual bun. She looked like hell. Behind her fluttered several shirts of varying degrees of faded red, blue, and yellow, all hung on a long piece of rope tied between two trees. Beau was standing on a chair and hanging a pair of dripping brown canvas pants over the rope. A large pile of wood was neatly stacked on the grass alongside the creek and several tubs of water and a scrub board were nearby.

"I," answered Amberson coolly, "am washing clothes." She did not falter in her stirring. Flames shot out under the sides of the tub. When Justin didn't leave, she stopped stirring, wiped her forehead with an arm, and snapped, "What does it look like I'm doing?"

Exasperated, Justin could only stare at her. The woman would drive him mad if he let her.

"Well?" she demanded. "Richard has already been by to sneer and mock me. Have your say and be done with it!"

Justin frowned. "I'm not here to mock you." When

she began stirring again, he added, "Where's the baby?"

"Sleeping. Mrs. Cooper is looking after him."

Justin relaxed a little at that. "How long you been doin' this?"

"Since dawn this morning."

"It's noon now," he said, squinting at the sun. "How long do you expect to keep doin' this?"

"Until I make enough money to feed and house and clothe my son until my brother gets here."

"When's that?"

She shrugged but kept stirring.

"Not soon," he guessed aloud.

"No."

He sighed. He was heading out to his new ranch and he'd stopped by to see if Amberson and Gerald wanted to come with him. No particular reason, he told himself. Just wanted to show her his ranch. His home.

"Miss Amberson, would you care to ride out and see my ranch?"

She stopped stirring and wiped her forehead again. She dropped one arm, then went back to stirring. "I can't."

"Don't want to, you mean."

"I have laundry to do, Justin. My son and I have to eat," she answered wearily.

"At this rate, you'll be flat on your back by dinner time."

"I will not resort to prostitution, sir!"

He stared at her. "That's not what I meant, ma'am. I meant that you'd be so tired from this dang laundering that you would faint. Or fall unconscious."

"Don't make the mistake of thinking I'm weak," she said contemptuously.

He thought about that. "No, I can see you're not weak," he allowed after a while.

She glanced at him then but said nothing. Just kept stirring the boiling blue mass of clothes.

"Well," he said, "no point in sticking around here."

"No."

He could see she'd be real sorry to see him go. Real sorry. "Look," he said. "I'm not trying to make this difficult. I just thought you might like to see my ranch."

"Why?"

Surprised, he replied, "Well, I just did."

"Some other time," she said.

"Yeah? Do you take any time off from this laundering chore?"

She nodded.

"When?"

"Sunday."

"Sunday it is then, ma'am. I'll pick you and the baby up in the morning and take you out to my ranch. For the day."

She kept stirring and didn't answer. Finally he walked away, wondering if she'd even heard him.

He glanced back over one shoulder and saw she'd stopped stirring the dang clothes and was staring after him. She'd heard, all right.

Sunday dawned clear and fresh.

By nine A.M. Justin was walking up the path to Dr. and Mrs. Cooper's residence.

He knocked on the door. "Hello, ma'am. Is Mrs. Rowan in?"

"Oh. She's sound asleep," apologized gray-haired Mrs. Cooper. She was dressed in some kind of gray-and-white-dotted go-to-meeting dress. "Mrs. Rowan was very tired last night. She didn't finish her washing chores until midnight."

"Midnight?"

"Yes. She works every night until then."

Justin frowned. The woman was working cowboys' hours—the long hours worked when men rode a cattle drive. He wondered how long she could keep that up. Kingsley had better get here soon. "Is the baby awake, ma'am?"

"Yes, I've been feeding him his breakfast. I was just about to get ready to go to church."

"There's a church in this town?" asked Justin in surprise.

"Yes. Reverend Pippin sets up a tent every Sunday morning. Would you care to join my husband and me?"

"No, thank you, ma'am," answered Justin as politely as he could. "I'm not really a church-goin' man."

"Few are, around here, from what I've noticed," commented the woman. "Would you care to come in?"

Justin stepped over the threshold into the kitchen and looked over at Gerald, propped on a chair. "I believe I'll stay and look after my son while you go to church, ma'am."

"Very good, Mr. Harbinger," approved Mrs. Cooper. "Mrs. Rowan could use the rest."

Justin fidgeted guiltily. Washing laundry from dawn until midnight, six days a week. No, no one could call Amberson Hawley Rowan weak, he thought. Why, a regime like that could kill a horse.

Doctor and Mrs. Cooper went off to church and Justin carried Gerald outside to show him around the town. Gerald started to cry when they passed a man standing on a wooden box at the corner of Gold Fever Street and Muleskinner Alley. The man was waving his arms and yelling at innocent and not-so-innocent passersby. "You! You are going to burn in hellfire, sir! You must mend your evil ways!"

"Me?" A passing miner laughed.

"The Lord will persecute mine enemies, sir. And he will persecute them good. The way He was persecuted!"

"He won't prosecute me," chortled the miner, who sounded like he was already tipsy this morning. "And I ain't gonna pay no lawyer."

"The Lord will rid the earth of sinners and idol worshippers, sir! Sinners like you!"

"Aw, shut up," snarled the miner, no longer seeing any humor in the situation.

"He will plunge you down to the depths! He will lift you up to the heavens! Which will it be, folks? You choose."

Justin realized he was probably seeing Holy Harry, one of Pa Parker's sons. "Come on, Gerald," Justin told the baby. "We'll find someone else to watch." They started to stroll down the street.

"Mister!" Holy Harry called after him as Justin moved away. "You can have heaven right here on earth! Or you can have hell! You choose!"

"That so?" murmured Justin to Gerald. "Well, so far, I feel like I've been livin' in hell."

He and the baby walked around the town, and by the time they returned to the Coopers' home, the doctor and his wife had still not returned from church. Amberson still slept, though the hour approached noon.

"Let's go wake your mama," Justin told Gerald. He opened the door to her room and stopped in his tracks. Clear light shone through a window, haloing Anberson's brown hair in gold while she slept. Her eyelashes lay long and dark against her cheeks. Her smooth skin looked pale and unsullied in the morning light. She looked so young. Only a girl, really.

Like the girl he'd met so long ago. The girl flying across the field on horseback, inviting him to dinner. His eyes lingered on her, tracing the outline of her slim body under the white coverlet. She was so beautiful. Always had been. Why hadn't he seen her innocence before?

Because he'd been too dang angry at her for her betrayal, that's why. He wondered now if perhaps he'd judged her too quickly. Perhaps there was more to why she'd chosen to marry Rowan. Only he, Justin, had never asked her about it, had he? He'd been content to nurse his anger at her for not waiting for him, to feel his fury about her hiding his son from him, but he'd never actually listened to what she had to say.

He sighed. Neither of them had listened to the other, truth be told. Whenever they were together, it seemed, logic and common sense flew out the window. They both just reacted. Angrily. Impulsively.

He glanced down at the sandy-haired child in his arms. And together, impulsively, he and the woman under the white quilt had created this child. A precious human being.

"Time to get up, Miss Amberson," he said softly. Her eyelashes fluttered against her cheeks and he wished he was beside her, kissing her awake to greet the morning.

But he wasn't. He was standing in the doorway, holding their son in his arms and hearing the Coopers walking up the path to the front door.

"Miss Amberson," he called again, "time to get up. Gerald wants you to get up and play."

Then he closed the door, knowing the Coopers would not look kindly upon his being in their guest's bedroom, no matter how much he wanted to be there.

Justin and Gerald were in the kitchen by the time Dr. Cooper opened the front door. The older man nodded a greeting to Justin and then Mrs. Cooper entered, her wise gray eyes taking in everything about him.

Justin shook off the feeling of guilt he had, as though he'd been doing something he shouldn't have.

When Miss Amberson entered the kitchen a few minutes later, the feeling was still with him. The sleepiness clung to her, and he bet if he went over and took her in his arms he would be enveloped in the warm, sweet scent of her. Just once—to see her, touch her, in the way he truly wanted to touch her. A sudden, piercing longing swept through him, a longing for things to be made better between them. Somehow.

"Saw Mr. Rowan after church," said Dr. Cooper to Miss Amberson. "He was passing by. Said to tell you to go and get the rest of your things from the Triple R."

Justin would bet that Rowan had not put it quite as politely as Dr. Cooper said it.

"Oh." Amberson blinked, and an expression passed over her face, as if she was waking from a dream. Her hazel eyes shuttered and her mouth thinned. Justin recognized the protective stance. The sweet, warm girl in the bed had just turned into a hard woman who took care of her own.

As he watched the transformation, Justin felt an aching sadness. For her. And for himself.

Chapter Twenty-seven

Justin and Amberson sat on a red blanket on a small, grassy knoll that overlooked Justin's new ranch. Beside them rested a picnic basket. Behind them sprawled the ranch house, built of long, solid lengths of log. A chimney made of black stones carried from the river graced the far wall of the house. A covered porch wrapped around the dwelling on three sides. Gerald slept in his wicker basket on the shaded side of the porch.

Below them, at a little distance to the east, a bubbling creek ran past the house. Over to the west, two thin red cows grazed on the fenced portion of the ranch. They were the remnants of Old Man McManus's herd, too scrawny even for rustlers to steal. The old man had thrown the cows into the deal for free, elated at selling his ranch.

Amberson looked out over the land. "It looks like a good ranch," she admitted. Not as large as Richard's Triple R, of course, but from what she'd learned about ranching, this spread of Justin's would probably make him a good living.

She turned to ask him, "When will you be getting some cattle?" and saw that he'd been watching her. She flushed, then reproached herself. She was no longer a green girl. She was a mature woman and should conduct herself like one, not turn red every time a man stared at her. Still, that it was Justin staring pleased her.

The sharp planes of his cheekbones shadowed his face. And how well she knew the strength of those arms . . . Flustered, she reached for the picnic basket and sliced off thick pieces of bread and cold beef from last night's dinner at the Coopers'. She offered the bread and meat to Justin.

He took off his brown slouch hat, set it aside, and reached for the food. He glanced over at the two cows. "I'll get some cattle after I pay off the ranch," he said. "Probably next spring." He squinted at the cows. "In the meantime, there's my herd."

She smiled at his small joke. He hadn't made a joke in a long time. Not since he'd returned to Montana Territory, now that she thought of it.

"Maybe you could buy some cattle from Richard."

He glanced at her. The tiny smile at one corner of her mouth must have given her away. Seeing she was joking, too, he smiled, his white teeth flashing. "Yes, ma'am. I bet Richard would give me a good price."

She laughed and cut herself a slice of beef. Inside the basket were two precious bottles of sarsaparilla. She offered him one. They ate, and Amberson thought the meat and bread and drink tasted better than anything she'd eaten in a long time.

When she and Justin had finished their meal, she

set aside the picnic basket. "You should have seen Richard the day he stopped by while I was laundering clothes. You'd have thought laundering was the lowest form of work a woman could do."

Justin shrugged.

"He said he was glad I was working so hard. Said he hoped I drowned in my tub of dirty water." She held up her hands, the skin rough and reddened from the past week's work. "He laughed at my hands." She shuddered. "I don't like Richard, but I hope I never fill with hate like he's done. I don't understand him." She shook her head.

"I'm going to get a divorce from him," she said with determination. When Justin didn't say anything, she thought he was uncomfortable talking about Richard.

"Why did you marry Richard?" Justin asked. So, he was just quiet, not uncomfortable. She glanced at him, trying to read his green eyes. But he was watching the cows.

"I was pregnant. I was desperate."

"Where were your parents?"

"They were dead by that time. Burned out by Indians."

"And Kingsley?"

She glanced at him. Something about the way he asked the questions told her that he truly wanted to know the answers. He wasn't angry, as he had been all the other times they'd spoken. This time he was . . . more thoughtful.

"Kingsley couldn't take their deaths. Seeing them dead like that. He—he went a little strange. . . . I guess he had to get away . . ." she said. Even now, tears welled in her eyes when she thought about her parents' brutal deaths. "He left before the townspeople even buried them."

When Justin said nothing, she added, "That's why I chose to stay near Gunpoint. The people of Gunpoint helped me bury my parents. I—I thought it was kind of them. Reverend Pippin said the words over their graves."

Now she was the one staring at the cows, blurred red and fat by her tears.

"When did you find out you were pregnant?"

She swallowed. "I knew the day you told me you were leaving for Virginia."

His green eyes swung abruptly to meet hers. "You knew then? Why didn't you tell me?"

"Because you wanted to go. You couldn't wait to leave. You had your *orders*."

"But if I'd known—"

"You'd what? Stay? I tried to get you to stay. Remember?"

"I remember." He hesitated. "Did your parents plan to help you?"

"My parents never knew, thank the Lord."

She saw a muscle clench in his jaw.

"It's the truth, Justin," she said. "They would have thought very little of me, giving myself like that to a man I barely knew, a man I was not married to—"

He turned to her. "I would have married you," he said hoarsely.

She shook her head. "I didn't know where you were. You said you'd return. I thought you meant two months, three months at the most. I waited—"

The pain she saw in his green eyes halted her words.

Swallowing past the lump in her throat, she continued, "I—I had no money. Kingsley was gone. The rest of my family was dead. I had nothing." She felt hot tears swell in her eyes.

"It was very difficult for me, Justin. And Richard Rowan was here. He said he loved me, offered me marriage. I—I thought I could love him, in time—" She heard the imploring note in her own voice and stopped. How could she be asking this man for understanding? He was the man who'd abandoned her, who'd caused her woes.

She stared at the cows. When the pain in her throat finally subsided, she gave a fake little laugh and said, "I'll manage. I always manage."

She looked up at Justin and was surprised to read admiration in his narrowed green eyes. "You will," he agreed.

But not with your help, Justin, she added silently. Last time I had to marry Richard. What will I have to do this time?

She bit her lip. She hadn't heard anything from Kingsley, so she'd sent another telegram, borrowing against the credit she still had at Hinckley's General Store. Richard had forgotten to revoke her credit and she was able to use it to buy things like cloth for diapers and get money for telegrams and milk for the baby.

But Kingsley had to answer soon. She didn't think she could keep up this laundering business for long. She was getting too worn out, even with Beau's occasional help. And she rarely saw Gerald anymore. Lord, what was she going to do?

"We'd better get back to town, ma'am," said Justin. "You've got a long day ahead of you tomorrow."

She gave a bitter chuckle. He was glad to get rid of her, as soon as the problems came up. She shrugged, as if cheerfully careless, and said, "Let's. I do have another busy day tomorrow."

She bit her lip. Tomorrow wasn't only a laundry day. She also had to find a place to live. Dr. and Mrs. Cooper had been kind to her and Gerald, but she had to find her own lodging, not continue to impose on them.

At least Justin hadn't said anything about taking Gerald away from her. Finding Gerald on the floor of the Plugged Nickel Saloon had actually worked in her favor. So, if she could find a place to live, and the customers kept bringing her their dirty laundry, she should be able to feed herself and Gerald until Kingsley arrived.

She struggled to her feet and carried the picnic basket over to the wagon.

Justin retrieved the sleeping Gerald from the porch and put him in the wagon behind the seat. Then he offered Amberson his hand to help her step up and into the vehicle. She met his eyes. She saw a warmth there, a warmth she hadn't seen since the days when she was a girl.

She smiled shyly, then placed her hand in his. He glanced down at her work-worn, red hand and she, too, glanced at it. The skin was cracked and red, not the hand of a lady. She started to withdraw her fingers, but his hand gently closed around hers. He brought her hand to his lips and pressed a kiss on the back of it.

She stood there, in shock, and her heart pounded. Justin Harbinger, kissing her reddened hand? Then he lifted her up into the wagon. She sat on the seat, numb. What did he mean by that kiss? Why had he done it? And why was her heart fluttering like a butterfly caught in a net?

Justin's big horse, Samson, stood in the traces. Justin took up the reins and clicked to the horse, and they started off. He guided them down the curving dirt lane to the bottom of the hill, then turned the wagon east, back toward Gunpoint.

Neither of them spoke on the ride. Amberson couldn't think of what to say. The silence, at first, made her feel relieved. Then she felt nervous, then she felt shy, all the while reliving his kiss on her hand, over and over. Oh, why had he done it? Wasn't her life confusing enough?

Evidently Justin didn't think so, for when they arrived in front of the Coopers' house, he turned to her and said, "Miss Amberson, why don't you and Gerald move out to my ranch with me?"

Chapter Twenty-eight

Stunned, she felt the blood drain from her face. Then she scrambled down from the wagon seat—without his help, thank you very much. "What," she demanded, hands on hips, "do you think I am?"

"A very desirable woman. The mother of my child."

She wanted to scream at him but satisfied herself with a toss of her head. "Do I look like a fool?"

He frowned. "What do you mean? I asked you and the baby to come and stay at my ranch with me. What's wrong with that? It seems to me it will help both of us. I'll have my son in my own home, and you'll have a place to stay without having to work as a laundress."

"I like working as a laundress!" she burst out angrily.

He raised a dark eyebrow at that. His green eyes laughed at her.

"I do!" she cried. "It—it supports me at a difficult time."

"It *is* lovely work," he said sarcastically.

She glared at him. "I know what you want," she snarled.

He grinned. "Good, that will make it easier for both of us."

"Oh no, you don't! I fell for those green eyes and that handsome face once! I will not, will not—" here her voice took on an inordinately high pitch—"ever sleep with you again!"

"Well! I am certainly relieved to hear that!" said Mrs. Dorothy Reedy to Mrs. Hyacinth Stanton as they walked by on the boardwalk.

Mortified, Amberson's eyes widened. Where had those two gossips come from? Horrified, she saw the two talking, hands to cheeks to preserve privacy—theirs not hers.

"Oooooh," she hissed at Justin. "You could have told me they were coming this way!"

"And ruin a perfectly fine tantrum? Not me." He raised his hands as if to deflect her angry glare. "Think about it, Miss Amberson. It would work well for us. You could take care of the baby and have a decent place to stay. I'd have the satisfaction of knowing my child is safe."

"Oooh! I know what you want!" she yelled. Glancing down the boardwalk at the receding backs of the two members of the Ladies' Culture Club, she lowered her voice. "You just want me to come and live with you so you can sleep with me!"

"And do my laundry."

"Aaarrggghhh!" she cried. "You are positively insulting!"

He laughed.

"You think this is funny!"

"I do."

"Well, let me tell you something!" Just then the baby awakened and started to cry. Hurrying over to him, she lifted him out of his basket and rocked him on her shoulder, unfortunately rather vigorously because of her agitated state. This made Gerald cry louder. "There, there," she consoled him. "Don't cry, Gerald. Mama's here."

Justin watched her, his green eyes twinkling. "You were saying? Mama?"

"I was saying," she said, "that unlike you, I learn from my mistakes."

"Do tell." His lips twisted in an amused, arrogant grin.

"I, sir, have learned not to kiss—or do anything else—with *anyone* in the moonlight. It results in babies!"

"Oh. And I haven't learned that?"

"You certainly have not! Why else would you give me such a sordid invitation?"

"Sordid invitation?" His grin vanished and he looked truly startled. "All I did was offer you the safety and sanctuary of my home."

"Aaaaaarggggh!" she cried. "You made me an indecent proposal!"

"I did?"

"Yes! I have received several of them and I know exactly what they sound like. And what you said, sir, is very definitely an indecent proposal!"

"Well, thank you for setting me straight about that," he said with a sneer. "Why should a man offer the mother of his child a home? What a perfectly terrible thing to do to a poor woman."

"I am not a poor woman!" she screeched.

He smirked.

She was so angry she could hardly speak. "Wipe that smirk off your face!"

He tried, but not very hard. "Miss Amberson," he said reasonably, "listen to me."

"No." She covered one ear with her hand. Gerald howled in the other ear.

"I said I wanted you to come to the ranch because it seemed to me we could help each other—"

"I am not listening!" And indeed she could not in fact hear what he was saying, could only see his lips move, because Gerald was crying so loudly.

"I will not!" she cried. "You seduced me! You left me pregnant and alone—"

"Miss Amberson." It looked as if he was pleading and saying her name, but the baby was still yelling so she couldn't be sure.

"No!" she cried. "You seduced me once! I will *not* sneak around to meet a man! Never again!"

The baby was yelling so loudly she didn't hear Mrs. Reedy and Mrs. Stanton walking behind her on the boardwalk. Why they had decided to return and walk past her again she could not imagine.

"Really!" exclaimed Mrs. Hyacinth Stanton.

"See if he'll give you his laundry to do," urged Mrs. Dorothy Reedy with a giggle. The two hurried off down the boardwalk, leaving a furious, embarrassed Amberson, a howling Gerald, and a frowning Justin Harbinger behind them.

Unable to take another minute of this madness, Amberson whirled and ran for the Coopers' front door.

Chapter Twenty-nine

By midmorning of the next day, Amberson was hard at work, stirring a steaming tubful of miners' pants. The smell made her want to gag, but she kept stirring.

Mrs. Cooper had had to call her three times to get up because she was so tired. Evidently laundering, or early rising—she didn't know which was worse—did not agree with her.

Fortunately Beau had brought a wagonload of wood for the fire. He'd stayed to help hang the washed clothes up on the line. Though he had to use one of Mrs. Cooper's chairs to stand on to reach the rope line, he never complained.

At least someone was helping her, she thought, stirring miserably.

No, she couldn't say that. Besides Beau, Doctor and Mrs. Cooper were helping her too. The kind couple had yet to say a single word about Amberson finding somewhere else to stay. And Mrs. Cooper continued to watch Baby Gerald for her.

At eleven-thirty, Mrs. Cooper brought Gerald by. Amberson kissed him and hugged him. She spent a few precious minutes with her son and it was so difficult to let him go when Mrs. Cooper had to take him back to the house for his lunch.

At noon, instead of eating her lunch, Amberson hastened over to the stables. She patted her beloved horse, Jessie, kissed her on the nose, and hugged her. Then Amberson hurried off to the telegraph office.

"Any word from Mr. Kingsley Hawley?" she asked old Mr. Tibbets as cheerily as she could.

"Nope. No word." He glanced up at her through round-rimmed glasses. Perched on his balding head was a green telegrapher's hat and behind one ear was lodged a chewed pencil.

"Are you sure?"

"No telegram has arrived."

It was the same answer he'd given her every day for the last week. She could feel her smile falter. "Are you absolutely certain, Mr. Tibbets? Perhaps he telegraphed something—"

"Nope." Methodically, Mr. Tibbets kept searching a stack of papers.

"I want to send another telegram then," she said firmly.

He shrugged. "Same thing?"

"Yes," she sighed, dispirited for the first time. What if Kingsley didn't ever answer? She caught herself. No! She mustn't think this way, she mustn't. He would answer. It just took a little time. She remembered clearly that he'd said he was going to Bodie, and that was where he must be. Kingsley always did what he said he'd do, didn't he? She paused. Well, there were a few times when he didn't. . . .

"To Bodie, Mrs. Rowan?" Mr. Tibbets took the chewed pencil from behind his ear and began to write slowly and methodically on a piece of paper.

"Yes, please."

He finished writing, then sent the message while she waited, loitering, absently reading maps posted all over the walls. She located Bodie on a map. The town was situated in the middle part of California, in the mountains. Perhaps Kingsley was in the telegraph office in Bodie at this very moment, getting ready to send her a telegram. . . . Why, he'd get this one and answer her right away! But though she lingered a good fifteen minutes, no message came clattering over the wires.

She edged toward the door. "Good-bye, Mr. Tibbets," she said forlornly.

"Good-bye."

Before she could open the door, it swung wide and Sheriff Logan walked in.

"Good day, ma'am," he said, lifting his hat politely.

"Good day." Curious, she decided that perhaps the maps on the wall required one more perusal.

The sheriff strode up to the counter. "I need to send a telegram, Tibbets."

"Yep. What's it say?" Mr. Tibbets took the chewed pencil from behind his ear and set it to paper.

"Send it to the governor's office," said Sheriff Logan importantly, giving Amberson a sidelong glance to see if she'd noted where he was sending his telegram.

She smiled.

"Tell the governor this: 'Been another Celestials killed. Advise. Sheriff Logan.' "

Tibbets looked up from his writing. "Them Celestials are killing one another off, sounds like. Got somethin' to do with that opium?"

"Yeah, it probably does," agreed the sheriff. "Did you spell 'Celestials' correctly?"

Tibbets gave him a withering look.

Amberson decided she'd lingered long enough. She'd be up again until midnight if she didn't get the laundry done.

She slipped out the door while Tibbets and the Sheriff were arguing about the first letter of the word. Tibbets said it started with a *C*, while the sheriff favored an *S*.

She trudged back to the vacant lot where she had her washtub and line set up next to a small creek where she could easily fill her buckets with water.

Beau had returned to the ranch to do his chores and the fire had burned low during her absence. She built up the fire again and set the tub on it. Then she filled the tub with several buckets of water. She set aside two big buckets of cool rinse water. While the washing water heated, she ate her meager lunch of a hard-boiled egg and a dried apple. She hadn't wanted to take much from Mrs. Cooper's larder this morning, only what she thought the Coopers could easily spare.

Her lunch finished, she went over to the pile of filthy clothes, fished out some of the shirts with the paddle, and carried them over to the tub. She was on her third trip to the tub when she heard a low laugh.

"Mercy goodness, is that truly you, Miss Amberson?"

Amberson turned wearily and gazed into the contemptuous, ice-blue eyes of the lovely Miss Madeline Mueler.

"Yes," she answered warily.

Madeline laughed and clapped her hands together—hands, Amberson noted, that were white and smooth. "Richard told me, but I didn't believe him."

A soft Southern accent betrayed her origins. Strange, thought Amberson, how Justin's drawl did not grate on her nerves the way Madeline Mueler's did.

Amberson kept pushing shirts into the hot water while Madeline simpered on the walkway.

"Richard just raved on and on about you doin' laundry chores," said Madeline. "I finally had to come and see for myself."

"Well, now that you've seen, you can leave," said Amberson shortly. Perspiration beaded on her forehead. Lord, but it was hot.

"I think I'll just stay and watch this fine sight, if you don't mind." Madeline giggled.

"I do mind," said Amberson pointedly.

"Oh, my. A short-tempered laundress. How ever do you get any business?"

"I get business the old-fashioned way," said Amberson between gritted teeth. "I do a very good job of washing clothes." She glanced up at Madeline and said, "And how do you get your business, Madeline?"

"Why, whatever do you mean?"

"I mean, what do you do to survive? You live in that fancy Two Star Hotel down the street. You eat at the hotel's restaurant. And they don't serve pig's feet at that restaurant, last I heard." Amberson eyed the ice-blue dress Miss Mueler was wearing. "You wear expensive dresses. How do you pay for them, *dear?*"

"Why, with Richard's money, of course," answered

Madeline sweetly. "We reside at the Two Star."

Amberson stabbed at the shirts and killed several of them.

"Do you do ironin' too?" asked Madeline.

"No!"

"I declare. Watching you work so hard does give me vapors."

"Perhaps you'd better get out of the sun then. Go back to Richard." And bother him, not me, Amberson added silently.

"Poor, dear Richard. He's feelin' poorly this afternoon."

Amberson glanced up. "What's the matter with him?"

Madeline shrugged, unconcerned. "A little matter of a sore belly, he says. He's always holdin' it and complainin'."

This was the first Amberson had heard that Richard had stomach problems.

"How long has he been like that?"

The blond woman shrugged. "Heavens, I'm sure I don't know. Days, I suppose."

"Sorry to hear that," said Amberson unsympathetically. As she stirred the shirts she thought about the times Richard had hit her. He deserved some pain.

Madeline gave a long, exaggerated yawn. "Time for me to go. I do see how Richard found you lacking in sympathy. That's what he always told me. That you didn't understand him," she said gleefully.

"Richard always liked roaring good times, I understood that," said Amberson. "A wife and child merely bored him." Slyly, she added, "Even a *mistress* and child would bore him. Be careful you don't get pregnant," she warned.

"Oh, I'd never do anythin' like that. I'm too smart." Madeline smiled sweetly. "Good-bye. And do put somethin' on that red complexion of yours. The sun is burnin' you somethin' awful." With false sympathy she gave a little wave and sashayed on down the boardwalk.

Amberson fairly attacked the shirts with her paddle until the water churned.

Chapter Thirty

Friday night, Amberson decided to quit her laundry chores early. Though she knew she should work until midnight, she'd been too tired and unhappy to be able to wash another shirt. She missed Gerald. She had to see him when he wasn't asleep.

"Thank you, Beau, for standing guard," she told him.

Beau nodded and scrambled down from his chair, careful to keep hold of his rifle. As her self-appointed guardian, every night he chased off miners, cowboys, soldiers, and mule skinners—drunk or sober—who thought a woman washing clothes was an open invitation for heavy-handed flirtation.

Amberson had been the Gunpoint laundress for two weeks now and it was taking its toll on her. She almost never saw Gerald, relying on Mrs. Cooper to care for him. Gerald was asleep when Amberson kissed him good-bye every morning and he was asleep when she kissed him good-night every midnight. The midday visits were the only times she saw him awake.

It was a hell of a life. Even her language had gone downhill, associating as she did with mule skinners, miners, and soldiers. They made cowboys seem like choirboys. The occasional curse word that slipped from a cowboy's mouth was mild compared to the daily fare she heard from her other customers.

So she tottered back to the Coopers' house at the early hour of seven P.M., just in time to eat the leftover dinner provided by Mrs. Cooper, who was as kind as ever. What Amberson had done to deserve the friendship of this wonderful woman she would never know, but she prayed for the Coopers every night before falling, exhausted, on her bed.

Tonight, Amberson dandled the baby on her knee. She cooed to him and told him she loved him. She sang songs to him and told him a story. That he couldn't understand a single word bothered her not one whit; his big blue eyes followed her face and eyes and she knew he'd missed her, too, but not as much, never as much, as she'd missed him. There had to be something else she could do that wouldn't separate her so much from her child. But what?

Mrs. Cooper made her a cup of tea and served her a generous piece of spongy spice cake. They sat at the kitchen table and chatted about the goings-on in the town. Finally Mrs. Cooper asked, "Have you heard from Kingsley?"

Amberson bounced Gerald on her knee another time or two before answering. Then, with a sigh, she brought the child to her and hugged him, answering, "No. I've sent so many telegrams, I've lost count. But he hasn't answered me."

"Oh, dear. I'm sorry to hear that," said the older woman. She sipped her tea. "Perhaps he's moved away from Bodie."

"Perhaps," said Amberson, troubled. She had wondered the same thing. "But surely he would let me know, or write to me . . ." Her voice trailed off. It had been a year and a half since she'd last seen Kingsley and he'd yet to write to her. There'd been no letters. No telegram. Nothing. It was as if the earth had swallowed him up.

"I'm going to try one more time," said Amberson stubbornly. "I am going to the telegraph office in the morning. I'll send one more telegram. After that, I—I, why, I'll think of something."

Mrs. Cooper daintily sipped her tea. "Yes, of course you will, dear."

At noon the next day, Amberson entered the telegraph office. Mr. Tibbets glanced up, and when he saw it was she, he nodded blandly. If nothing else, she was his best customer.

"I'm going to send one more telegram, Mr. Tibbets."

"Yep." He pulled the chewed pencil from behind his ear and waited, tip poised over a clean piece of paper. "Ready."

" 'To Mr. Kingsley Hawley, Bodie, California. Mr. Hawley. Please get in touch with your sister in Gunpoint. It is urgent.'

Mr. Tibbets peered at her from behind his round-rimmed glasses. " 'Urgent,' Mrs. Rowan?"

"Urgent," she confirmed. "U-R-G-E-N-T."

He wrote. "I know how to spell it."

"Very good, Mr. Tibbets," she said politely. "Please end the telegram with, 'Answer immediately.' "

When he finished writing, she thanked him and turned away to study the maps on the wall, waiting for him to send the message and waiting, as had become her habit, for a return telegram.

The door opened suddenly and Sheriff Logan entered. He grinned at Amberson. "Say," he said in a friendly manner, "you send a lot of telegrams, don't you? Seems like every time I come in here to send one, I find you here."

His hearty greeting made Amberson want to run away and hide.

Sheriff Logan stared at the paper on Mr. Tibbets's desk behind the counter.

"Good thing I can read upside down," said the sheriff. "I see you're still looking for Mr. Hawley."

"You knew?" she asked, offended that he would know her business.

"Not much goes on in this town that I don't know," he bragged.

"Oh." She turned away, pretending to be engrossed in a large map of Gunpoint.

"But there is one thing I don't know," he said, removing his hat and scratching his head. "I don't know who is killing all these damn Celestials."

Amberson ignored him.

"Take a telegram, Tibbets," ordered Sheriff Logan when he saw that Amberson had no interest in all his knowledge of what went on in Gunpoint.

"This one's to the governor. Again." Sheriff Logan slid a glance at Amberson to see if she'd heard the tired, bored note in his voice. He was an important man, sending telegraphs to important people. Again.

Amberson leaned toward the map, studying intently.

Mr. Tibbets waited, pencil poised.

" 'To the governor. Another dead Celestial. No one suspected.' " He paused.

"Wait, Tibbets, scratch that part out. Don't want the governor to think we don't know what we're doing here in Gunpoint." He cleared his throat and began again.

" 'Another dead Celestial. Suspect Lee Fung.' "

"Lee Fung," announced the sheriff to the room at large, "is probably the biggest opium dealer in this town. He owns at least two dens. But I think he has a white partner, 'cause whenever I happen to stop by and, ahem, *visit* Lee Fung, that cunning Celestial has nobody and no opium in his house. I think his partner must be warning him. And I aim to find out who he is!"

"Good for you, sir," encouraged Mr. Tibbets.

Amberson said nothing, only moved over to study the map of Gunpoint more intently than ever. She never knew there were so many canyons in the area.

"We're going to raid every opium den in this town!" promised Sheriff Logan.

"The telegram, sheriff?" The poised pencil hovered over the paper.

"Oh. Yes. Let us continue. 'Send men to help.' " He scratched his chin. "That should be all, Tibbets."

"Very good, sir." By the deferential treatment he was receiving, Amberson suspected that Sheriff Logan was Mr. Tibbets's second-best customer.

She waited until after the sheriff left, and then another ten minutes besides. But the telegraph clacker remained silent. There was no answering message from Kingsley.

Chapter Thirty-one

Amberson edged into Hinckley's General Store. There were three men purchasing dry goods and tobacco, so she waited by the pickle barrel, pretending to examine a bolt of lovely green satin. Finally they left, and she ambled up to the counter.

Hinckley asked, "Can I help you this morning, Mrs. Rowan?"

"Yes," she said, with her head held proudly. "I'd like to settle my bill."

He nodded and pulled out his ledger book. Frowning thoughtfully, he ran his finger down the long list of inked entries.

"I believe Mr. Rowan gave you some money so I could have credit," explained Amberson. "I've come to pay it back." Pride warmed her heart. She'd worked long hours and very hard for her money, but she would not be beholden to Richard any longer. Not for anything! With her earnings from her laundry business she could now afford to pay him back.

"There must be some mistake, Mrs. Rowan," said Hinckley, peering at her over his glasses. "My ledger shows that it was Mr. Harbinger who advanced the sum of twenty dollars for you, not Mr. Rowan."

"Twenty dollars? Mr. Harbinger?" she exclaimed, shocked. "Mr. Justin Harbinger?"

"I believe that is his name."

"I—I can't believe—there must be some mistake—"

Hinckley was staring at her strangely.

"I—I—Thank you, Hinckley." She took a deep breath, trying to recover from her surprise. "I will settle up my account with you now."

"Very good, Mrs. Rowan. That will be six dollars and seventy-four cents."

She gasped. It was a goodly sum and would take most of her laundry earnings for the past two weeks. But she pulled the bills and coins out of her pocket and, with trembling fingers, handed them over to Hinckley.

He made a notation on his ledger and put the money in a drawer. "Thank you, Mrs. Rowan. Will there be anything else?"

"No, Hinckley. That will be all." She tottered from the store on shaking legs. Whatever had happened? Justin Harbinger? Actually helping her? Twenty dollars was a large sum. Why, it would buy him some cattle. . . . Yet he'd seen fit to use the money to help her and Gerald. She halted in midthought. Gerald. That was who he was doing it for. He was helping his son. Not her. She would do well to remember that.

On unsteady legs, she made her way up the boardwalk. She had one more stop to make.

*   *   *

She walked through the gilded front doors of the Two Star Hotel. The lobby was large, and fitted with comfortable, overstuffed wine-and-gold-striped chairs. Beige and gold curtains, in a fleur-de-lis pattern, were pulled back from the windows and at doorways.

She tiptoed past the dining room where two elegant gentlemen sat eating at a white linen–covered table, and found herself at the counter.

The hotel clerk looked up from some papers he'd been shuffling. "Can I help you?" His voice was cool and his blue eyes only a fraction less so. He reminded her of a small, fierce pug dog, the kind she'd seen in ladies' magazines.

"Mr. Rowan's room number, please."

The clerk eyed her, then coughed. "Room Eight. Upstairs, left at the first landing." He caught sight of a young Oriental man hovering near the stairs. "You! Boy!" he barked. "Go clean Room Number Six. Now! Chop-chop!"

The young man scurried off.

"Go on up," the clerk told Amberson.

She took the stairs to the landing, then walked across the wine-and-yellow-flowered, thickly carpeted floor of the hall. Richard was staying in a lovely place, she thought with a sigh.

A man was walking down the hall toward her. His back was to the light filtering in through a window at the end of the hall, so she could not determine whether she knew him.

She stepped aside to let him pass and was surprised when he spoke her name.

"Mrs. Rowan?"

She blinked. It was Fred Knox, looking as surprised as she felt, but far more delighted. "Mrs. Rowan, what are you doing here?"

"I've come to talk to Richard," she said. "He lives here."

"Ah, yes, yes, he does, ma'am," agreed Mr. Knox amiably. She waited for him to pass by, but he seemed content to stand there. "Mrs. Rowan," he said, lowering his voice to a whisper, "I have been meaning to speak with you."

"You have?" she asked warily.

"Ah, yes." He glanced around, as if making certain they were alone. They were.

"It has come to my attention that Mr. Stanton is the owner of the property where you have set up your washtub and line." Fred Knox coughed. "It seems," he said delicately, "that Mr. Stanton does not like having clothing strewn all over his property. I presume that you forgot to ask him if you could set up your tub on his premises?"

"Why, I never thought—I—That is where Mrs. Cleo Throgmorton set up her business. I thought—"

"Ah, yes, I see." Fred Knox's brown eyes were warm with understanding. "So of course you do not know anything about the charges Mr. Stanton wishes to press."

"Charges?" she asked in dismay.

"Ah, yes, the trespassing charges. The cease and desist order."

A sick feeling curled in Amberson's stomach.

"There, there, now, Mrs. Rowan. Perhaps I can speak to Mr. Stanton for you. Tell him you had no intention of harming his property. No intention whatsoever, am I correct?"

She nodded numbly.

"Ah, yes. Perhaps I can get him to calm down. After

all, taking someone to court is not always the best way."

"Court?" she gasped.

"For money." He pulled a gold watch out of his vest pocket. "Ah, I have to go. I have a business meeting," he explained pleasantly. "There now, Mrs. Rowan. Don't look so upset."

Her mouth worked as she tried desperately to rearrange the grimace she knew must be on her face.

"You always have the chance to work at my Hurdy Gurdy Palace, ma'am," he said earnestly. "I would provide employment for you. I would never stand by and see you tossed out of your laundress job, with nowhere to go."

She stared at him, aghast.

"Tell you what, Mrs. Rowan. Come by the Palace one night. Say, seven thirty. I'm usually there, making sure the girls are ready for a night of dancing." He smiled. "It's all harmless fun, Mrs. Rowan. Truly. And did you know that Hurdy Gurdy dancers make more money in one night than laundresses do in a week?"

Appalled, she could only open and close her mouth silently, like a hooked trout.

"No? You didn't know that, did you, Mrs. Rowan? And the dancers work at night. Children sleep at night. You do have a child, don't you, ma'am?"

Her eyes were so wide, it hurt.

"Well, I must be going. Enjoyed visiting with you, Mrs. Rowan." He hurried off down the hall to the landing.

She gaped after him. Then she turned and finished the walk down the hall on wooden legs. Arriving at Room Eight, she had to wait for several minutes, while her madly beating heart calmed.

What Fred Knox had said had shaken her badly. Mr. Stanton, wanting to take her to court? For money? What would she do to make a living in this town? Despite Fred Knox's kindness today in telling her about Mr. Stanton, she still did not want to dance in his Hurdy Gurdy Palace.

Summoning the little that remained of her courage, she knocked on the door of Room Eight. The door opened and there stood Miss Madeline Mueler.

"What do you need?" asked the cool-eyed blonde. Behind her, the large room was well appointed, with a wine-colored couch and armchairs and a low table. The walls of the room were painted in cream with gold trim. On the dining table sat a bowl of carved wooden fruit. The peaches looked so real that Amberson felt saliva come to her mouth.

She drew her eyes back to the watchful Miss Mueler. "I'd like to speak to Richard, please," said Amberson.

"What about?"

Amberson flushed. "I do not see that it is any of your business."

"I declare. The little wife has vinegar."

Amberson glared at her.

"Who is it?" called Richard from one of the rooms.

"It's Miss Amberson," answered Madeline. "You remember her? You were married to her." She winked at Amberson, as if they shared a joke.

"We are still married," Amberson pointed out.

Madeline made a little moue of distaste.

"Let her in," ordered Richard.

Madeline stepped aside and watched Amberson, as if daring her to step across the threshold.

Amberson dared.

Madeline closed the door with a final click. "He's in there."

Amberson walked through the open door of a bedroom. Richard lay in the wide bed, cotton quilts drawn up to his chest. The curtains had been drawn so the room was dark. The only source of light was an oil lamp on the bedside table. Amberson closed the door behind her. What she had to say was not for Madeline Mueler's ears.

"What do you want?" Though he was on his back, Richard sounded as belligerent as ever.

"I've come to talk to you."

"What about?"

She took a breath. "I want a divorce, Richard."

He laughed, a croaky chuckle. "A divorce? You'll be the talk of the town. Those old ninnies you think are your friends will cross the street to get away from you when they see you coming."

"That should make you happy."

"It would." He eyed her.

She eyed him. He looked awful. There were dark circles under his eyes and he looked as though he hadn't shaved in three days. There was a stuffy, medicinal smell to the room.

"I want a divorce, Richard," she pressed. "There is no reason for us to stay married any longer. Surely you must have your own plans . . . with Madeline."

"What I want is none of your business. And leave Miss Mueler out of this. You aren't fit to button her boots."

"I didn't come here to argue with you. I came to ask for a divorce. It would be best for both of us."

She waited, giving him time to think about it. The bedroom was also well furnished, and she saw tall bottles of perfume—expensive perfume—set on the low, ornate bureau. Gifts to Madeline, she realized.

There was a fumbling sound at the keyhole and Amberson glanced over.

"Madeline, I'm sure, would want you to divorce me," said Amberson, raising her voice just a little. "Then she could marry you."

"To hell with what Madeline wants," barked Richard. "To hell with what you want too!"

"What do you mean?"

"I mean, get the hell out of here!"

"But, Richard, a divorce—"

"Madeline!" he shouted. "Throw her out! She's disturbing me."

The door opened, and Madeline, a petulant look on her face, hurried over and grasped Amberson's arm. She dragged Amberson through the door.

"Let go of me," demanded Amberson.

"He said to get rid of you," puffed Madeline. "And I will."

"Let go," cried Amberson, pushing the woman's hand away. "I can walk out of here on my own!"

She marched to the door, opened it, and went through, slamming it behind her.

The door opened again. "Good riddance!" yelled Madeline.

Amberson stalked down the hall. She'd had all she could stand of Richard Rowan and his paramour.

Madeline glided into the bedroom. "What did she want, sugar?"

"You heard," he said. "You were at the keyhole."

"I? Not I," she protested.

He chuckled. "Don't think I don't know," he said indulgently. "She wanted a divorce."

Madeline came over and sat on the side of the bed.

"Did you agree?" she asked, stroking his arm, which lay above the coverlet.

"No."

The stroking stopped. "Why ever not?"

"I want her to suffer, the snake. She told me that brat of hers was mine and I believed her." He turned tortured eyes on Madeline. "Do you know what that does to a man? To find out the kid he loves isn't his?" He fought to get his voice under control.

"Why, surely she is a snake," agreed Madeline. "But a little old divorce would set you free. Take a load off your mind. Help you regain your health." She smoothed the hair back from his forehead, running her fingers over and over again through the graying strands.

He turned to her and put his face in the palm of her hand. "You are so good to me," he said. "So good. *She* was never good to me, not like you are."

Madeline smiled. "You'll get the divorce then, darlin'?"

"Hell, no!"

Madeline withdrew her hand from his hair.

"I want her to be as miserable as I feel. Oh, God," he groaned suddenly, holding his stomach. "My gut hurts. It hurts bad."

"Yes, sugar," she said soothingly. "I'll get you a glass of water."

"To hell with water, make it whisky."

"Yes, sugar." She hurried from the room and went into the tiny kitchen. Taking a bottle of whisky from the cabinet, she splashed several inches into a cup.

A small smile played about her ripe lips. "You'll divorce her, Richard," she muttered to herself. "You'll divorce her because if you don't, your gut will hurt much worse. Much, much worse, *darlin'*."

267

Chapter Thirty-two

"You still here?" asked Justin. He couldn't believe his eyes. It was ten P.M.—the sun had set an hour ago—and the woman was washing clothes by the light of a lantern. If it weren't for Beau, sitting on a chair with a Hawkens rifle across his lap, Justin would question her sanity, being out here at night alone.

He had to repeat himself because she couldn't hear him above the noise of two men shouting and punching each other a few doors down at the Plugged Nickel Saloon.

He heard Sheriff Logan's deep voice, breaking up the fight, so Justin turned his attention back to Miss Amberson. He pulled out his watch. "Midnight in two hours," he said.

"Good," she answered sweetly, on her knees, scrubbing a shirt against the scrub board. "Then I'll have time to get all these shirts washed."

He shook his head, marveling at the woman's stubbornness. "How's the baby?"

"Why don't you come by and see?"

Was that sarcasm in her voice? "I've been out of town," he explained. "Riding shotgun on a freight line."

"Richard hired you?" she asked in astonishment.

He grinned. "Not Richard. Whiskers. Said what the boss didn't know wouldn't hurt him."

She nodded. "Richard's up in the hotel. Sick."

"How do you know?"

She tossed her head. "I went to see him."

"Just can't stay away from the man, hmmm? Launderin' would drive any woman back into his arms."

"I went to ask him for a divorce," she explained coldly. "Not that it's any of your business."

"You're right," he said shortly. "It's not." Dang. Why did they always get into arguments? He couldn't be near the woman for two minutes before they were fighting. Her hair had half fallen out of its usual bun. She looked tired, but oh, she looked good to his hungry eyes.

He took a breath. "Look," he said evenly, "I didn't come here to argue."

"What *did* you come here for?"

"To see how you were doing."

"Me? Are you certain you don't mean Gerald?"

"Gerald too. But I was hoping you were doing all right."

"I am." She threw the shirt into the rinse tub, then turned back for another one to scrub.

He watched her, at a loss for words. "Heard from Kingsley?" he asked idly.

"No."

He cast around for another topic. Dang it, why couldn't she look at him, instead of the tub of washing? "Seems you got plenty of customers."

"Yes."

Well, that killed that topic. "I want to come by and see Gerald tomorrow."

"Fine."

"How's the baby doing?"

"Fine."

Justin waited. She kept scrubbing. Finally he said, "Miss Amberson, are you going to talk to me or not?"

"No."

In exasperation, he said, "I'll be by to see the baby tomorrow."

"Fine."

He shook his head and slammed his slouch hat back on top of it. "I need a drink."

She didn't answer that, just kept scrubbing. Seeing he wasn't going to have any decent words with her, he stormed down the boardwalk, headed for the Plugged Nickel.

He heard footsteps coming after him. Short steps.

"Mr. Harbinger?"

He stopped and turned. "Yeah?"

It was Beau. "Missus Rowan, she doesn't want to tell you what's truly goin' on."

"Oh. And what might that be?"

"She can't do no more laundering. Mr. Stanton owns the property she's using. Mr. Stanton complained to Fred Knox about trespassin'. And any other place is too far from the creek for carryin' water. So tonight's her last night of laundry business."

"What?"

"It's true." The dwarf nodded seriously. "Otherwise Mr. Stanton's taking her to court."

Stunned, Justin stared at the man. "What's she going to do?"

Beau shrugged. "She's goin' to go work at the Hurdy Gurdy Palace."

Chapter Thirty-three

Amberson pulled Mrs. Cooper's big gray cloak tighter around herself.

"No, no, Mrs. Rowan. We must let the men see what's under that cloak. They want to see what they're dancing with. My, but your hair looks fine this evening. Here, it will look even better if we take it out of this tight bun." Fred Knox pulled out her hairpins, and she felt her long locks tumble loose. "Much better."

Mortified, she felt him tug at her cloak. "Mrs. Rowan," he said patiently, "I don't believe that you would present yourself in my establishment unless you intended to take me up on my offer. Am I correct?"

She nodded, clutching the cloak tighter.

"Then, Mrs. Rowan," he said reasonably, "you must be ready to dance. I don't know of any man who frequents this palace who will dance with a woman cloaked from her neck to her feet."

Amberson glanced around the Palace. A piano player sat playing tinkly songs in one corner of the dance floor.

There was a wooden stage set higher than the floor, and it even had red velvet curtains. But most of the room was filled with tables and chairs. And men; many men sat drinking, talking, and mostly ogling the three women who moved about the room, sitting at tables, jumping up now and then to dance with men who could afford to pay for it.

"Watch Lily of the Valley, Mrs. Rowan," urged Fred Knox, pointing to a thin blond woman with a slight overbite that made her attractive. She wore a tight yellow and black dress that opened at the front, the better to display her long thin legs. "Lily's a fine dancer.

"So is Velvet Susie." Susie was short and stocky, with lush dark curls falling below bountiful breasts that spilled out of her black-and-purple dance costume. "Susie used to work at Estelle's House of Beautiful Ladies, but we have the satisfaction of her presence at our establishment now that her baby's been born. Of course, Estelle wants her back. Ah, yes, and there is Fancy Francie. Isn't she lovely?"

Amberson looked over. Red-haired Fancy Francie looked tired, her bright makeup blotchy red on the lips and dark pink on her cheeks. Her highlighted mouth sagged unhappily. And that, unfortunately, was not all that sagged in Francie's black-and-pink lacy costume.

"These girls all know what to do," continued Fred Knox. "Ah, they'll do a little dance on stage now and then. And they are always available for any gentleman who wishes to pay a small price for the immense privilege of dancing with them."

"How small a price?" asked Amberson.

"Whisky's five cents a glass; a dance with a lovely lady is a dollar." He smiled with his brown eyes. "I'll get sixty cents of that dollar and you'll get forty. Agreed?"

She shrugged. "I suppose."

"I do believe Francie makes about thirteen dollars a night." He called over the tired woman. "Francie," he said in a cajoling voice, "how much did you make last night?"

"Fifteen dollars," she answered promptly.

Fred Knox turned to Amberson and smiled. "Ah yes, it's even better than I said, isn't it?" He looked up then, toward the door. Amberson followed his gaze.

A tall, elegant, dark-haired woman, her hair swept up in swirls and curls on top of her head and wearing a dark blue gown, had wandered in. Abruptly, Fred Knox said, "Why don't you talk with Francie, Mrs. Rowan? She'll show you around."

Amberson glanced at Francie, who rolled her eyes.

"And Francie," he said sternly to the woman, "don't let Estelle see her."

He hurried off.

"Ol' Fred doesn't want Estelle to see you 'cause he's afraid she'll want you for her House."

"I will never go and work at Estelle's," said Amberson.

"She don't know that," Francie said with a smirk. "And neither does he. Take my advice. Better to keep him guessin'."

274

She seized Amberson's hand and led her backstage. "Take off that cloak," she said.

"I—I like this cloak."

"You wanta be a hurdy-gurdy dancer or not?" Francie looked like she didn't care either way.

"I don't know any other way to make money," admitted Amberson miserably.

"Well, then, take off your cloak." Francie was remorseless.

Slowly Amberson removed her cloak.

"Turn around."

Amberson did so.

Francie let out a whistle. "No wonder ol' Fred doesn't want Estelle to see you."

Amberson moved her hands to cover up her breasts and any other part of her anatomy that she could reach quickly.

"Pretty color," complimented Francie. "I like that green. Kinda see-through, ain't it? The cape looks good, too. Where'd you get the outfit?"

"From—from a friend," whispered Amberson. Truth was, she'd begged the Titania costume from Annabelle Simmons after the play. Amberson had had to cut off the fairie wings and take it in a little in the bosom, but otherwise, it fit quite well.

"You look like an angel," said Francie in awe.

Amberson blushed.

Feeling thoroughly embarrassed in her green dress with the green cape and tight bodice, she said, "What do I have to do on stage?"

"Oh, we just line up and give a few kicks. Gets the men so excited they can't see straight." Francie grinned. "Then you go and corral a man or two and make him pay to dance with ya. It's easy." Her brown eyes narrowed. "What's ol' Fred payin' ya?"

"He said he charges a dollar a dance and he keeps sixty cents and I keep forty."

"You're a fool, girl. I get to keep fifty cents. So do all the girls here. Hee hee." Francie laughed.

Amberson spitefully noted that she had a tooth missing in the upper left side of her mouth. "Seems ol' Fred is taking advantage of me," she muttered.

" 'Fraid so," agreed Francie easily. "Hey, don't take it so hard. At least it's a job."

"It is that," agreed Amberson, glancing down at her green costume.

"Tell you what," said Francie. "I like you. You got spunk. So I'll tell ya somethin'."

"What's that?"

"Business," said Francie. "Don't dance too long with one man. You go stale. Keep movin' on to new dance partners. They're willin' to pay full price and that way you get in more dances. Try and dance every dance. By the end of the evenin' you'll make ten or fifteen dollars."

Amberson pondered the advice. "That's more than I made in two weeks of laundering."

"That's how I do it," explained Francie. " 'Course you can make more at Estelle's, but hey, who wants to spend all night on your back with some pig pantin' over ya?"

Amberson nodded sickly. "Not me."

"Me neither," said Francie. "Now let's go out there and rustle up some men to dance with. Watch for the ones who are only a little bit drunk. You can usually squeeze an extra fifty cents out of them for drinks."

"Drinks?" asked Amberson weakly. "I don't drink."

"You drink water. They drink spirits." Francie grinned and gave Amberson a swat on the backside. "Get out there, girl."

Chapter Thirty-four

Kicking her way across the stage with the other women was good exercise and a bit of fun, Amberson decided. Trying to dance the waltz with a man who smelled like he hadn't bathed in a month was another matter. She held out her arms stiffly, hoping the balding miner she danced with would keep some distance between them, but the miner merely pulled her tighter to him and she found herself staring point-blank at his food-covered shirt.

His smell was very strong. She wanted to throw up.

"Say," he said. "You're a good dancer. Let's dance another one."

She summoned Francie's advice and faked a smile. "Hmmmm. I must dance with some of the others now. Good-bye." She hurried away before she could hear his protests.

She made it to the bar and ordered a water. A tap

on her shoulder told her the next customer was ready. This one was a lanky fellow, a freckled, red-haired cowboy who looked vaguely familiar.

"My turn," he said.

She nodded and he paid his dollar to the bartender for their dance. When they got out on the dance floor, she discovered that this one was a talker. "Haven't I seen you before?" he asked.

"I do not believe so," she answered. With her luck, he'd probably worked for Richard. All her good intentions about speaking the truth had evaporated in one night on this job. She was, however, still telling herself the truth, so perhaps that counted for some-thing.

"I told that piano-playing 'professor' to play a waltz," he complained when the tune speeded up. He danced faster and asked, "What's your name?"

She thought quickly. All the hurdy-gurdy dancers that Fred had introduced to her had nicknames. She would have one too. "Montana Angel."

"You *do* look like an angel," he complimented.

She simpered.

"Well, now, Angel, and it's sure you're a lovely girl."

She could hear the Irish brogue in his accent. She simpered again.

"Angel, me girl, I want to ask you something."

Warily she asked, "What?"

"Run away with me. I can take you out of this place. You can help me and me brothers with our mining claim."

"I thought you were a cowboy," she hedged.

"I've switched professions," he explained with an easy laugh. "By the way, me name's Sean Coyle."

Now she remembered: He'd proposed to her when she was starting her laundry business. Bracing herself for what was coming she said, "Hello, Sean."

"Say, do you want another dance?" he asked eagerly as the music ended.

"No, thank you." She smiled. "I have another customer waiting."

"Don't go to him, me girl," pleaded Sean. "Dance once more with me and you'll no' regret it. I have somethin' important to tell you."

Curious, she paused. "And what might that be?"

"Marry me," he encouraged.

"Don't you already have a wife?"

He looked deflated. "How did you know?"

She affected a mysterious air. "I know these things. In fact," she pressed, "you are one of the triplet cowboys who brought in the Mormon preacher so you could marry more than one wife each."

He frowned. "You do get around, Angel."

"I do."

"Excuse me," interrupted Fred Knox, "but this dancer has another customer. One who has already paid," said Fred Knox pointedly.

"Good-bye, Angel," said Sean, holding his cowboy hat over his heart, a look of intense longing on his freckled face. "Farewell."

"Farewell, Sean," she said gaily, following Fred Knox through the mostly male crowd.

"Angel?" asked Fred.

"Montana Angel," she corrected.

They reached the bar. "You're doing well," Fred Knox commented, his brown eyes warm with approval. "You're our most popular dancer."

She smiled. "In that case, you'll be willing to give me a raise."

"Oh?" He signaled to the bartender. "Give me a whisky."

"Yes," she said. "Fifty cents on the dollar for me, fifty cents for you."

He eyed her. "And if I don't?"

"I don't dance tomorrow night."

The bartender plopped a glass of whisky on the counter in front of Fred. "Ah, you drive a hard bargain, Montana, but it's a deal." He took a quick swig of his drink. Glancing around, he lowered his voice, "I want to warn you about someone."

"Who?"

"Estelle."

"Estelle of the House of Beautiful Ladies?"

"Ah yes, the same. Now, I have nothing against Estelle, you understand. She's a lovely woman, lovely. Joe Parker certainly thinks so, and he ought to know. But here's the truth of the matter: She is a woman to beware of. She's taken three of my best dancers." He took another swig of whisky.

"You think she'll ask me to whore for her?"

"She might. Only she won't put it that way. She'll say something like she wants you to come and be a pretty waiter."

"Pretty waiter?"

"Ah yes, one of the barmaids in her House. Bring food, drinks to the customers, things like that."

"Oh."

"But don't you fall for it. Oh, no. Because once she gets you in there, she'll have you working the night shift, flat on your back. She's as slick as a pair of silk drawers, that one. And that big fellow—McIver—have you seen him?"

"He brought his laundry to me a time or two."

"Ah yes, well, he's her bouncer. Keeps the bad girls in and the bad boys out." He winked. "Understand?"

"I see." Amberson glanced around. Gunpoint at

night seemed a little more dangerous than she'd realized.

Fred Knox patted her shoulder reassuringly. "Now, now, Montana, I didn't want to alarm you. Just a friendly little warning, is all."

"Thank you," she muttered, getting more alarmed by the second.

"Here's your customer," he said cheerily. "This is Sheriff Logan."

"Sheriff Logan?" She turned to greet him. He was swaying on his feet, obviously very drunk. "Sheriff?"

"Whassa matter with the floor? Whysssh it moving around so mussshhhh?" He blinked, peering at her. "Fred promisshed me a dansssh with the new girl. That you?"

From the way he was acting, he didn't recognize her from the telegraph office. The dim light hid her features. Relief settled over her.

"My name's Montana Angel. Let's dance." She seized his hand and dragged him out onto the floor, anxious to get the dance over with. This night, she realized, was turning uncommonly long.

The sheriff pinched her buttocks as they moved across the dance floor.

"Sheriff Logan," she squealed, "stop that!"

He laughed. "You like it," he chortled and pinched her again.

She moved his hand away and scolded, "If you do that again, Sheriff, I won't dance with you!"

"Aaaw, I wasssh only havin' some fun. Whatsshhh wrong with havin' a little fun?" he whined.

She rolled her eyes and kept on dancing. Mercifully, the dance was over soon and she sidled away from the lawman and back to the counter.

"Keep Sheriff Logan happy," whispered Fred Knox

in her ear. "He's an important customer."

To you, but not to me, she thought.

A warm hand settled over hers. "I claim two dances," said Justin Harbinger, throwing several coins on the counter.

She stared at him in surprise and her heart beat faster. "Justin? What are you doing here?"

"I came to dance," he said shortly, leading her out onto the dance floor. "The whole room's talking about the new dancer: Montana Angel."

She smiled.

"I thought you were an angel—once," he said.

Her smile froze. Those days were long behind her now. "How kind of you to remind me," she murmured.

He winced.

The "professor" at the piano chose this moment to play a slow waltz. Amberson moved into Justin's arms, not sure she should, but wanting to. He didn't say anything, but his arms around her felt solid and she let herself relax for the first time that evening.

"How do you like hurdy-gurdy dancing?" he said, his voice rough.

She closed her eyes and sidled a little closer against his hard chest. "I like it."

She could feel his corded arm muscles tense as he puller her closer. She opened her eyes and gazed into his, darkened with desire in the dim light.

"Justin," she said seriously, tilting back her head to get a better view of him, "I lied. I don't like it. I don't like being here. I didn't like doing laundry either, but I have to make a living for Gerald and myself."

"Come to my ranch," he said. "Stop this hurdy-gurdy dancing, and you and the baby come to my place. We'll have enough food, you'll have a roof over your head . . ."

She wanted to. Lord help her, but she wanted to. She sought his green eyes. "Justin, I am still married. I am not going to live with you. For once in my life, I am going to live a moral life. I let you seduce me and I paid a high price for not living right. I lied to Richard about Gerald, and I lied to you too. I will not live a life built on lies. It got me into nothing but trouble. And living with a man I'm not married to is a lie. I won't do it."

He was silent. They moved about the floor and she snuggled closer. She caught a whiff of him. He smelled of leather and man. She found she had a new appreciation for a clean man.

"I admire your strength," he said, and she heard a new note in his voice. "I respect that you want to lead a good life, an honest life. But Amberson, what if you are destroyed in the process?" He gestured at the miners and cowboys around them. "Your laudable goals have led you to a very risky place. The next stop on this road is Estelle's."

"Pooh," she said.

"It is," he warned. "And she's right over there. Waiting." He gestured with his chin. The dark, curly-haired woman stood at the bar, watching them. A small smile played on her wide mouth. Whispering in her ear was a big man with a black handlebar mustache. Amberson recognized him as the bartender from the Plugged Nickel Saloon.

"I am not going to work for Estelle," she said.

"Yeah? I believe you also told me you weren't going to work in the Hurdy Gurdy Palace."

She clamped her mouth shut. It was true, unfortunately. "You have an awfully good memory," she noted.

"Flattering the customers, ma'am?" he asked snidely.

She smiled at him. "If it's good for business, I do."

He drew her closer. How good it felt to be in his arms. She could let herself have this little time with him, only this little time. She must remember every moment, impress it on every heartbeat. . . . Her smile disappeared. "I don't want you throwing your money away on dances with me, Justin. I know you're saving for your cattle herd."

"I'll decide what I throw my money away on."

At that moment, the "professor" broke into a wild dance tune and Amberson found herself out of his arms and moving swiftly to the fast beat. She and Justin danced until she was out of breath. "Oh, Justin!" She laughed up into his green eyes. "I am plumb worn out."

His green eyes glowed with warmth and he bent down and kissed her on the lips. She clung to him until she remembered where they were, who he was, who *she* was. She pushed him away, gasping. "I don't want anyone to get the wrong idea. . . ." she mumbled.

"Let's get out of here," he pleaded. "Come with me, Miss Amberson. We'll take Gerald and go to my ranch—"

She let go of his hand and moved out of the warm circle of his arms. "I can't, Justin," she said sadly. "I am putting my life in order. I can't do anything with another man until I divorce Richard."

The warm glow in his eyes disappeared.

"Even if I want to," she whispered.

"Do you want to?" he whispered, the glow back.

She stood on her tiptoes and kissed him. "Yes."

Shouts and cries and whistles broke out. "Whhooooeee, I wanna dance with her!"

"My turn, my turn!"

"Get out of the way, all of you! That dancer is *mine!*"

The throng of eager men tore them apart and she watched with stricken eyes as Justin was pulled away from her by a laughing Lily of the Valley. Fred Knox beamed his approval at Lily.

A burly miner grabbed Amberson and danced a jig, his arms pumping hers up and down. She soon lost sight of Justin altogether as she was whirled and flung to and fro by her new partner.

The evening passed quickly from then on. Justin, she saw, spent the evening sulking in a corner. Whenever he thought she noticed him, he'd go over and ask Lily of the Valley to dance.

It was two a.m. when Amberson finally departed the Hurdy Gurdy Palace. She was twenty-three dollars richer than when she'd entered and sadder but wiser of heart.

Chapter Thirty-five

"You look lovely, Mrs. Rowan," Sheriff Logan said, tipping his hat to her. "Baby is cute too," he added in his gruff voice. If one excluded the sheriff's bloodshot eyes, there was no sign of the inebriation he'd displayed the night before. Evidently he did not make the connection between Montana Angel and Mrs. Amberson Rowan.

She smiled. "Good day, Sheriff." He held the door of the telegraph office open for her and she preceded him in.

Mr. Fred Knox was inside, sending a telegram. He looked up and nodded politely when he saw the sheriff. He took off his hat and bowed to Amberson. "Good day, Mrs. Rowan." One would never suspect that she was his employee at the Hurdy Gurdy Palace, so smooth did he act.

"Good day, Mr. Knox." She nodded regally. Gerald

stared at both men out of big blue eyes, but mercifully, kept silent.

"Be sure to send that telegram immediately," Fred Knox said to Mr. Tibbets. He nodded once more to the sheriff and Amberson as he left the telegraph office.

Sheriff Logan sidled up to the counter and was staring at the paper in Mr. Tibbets's hand. "That's odd," he muttered. "Why is Fred Knox sending telegrams to the governor too?"

Mr. Tibbets snatched the paper away. "You're not supposed to be reading other people's telegrams," he scolded.

"Aw, come on, Tibbets," said Sheriff Logan. "I'm the sheriff of this town. How am I supposed to keep the peace if I don't know what's going on?"

His reasoning must have made sense to Mr. Tibbets, for the old man answered, "All right then, Sheriff, but you didn't hear it from me. Fred Knox has been sending telegrams to the governor about the opium situation, just like you have."

"That so?" Sheriff Logan frowned.

Amberson waited patiently. This was her last attempt, her very last, absolutely last, attempt to contact Kingsley. She wished the sheriff and Mr. Tibbets would hurry up with their talk and let her send her telegram.

"But Fred Knox, now," said Tibbets, "he takes a little different aim than you do."

"And what aim might that be?" inquired the sheriff pleasantly.

"Well, Mr. Knox now, he complains about the opium fiends in this town, too, just like you do. And he tells the governor he needs to close down those opium dens, just like you do. But Mr. Knox likes to be kept informed about what dens the governor's ordered raided, who's been caught, little things like that."

The sheriff's face, to Amberson's bewildered eyes, turned a flushed red. "And the governor's been telling him?"

Tibbets shrugged. "Seems like it. He always sends a telegram answering him."

Sheriff Logan's face was now dark purple. "You pinheaded pig knuckle!" he cried. "Why didn't you tell me this before now?" He glared at the little man. "Every time I raid Lee Fung's opium den, there are no customers and no opium! And now I know why!"

He stormed out of the telegraph office, leaving Amberson and Mr. Tibbets wincing from the slammed door.

"Whew," said Mr. Tibbets. "I wonder what got him so angry?"

Amberson stared at him. "I don't think he likes it that the governor was telling Fred Knox which opium dens the sheriff was going to raid." She paused. "There was something about a Lee Fung . . ."

But Mr. Tibbets wasn't listening. He scratched his head. "Why should it matter if the governor let Fred Knox know? After all, he's on the side of the law. He's an attorney."

"That's not all he is," muttered Amberson.

"Beg your pardon, ma'am?"

"Nothing." Amberson smiled sweetly. "I want to send a telegram."

Pencil poised above a clean sheet of paper, Mr. Tibbets waited. "To Kingsley? In Bodie?"

"Yes," she answered with her chin up, refusing to be defeated.

288

*   *   *

The telegram sent, for the last time, Amberson wandered down the boardwalk toward Hinckley's General Store. The sun shone bright, she did not have to wash anyone else's laundry ever again, and seven o'clock tonight was a long time away. She and Gerald would celebrate the day with a sarsaparilla.

She was walking past the bank when someone called her name. She turned.

Justin.

Her heart beat faster. She swallowed and stood her ground, watching him stride toward her. Would her heart ever cease to thrum when she saw him? He looked so tall and rugged in his brown-and-white vest and leather chaps. The jingling sound of his spurs fascinated Gerald, who reached out a little arm to him.

Justin bent over and nuzzled the baby. He lifted his head, green eyes sparkling. "Hello, Miss Amberson."

Had his voice always sent such delicious shivers up her spine?

"Hello." She glanced down at the baby, suddenly shy, afraid Justin could read the feelings he incited in her with only a single glance. "Gerald and I are going to Hinckley's General Store to get a sarsaparilla. Would—would you like to join us?"

"That would be fine. Thank you, I will." They had walked about two steps when suddenly a bullet zinged past her elbow.

"Justin!" she gasped.

"Quick!" He pushed her and the baby into the alley between the bank and Eddie's Embalming Emporium. Two more bullets kicked up dust beside them.

A hail of bullets peppered the side of the embalmer's.

Amberson found herself thrown to the ground, the baby cradled beside her, and Justin hovering over both of them, shielding them with his body.

Several more bullets whined past them and thudded into the wall above her head. Her heart pounded in fear and all she could do was watch her baby's face. Gerald. The light of her life.

Oh, God, a bullet could hit the baby. Above her, Justin stirred as another bullet pinged nearby.

Justin. If anything happened to him, oh my Lord . . . She sobbed her fear into the baby's stomach.

Several yells came from the bank; then there was the pounding sound of feet running on the boardwalk.

"Stay down," whispered Justin. She clutched the baby tighter.

They stayed frozen like that for several minutes, and finally she heard horses galloping down Gold Fever Street, headed for the outskirts of town. Several more gun blasts echoed up and down the street.

Justin rolled off her. "Sounds like the bank has been robbed. It looked like those rustlers, the four of them."

"The rustlers?" She blinked several times, trying to make sense of what had just happened.

"How's Gerald?"

"He—he's fine." She traced the baby's face with shaking fingers. "He's fine." She hugged Gerald to her, her eyes riveted on Justin. "Oh, Justin, I was so scared. . . ."

The baby started to cry.

Justin patted her shoulder awkwardly, then took her hand and squeezed it reassuringly. "Good thing

Gerald kept quiet during the robbery," he said finally, as he helped her to her feet.

They dusted off their clothes as best they could and remounted the boardwalk.

Still shaking, Amberson drew near the bank door and peeked inside. Sheriff Logan was in the bank, talking to banker J. V. Simmons. Fred Knox, Joe Parker, and most of the men of the town milled around in clusters, talking excitedly. Amberson was surprised to see Annabelle Simmons there too. She looked white-faced and clutched her husband's arm as he spoke with the sheriff.

Justin opened the door and went inside; Amberson hurried after him. Her legs still trembled.

"How much did they get away with?" Justin asked Joe Parker.

"Too damn much," said Joe. "They made off with two thousand dollars—"

"Two thousand dollars," gasped Amberson.

"—and half of it was my money!" Joe Parker looked angry. This was the first time Amberson had heard that Joe was a partner in the bank.

"Listen, men," said Sheriff Logan, "we're going to get up a posse and hunt those robbers down. All the men who want to join the roundup party, go and get your horses. Meet me here in five minutes."

Men hurried out the door and soon there was only Amberson and Justin standing in the doorway.

"I'm going to go with the posse to catch those men," said Justin. "We can't be having lawlessness in this town. It's not safe for women and children." The glitter in his green eyes warned her. "As for you, Miss Amberson, I think you've seen that this town is not a fit place to raise a child. I want you packed and ready to ride to my ranch tonight."

"But I have to dance—"

He held up a hand. "No. It's my child. And your life is at stake. You were lucky I happened by. Next time you might not be so lucky."

She heard the implacability in his voice. He was not giving her a choice. She remembered the weight of him pressing against her back as bullets winged by. He'd risked his life, not only for Gerald, but also for her. No longer could she tell herself that he only cared for Gerald. He'd proved the strength of his caring today, without words.

And some strong part of her was too tired to fight anymore. Besides, she found she agreed with him. She wasn't safe on the streets of Gunpoint, never mind the Hurdy Gurdy Palace, where fights were a nightly occurrence. It didn't take much for bullets to fly in this town.

"Gerald and I will be ready," she said, and she was surprised that her capitulation came so easily.

When she saw the little smile on his lips and the sparkle in his eye, she added, "I'll be bringing Beau with me. He'll be my chaperone."

Justin laughed out loud.

"He'll sleep outside my bedroom door with a rifle across his lap," she promised. "And guard me the same way he guarded me at the laundry tub."

Justin stopped laughing.

Chapter Thirty-six

Amberson halted her packing in the late afternoon. While Gerald slept under Mrs. Cooper's watchful eye, Amberson went to Fred Knox's office to tell him she would no longer be dancing at his Hurdy Gurdy Palace. He professed great disappointment, but seeing she was firm in her decision, he told her if she ever needed a job, she could always come to him. She thanked him and left, glad to be out of his office.

Next, she walked over to Hinckley's General Store to buy four bottles of sarsaparilla. On the way back from Hinckley's, she stopped at the telegraph office. One look at Mr. Tibbets's wrinkled face confirmed her fear: no word from Kingsley.

She returned, feet dragging, to Dr. and Mrs. Cooper's house.

"Would you like a sarsaparilla, Mrs. Cooper?" Amberson asked.

"Yes, dear, that would be nice."

Amberson produced two bottles and poured the contents of one into a cup for the older woman. The two women sat at the kitchen table while Gerald slept soundly in the back bedroom.

"Are you sure you're doing the correct thing?" asked Mrs. Cooper. "You know you're welcome to stay here." She took a sip of the fizzy drink. "My, but that tastes sweet," she said.

"Yes, doesn't it," answered Amberson happily. She had her drink of sarsaparilla, though not quite the way she'd envisioned it before the bank robbery. "I hope they capture those robbers," she said. "The whole town is talking about the robbery. I saw a poster from Banker Simmons. He's offered a reward of one hundred dollars for the capture or death of each robber."

"My goodness," said Mrs. Cooper, drawing her gray shawl tighter about her shoulders.

Amberson shivered too. "I hope that Justin returns soon. The posse has been gone a long time."

"They'll probably stay out until they find those desperadoes or until they lose the trail," said Mrs. Cooper.

The two woman sat in companionable silence. The decision to go to Justin's ranch had been made. Amberson had hoped to ask Beau to accompany her so that she could make good on her threat to Justin about Beau guarding her door, but she'd been unable to find the short cowboy. He'd probably ridden off with the posse.

The women finished their drink, and then Mrs. Cooper started to make the evening meal. "You must stay for supper," she encouraged as she dredged the chicken with flour and herbs. "I'm making spice cake," she teased.

Amberson smiled. "I do prefer your spice cake to any other I've tasted."

"Why, thank you. And if the posse gets back late, you don't want to be out at the ranch and have to cook a meal at midnight."

"I've done worse," said Amberson.

"You've done very well," said Mrs. Cooper. "You've managed to work and make some money for yourself and your son. I dare say you've even managed to save some."

Amberson nodded. "I was going to put it in Mr. Simmons's bank. But that was before the robbery."

"Under your mattress is safer," assured Mrs. Cooper.

"Is it?" asked Amberson.

"That's where I keep my money," said the prim old woman.

Amberson smiled. She was going to miss kind Mrs. Cooper. And Dr. Cooper had been kind too. Amberson was fortunate to have found such good friends in Gunpoint.

The chicken was baking and the spice cake cooling on the counter when there came a pounding at the door.

Alarmed, Amberson flew to the door and opened it.

Beau stood there, panting from a fast run. "Come quick, Missus Rowan," he cried. "You must come with me!"

"Beau! What is it?" she asked. Mrs. Cooper hurried to the door to join her.

"They caught the robbers," said Beau, starting to get his breath back. "They're the men been doin' the rustlin'. Some of the boys identified them."

"What about Justin? Is he all right?"

"Justin's doin' fine," said Beau. "It was him that sent me for you."

"Whatever for?"

Beau shook his head. "Don't have time to talk, Missus Rowan. Just come. Please!"

She glanced at Mrs. Cooper.

The older woman nodded. "I'll watch the baby."

Amberson grabbed up a shawl, flung it around her shoulders, and put on her boots.

"I got Jessie, your horse, from the livery stable," said Beau. "She's all saddled and ready to go. You can ride her."

They ran down the steps and through the garden to the boardwalk. She gave Jessie a pat on the nose, glad to see her again. Beau helped her into the saddle, then mounted his own pony. They galloped out of town, headed for the open range.

They rode for about forty-five minutes and Amberson was beginning to wonder if she'd been mistaken to go with Beau. After all, why would she be needed if they'd caught the robbers? He'd hurried her out the door so fast she'd not had time to think straight.

But every time she'd ask Beau a question about where they were going and why, the short cowboy just shook his head and kept riding.

They reached a canyon and he led the way through some of the brush. She followed. "Just ahead a little ways, Missus Rowan," Beau encouraged.

She nodded and guided her mare around a pile of rocks. A few minutes later they rounded a section of the canyon and came to where the Gunpoint posse had cornered the robbers. Three of the robbers sat on the ground, trussed up like plucked chickens, their arms and legs bound and Sheriff Logan standing watchful guard over them.

Behind them, two posse members lay on the ground.

The fourth robber slumped beside a big rock, his shirt bloody. Justin knelt beside him.

Justin looked up when he saw her and motioned for her to approach.

"Justin?" She dismounted, staring at him. Whatever did he want?

She glanced briefly at the men standing around. They all watched her.

Something was wrong. Very wrong.

She walked up to Justin, and it was then she saw the face of the wounded robber. "Oh my God," she screamed. "Kingsley!"

She threw herself down beside her brother. "Oh, Kingsley! Kingsley!" She started to cry. She ran her hands over his face, his arms. She stared at his stomach. "Oh my God, Kingsley, what have they done to you?"

"He's shot bad," said Justin. "He's gut shot and he isn't going to last long."

"Oh no, Kingsley," she cried, cradling his head. "Oh God, no!"

Justin put his hand on her back, but she shrugged him off. "Who shot him?" she cried. "Who did this to my brother?"

"We don't know who did it," said Justin quietly. "Kingsley and his men were shooting at the posse, and the posse shot back. Two townsmen from Gunpoint are dead."

"My brother!" she howled. "Not my brother! He's all I have!"

"You have Gerald," said Justin quietly. "And you have me."

She started to cry. "I want my brother too."

Kingsley moaned. "That you, Ammie?" He'd always called her that. Ammie. Since they were little.

"It's me," she said. "Oh, Kingsley, don't die. I love you!"

"Don't start in on that stuff, Ammie," he gasped. "It's too late. Too late for me. Too late for you."

"No," she cried. "It's not! I'll help you. You don't have to die!" She glanced wildly around. "Justin! You have that knife. Use it to get the bullet out. We can save him. I know we can!"

Justin pulled his obsidian knife out of his boot. "I'll try," he said. "But he's been shot bad."

She nodded. "We've got to do something," she answered. "He can't just die!"

"He's shot bad," Justin repeated.

"You were in the war," she answered. "You even helped in field operations. You told Dr. Cooper so. And you helped Gerald. Help my brother," she pleaded.

His green eyes met hers, and she saw the compassion in them.

"I don't want him to die, Justin," she said fiercely.

"Anyone got any whisky?" Justin called. One of the men produced a bottle.

Amberson peeled back Kingsley's shirt. Some of it was stuck to his skin, so she pulled carefully.

Justin poured some of the whisky on the gaping wound. He glanced at her, then at the wound. "The bullet's in there, somewhere," he said. "It tore his guts apart."

"Justin, as God is my witness, help him!"

She stroked Kingsley's forehead while Justin used

the point of his knife to carefully push aside some skin. One of the men took the bottle from Justin. "Let's give him a drink," the cowboy said.

She saw he meant Kingsley. His face was pale and contorted with pain. "Drink this," directed the cowboy. "It will help."

He poured the whisky over Kingsley's mouth. Some ran into it, some down his chin. He shook his head.

"I wanted—" he gasped. "I wanted to come back to you a big man. Money, horses, all that stuff. Like Father had."

"Hush, Kingsley," she said. "No need to talk. Save your strength."

He shook his head, weakly. "Ain't gonna make it, Ammie," he told her.

"Found it," muttered Justin. There was a *clink* sound as the knife touched the bullet. He gritted his teeth and dug a little deeper for it.

Kingsley let out a cry.

"Oh God, Justin," she said. "Don't hurt him!"

Justin laughed bleakly. "I can't *not* hurt him, Amberson." He continued fishing with the knife, trying to scoop out the bullet. A few seconds later, he brought it to the surface. The bullet was hard to see in all the blood.

Amberson couldn't look. She turned back to her brother. "You told me you were going to Bodie. Why didn't you go there?"

"I let you think that. I stayed here. Didn't go west to seek my fortune after all." He gave a chuckle, more of a groan. He opened his eyes. "Ammie," he said, "I couldn't wait all that time to earn my fortune. I had to steal it."

"No, Kingsley," she protested. "I would have helped you."

"You—" he gasped, and she sensed he was fading, "had problems—of your own—"

She ignored that. She didn't want to bother him with her little problems, not now, not when he might be dying.

"Kingsley," she pleaded, "don't go. Stay with me. Stay here in Gunpoint. I'll help you get some money."

He laughed weakly. "A man's—gotta—get his own—money—"

His head rolled limply and she saw how weak his breathing was. "Justin," she hissed, "do something!"

"I can't, Amberson," he said soberly. She felt his hand on her arm. "He's going to die, Amberson. Make your peace with him."

She started to cry again. "Kingsley," she sobbed. "I want you to stay—"

"What for?" he gasped. "So they—can put—a noose—around—my neck?" His voice sounded stronger and she took hope.

"I'll care for you," she cried. "I'll help you get better."

"I ain't—gonna—swing—on no rope, Ammie—"

"You won't swing," she assured him. "You didn't do it. You didn't rob the bank."

"He did," said Justin soberly. "There're witnesses. His saddlebags have two of the sacks of money from the bank."

"They're lying," she snapped. "You're all lying!"

"He stole the cattle too," said Justin. "More witnesses."

"He didn't!" she cried. "Kingsley, tell them! Tell them you didn't do it!"

He chuckled, and blood dribbled out of the corner of his mouth.

"Oh, Kingsley," she cried. She dabbed at the corner of his mouth with the hem of her dress, wiping away the blood.

"They got reason to hang me—" he told her. "Good reason—"

"Kingsleeeeey," she cried and sobs shook her.

"He did it," said Justin soberly. "And he's dyin'."

She glared at him, lifting her hand to strike him for what he was saying. But when she saw his steady gaze, the sadness and the compassion in his green eyes told her the truth. Kingsley *had* robbed the bank; he *had* rustled the cattle.

"Two men lie dead because of him and his men," said Justin quietly. "I'm sorry, Amberson."

Tears rolled down her cheeks. "I loved him," she sobbed.

Justin put his arms around her. "Of course you did," he said. "He was your brother."

"Not—gone yet—"

"Kingsley," she said, wiping at her tears. "Before you go, I want you to know I love you—"

"Always—knew—Ammie—"

"I love you, Kingsley." She looked at her brother. He was dying. There was nothing she could do to stop it. Nothing any of them could do. He was dying and she loved him. Would always love him.

"Kingsley," she choked out, "say hello to Mama and Papa for me—"

"They're here—" he said.

"Where?"

"Over—there—smiles—" He tried to raise a hand, but only his fingers twitched. "Want me—go with them—"

"Yes," she said slowly, holding his hand. "You go with them. Go with them, Kingsley. Tell them I love them."

She felt how cold his hand was. The blood on his stomach was growing cold and black. "Oh, Kingsley," she whispered. "I don't want you to go." She closed her eyes. God, give me strength, she prayed. Give me the strength to love him and let him go.

"He's gone," said Justin quietly. He reached over and closed Kingsley's staring eyes. He put his arm around Amberson. "He's with your parents now."

She crumpled against his chest and sobbed.

Chapter Thirty-seven

Amberson sat in a rocking chair on the wooden porch of Justin's ranch house and stared out over the flat grasslands below. A newly filled grave, its hump of brown earth a rectangular contrast against the green of the grass, drew her eyes. She sighed sadly. Kingsley. He'd sought his fortune and now rested beneath a shade tree on Justin Harbinger's ranch.

In her arms, Amberson held Gerald. Since Kingsley's death, she'd held the child every waking moment she could. She'd been unable to let go of Gerald. Some wretched part of her had to hang on to the only person she still had left on this earth: Gerald. And . . . tentatively, unbidden, came the thought, Justin . . . She had Justin in her life too.

She closed her eyes and leaned back against the hard wooden boards behind her. Life had won, she decided. She had nothing left to ask of it, or give to it. Nothing. She was beaten. She surrendered. All she wanted from life now was to hug her child and sit on this porch.

Evening shadows were lengthening when Beau climbed up on the porch. "Evenin', Missus Rowan."

She nodded.

"Baby's gettin' big," he observed.

She saw the twinkle in his eye and wondered wearily why he was her friend. There wasn't anything she'd ever done for him, anything she could remember doing. She sighed. Sometimes it was best just to accept what was. Beau was her friend. Kingsley was dead.

"Goin' into town tomorrow, Missus Rowan," continued the irrepressible cowboy. "Wanta come along?"

"I don't care, Beau," she said and gave a long sigh.

"Maybe you can visit that Ladies' Club, talk to the ladies."

"I don't think the ladies want to talk to me," she answered. "Not since my hurdy-gurdy dancing."

"Oh, pshaw, Missus Rowan. You were a good dancer. I saw you."

"I don't believe the quality of my dancing is what concerns the ladies of the Gunpoint Culture Club." She yawned. Gerald squirmed in her lap, wanting to get down. She set him down on the porch beside her chair.

"There's always Mrs. Cooper," said Beau.

She blinked. "You want me to go into town, Beau?"

"Well—" he turned his hat nervously in his stubby fingers—"I think it might be good for you to get out and see people. It's been three weeks since your brother died."

She thought about that. Three weeks since Kingsley had died in her arms? It didn't seem possible. It seemed more like three centuries.

"Where's Justin?"

Beau blinked. "He's gone on a freight run, Missus Rowan. Remember? He told us he was gonna be gone for the next three days."

She didn't remember. At his worried look, she said, "Oh, yes, I forgot."

Beau looked relieved and she almost laughed. Almost. It must be odd for him to be trapped on a ranch with a grieving woman who wanted him to sit all night with a rifle across his lap, guarding the door. Not that he'd shoot Justin if Justin tried to get into her bedroom.

She'd already realized that. Beau and Justin were good friends and she doubted either would ever shoot the other. What a morose direction my thoughts are taking, she thought in a moment of self-realization. All my thoughts are about death and dying. Kingsley's death had affected her strongly.

Though she'd been able to accept that he was gone, still she missed him. And regret that they'd not spent more time together ate at her. If only he'd let her know where he was ... they could have ... She halted. There was no point in trying to change the past. What had happened, had happened.

She sat up a little straighter. "Very well, Beau," she said. "I'll go into town with you tomorrow."

He brightened. "Good for you, Missus Rowan." He put his hat on his head. "I'll go make dinner."

As the door banged shut behind him, she realized she'd abdicated most of her household duties. Beau made the meals, Justin worked on fencing his property and Amberson sat in her rocking chair on the porch.

Feeling as though she was awakening from a bad dream, Amberson slowly stood up and reached for Gerald just as he was crawling down the steps. She took him back into the house with her and set him on the kitchen floor.

"I'll help," she announced to Beau.

He was standing on a chair, scooping water from a bucket into a sturdy pot. Sliced potatoes and carrots lay on a board.

"Stew for dinner?" she asked.

He nodded. They worked together making the meal.

"How long did Justin say he was going to be gone?"

"Three days," answered Beau patiently.

Three days. "Why is he freight hauling?" she asked as she sliced a portion of beef.

"For the money," said Beau. He carried the pot over to the stove and climbed up on another chair, carefully lifting the pot and setting it on the wood stove to heat.

Then he climbed back down. "He wants to buy some cattle."

"Oh."

"After this trip, he'll have enough to buy ten head," boasted Beau.

She thought of all the cattle Richard owned. Cattle and land and freight lines and contracts with the military. And then there was Kingsley. He'd said he didn't want to take the time to *earn* his fortune, so he stole it. "Money makes men do strange things," she said.

"Yes, ma'am," he said, looking at her askance.

"I'm thinking of Kingsley," she explained. "He stole from the bank, robbed people of cattle, and look where it got him."

Beau nodded. "Dead."

Amberson didn't say any more, but that night, when she put Gerald to bed, she was still thinking about the choices people made in their lives. Richard, who owned property and cows and lived with Madeline, was unhappy. Kingsley, who'd owned nothing but his horse and saddle and red bandanna, was dead. Men weren't happy when they were rich; they weren't happy when they were poor. What was happiness about, anyway? she wondered.

And what was her life going to be like from now on? She had neither the wealth of a Richard Rowan nor the desperate poverty of a Kingsley Hawley. She had only herself and Gerald. And perhaps Justin.

Pondering, she said a quiet good night to Beau and returned to her bedroom. She undressed and got into bed and blew out the lamp. Sleep refused to come, so she thought some more. Finally she decided it was up to her to make a life for herself. She had to decide what was important to her, Amberson, not go by what was important to other people.

She started with the truth. It was important that she tell herself and other people the truth. She'd learned that lesson when Gerald was taken from her.

Then there was Gerald. He was the one she loved, the innocent child she loved with all her heart. He made her day bright and gave her something happy to look forward to.

There was Justin. He'd treated her well, lately. He'd helped her with credit at Hinckley's store, he'd protected her and Gerald, risking his own life by throwing his body across them during the bank robbery. And then, when Kingsley was dying, he'd been honest and truthful with her. Even tried to save her brother's life for her. Now he was giving her a place to stay. Yes, Justin was important to her, she realized.

And what about Beau? He'd been her friend when she had no one. He'd dragged wood to the laundry tub, hung up clothes, fetched her when her brother was dying, and tonight he'd made her a meal. And all because of friendship.

And there was Mrs. Cooper and Dr. Cooper. They'd proven themselves as friends to her, taking her and her child in when they'd needed a place to stay.

Amberson sat up. She had all the things she needed to build a life. She had herself, a child to love, a man to love, and friends. That was going to be the basis of her life: truth and love and friends. That would be what she would build her life on.

And she would start tomorrow morning.

Chapter Thirty-eight

Amberson walked through the front doors of the Two Star Hotel. She walked past the overstuffed chairs, past the gaping hotel manager, and past the silent, wary Celestial houseboy. She went up the stairs and turned left at the landing. At Room Eight, she pounded on the door.

"For Jersey's sakes, open the door," she heard Richard yell.

The door swung open and Madeline stood there, a blond, blue-eyed succubus.

"Oh. It's you." Madeline opened the door a little wider. "Are you here to ask Richard for a divorce?"

"Yes, I am," stated Amberson firmly. "I do not wish to be married to Richard any longer."

"Well, now, that's just fine with me." Madeline stepped back, letting a surprised Amberson stumble over the threshold.

"In there." Madeline moved her head in the direction of the bedroom. Feeling strangely like a cocon-spirator with Madeline Mueler, of all people, Amberson entered the darkened bed chamber.

Richard lay propped up on several beige-colored, lacy pillows.

"How are you, Richard?" Amberson greeted him.

He peered at her. "Not so good," he muttered. "What have you got to be so cheery about? Are you glad your brother is dead?"

The man was mean. How could she have forgotten? "No, I am not glad Kingsley's dead."

"Oh." He looked tired and moved his hand slowly to rest on his stomach. "What do you want?"

"Are you feeling better?" she asked, wanting to postpone their confrontation a little longer. She slipped into a chair at a little distance from his bed.

"I feel rotten," he said. "My gut hurts, my head hurts. But you didn't come here to talk about me, did you? Say what you came to say and get out."

She took a breath. "I want a divorce."

"I already told you, no! I want you to be as miserable as I am!"

"Richard," she said, keeping her tone as reasonable as she could, "a divorce will be much better for you too. You can make a happier life for yourself—"

"I don't want to make a happier life for myself!" he shouted. "I've already got a life—or will have, once my gut stops aching."

"Has the doctor seen you?"

"Yes, he's seen me," he said sullenly. "The old fool's no help. He tells me he doesn't know what's wrong with my gut."

Amberson cast around for words. Richard's face

was drawn and thin, the circles under his eyes darker than the last time she'd seen him.

"Gerald's doing well," she said at last, not knowing what else to say.

"I don't give a buffalo snort what Gerald's doing." Angrily, he picked at the coverlet. "And I'm not giving you a divorce! You had the stupidity to foist him off on me as my son!" She could see Richard getting angrier by the minute.

"I was wrong," she said, looking at the coverlet. Even she was surprised at her admission. She looked up at him and saw the fury in his eyes. "I lied to you. I am sorry, Richard."

"Too freight-haulin' bad!" he cried. "You lied to me and what's done is done! You lying snake!"

She got up from the chair. "I believe we've said enough to each other."

"Not so fast, you two-bit, hurdy-gurdy dancer!"

"Madeline keeps you well informed, Richard."

"Doesn't she, though?" he sneered. "And that's not all she does."

"I don't wish to know the details, Richard," said Amberson. "I just want a divorce."

"Well, you're not getting one! Anything that will make your life difficult is fine with me!"

She paused at his bedside and glared at him. "Do you hate me so much?"

"Yes! Yes, I do!" he cried. "You made a mockery of our wedding vows."

"Wait!" she cried. "It was you who made the mockery of our vows. It was you who was chasing Madeline while I was at home with the baby!"

"Another man's baby!" he cried.

Wearily, she answered, "You're right, Richard. I made a mockery of our vows. You made a mockery of our vows. There, we're even. We both destroyed our marriage. Now will you give me a divorce?"

"No," he answered sullenly. "You have to suffer first."

She laughed bitterly. "I am suffering, you son of a prairie dog. I *am* suffering!"

"Kingsley's death doesn't count," he said. "I want you to suffer more."

She glared at him. "You are a sick man," she said at last. "And I'm not talking about your stomach."

Madeline entered the room. "Now, what do we have here?" she asked in her southern drawl.

Amberson gritted her teeth. "I was just leaving."

"Well, now, hold your horses. I'm sure Richard will see reason about the divorce."

"Don't *you* start in on me," Richard warned her.

"But Richard, aren't you forgetting somethin', darlin'?"

"What's that?"

Amberson watched her warily. How unlike Madeline to aid her cause.

Madeline slanted a malicious glance at Amberson. "Why, since you refuse to sign those wills Fred keeps makin' for you, darlin', if you die and she's still married to you, she gets your ranch and a third of everythin' you own."

There was a stunned silence in the room.

"I know your parents are dead, darlin'. Do you have any sisters or brothers or other children?"

"No."

"Tsk, tsk. Then she gets the whole thing. And when she dies, her bastard child inherits it all. Every tiny bit of your property, darlin'."

"Fred told you that?"

"Uh-huh, he did."

"Fred talks too much."

"She'll get your freight-line business, sho' nuf," added Madeline.

"I worked hard for that freight business!" Richard picked furiously at the coverlet. "Well, you listen to me. I ain't gonna die! You hear me? I'm going to live a long time—outta sheer spite, if I have to. And no unfaithful hurdy-gurdy prancer and her sniveling boy child are going to get my things."

"Then give her the divorce," Madeline shot back.

Amberson stared at the woman in awe. It seemed that Richard had met his match. "She's right, Richard," said Amberson. "If you die and we're still married, I'll get the ranch."

"I won't die!" Richard repeated stubbornly.

Both women kept quiet. Amberson thought of Kingsley. Life was fragile. One never knew when it would end.

"There will be no divorce," said Richard stubbornly. "And I'll figure out a way to fix it so you don't get anything," he told Amberson.

Wearily, Amberson shrugged. This was a battle she'd never expected. As long as she was tied to this man, she could never be free to pursue a life, or love, of her own.

She tried one more time. "Richard, I don't want the ranch. It's your ranch. You deserve it. All I want is a divorce. Give that to me and I'll never bother you again."

"Hah," he snorted. "You lied before. Why should I believe you now?"

"Because I'm telling the truth."

"Bah! You don't know what the truth is."

"Yes. I do. The truth is, I want a divorce," she said.

"You want, you want. What about what I want?"

"What do you want?"

"I want you to be miserable," he cried. "I want you to suffer like I have!"

They were getting nowhere. She walked to the bedroom door and put her hand on the doorknob. "I'll be back, Richard. I will not give up on this until you change your mind. I can't."

"You're wasting your time!"

"It's my time to waste, isn't it?" She went out and closed the door behind her.

"Richard, sugar, give her the divorce."

"Not you, too. I'm warning you, Madeline, I don't want any more divorce talk."

"But you're tied to the woman. You're not free. If you get a divorce, everyone will side with you. They'll call her names every time she shows her face in town."

"Would you like that?"

"Yes," said Madeline thoughtfully. "Yes, I would."

He laughed. "Well, the things it takes to make a woman happy."

She smiled. "You're such an intelligent man, sugar pie," she said. She sat down on the bed and put her arms around him. "Divorce that ol' hag and marry me. I'll take good care of you."

"Oho, so that's what you want, Madeline? To marry me?"

"You know I love you."

He smiled. "You do take good care of me," he allowed.

"I'll take even better care of you when we're married," she promised, clapping her hands together happily.

"I don't want to think about it."

"Richard, darlin', you must. That woman isn't going to go away. You've seen her. She's determined. Give her the divorce and you and I can get married and be happy."

"No."

"No?" She sat back, stunned.

"I said no," he stated deliberately. "Even if I divorced her, I wouldn't marry again. I've had enough of marriage to last a lifetime."

Cold rage crossed her face. "I have to leave for a few minutes, Richard," she said softly. "I am gravely—disappointed."

"You'll get over it," he snorted. He yawned. "I'm hungry. Bring me something to eat."

She bared her teeth at him suddenly. "I certainly will do that." She slipped from the room.

She went down to the hotel kitchen and returned with a tray of cornbread and jam. Going to a polished glass and wood cabinet in the sitting room, Madeline reached for a small pestle. Inside were ground fragments of glass, expensive glass from the Parisian perfumes Richard had given her. She smiled as she ground the pieces of glass a little finer in the mortar with the pestle. She hummed as she sliced the cornbread and carefully blended the glass in with the jam, then spread the jam on the cornbread.

What Richard needed was more ground glass in his food; the amounts she'd been using obviously weren't making him sick enough. The man had the constitution of a mule. And sometimes he made her so angry, like today. And then she had to punish him by putting even more ground glass in his food.

Richard should be agreeing to the divorce any day now. She had it all planned. He'd divorce that tacky hurdy-gurdy dancer and marry her, Madeline, the love of his life. After their marriage, she'd kill him off quickly by increasing his dose of ground glass. Yes, she had it all planned. Even Fred didn't know about it.

But Richard was a stubborn mule, and he needed a few more stomach pains to change his mind.

Still humming, Madeline ground up another piece of glass. One day that ranch would be hers!

Chapter Thirty-nine

Two days later, hot, tired, and dusty, Justin slowed Samson to a trot as they reached the borders of his ranch. The rest of the boys on the freight line had ridden off to Gunpoint to celebrate their payday. But Justin wanted to go home.

Home.

He rode slowly so he could savor the land, *his* land now. The grass was green and thick, as high as a man's knees. It would make excellent feed for many cattle. His ranch should do well.

It made a man feel good to have his own land. For the first time since the war had ended, Justin felt he belonged. He had a right to a place. He owned land. It was hard-won and it was his. His family had always owned land, ever since his great-grandfather had first settled in America. Justin was keeping that powerful family tradition alive. He had his own land.

On the freight line, Whiskers and some of the boys

had teased him about buying the ranch. Why, set- tlers could get 160 acres of free government land just by putting a sod house on it and planting some wheat!

But Justin didn't want to grow wheat. He wanted to raise cattle. And he needed a reliable source of water on his property to do so. His creek supplied that. And his ranch had a house, a fine log house, already built. Yes, he'd paid top price for the land, but he'd gotten a good bargain.

And, best of all, he had a safe place to keep his son and the mother of his son. It had taken the bank robbery in Gunpoint to show him just how danger- ous that town was for a woman and child.

Warm satisfaction spread through his breast at the thought of Amberson and Gerald. His time away from them on the freight line was worth it if he could make a better life for them.

With the money he'd made on the freight line, he'd made arrangements to purchase twenty head of cat- tle. The cattle should be arriving next week. And he'd already saved enough money to pay off the rest of what he'd owed Old Man McManus. Yes, life was good.

Samson trotted along at a good pace and soon they came abreast of the stream that ran through Justin's land. Here and there a few cottonwoods and aspens grew along its banks, but mostly it was grass that bordered the creek. The spring, where his water sur- faced from the ground, was quite some distance from the house and the creek meandered along, so he followed it, listening to the birds calling out in the cottonwoods in the midday heat. He surprised a pair of ducks who flew off, quacking.

He rode out from behind a cottonwood and sawed on Samson's reins. "Whoa, boy."

There, standing knee-deep in the middle of the stream where it widened into a pond, stood Miss Amberson. With her dress hiked up to her thighs, she grimly wrung out one of his shirts.

He smiled to himself. She looked a picture, she did, with her hair loose and her dress wet and clinging like that. "Giddap, Samson," he murmured. They moved forward and he gave a few bird whistles, so as to warn her of their approach.

She looked up and saw him, and he was pleased to see a happy little smile cross her face before she could hide it.

"Afternoon, ma'am," he said politely, touching the tip of his hat as he rode closer.

"Afternoon," she said, and he was surprised that she seemed so shy.

He reined in Samson and dismounted. He let the reins drag on the ground and walked over to her, watching her all the while. My, but she was a sight for his eyes. He'd been away too long.

Shivers raced up and down Amberson's spine as she watched Justin prowl toward her. He looked so strong, his broad shoulders filling out his brown-and-white vest admirably, and she could see the canvas-clad muscles of his legs flex as he walked. His green eyes glittered and she found herself catching her breath.

"Just can't stay away from doin' laundry, can you?" he asked.

She laughed. She felt so free, here, in the sun, standing in the cool water, and having this man so close to her. "I thought I'd try washing clothes without all the hot water and the tub."

He glanced around at the clothes spread on the grass. "Seems to work all right," he observed. He took off his hat.

"Want me to wash your hat?" she asked playfully, walking toward him. She reached for it. Dusty, brown, it had been punched several times and definitely needed a cleaning.

"Don't you touch my hat," he growled, snatching the hat out of reach.

"It needs a good wash," she said seriously.

"Doesn't."

"Does." She lunged for the hat and grabbed it, running out of his grasp.

She waded out to the middle of the pond, holding the wretched hat above the water. "In it goes," she cooed.

"Come back here."

"Come and get it," she taunted.

"If I go in that water, I'm going to get more than my hat back," he warned.

She smiled in anticipation and licked her lips.

He pulled off his boots, watching her the while. Next, he peeled off his brown-and-white cowhide vest. Now he was wearing only his shirt and pants. He was serious about getting his hat back, she could tell.

She glanced at it. Maybe she shouldn't wash it; maybe the water would destroy it.

He waded in and she started backing up, deeper into the pond. She waved the hat coyly, almost unable to believe it was big, bad Justin she was teasing. But the playful light in his green eyes told her he was challenged, and he wanted his hat back. He reached for her and she jumped aside, though the water made her movements clumsy. His, too, she noted.

"Your pants are wet," she observed as he circled closer.

"Saves you the trouble of washing them."

"Who says I was going to wash your clothes? I only wash mine!"

"That so?" He grinned and lunged for her again.

"Hey!" she said. "You're supposed to go after the hat."

"Not me. I've got better things to go after." He swiped at her, barely missing her.

"No fair, Justin," she said nervously. The water was getting deeper, almost to her hips, and she had to move slowly.

He managed to grasp her dress this time, but she pulled away from him by going a little deeper in the water; he let go. "Oh. As soon as the little lady starts losing the contest, it's not fair."

"I'm not going to lose," she said mischievously, holding the hat higher and waving it.

"We'll see about that." He was moving toward her steadily. "Know how to swim?" he asked conversationally.

She glanced around. How deep was this water?

"I can swim," she assured him. "Oooh," she squealed. "A fish just brushed my leg!"

He threw himself at her, startling her, and she tried to plunge away from him, but he caught her up. "You can't have your hat," she cried gaily.

He lifted her up in his arms. "To hell with the hat."

He started wading toward the shore, with her in his arms. "Put me down!" She giggled. "Put me down, Justin!" Fortunately, she still had his hat. She whapped him softly across the head with it. He pretended to fall backwards, taking her with him. There was a huge splash.

"Justin!" she cried, struggling to get to her feet. "Look what you've done!"

"What?"

"My dress!" She pulled the dripping, sopping mess away from her skin. Her hair streamed down her breasts and back.

He laughed. "Give me my hat, woman."

She threw it at him and it plopped in the water. He winced. "It was a good hat," he said mournfully.

"It was wretched!"

"I'll have to get you now," he said, moving toward her.

She began backing toward the bank of the pond. "No, Justin!" Hands out in a futile gesture to stop him, she tried to turn and run, but the water slowed her down.

He grabbed her again. "Aha! Got you!"

"No, no," she squealed, kicking water into foam.

"Yes, yes," he mimicked. Holding her firmly in his strong arms, he carried her to the bank of the pond. Then he set her on her feet, but he didn't let her out of the circle of his arms.

She squirmed, trying to get loose, but he only held her tighter. Their wet bodies slid against one another. She stopped squirming when she felt his leg between hers. She'd been a married woman. She knew what else she was feeling.

"Uh, Justin . . ." she whispered, looking up at him.

His laughing green eyes gazed into hers. He lowered his face, bringing his lips to touch hers.

His lips were soft, then firmer. He pressed the full length of her against him as his mouth plundered hers.

"Oh, Justin," she murmured, weakening. His lips

felt so good. His touch . . . she hadn't realized how much she'd longed for him to hold her.

He kissed her again, then his lips moved up the side of her cheek, along her ear line.

"Justin, we must stop—"

"Can't—" he muttered, kissing her avidly.

"Justin." She sighed, and pushed at him. He didn't budge. "We must stop."

"We're adults," he said, his voice low. "We can do what we want."

Gripping his shoulders, she gave in to his kiss. His hands moved up and down her back, caressing her. She felt herself melting in his embrace. He put his hands on her buttocks and pulled her into his need. "Ah, Justin," she sighed. "You feel so good."

"So do you," he murmured. His hands were doing treacherous things to her body. Her head felt heavy and she pressed herself closer to him, wanting everything she knew he could give her.

"I've got to have you," he murmured raggedly.

"Oh, yes," she whispered, straining against him. He kissed her neck and she arched back to allow him better access to her throat.

Lord, he felt good. His hands cupped her breasts, breasts that were fuller since Gerald's birth. Gerald.

Wait a minute, thought Amberson. This is Justin. I can't let him seduce me again. I can't!

Desperate to stop him, because her own body was acting such a traitor and her head still swam from the powerful tonic he was to her, she said, "All right, Justin, let's have another baby."

He drew his head back. "What?" Confusion reigned in his green eyes. "What did you say?"

"I said, 'Let's have another baby.' "

He dropped his arms. "Let's think about this, Amberson," he said seriously.

She smiled a crooked little smile. Her body still throbbed from his touch. "Don't you want to make another baby with me, Justin?"

"It's not that I don't—that is—I want—"

Reluctantly, she pushed him away from her. "Not exactly seduction in the moonlight, is it?"

He looked rueful. "No," he answered finally, "it's not."

"I will not make love to you without marriage, Justin. I did that once and it was disastrous for me, as you know. I want a secure home for my child or children, not some happy little romp now and then."

He frowned. "It wasn't going to be a happy little romp—"

"It was starting to be."

He grinned. "It was, wasn't it?"

She smiled slowly. He was a rogue, for sure. "And until I'm divorced from Richard," she said sadly, "I'm not free to marry another man."

Are you crazy? cried a little voice in her mind. Look at him! Don't give up a man like this for such a paltry reason!

But it wasn't a paltry reason. Gerald wasn't paltry. And it had only taken one time in the moonlight to make Gerald. If she was going to live a better, honest life, she had to start now.

Justin searched her eyes, but she held firm. He didn't answer her. He walked gingerly over to the water's edge and picked up his hat. It was a soggy mess.

"This is yours," he said and threw it at her.

She jumped aside. The hat was ruined.

He walked over and picked up his vest and boots. "Want a ride back to the house?"

He didn't want to talk about it—didn't want to talk about what they'd almost done—again. Very well, she would keep quiet too.

They walked over to the horse. Justin climbed on, then helped her up onto Samson's back. She put her arms around Justin's waist and settled her chin on his shoulder. Closing her eyes, she tried to imagine they were lovers.

"Have you talked to Richard?"

Her eyes flew open. "What about?"

"About a divorce."

"Yes, I have." She told him about going twice to see Richard at the Two Star Hotel and of her lack of success in getting him to agree to a divorce.

"Stay away from him, Amberson," warned Justin. "Richard is cruel. I don't trust him and neither should you," he reminded her.

She was silent for a time. "Richard has hit me before," she said in a small voice.

Justin halted Samson "When did he hit you?"

"Various times. Twice after you arrived at the Triple R."

Justin swore a savage oath. "That day, when you came in from the barn—"

"And one time when you were out in the yard. I—I kept to myself. We'd had a fight—"

"I remember," said Justin shortly. "That son of a bitch. Stay away from him, Amberson. He's a sick man, and I'm talking about his mind."

She kept silent.

"Promise me you won't go and talk to him. He's dangerous." She heard the concern in Justin's voice. He nudged the horse forward.

"But Justin, if I don't go, he won't give me a divorce. And then I'll die alone," she wailed. The words slipped out before she could stop them.

"Is that what you're afraid of? Dying alone?"

"No," she answered steadily. "Living alone."

"I can fix that."

"I'm sure you can."

"Let me."

"No."

Now it was his turn to be silent. She wondered what he was thinking, but when they reached the ranch house, he had given her no sign of his thoughts. He slid off Samson, then helped her down. "We'll go back later for the clothes, after they've dried," he told her.

She nodded and went into the house. Beau and the baby were on the floor, playing with a set of wooden blocks.

Beau glanced up at her and stared. "Missus Rowan! You—why you are all wet. Your hair—" He turned to see Justin enter. Justin, hair and clothes soaked, winked as he disappeared into his bedroom.

Beau's eyes narrowed. "I'll be sleeping in front of your door tonight, Missus Rowan. With my rifle."

"Good idea, Beau," she said. "*Very* good idea."

Chapter Forty

Justin knocked on the door of Room Eight.

Fred Knox opened the door.

"I've come to speak with Richard Rowan," said Justin. What the hell was Fred Knox doing here?

Knox opened the door wider. "Come in. I was just leaving." He held a handful of papers to one side, as though hiding them from Justin.

Justin stepped inside. The place was fixed up nice, much better than the Hank Parker Hotel room he'd rented for himself and Gerald.

The attorney put on his hat, nodded to Justin, and went out, closing the door quietly behind him.

"Fred?" called a woman's voice from the bedroom.

Justin cleared his throat. "He's gone."

A blond woman hurried from the bedroom. She halted. "Who are you?"

He went to touch the tip of his hat. Dang, he'd forgotten he wasn't wearing one. "My name is Justin

Harbinger," he said. He recognized her from Hinckley's General Store, that day long ago. Rowan's mistress.

Her eyes narrowed. "Justin Harbinger? And what brings you to these rooms, sir?" She backed up a little and glanced at the bedroom door. "State your business."

"My business is with Mr. Rowan," he answered. "I'd like to speak with him."

She eyed him. "What about?"

Rowan's mistress was a curious one. "Well, now," he said pleasantly, "that's between Mr. Rowan and myself. Isn't it?"

She smiled. "I like a man who's tall and strong." Again she slanted a glance at the bedroom. "I'll tell Mr. Rowan you're here to see him." She disappeared into the bedroom.

He waited and could hear low murmurings coming from the room.

The mistress reappeared. "Mr. Rowan will see you now."

"Thank you." She gave him an approving glance as he walked past her. He shut the door firmly behind him.

"Harbinger, you stinking skunk. What are you doing here? I told you I never wanted to see you skulking around again!"

Rowan looked sunken and pale, lying in the bed like that. Justin had seen better-looking corpses on the battlefield. "Good day to you, Rowan." He didn't want this visit to turn into a name-calling tirade.

"I paid you every cent I owed you in wages," said Rowan. "Don't you come whining to me for more money. I'll throw you out on your—"

"You still owe me back wages, Rowan," interrupted Justin. "But I didn't come looking for money."

"What did you come for?" fretted Rowan.

"I came to ask you to give Mrs. Rowan a divorce."

A cagey look crossed the sick man's face. "Oh? So you can marry her, I suppose?"

Justin shrugged. He had no intention of sharing his future plans with Rowan.

There was a tiny rattling sound at the keyhole of the door. Justin shifted, so his back was between the door and the sick man.

Rowan was laughing, a coughing, hacking laugh. "Hah! That is good," he chortled, when he could finally speak. "The lovelorn cowboy coming to appeal for the virtuous woman's release." He started laughing again.

When he was done, he said, "Get out of here, Harbinger."

"You haven't heard me out yet, Rowan." Justin kept his feet planted on the carpet.

"There's more?"

"Yes. I didn't come just to ask you to divorce her."

"Oh?"

"No. I came to make you a deal."

"What kind of deal?" The sick man sat up a little straighter on the fluffy cushions. His wan face showed interest.

Justin took a breath. "I'll give you my ranch. You give Amberson her freedom."

"Madeline!" yelled Rowan. "Get in here!"

The door opened immediately and Madeline hurried in. "Yes, sugar?" She went over to the chair by the bed and sat down in it.

"Listen to this, Madeline," chortled Rowan. The man was so excited, he was squirming around in the bed. "Tell her," he ordered Justin.

Justin tightened his lips. He wasn't about to make a fool of himself for the benefit of entertaining Rowan and his mistress.

When Justin said nothing, Rowan told her, "This cowboy here just offered me his ranch in return for me giving that snake a divorce! Isn't that funny?"

Madeline beamed at Justin. "Why, I think it's a charmin' idea. I'll have Fred draw up the papers right away."

Justin smiled grimly at her.

"You nitwit!" replied Rowan. "I'm not going to give that two-timing snake a divorce and that's final!"

Madeline's lips pressed shut and she said nothing, but she radiated disapproval.

Justin spoke up. "There's twenty head of cattle coming next week. I'll throw them into the deal. Think about it," he told Rowan. "That will increase your herd by another twenty percent."

Rowan glared at him. "I've thought about it and the answer is still no!"

Justin shook his head. Rowan was determined; he'd give him that much.

"That hurdy-gurdy dancer doesn't deserve to be free to do what she wants. She lied to me about that b—" he slid a cautious glance at Justin "—baby, and I want to see her suffer. If she wants a divorce so bad, she can damn well go without!" He looked almost gleeful.

"Darlin'," said Madeline, in a low, husky voice. Both men turned. She smiled, basking in the attention. "Think about this, darlin'. Think about your land and holdings. Here's a chance to increase the size of your ranch. You need more cattle," she pointed out gently. "What kind of cattle did you purchase, Mr. Harbinger?"

"Longhorns."

"Longhorns. How lovely." She beamed at Rowan. "You always liked longhorns, darlin'."

"Yeah. But I like revenge better."

A tiny frown marred Madeline's perfect forehead. "Richard," she said, "I beg you to reconsider. This is an important matter that Mr. Harbinger has brought to your attention."

"Not to me." Rowan actually looked happy.

Justin winced. He was getting nowhere with Rowan. The man would never give Amberson a divorce. Sadness enveloped Justin. When he'd come here with the idea of offering Rowan his ranch, it had meant giving up everything he valued so Amberson could be free. He didn't even know if she'd marry him if she was free, but he'd hoped to have that chance. Rowan had killed even that slim hope.

"I'll be leaving now," he told them both. Rowan looked gleeful, Madeline disappointed.

"But before I leave, I've got one more thing to say to you." He paused and eyed Rowan. "Stay away from Miss Amberson. I know you've hit her in the past. That stops now! If you even touch her . . . let me put it this way—you won't need to worry about your old age."

"You threatening me, Harbinger?" demanded Rowan.

"I am," answered Justin. "Stay away from Miss Amberson."

Rowan kept quiet.

"I will see you to the door, sir." Miss Madeline rose from her chair, a determined look on her face.

Justin nodded and turned his back on Rowan. He followed Miss Madeline out of the room.

She paused in the larger room. Her face was a

stolid mask, but he could see lively anger glimmering in those blue eyes. She didn't bother to walk him to the door, but ignored him and went to a highly polished wood and glass cabinet. Knickknacks of shepherds and princesses sat on the top of the cabinet. Inside were red, blue, white, and green glass bottles lined along the back of it.

She took out a little stone cup and some fragments of glass from the cabinet and set them next to a stack of cornbread. Seeing she was preoccupied, Justin went over to the main door to leave. As he did so, he saw Rowan staggering to the chamber pot. Rowan scowled at him and glared at his mistress.

Suddenly Rowan's face blanched and Justin thought the man would pass out. He's weakened from lying around in bed, thought Justin. He started to approach Rowan, to offer him help, but the man, rage in his eyes, waved him away, all the while keeping his furious gaze on his mistress.

Madeline, unaware that Rowan watched her, noisily ground something in the little stone cup. Pieces of broken glass lay on the top of the cabinet.

Something is amiss between those two, thought Justin, as he hastily slipped out the door.

He clenched his fists as he walked out the hotel's double doors. Amberson was trapped. Rowan's refusal to give her a divorce trapped her as neatly as any snare he knew of. And her determination to live an honorable life, not to involve herself with another man until she was legally free to do so, further trapped her. It was a bleak outlook for them all, he realized—for Amberson, for their child, and for Justin.

Chapter Forty-one

"To what do I owe the honor of this fine supper, darlin'?"

Richard grunted. He's puny tonight, thought Madeline. And mean and peevish and spiteful. I'll be glad when he's divorced that hussy and married me. Fred promised me he'd draw up the divorce papers and the will.

"It's unusual for you to order a special supper," she pressed.

Richard tried to smile, but his attempt was feeble. Mostly he just looked tired. "I realize this has not been the best of times for you," he answered.

Since when did he think about what was best for her? "Are you feelin' poorly, darlin'?" He looked terrible. And she was amazed that he was showing so little effect after all the glass she'd been feeding him. As well as putting the glass in the cornbread, she also put it in his vegetables and meats and puddings. She longed for the day when he would be so sick that he'd grovel and do anything she told him to do.

And though he'd surprised her with this meal, she'd been able to sprinkle some glass in the food just after the hotel houseboy left and while Richard was fussing in the bedroom.

"You've been holed up in this hotel room for quite a few days," he told her. "I thought, since I couldn't take you down to the dining room, that we could have a special little celebration up here. Just the two of us."

She smiled. How unlike him.

"Ever since that man visited us—what was his name?"

"Harbinger," Richard prompted.

"Yes, ever since Mr. Harbinger visited us you've been different."

Richard pinned her with gleaming blue eyes. "Have I?"

"Yes, darlin', you have. Tell little ol' me what you're frettin' about."

He grimaced. "Nothing that a little wine won't fix."

That sounded more like the old Richard. She smiled and poured a glass of wine for him.

"Pour one for yourself, too," he said. She poured.

He took a gulp of his wine. She smiled. He gasped a little and said, "I'm cold. Get me my shawl."

Amused that he would even admit to having a shawl, she sauntered into the bedroom and returned with a knitted pea green shawl. He looked like an old woman in it, a foolish old woman.

"Here, sugar." She placed it carefully around his shoulders, as though he was the most precious thing in the world to her, and bent down to kiss the top of his head.

He groaned and said, "I'm not feeling so good, Madeline."

"I know, darlin', I know," she answered softly. "We'll have that doctor come and look at you again. Maybe he can tell us what's wrong."

"Pshaw," muttered Richard. "That doctor doesn't know anything. He's been here three times and he still can't tell me what's wrong."

There was a distinct, unpleasant whine in Richard's voice. It set her teeth on edge.

"What was Beau doin' here today?" she asked, to change the subject.

"What do you mean?" Richard glanced up at her from under bushy brows.

She shrugged. "Nothin', sugar. I saw him leaving here when I returned from shoppin' at the mercantile."

"Oh, that." Richard picked at his stew. "He was just visiting, for old times' sake. Beau was always my best cowhand, you know."

"No, I didn't know," she answered idly, picking at her stew. "I thought that Mr. Harbinger was your best cowhand."

He almost choked on his food and she had to hide a laugh. Needling him about other men, especially other virile, handsome men, was always entertaining. Maybe once she was married to Richard, she'd take up with Harbinger. She'd have to pick some young stud for her pleasure. Richard was useless.

"Did you sign those papers Fred brought over, darlin'?" she asked. She chewed on a piece of cornbread, careful to keep to the edges of it. The glass was inside, in the middle. She offered Richard some cornbread. He was just about to bite into it when he said, "What papers?"

"The papers Fred brought. I put them on the bureau, in the bedroom. Fred wanted you to sign them."

He set down the cornbread and waved a hand. "Fred's always havin' me sign papers," he said. "I didn't sign them, no."

She frowned in disappointment. Those papers were for the divorce action against that two-bit hurdy-gurdy dancer. There was also a will slipped in there that she hoped he'd sign without knowing. The will left everything to her. She'd have to get him drunk tonight and have him sign the papers then. That should work.

"Your appetite is healthy tonight, sugar pie."

He ignored her and lifted his glass of wine. "A toast," he proclaimed.

She grimaced. "I don't really like wine, sugar."

"Aw, drink it tonight," he told her. "It's my little way of treating you to something nice."

"I'd like perfume better," she said, pouting. "French perfume."

"This is French wine." He chuckled. "I know you like that perfume, sweet thing. Haven't I bought you enough of it?" He waved a hand at the glass bottles lining the cabinet.

She lifted her glass. "You can never have enough perfume," she said coquettishly. He hadn't called her "sweet thing" for at least a fortnight. It was a name she detested, but he always said it when he was feeling in the best of moods toward her.

"My toast tonight," he said, looking fondly into her eyes, "is this: to someone who deserves the something special she's going to get." He smiled lovingly and took a drink of wine.

"Why, darlin'," she said, taking a sip, "whatever are you goin' to buy me?"

"You'll see."

She clapped her hands together. "You have a surprise for me? For little ol' me?" He hadn't bought her a gift in so long, she thought he'd forgotten how.

"So that's what Beau was doin' here today," she crowed.

"You bright little sweet thing. You figured it out." He reached across the table and they clinked glasses. She smiled at him and tasted the wine, happy that he was at last paying some attention to her. She hoped her gift was something expensive. "I like jewelry," she reminded him.

He chuckled. "I know you do."

"Necklaces, especially." She touched the gold filigree leaf on a gold chain that encircled her neck.

"You want another necklace?" he asked casually.

"Is that what the surprise is?"

"No. But you'll find out," he assured her. He took a drink of his wine.

She took another sip of the wine and made a face. "I don't usually drink. . . ."

"Sweet thing, if you want your present, you have to be good to Daddy," he told her.

She smiled. "I'll be good," she promised. "I'll be very, very good." She took a drink of wine, bigger this time. Seeing him beaming at her, she drank again.

He looked satisfied under those bushy brows. She was careful to eat only the potatoes and carrots in the stew. She reached across his plate and daintily sliced up a large piece of meat for him. She distinctly remembered sprinkling glass on it. "Here," she said solicitously, holding a forkful of meat to his mouth. "Eat this fine stew."

He eyed her, then took a big bite. He chewed it slowly.

She smiled, careful to look lovingly at him. "If you eat well, I'm sure you'll get strong again soon."

"Think so?" he asked.

"I'm certain of it," she said.

He lifted a forkful of carrots to his lips. He reached for his cornbread again and she followed it with her eyes as he raised it to his lips. "You like cornbread," she said.

"Always have," he agreed. "Here, you have some." He handed her a piece of cornbread from the plate.

She giggled and clapped her hands. "Why, darlin', I already have some."

"Have some more."

"If you insist."

"I do."

With a grimace she took the second piece of cornbread, trying to make sure she ate only from the edge.

He took a sip of his wine. "Here, sweet thing," he said, "wash it down with this." He held her glass up to her lips, and she had no choice but to drink. Some of it spilled down her chin.

"Richard," she exclaimed. "Not so much!" She dabbed at her chin with her white linen napkin which was embroidered with two white stars.

"Sorry," he said, unperturbed. "I guess I'm just so anxious for you to see your present."

"Can you give me a hint?"

"No. No hints."

"Not even one?"

"None."

She pouted while they ate the rest of the meal in silence. He refilled her glass and she drank some more wine, but it didn't taste very good so she only drank half a glass. "Richard," she said, putting her hand to her forehead. "I—I don't feel very well."

"No?" he asked. "Why don't you lie down on the bed? Maybe you'll feel better."

She got up and staggered toward the bedroom. She gasped and held her stomach. "My belly hurts," she complained.

He rose, too. "I'll help you," he offered. He took her arm and, shuffling, led her to the bed.

"I feel sick," he complained, after helping her onto the wide, comforter-strewn bed. "My gut hurts."

It should, she thought. You swallowed about six pieces of ground-up glass tonight.

He lay down beside her, bent over and holding his stomach.

"Everything's blurry. I can't see very well," she said. "And my stomach, it hurts so bad. God, Richard, it hurts!" she cried. "Call the doctor. Do something!" Her head rolled back and forth as she tried to shut out the pain.

"I already have." His quiet answer awoke a sense of danger in her. Wordlessly, he huddled on the bed beside her.

"What? What have you done, Richard?" she asked wildly. "Water! I need water!"

"You're not getting any." He groaned.

"Get me some water, Richard," she pleaded.

"How about some wine?"

"Water," she insisted. "Oh, God, I'm thirsty, so thirsty." She lay back moaning, pressing her stomach with her arms.

"You're getting what you deserve." He laughed.

"Your gut hurts, does it? What about my gut? What about the weeks of pain I've endured?" He stifled a groan.

"What are you talking about? I *need water!*"

"Forget the water, Madeline. You just drank rat poison. A fitting end to a rat like you. You're going to die!"

"What?" she screamed. "Goddamn you, Richard!"

"He already has. He gave you to me, didn't He?" said Richard. "But He'll damn you too, sweet thing, just see if He doesn't. Ooh, my gut. It shouldn't be hurting me."

"Why?"

"I didn't eat the cornbread."

"You knew!" She held her stomach, trying to stop the terrible pains that were ripping at her very center.

"Yeah, I knew, you lying bitch. You poisoned me. You fed me ground glass in the cornbread. I saw you."

"So that's it," she gasped. "That's why you didn't eat it." The pain in her stomach receded a little, now. Her mouth felt dry, dry as a desert. She gripped her belly. The pain would come back again. She knew it would. It was coming in waves.

"Yeah. I know you, Madeline."

"No, you don't, you bastard," she snarled. "You're going to die too. I put ground glass in the meat!"

"You bitch!"

"If I'm going to die, Richard—" She could feel the pains coming again. Bad, oh God, they were bad. "I'm going to tell you something. I hate you, Richard. I detest you. You can't do anything! You can't kiss, you can't perform like a man! I loathe you. There's nothing about you I ever liked." God, the pain was ripping at her; she wanted to die. Get the pain over with. Over with. "It was all an act. . . . I wanted your money. . . ."

Moaning, he brought up his legs. "Yeah? Well, you're the one dying, not me!" He stifled a groan. He was clutching his stomach too.

"I was going to marry you and kill you off . . . get the ranch—" She grimaced. "Maybe marry Harbinger. Oh, God."

"Harbinger? That two-bit saddle bum?"

She gave a groan. "So now Miss Amberson, the two-bit hurdy-gurdy girl, gets it—" The pain ripped through her. It felt like her stomach was being turned inside out. "Miss Amberson gets the ranch—"

"Shut up!" he cried. "I'm not gonna die!" He held his gut. They were both holding their innards. His face looked strange. Pale, wan, and he kept grimacing.

He writhed around, flinging out his limbs now and then. She could barely feel where he struck her with his flailing legs.

"Her baby . . ." She was losing her fight; she could feel her life slipping away. "Bastard's . . . gettin' . . . the ranch . . ." She felt a croaky laugh well up.

"Shut up!" he howled. "Shut up! Oh, my gut, my gut . . ." His legs hit hers, his body jerking in spasms.

She could feel something burgeoning up inside her, trying to get out. Suddenly she blurted out a last, horrible chuckle; then everything went black.

Chapter Forty-two

"Where are you going, Justin?" Amberson was watching him. He'd been restless all morning.

"I'm going into town."

Fear spiraled through her. This was what Richard would do—go into Gunpoint.

She fell silent and tried to concentrate on spooning the baby's mashed carrots into his little mouth. If Justin was going into Gunpoint, she wouldn't stop him.

Justin put on his brown-and-white cowhide vest and the new brown slouch hat he'd bought at Hinckley's General Store. She smiled sadly, thinking of the day they'd played in the river, when she'd ruined his old one.

Beau spoke up. "I'll come with you."

Amberson glanced at him, wondering if her self-appointed protector was trying to keep Justin from looking for another woman in Gunpoint to satisfy

342

his needs. She fed another spoonful of carrot mush to Gerald; her hand shook.

Justin walked over to her. "I'm not going to Gunpoint to chase women," he told her. "So get that thought out of your head."

She stared at him. "I—I—"

He grinned. "I'm not Richard." His green eyes were warm.

She smiled back. "No, you're not. Thank the Lord."

He stroked her hair and then he said to Beau, "Let's go."

She missed the touch of his hand.

He paused in the doorway. "I'm going to call on Richard," he told her. "I've got some business with him."

She nodded. She didn't think she wanted to know what his business was.

The short cowboy pulled on his boots. "I'm gonna visit Richard too," he told Amberson. "He wasn't feelin' so good last time I saw him."

"Yes, I know he's not been well."

"There's rats in that hotel," said Beau. "He had me bring him some rat poison."

"Rats? Such a nice hotel too," marveled Amberson.

She and Gerald stood on the porch and watched them ride off, Justin on his big bay and Beau riding his paint pony. "We're very fortunate," she told Gerald. "We have people who care about us."

Justin mounted the stairs two at a time. He heard Beau puffing along behind him, several steps below. The sooner this interview was over, the better.

He waited at the landing for the little cowboy.

"What's the hurry?" demanded Beau.

"Sorry. Just anxious, I guess," admitted Justin.

They knocked on the door of Room Eight.

"Must have gone out," said Beau when no one answered.

"I didn't think Richard was healthy enough to go anywhere," answered Justin. He knocked again.

They knocked several more times. Finally, Justin said, "Let's come back later. Maybe they're downstairs in the restaurant or over at the General Store."

They checked the dining room and walked around town, but they didn't find Richard or Madeline. When they'd been to all the likely places, Justin said, "Let's go back to the hotel. Maybe they're there by now."

They returned to the hotel and knocked several times on the door of Room Eight. There was no answer.

Justin, puzzled as to where they could be, said, "Maybe we should talk to the hotel clerk."

Beau held up a key.

"Where'd you get that?"

"Richard gave it to me the other day, when he asked me to bring him the rat poison. Gave me a key and said I could come in whenever *she* wasn't home."

By "she" Beau meant Madeline, guessed Justin.

Justin snatched the key from the short cowboy. He unlocked the door and swung it open slowly. "Madeline? Richard?"

"Are you in there?" called Beau.

"Something smells bad," said Justin. A feeling of dread washed over him. He'd smelled that odor in the war, after battles, when dead bodies covered the fields.

"I don't think this is so good," he muttered, walking slowly into the suite. On the table were the dried remains of a meal.

"Mr. Rowan? Miss Mueler?"

They went to the bedroom; the door was half-open.

"Smells bad," observed Beau. "Real bad."

Two bodies lay on the bed, Madeline on her side, in a curled up position, and Richard on his back, one arm over his head, the other holding his stomach. His wide open, glassy eyes stared at the ceiling.

"They're dead," muttered Justin.

"My God!" whispered Beau. "What happened?"

"I don't know. I think we'd better call the sheriff," said Justin.

"What about?" came a voice behind them. Justin whirled. Standing in the suite was Fred Knox, and behind him hovered one of the Celestial houseboys.

Knox approached the bed. "So they're both dead," he said slowly. He did not seem surprised.

Beau edged over to the bureau.

Knox glanced around the room and spied Beau. "What are you doing? What's that you put in your pocket?" He hurried over to the bureau and absently scooped some papers off the top, keeping his attention on Beau the whole time. "Show us what you put in your pocket!" he demanded.

Reluctantly, Beau pulled his hand out and showed the half-empty brown bottle.

"What's that?" asked Fred Knox with a frown.

"Rat poison," said Beau with a sigh.

"Rat poison!" Knox's narrowed gaze went to the bed and back to Beau. "That's how they died?"

Beau shrugged.

Justin said, "We don't know how they died. That's a matter for the sheriff."

"Tell me why you were hiding that bottle of rat poison!" Fred Knox demanded of Beau.

345

"I wasn't hiding it," protested Beau. "I lent it to Mr. Rowan. I want it back, is all."

Knox regarded him suspiciously, then said, "All right, it can't be that important. You can take it."

Beau stuffed the brown bottle back in his pocket.

Fred Knox turned to Justin. Justin saw a cunning in those brown eyes that he immediately distrusted. The rat poison *was* important. Why was Knox pretending it wasn't?

Justin was inclined to let Beau take the poison away. That way the cowhand would not be under suspicion of murder. But why would Knox let it go?

"I'll go call the sheriff," Fred Knox told Justin. He headed for the door. "You, get out of here!" he ordered the thin houseboy. The man ran.

Knox chuckled and said, "Sheriff Logan will want to ask you folks some questions. Wait here." Then he was gone.

"That attorney fellow seems to think he's in charge," said Beau.

"Yeah," answered Justin. "Let's wait out in the hall."

They waited a short while and then Fred Knox arrived with Sheriff Logan. "What's this I hear about two dead people?" cried the sheriff.

"In the bedroom," pointed out Justin.

The sheriff went in. "Whew. Smells pretty bad," he said. "I wonder how long they've been dead?"

"Last time I saw them was a week ago," Justin said with a shrug.

"What were you doing here today?" asked the sheriff.

"Came to discuss business with Mr. Rowan. There was no answer when we arrived the first time. So we came back about twenty minutes ago and found this."

The sheriff frowned. "Well, something sure as hell happened. And by the smell of it, they've been dead at least a day."

"Or longer," added Justin. "Smells like the battle-field," he explained at the sheriff's curious glance.

The sheriff glanced around the room. "There's no gunshot wounds," he mused aloud. "There's nothing to show how the hell they died."

Justin didn't say anything. If he mentioned the rat poison, Beau would be under suspicion of murder, and Justin knew the short cowboy was not the mur-derer. Someone else was.

Sheriff Logan scratched his head. "Well," he said at last, "can't say what I'm going to do about this. Mr. Rowan was well-known about town and folks will wonder how he died. The woman, though, I don't recognize. Anyone know who she was?"

Knox spoke up. "She was my sister."

Justin glanced at the attorney. Knox stood, hands folded together quietly, in a respectful pose.

The sheriff sighed. "Well, can't do much else around here," he said dismissively. He waved a hand. "I guess we'd better go ahead and bury them."

Fred Knox said he would be making arrangements with Eddie's Embalming Emporium. That taken care of, Justin and Beau left.

When they were out on the boardwalk Beau asked nervously, "You reckon the sheriff thinks anything's suspicious?"

"Yeah, he probably does," answered Justin. "But he doesn't know what happened the way you and I do."

"What happened?" asked Beau.

Justin halted and looked at him. "Why, Rowan and his mistress drank rat poison. Probably murder-suicide or suicide-suicide. What else can it be?"

Beau regarded him thoughtfully. "Yeah," he agreed. "I sure wish I hadn't brought him that rat poison, though."

"Yeah," said Justin grimly. "Well, don't worry about it. I won't be telling anyone," said Justin.

"But what about Fred Knox?"

"That remains to be seen," answered Justin uneasily. "But I bet Knox wants it hushed up. It was his sister. He probably doesn't want the scandal of folks knowing what happened to her."

"Maybe Knox killed them."

"Hell," muttered Justin, "if you think about it, anyone could have killed them. Someone could have visited them in their hotel, poured the rat poison in their food or drinks, and there you have it . . . dead. Anyone in the town, anyone at all."

"Someone they know," said Beau. "Not just anyone."

Justin glanced at him. "You or me too," he said. "I hope the sheriff just lets this go and doesn't pursue it."

"I hope so too," answered Beau.

Chapter Forty-three

It was a solemn occasion, thought Amberson, on the day that Richard Rowan and Madeline Mueler were buried in Gunpoint's small cemetery on a dusty hillside a mile from town. The Reverend Pippin presided over the town's motley inhabitants—at least, those who showed up to mourn the passing of one of its richest citizens.

The Parker family was there; Hinckley, his gaze behind his round glasses vacant and staring; Loser Larry, looking lost as he stood back a little from the rest of the family; Hank, a young man with thinning hair and a nervous manner; Joe, standing next to tall Estelle, who looked elegant in black, and Pa and Ma. Pa parked Ma in a chair and proceeded to move through the crowd, visiting here and there. The Parker daughter, Annabelle, clung to her banker husband's arm. Only Clive was missing.

Holy Harry Parker approached the coffin, and Amberson overheard him mutter something about hell-fire and damnation. Amberson thought he probably had the right of it, at least in Richard's case.

Fred Knox stood alone by Madeline's grave. Amberson had to turn away when she saw him wipe a tear from his eye. She hadn't known until Justin told her that Madeline was Fred's sister.

Scattered through the crowd were various members of the Gunpoint Ladies' Culture Club and their husbands. Several of the women nodded to Amberson, though she noted that Mrs. Stanton and Mrs. Reedy avoided her gaze.

Sheriff Logan was there, watching the throng through narrowed eyes. Even Mr. Tibbets was there; Amberson almost didn't recognize him without his green telegrapher's shade.

Whiskers nodded to Amberson across the coffin. The Coyle brothers, with five wives in tow, arrived when Reverend Pippin was ten minutes into his oration.

The day was hot and Amberson's black widow's weeds and hat with netted veil made it even hotter.

Reverend Pippin droned on and on. His lofty descriptions of Richard and Madeline bore little resemblance to the two people Amberson had known. Finally Reverend Pippin was done.

She had been unable to shed a single tear upon first learning of Richard's death, nor did Reverend Pippin's oratory summon any grief now. But she was determined to get through the occasion with her dignity intact.

She kept Gerald with her and spoke quietly with the well-wishers who stopped to give her their condolences.

Dr. and Mrs. Cooper spoke to her, lingering near

her side, as did Beau, who took the baby from her now and then. Justin hovered behind her for most of the time she was there. He was a presence she felt, rather than saw.

She was a little surprised when Annabelle Simmons and her husband walked over.

Mr. J. V. Simmons bowed over her hand and murmured, "Our sincere and deep condolences on your terrible loss, Mrs. Rowan."

She said, "Thank you, Mr. Simmons. How kind of you to attend."

"I have not had a chance to tell you before this, Mrs. Rowan," continued the banker, "but you will be receiving the hundred-dollar reward from your brother Kingsley's death."

"I do not wish to profit from my brother's death," answered Amberson, recoiling.

"Very understandable, I am sure," said J. V. Simmons. "But the sheriff and the men of the posse thought that the sum would be of help to you. It was never established as to who actually killed Mr. Hawley," he added delicately, "and every member of the posse declined the money. They asked that it be given to you."

She regarded him consideringly. His gaze was most earnest, and Annabelle touched her on the arm. "If it would help you and your son, please take the money."

She stared at them. It was obvious that the gesture was well meant. Finally she said, "I thank you, Mr. Simmons. I will accept the money." Now she could buy a headstone for her brother.

"Good, good," he said heartily. "And of course," he said, "now that you are the widow of the owner of the Triple R, I expect we will be sitting down to business now and then. Heh, heh."

"I expect we will," Amberson answered carefully.

She watched the banker and his wife walk away, and pondered how quickly one's fortunes could change.

Other town notables drifted over to murmur about the great loss to the community that Richard's death meant. She accepted their comments and greeted each one respectfully. Finally, as the last of the funeral visitors trailed away, she turned to Justin.

"I want to thank you for giving Gerald and me a place to stay," she said quietly. "I will always remember your kindness."

He looked surprised. "What's this? You're moving?"

"I can impose on your generous hospitality no longer," she answered. "Gerald and I will be moving back to the Triple R."

"I see," he answered slowly, and she could hear the disappointment in his voice. Was he sad to see her go?

"I believe it is for the best, Justin," she told him, hoping he would understand that she did not wish to be a burden to him any longer. "I will never forget your help," she told him earnestly. "You and Beau helped me when I needed it so desperately."

"Beau is moving with you?"

"If he wishes to," she answered. She hadn't actually talked to him about it, but she hoped he would go to the Triple R with her.

"What about Gerald?" Justin's voice was guarded.

"You may visit him whenever you like," she answered. "And of course, as he gets older, he'll be able to stay for longer periods of time with you." Lord, but it hurt to think about Gerald staying away from her, but she loved him, and part of that love was making sure that he had a loving, caring father in his life.

"Your offer is generous," Justin conceded. It appeared he was about to say more, but Beau came up to them and she told him of her plans. He consented at once to go to the Triple R with her.

"Good-bye, Justin," she said softly. "Thank you for all your help." She hesitated, then smiled. "Thank you, too, for arranging the twenty-dollar credit with Hinckley when I needed it so badly."

He smiled sadly. "Glad to help out," he said.

She nodded. "We're leaving for the Triple R now. Beau will take the wagon over to your ranch tomorrow and get the rest of our things."

Justin nodded, and she thought she saw a bleak look in his green eyes. "Good-bye," she said impulsively, reaching for his hand and squeezing it.

Wordlessly, he squeezed back, the warmth and strength of his hand reassuring her. Then he slowly let go of her. She relinquished his touch reluctantly, too, still feeling his warm skin.

She watched him walk toward his horse. Why did she feel as though she was watching part of her life walk away?

Chapter Forty-four

Amberson looked at the sign above her head as Beau drove the wagon up the lane. TRIPLE R RANCH. For better or worse, she'd married Richard. For better or worse, the ranch was hers now.

Beau halted the wagon, jumped down, and untied Jessie and his paint pony from behind the wagon. Amberson carried Gerald up the front porch steps and opened the door. Stepping inside, she half-expected to see Richard come staggering out of his study. But all was silent in the house. There was no Richard. There would be no Richard, ever again.

She glanced around, breathing in the still air and with it the knowledge that the house was hers. The house, the land, even the freight-line business was all hers.

She set the baby down and he crawled toward the kitchen. She pulled off her black gloves as she wandered from room to room, surveying her "new" home.

To think that Richard had died and she had ended up with the ranch. Why, the poor man must be turning over in his grave. She shook off a feeling of guilt; it all came from his not wanting to give her a divorce, so she would not waste any more time on what Richard did or didn't want.

She spun on her boot heel. Beau was coming in the door and he grinned at her. "It's all yours, Missus Rowan."

"Yes, it is," she agreed gravely. "And I will make a home for Gerald and myself here. With your help," she added quickly.

"Yes, ma'am." He picked up the baby.

"Gerald and I will take the upstairs bedroom as we did before," she told Beau. "You may move into the study. I'd prefer to have you here, in the house, instead of in the bunkhouse."

"Yes, ma'am," he agreed. "I'll keep my rifle handy."

"You do that." She went over to inspect the kitchen. Evidently Richard had spent very little time at the ranch recently. A layer of dust covered everything.

She ran a finger over the dusty counter. "There's some work ahead of us," she warned Beau.

"Fine with me," he said. "I expect Whiskers will get here afore long."

"Oh?"

"To talk about the freight line and what you want to do with it," Beau explained.

She smiled. "Good," she agreed. "I want to keep busy."

* * *

Whiskers appeared two days later. She invited him in to have a cup of hot coffee and they sat at one of the tables. As she listened to Whiskers, it became obvious to her that running a freight line was a big undertaking.

"Do you want to sell it, Mrs. Rowan?" asked Whiskers at one point, when he'd finished explaining that two military contracts were up for renegotiation. "Just sell the whole freight line, kit and caboodle, and be done with it?"

She thought about it.

"Don't blame you if you do. It's work, no doubt about it." He scratched his chin. "And we need more mules, if we renew one of the military contracts. Someone will have to purchase the mules. Also, a couple of the boys quit, so I've gotta hire two new men."

Her head spun from all he was telling her, but, bravely, for Gerald's sake, she said, "I want to keep the business, Whiskers; that is, if you're willing to continue on."

"I am."

"Good, then between us, you and I, we should be able to keep the freight line running."

So it was decided. They spent the rest of the morning working on the details, and when Whiskers left after lunch, she felt that she had at least a glimmering of understanding about what it took to run a freight line.

In the quiet of the evening, she walked around the house once more, and then out onto the porch. She had a place now for herself and Gerald. A home. Lord, how strange life could be. Everything Richard owned was now hers. She was a wealthy woman.

She smiled. She would use her wealth wisely, to

help herself and her son have a better life and to help the people around her. She would pay an honest wage and treat the men who worked for her fairly.

Stars twinkled above her head as she stared out at the huge sky. Montana Territory was a good place to live. She and Gerald would thrive here.

She said a quiet prayer of thanks and went back into the house.

Bright and early the next morning there was a sharp rap on the front door. Beau and Amberson were having their breakfast, and she glanced at Beau with a frown. "Who could that be?"

He shrugged and she went to the door to answer it.

"Why, Mr. Knox," she said, stepping back in surprise. "Do come in."

He crossed the threshold, a smug look on his handsome face. In his hand he held a sheaf of papers.

"May I offer you a cup of coffee?" she asked politely.

"I'm not here to socialize, Mrs. Rowan."

Taken aback, she straightened. "What brings you here then, Mr. Knox? It is a long ride from Gunpoint."

He held up the papers and started leafing through them, for her benefit.

"I have here the divorce papers of Mr. Richard Rowan."

"Divorce papers?" she gasped.

"Signed. And the will," he added importantly.

"The will? What will?"

Beau stomped over. "What's the meaning of this, Knox?"

"Don't talk to me like that, Shorty," sneered Fred

Knox. "I just came over to tell you two to get the hell off my ranch."

"Your ranch?" She felt like a prizefighter reeling from body blows. It was all too much to take in. . . .

"That is correct," said Fred Knox. "This will, the last will and testament of one Richard Rowan, late of Gunpoint, leaves everything he owns to Miss Madeline Mueler."

"But she's dead!" cried Amberson.

"She's dead, and I, as her brother, am next of kin. I inherit. Everything." He waved the papers triumphantly. "Get your things packed," he told Amberson. "And get out!"

Chapter Forty-five

Under cover of darkness, Amberson slipped into the Hank Parker Hotel. Beau carried Gerald, bundled in his arms. Nobody was behind the hotel counter.

Amberson sat down to wait in a green overstuffed chair in the tiny lobby. Beau sat down across from her in a brown chair. In the corner next to him sat the mummified miner in a mustard yellow chair with the sign advertising EDDIE'S EMBALMING EMPORIUM.

"I'll stay here tonight," Amberson told Beau. "I have to find work tomorrow."

"Let's tell Mr. Harbinger," suggested Beau for the fourteenth time.

But Amberson would not hear of it. "Mr. Harbinger was a good friend to me," acknowledged Amberson. "But I can't go running to him every time I have a little problem."

"I would not call this a little problem, Missus

Rowan, beggin' your pardon. I would call this a *big* problem."

"I will not go crawling to Justin for help," said Amberson primly. "And that is that."

Beau subsided into a sullen silence. She waited, glancing around at every corner of the room except where the mummified miner resided. She managed to ignore Beau's unhappy face, until finally Pa Parker came out of one of the rooms. "Ah!" said Pa, rubbing his hands gleefully. "Customers!"

Amberson took the sleeping baby from Beau and walked up to the counter. "I'd like a room, please."

Pa hesitated, glancing at Beau. "We don't rent to no short people. Hotel rules."

"Beau will be staying—elsewhere." The wagon, actually.

Amberson glared up at Pa. She huffed, "Anyone who keeps a dead body in their lobby should not be particular about who they rent to!"

"Dead body! Why, that's old Warren. Loser Larry found him in a cave one day. All dried up and wrinkled like a prune. Don't you talk about old Warren like that."

"I've a good mind to go elsewhere!"

Pa regarded her. "Well," he said slowly, "there's always the Two Star, down the street. Guess you could try them. Say," he said, leaning closer, "ain't you the Widder Rowan?"

At Amberson's reluctant nod, he said, "I thought so. I was right sorry to hear about your husband's death, if you get my drift."

"Thank you," she said. "Now, about the room?"

He frowned. "Beggin' your pardon, ma'am, but if you're the Widder Rowan, why ain't you stayin' at the Two Star? Of course, they are a little more expensive than we are here, but you can afford five dollars a night. That's their goin' rate."

"Five dollars!" exclaimed Amberson.

"Oho! I get it." Pa grinned. "You don't wanta pay so much. Can't say as I blame you. Rooms is expensive."

Amberson said impatiently, "I'd like the room, please."

"Sure, ma'am. Big, middle or little?"

"What are you talking about?"

"The size of the room, ma'am. You keepin' that baby with you?"

"Yes."

"Then I recommend the big room. Babies need lots of room."

She sighed. "I'll take middle, thank you."

He sighed. "All right, ma'am, but I just hope you know what you're doin'. What with the baby and all." He reached slowly for the key, as if giving her an opportunity to change her mind. She gritted her teeth and kept silent. She was tired, and the baby was exhausted. It had been a most trying day, most trying. She would not end it by screaming at this—this—

"Here you go, ma'am." He walked over to the door behind the counter and handed her the key. "It's all yours." He grinned. "For this evenin'."

He eyed Beau, who was still sitting in the chair. "By the way, ma'am, we have strict rules about gentlemen callers."

"And what," she ground out, "might those rules be?"

"No gentlemen callers before ten in the morning and none after six in the evening. Them's hotel rules."

"Thank you," she said, unlocking the door. "I'll see you in the morning, Beau," she said. Then she and the baby entered the tiny room and she slammed the door behind her. Very hard.

At ten o'clock the next morning, Amberson sauntered out of her room, carrying the baby. She spotted Beau sitting in a red chair in the lobby. And seated in the brown overstuffed chair was Justin Harbinger.

"How did you—?" she began. Justin rose from the chair, his big body a reassuring sight in the tiny lobby. She couldn't take her eyes off him. Justin! Here, to help her. Oh, Lord, he looked so handsome. . . .

"I fetched him," explained Beau cautiously. "I know you didn't want me to, but I fetched him anyway."

She tightened her lips and glared at Beau. "I will speak with you about this betrayal later," she told him.

She wondered how much of her circumstances Beau had discussed with Justin. The little cowboy refused to meet her eyes. Not a good sign.

She lifted her chin. "I will do fine by myself, Mr. Harbinger," she said. "I do not need your help."

"Well, now, ma'am," he said, "I was just going over to Hinckley's General Store and thought I'd stop by to see if you needed anything."

"Nothing," she answered, chin still high.

His green eyes spoke his frustration with her. "Do you have any plans?"

"Plans?"

"For the future?"

"None that I care to tell you at this time."

"That's just fine, Mrs. Rowan," he sneered. "And what about Gerald?"

"Gerald will be fine. I will be keeping him with me."

He looked angry. But she was not going to let him know how humiliating this whole situation was for her. She'd thought she had a home at last for herself and Gerald at the Triple R; thought the ranch was hers, and the freight-line business too. She'd talked with Whiskers, made arrangements to hire men, buy mules . . .

No, she could never let Justin know how thoroughly humiliated she truly was. Gone, all of it gone, in one stroke of Richard's quill pen. Amberson would die, literally die, before she would ever say a word to Justin Harbinger about her true position. She would not be humiliated before the man she loved.

"Of course, I will bring the baby out to visit you at your ranch," she offered.

His eyes glittered. "That will be fine, Mrs. Rowan," he said. "I'll expect to see you out there tomorrow."

"Tomorrow? That's a little too soon—"

"Not to me, it isn't. Tomorrow. Be at my ranch." He rammed his brown slouch hat on his head and left.

"Whew!" said Pa. "He's a hot one, isn't he? Big too." He glanced at Beau and Amberson. "I shoulda told him to go cool down at the Plugged Nickel. A whisky would do him good. It sure helps Ma Parker out." He laughed.

Amberson stormed out of the Hank Parker Hotel and marched up the street to the bank. The thought of staying another night at the hotel was truly daunting.

She had just reached the double doors of the Gunpoint Greatest Savings Bank when her way was suddenly blocked by a tall, elegant-looking brunette in a stunning jade green dress and jacket. Accompanying the woman was a hulking bald man whom Amberson recognized as McIver, one of her previous laundry customers.

"How—how do you do?" asked Amberson nervously.

"Very well," purred Estelle. "I believe it's time you and I talked business."

Dang that woman's pride! fumed Justin. He'd gotten around her dang pride last time when the bullets flew at the bank robbery; he'd told her the town was too dangerous for her and Gerald, which it was. But this time, this time was something else, and he knew he was going to have a dang hard time of it getting her back to the ranch.

He recognized a filly balking at the bridle when he saw one.

Cooling down somewhat, he began to think about what Beau had told him. Fred Knox had appeared at the Triple R, waved some papers at Amberson, and declared the ranch was his, because Rowan had signed divorce papers and a will leaving everything to Madeline Mueler. Therefore, by inheritance from his sister, Knox got the ranch. Justin remembered the papers Knox had picked up from the bureau in Rowan's hotel room. He had a sick feeling in his gut that they were the same papers Knox had waved around at the ranch.

Justin frowned. He should have demanded to see the papers then and there. Was that why Knox had been so eager to let Beau pocket the bottle of rat poison? To keep their attention off his own actions?

Still pondering as he walked, Justin happened to glance up the boardwalk. He halted abruptly.

There, in the middle of the boardwalk, stood Estelle and her mountain of a bodyguard, and they were talking to Miss Amberson! He watched as Miss Amberson shook her head and proceeded into the bank. Estelle and her escort said something to one another, then laughed as they walked away.

Justin's gut tightened. Every time he looked around, Miss Amberson was in worse trouble.

Walking slowly, he reached the bank. He was about to pass by when he looked inside and saw Amberson talking with J. V. Simmons.

This is interesting, he thought. The two were nodding heads together, having a fine old time. He saw Simmons hand Miss Amberson some money.

So she has some money, at least, thought Justin. Maybe he should just let her do whatever she was going to do and not try to help her and Gerald. But the memory of the bank robbery shootout was strong. And the image of Estelle talking to Miss Amberson wouldn't leave his mind.

He sighed. Dang it, but Gunpoint was no place for his son and the mother of his son. If ever a woman needed help, it was Amberson Hawley Rowan.

He sauntered down the street, waiting for her to leave the bank. When she did, he ducked inside the bank door. He'd find out what she was up to.

Mr. J. V. Simmons smiled at Justin across a tidy, expansive desk. "So you're looking for a loan are you, Harbinger? I hear you just bought the McManus ranch."

"Yeah," answered Justin.

"Good collateral," approved the banker.

Justin smiled. He had no intention of taking out a loan, but he was hoping he'd learn something about Amberson's business. He pushed his guilty qualms aside. Sometimes a man had to pry.

He and J. V. Simmons talked back and forth about some properties and how much Justin could borrow. Finally, when he figured they'd talked enough, Justin said, "I hear Fred Knox got the Triple R."

"Yep," said the banker, puffing out his chest. "Fine ranch too. Too bad the little widow couldn't keep the place. She was just in here, you know."

"Interesting how the divorce papers and the will turned up right after Rowan died," commented Justin.

J. V. Simmons leaned forward. "Even more interesting—" he lowered his voice confidentially—"is that Richard Rowan's signature didn't look quite right."

Justin sat up. "He was sick. Maybe his hand shook."

"No, the signature I saw looked firm, not shaky. And it didn't look quite the way Rowan usually signed his papers."

Justin pondered this. "Who was the witness to the will?"

"Loser Larry, ahem, excuse me, I mean Mr. Larry Parker," the banker answered.

"Is he reliable?"

The banker shrugged. "He's a Parker."

Justin lifted an eyebrow. The banker had said all he was going to say. Rising to his feet, Justin said, "Thank you for your information. I'll talk with you again later."

"Any time, any time," said J. V. Simmons heartily.

Justin found Loser Larry in the fourth saloon he

visited. Larry was in the Fool's Gold, a rundown saloon at the very edge of town. Most of the customers
were drunken miners, with a handful of drunken soldiers scattered here and there. Cowboys hardly ever
visited this particular saloon unless they were looking for a fight. That was because most of the cowboys
had fought for the Confederacy in the war, and most
of the soldiers had fought for the Union.

Justin walked over and pulled up a chair. Larry
was drinking a whisky by himself. Justin got a glass
of whisky from the bartender, a thin man with
slicked back hair and only one eye. There was a dark
hole where his other eye should have been.

The Fool's Gold had ten tables. Nine of those tables
had drinking miners sitting at them. Over in a corner
sprawled two men, passed out.

"Nice place you got here," lied Justin.

"Look, mister," said the bartender, "if you're looking for trouble, go talk to that buzzard over there.
He'll accommodate you."

He indicated Loser Larry.

Justin went over and sat down. "Howdy, Larry."
Justin nodded.

Larry glanced at him sullenly.

"This a good place to drink?" asked Justin.

"Company's lousy."

"You mean me?" asked Justin.

"If the shoe fits."

If there was anything Justin hated, it was a mean
drunk. He picked up his glass and moved back to the
counter.

The one-eyed bartender laughed. "You didn't last
long."

"Didn't want to," answered Justin, taking a drink.
"He always that pleasant?"

"Sometimes," said the bartender with a shrug. "He should be celebrating. He just found some gold."

"Wonder where?"

"Don't we all?" The bartender wiped at the counter. "If you talk nice to him, he'll spit in your eye." He laughed. "That's what happened to mine."

Justin sat at the counter for a while, wondering how to approach Larry. Suddenly a fight broke out at one of the tables. One miner accused another of cheating at cards. Fists flew.

Larry got up and moved to a spot away from the fight.

Justin ambled over. "Good fight," he remarked to Larry.

"I seen better."

"So have I," said Justin. "In the war. Now, there was a place for fights."

"I didn't go to war," said Larry. He took another drink of his whisky.

It wasn't much, but it was a start. Justin talked to him, quietly, now and then, and soon they were sitting at a table. He signaled for two more whiskies. Larry required delicate handling.

Larry was becoming more talkative the more he drank. Justin realized he'd been mistaken when he'd thought the fellow was a mean drunk. That was his sober side.

"Let's go to another saloon," said Justin after a while.

They staggered out of the Fool's Gold and down the boardwalk, past some very offended, familiar-looking, well-dressed ladies of the town, who whispered avidly to one another.

Justin and Larry entered Miss Honey's Place, a saloon run by a foul-mouthed, tough-looking, pimply blond woman who kept a butcher knife under the counter. She used it when she had to. Cowboys kept a respectful distance from Miss Honey. She could outcuss mule skinners, outshoot cowboys, and out-drink soldiers. Word around town was that she'd learned it all prostituting herself to sailors in San Francisco. The good thing about Miss Honey's Place was that Sheriff Logan was seldom called in to break up a fight. Miss Honey kept strict order.

Justin bought Larry another whisky and they sat down at a table.

"You find any gold lately?" asked Justin.

Larry looked at him. "Why you want to know?"

Justin shrugged. "Just asking."

Larry glared at him. "I been out to the Triple R. Looking for gold there. Fred Knox thinks there's something there."

"Yeah?"

Larry shrugged. Justin didn't press him.

"You like Fred Knox?" tried Justin.

"He's all right."

"Have another drink," said Justin, signaling to Miss Honey.

Three drinks later, Loser Larry could barely sit up. But he was talking, spilling his innards like a gutshot soldier.

"Come on," said a pleased Justin, hooking his arm around Larry's. "Come on. I want to introduce you to my friend."

"Where we goin'?" asked Larry.

"Not far," Justin promised.

They staggered out of Miss Honey's arm in arm, singing bawdy songs.

When they reached Sheriff Logan's office, Justin pushed open the door, singing at the top of his lungs.

Sheriff Logan looked up, and Justin signaled to him frantically. The sheriff nodded.

"Sit down," said Justin, pushing Larry into the sheriff's round chair. "This here's my friend. Tell him what you been tellin' me." He sang another verse of a filthy little ditty Larry particularly favored.

"Ha ha." Larry laughed. "Thassh a good one."

"Tell my friend," said Justin.

Sheriff Logan beamed at Larry and leaned closer.

"Wasshh it I wasshh gonna sshhay?" slurred Larry.

"You told me about the papers you signed for Fred Knox."

"What papers?"

"The papers," said Justin patiently, "the divorce papers and the will papers. Remember?"

"Yessshh." Larry nodded several times. "I sshhigned them."

"By yourself?"

"No. Ol' Fred tole me to sshhign."

"When?"

"After he sshhigned them."

"Aha," said Justin. "Fred signed them."

"Yesshh, he sshhigned them and then I sshhigned them."

"Forged!" exclaimed Sheriff Logan. "Let's go find Fred Knox."

He and Justin ran out of the office, leaving a snoring Larry slumped in the sheriff's big chair.

Chapter Forty-six

Sheriff Logan led his prisoner in handcuffs along the boardwalk to the sheriff's office that doubled as a jail. Justin trailed along behind Fred Knox. They were halfway to the jail when a short, middle-aged Oriental man, with his black hair in a long queue down his back, hurried up to them.

The Celestial bowed stiffly to the sheriff.

"What do you want, Lee Fung?" said the sheriff, pausing.

"Very honorable Sheriff," said Lee Fung, "this bad man your prisoner?"

"Shut up, Lee Fung," snapped Fred Knox. To the sheriff he said impatiently, "Just take me to jail."

But the sheriff hesitated. "You got something you want to say?" he said to Lee Fung.

The Celestial nodded.

Fred Knox grimaced at him. "You say anything

371

and you're going to end up like some of your boys—dead."

Sheriff Logan's eyes narrowed on Fred Knox. "What," he asked suspiciously, "do you know about the dead Celestials I've been finding around town? There have been four of them."

"I don't know anything," sneered Fred Knox. "Let's get over to the jail and stop all this useless talk."

"You're in an awful hurry to get to jail," observed the sheriff. He studied the short Celestial, who appeared quite nervous. "What do you want to tell me?"

"It concern this very bad man."

Fred Knox straightened. "Don't believe anything this dirty Celestial tells you. He lies."

"He's not the only one in town does that," commented the sheriff.

The Celestial bowed again. "Please," he said politely. "Most honorable Sheriff. You look in saddlebags of bad man. You find something. Important." He bowed, and hurried away.

"That's the man you should be arresting," snarled Fred Knox.

"Why?" asked the sheriff.

"Because he owns the biggest opium den in this town. He's taking over the whole opium trade in this town, that's why."

The sheriff said to Justin, "Bring Fred Knox's horse and saddlebags to my office. I'll get him to jail."

Justin went and retrieved Fred Knox's saddled horse from in front of his law office. The horse, a roan, went willingly with him over to the sheriff's.

Sheriff Logan walked out of his office door. "While Knox is sitting in jail, let's take a look through his saddlebags."

It didn't take long to find the brown bottle. The

sheriff opened the bottle and sniffed. "Rat poison!

"Now, how," murmured the sheriff, "did that Celestial know it was in Fred Knox's saddlebags?"

"And how did that Celestial know that rat poison killed Richard Rowan and Madeline Mueler?" asked Justin.

"You tell me," said the sheriff. So Justin told him about finding the bottle of rat poison in the Rowan suite.

The sheriff stared at the brown bottle a long time.

"What side of the war did you fight on, Harbinger?" he asked at last.

Surprised by the question, Justin answered, "I fought for the North."

"I'd have guessed the South, from your accent," said Sheriff Logan.

"My family is from the South, sir," said Justin. "I chose to fight for the North."

"So did I," said the sheriff. "Did you know that Fred Knox fought for the South?"

"No," answered Justin. "I didn't know that."

"He did. He's from a well known Southern family. He was a spy, out of Atlanta. A very successful spy. Probably killed off some fine men with his information."

"Probably," said Justin. "But the war is over, sir."

"It is, isn't it?" said the sheriff. He glanced back at the bottle. "I'm pretty certain that Lee Fung and Knox were in cahoots. They aren't any longer," he said at last. "I think Knox and Lee Fung were partners in the biggest opium den in town. Knox telegraphed the governor to raid the competition. I raided the Celestial leaders and their dens one by one, but I could never catch Lee Fung. His places were always clean: no opium, no opium fiends.

Somebody, a white partner, was warning him.

"But I kept trying, and the last time I raided Lee Fung's place, I found opium. I just missed capturing him. He ran out the back door."

The sheriff eyed Justin. "Do you see what that means?"

"Fred Knox didn't warn the Celestial."

"Yeah. Knox probably wanted the business all to himself. Looks to me like Lee Fung took a little revenge on his 'partner.'"

"A murder accusation is strong revenge," said Justin.

"Effective too," said Sheriff Logan. "And I'm certain Fred Knox is a murderer. A Celestial witness came forward and told me Knox had killed three of Lee Fung's men in an attempt to take over the opium business. Next day that witness was dead—Knox got him too. But I can't prove Knox is a murderer when my witness is dead. Looks like Lee Fung's doin' my job for me. He wants Knox out of the way."

"What are you going to do?" asked Justin.

"Do?" said the sheriff. "Why, arrest Fred Knox for the murders of Richard Rowan and Madeline Mueler, what else?"

"How about forgery of the will and divorce papers against Mrs. Rowan?" reminded Justin.

"That too," agreed the sheriff.

Together, they walked back to the sheriff's office.

Fred Knox laughed when Sheriff Logan formally charged him with murder. "You can't do that. I didn't do it."

"Richard Rowan and your sister died of rat poison," said the sheriff. "You killed them. After her death, you forged the divorce papers and the will so you could get the Rowan property. That's good enough for me. I'll see you hanged."

"You seem to forget," spat Knox, "that I'm a very good friend of the governor."

"You may be a very good friend of the governor," retorted Sheriff Logan, "and you may have gotten away with murdering four Celestials—"

"Ahh, who cares about dead Celestials?" spat Knox.

"They're people too," answered the sheriff. "And furthermore," he continued, "friend of the governor or no, when you start killing off your relatives and wealthy ranchers, even the governor will have nothing to do with you!"

"You hate me, don't you, Logan? You can't pin those murders on me, but you hate my guts," sneered Knox. "That's what's behind this. Your petty hatred."

"No," said the sheriff. "There's something else behind this. During the war you wooed a certain Union sympathizer in Atlanta. A woman. With sweet words and promises, you sucked all the secrets out of her, secrets you sold to the South."

"You son of a bitch!"

"You're the son of a bitch," replied the unperturbed sheriff. "That Union sympathizer was my sister. She committed suicide three days after she found out you'd betrayed her." He smiled. "You know, Knox, I'm gonna enjoy your hanging."

"Me too," said Justin.

Two weeks later there was a raid on the biggest opium den in Gunpoint and Lee Fung was captured by the governor's own agents.

Chapter Forty-seven

"Justin!" said Amberson. "What are you doing here?"

"I brought a friend of mine along to meet you," he answered.

She wrinkled her nose. "Your friend smells a trifle, er, strong."

"He's had a busy day," said Justin. "Sit down," he told Larry. Larry Parker sat down in the green chair, Justin in the brown one, and Amberson lowered herself into the red one, careful to keep her eyes averted from the mummy, which Beau had turned to face the corner. Beau now sat in the yellow chair, his feet not quite reaching the floor.

"Larry's got some news for you," said Justin conversationally. "I've been taking him around to all my friends. Seems he has something good to say to each one of them."

"Oh?" Amberson clearly didn't believe him.

Justin chuckled. "Can I hold the baby while you listen to Larry?"

She handed Gerald over to him and Justin held the child close. His child. Somehow he could never get over the miracle of his child.

Larry didn't say anything.

"You going to tell her, Larry?" inquired Justin after a while.

"I'll tell her," said Larry, "but I don't know what good it's gonna do." He glanced at Justin. "This your idea of a joke? Tricking a lady?"

"Just tell her, Larry," said Justin.

Larry began, "I was hired by Fred Knox to look for gold."

Amberson smiled and nodded. Justin was amused that she was being polite for his benefit.

When there was a long silence, she asked brightly, "And did you find gold, Larry?"

"I did."

She glanced at Justin. "*Where* did you find this gold?"

"On the Triple R spread."

She rose out of her chair. "I'll take the baby," she said. "I didn't think you would stoop so low, Justin. To flaunt my loss in my face! I hope your revenge is satisfying—"

"Hold your horses," said Justin, moving the baby out of her reach. "He found gold on the Triple R Ranch, all right, but that's not all."

"Spare me," she said, tugging the baby out of his arms. "I'll be in my room. Beau will see you out of here." She carried the baby with dignity, and kept her back straight all the way to the door of her room.

"Amberson," called Justin, "wait! Fred Knox was

jailed this afternoon. For forgery of the divorce papers and the will."

She whirled around. Her face was white. "What?" she cried, stupefied.

He grinned. "You own the ranch. The Triple R. It's yours!"

Pale and shaken, she made it back to the red chair. "The ranch?"

"It's yours," Justin said. "The sheriff knows Knox forged the papers." He gave her some time to let the information sink in.

Amberson put her hand to her mouth. "Oh, my word!" She turned to the baby. "Did you hear that, Gerald?"

"There's something else I need to tell you," said Justin solemnly. "It's about Fred Knox."

He had all their attention.

"Fred Knox is to be hanged for the murders of Richard Rowan and Madeline Mueler."

"Fred Knox? Murdered Richard and Madeline?" gasped Amberson.

"No!" exclaimed Larry. He gaped at Justin.

"That right?" asked Beau, his eyes riveted on Justin's.

"Sheriff figured it out," Justin assured them. Knox was a murderer, so justice had been served, though in a roundabout way. He turned his attention back to Miss Amberson.

"Justin," she said, "tell me the truth, no tricks. I—I can't bear it."

"No tricks, Amberson," he said, coming over to her. He put his arms around her and Gerald. She held on to him as if for dear life. "The ranch is yours. Yours and Gerald's. Fred Knox can't take it from you. No one can take it from you."

"You're sure?" She was looking up at him out of those big hazel eyes of hers.

He grinned down at her. "It's yours, Amberson." He thought, But you're lost to me now, Amberson. You have no need of me. You can offer Gerald a better life than I can.

"Mine?" She blinked, and he understood how difficult it was for her to believe it this time.

"Yours," he said softly. He wanted to kiss her, to let their lips touch one more time. He lowered his mouth to hers . . .

"Missus Rowan," interrupted Beau, "I think we should be heading out to the Triple R. Don't you?" The short cowboy tugged on her dress to get her attention.

She glanced at him, dazed. "Oh, yes, yes, of course, Beau. Let me pack up the baby's things. . . ." She thrust the baby at Beau and ran to the room she was staying in and shut the door.

Justin stared bleakly at the door. He was shut out of her life. She didn't need him now. It was over. Any hope he'd ever had of helping her, of marrying her, was as effectively closed as that door.

With a grim nod to Beau, he swung on his heel. "I'll escort you out to the ranch."

"That won't be necessary," said the cowhand. "I have my rifle."

"Rifle or not, I *will* escort you."

"If you must," shrugged the dwarf, with a knowing smile.

"Well," said Amberson, standing on the boardwalk in front of the Hank Parker Hotel, "I want to thank you, Justin, for all your help—"

"There's nothing to thank me for," he said gruffly.

"Oh, Justin, that's not true. You offered to help me so many times." She gave an embarrassed laugh. "Why, did you know I was running out of money at this hotel and I was about to ask you if I could stay at your ranch?"

She laughed and waved a hand at the silliness of it all. "I was going to impose on you once again, Justin. Today. I was going to ride out to your ranch and ask if I could stay there again."

He looked stricken.

"Justin?" Appalled, she stared at him. She hadn't realized what a burden she was to him. "Justin, I was only fooling. I wasn't really going to ask you—"

"No, no," he said hastily. "It's not that—"

"What then? You look positively sick. Is something wrong?" She glanced around. "Beau, get the wagon. Help Mr. Harbinger to the wagon. He's sick and we're taking him to the Triple R."

"God, no, Amberson," Justin protested.

He didn't want to go to her ranch. "Very well, Justin," she said sadly, "but you must do something to take care of yourself. You look—well, you look quite, quite ill."

He nodded.

"Perhaps Dr. Cooper—" she began.

"Good-bye, Amberson," he said, gritting out her name.

"Good-bye, Justin." She wanted to run and hide in the wagon. It was obvious he could barely stand her, while she, she loved him—No! For Gerald's sake she must be strong and not give way to womanly torments. "You must come and visit us soon," she said with as much dignity as she could. "Gerald would love to have you stop by."

"Gerald? Only Gerald?"

She gave a little laugh. "Well, I'd like it too, Justin, but I didn't think you wanted to hear that."

He glanced around at the people gathering about them, and she realized he was embarrassed. "I'll be going now," she said with a little wave. "Farewell."

He stood there watching her, his green eyes as hard as the gems they so reminded her of.

Chapter Forty-eight

The days were long now. Oh, she had the freight-line business to keep her busy, and the care of the ranch and the cattle. But the baby was increasingly fretful and she felt restless herself. She knew what was missing: Justin.

Tears welled in her eyes as she thought of him. Lord, she loved him. There was no doubt in her heart now. She loved him, always had, always would.

She looked out the ranch house window and sighed. It was a warm, sunny autumn day, one of the last they'd have before the cold days ahead. Her whole life lay before her, but without Justin it was as bleak as the winter promised to be.

And yet her needs were all satisfied. She and Gerald had the Triple R Ranch to live on. She had an excellent income from the freight line. Whiskers was doing a fine job of running the freight line, and Beau helped her at the ranch.

But she couldn't have Justin. He'd made that clear. She'd been back at the Triple R for a month and he'd yet to call upon her and Gerald. It was time she faced the truth: Justin didn't love her. Oh, he probably had some feeling for her, as the mother of his child, but the love she wanted, the honest, intense love between a man and a woman . . . no, that wasn't there. At least not on his side.

Determined to shake off her brooding thoughts, she decided she and the baby would go on a picnic. So she got Gerald ready and crammed some cheese and bread into a basket. Carefully, she laid two bottles of precious sarsaparilla in the basket. Gerald was too young to drink out of a bottle, but maybe she'd have the second one. She could afford it now.

She told Beau she was going down to the creek and headed off. Her steps gradually lightened as she went along. Now and then she'd set the baby down in the grass to play. He was getting heavier and squirmed when she carried him. He wanted to walk.

They reached the creek and wandered along its banks. The green depths of the water looked so clear. She and Gerald moved toward the point where the stand of aspens and cottonwoods grew.

She remembered the long-ago day when the four rustlers had burst out of the woods. Kingsley had been one of them. She wondered if he knew he was robbing his sister's ranch. She had a feeling he did know.

She spread the blanket and sat down, placing the baby in the center of it. "There you go, Gerald," she cooed. "You can practice crawling or walking."

He decided to stick with crawling and moved off the blanket.

She fetched him back several times. Finally, they

ate their lunch and she rubbed his back so he would fall asleep.

This could be a good life, she thought. I will just have to make the best of it, without Justin. Her heart fell at the very thought.

The baby gurgled in his sleep. She wished her mother and father were alive to see Gerald. And Kingsley, though if he were alive, she'd have to visit him in jail. Not so good, she thought.

Her life had settled down now that Richard was gone. She was sorry that he'd been murdered by that blackguard, Fred Knox, but she had to admit she liked her new peaceful life.

And the ranch and freight business were going well, she reminded herself. Larry Parker had prospected the northern margin of the ranch and that was where he'd found gold. She didn't need to work it now. She'd work it later, if she needed to.

Whiskers had the freight lines running smoothly enough.

Why, then, this sadness about Justin? She lifted her chin. She should be glad he was out of her life. The last thing she needed was a man to complicate things, especially one as frustrating as Justin. She could manage, she told herself. And she would manage. Without him.

She stared at the green waters of the creek. She was lying to herself, something she'd promised she would no longer do. No, the truth was that she loved Justin Harbinger and would love him to her dying day.

Suddenly her attention was caught by sunlight flashing on the silver bridle of a distant horse. She sat up and watched the rider come toward her.

"Justin," she murmured. "Oh, my Lord, Gerald, it's

Justin. What's he doing here?" She chuckled quietly, careful not to wake the sleeping baby. "I wonder what he wants." The baby stirred in his sleep.

Justin rode closer. How strong, how straight he looked, sitting atop the big bay horse.

"Hello, Justin," she greeted him. Her traitorous heart leaped in her chest.

Justin touched the rim of his brown slouch hat, and she was reminded of the day they'd played in the creek near his house. And further reminded of how he'd looked in his blue uniform when she'd first met him.

"Sit down," she said with a gesture at the blanket.

He dismounted and walked closer.

"Baby's asleep," she whispered. "He just went to sleep a few minutes ago."

Justin nodded. He held the reins and fidgeted with them. How unlike big, bad Justin to be so reticent.

She rose and walked toward him. "Justin?" she said.

He stared down at her.

She gave a shaky laugh. "You look so solemn," she said. "Don't tell me Fred Knox or someone else has claimed the Triple R again."

That brought a smile to his lips. "No, Amberson, nothing like that."

"What then?"

She looked into his green eyes and realized she wanted to stare into them for the rest of her life. Lord, but she loved him. She took a calming breath, so he wouldn't see the effect he had on her.

Her eyes played over his face. She could see how Gerald resembled him, around the eyes, the nose.

She swallowed. He thought her a burden. He was appalled that day when she'd told him she was about to seek him out and ask to stay at his ranch.

She smiled, her lips trembling. This is where true love comes in, she thought. True love would be happy with whatever made her beloved happy.

What would make Justin happy?

She hadn't realized she'd spoken the words aloud until he said, "You."

She gasped. "Justin?"

"You asked what would make me happy," he said. "I told you: you."

"What about Gerald?"

Justin grinned. "Yes, Gerald too. But it's you, Amberson, that I think about. It's your face I see as I fall asleep each night. It's you I want. My ranch is just a house and some land without you there. It's *you* I want for my life's companion. Come and live with me, Amberson," he urged. "Marry me and come and live at my ranch, you and Gerald."

Her heart pounded as she gazed into his wonderful green eyes. "Oh, Justin!" she cried, throwing herself into his arms. "That would make me so happy too!"

He laughed embarrassedly. "I guess it looks like I'm marrying you for your money," he said. "I remember I accused you of that with Richard."

"Oh!" She waved a hand at the land and the big ranch house. "I would give it all up in a minute for you, Justin."

"You would?"

"Yes!" Tears blurred her vision of him. "I love you so much," she whispered.

With a gentle finger he brushed away the wetness on her cheek. "Crying?" he asked.

"With happiness!"

He chuckled. "No need to give up anything, Amberson," he said. "Not anymore. Let's take what we have and make it even better."

"What do we have, Justin?"

"You. Me. Our baby. Our love."

"Do you love me, Justin?" She touched his cheek with a trembling hand.

He enfolded her in his arms. "I love you beyond words. Beyond anything." He kissed her. "I'm happy when I'm with you and I want you with me for the rest of our lives."

"Oh, yes, Justin. Yes!"

He grinned. "That settles it. Let's move to my ranch." He took her hand.

"Aren't you forgetting something?"

He regarded her thoughtfully, a question in his green gaze. Then he dropped to one knee. "Will you do me the honor of marrying me, Miss Amberson?"

"Oh, yes," she cried happily.

"Marry me and be my wife and do my laundry for always?"

When she realized what he'd said, she pushed at him, and he toppled over on the grass. He laughed and pulled her down with him. They rolled in the grass, laughing together.

Then he touched her cheek, serious again, and trailed his fingers down the side of her face. "I love you, Amberson. Ever since that day I saw you riding across the field on your horse. You were just a slip of a girl, but you galloped off with my heart."

She smiled back, her heart singing. "I can't remember when I first started to love you, Justin. I feel like I've always loved you."

They kissed.

"I remember now," she said. "It was in the Hurdy Gurdy Palace. When you asked me to dance . . ."

He gave her a swat on the behind. "That deserves a swim in the creek!" he exclaimed. He scrambled to his feet and pulled her up.

"No, Justin!" she cried as he lifted her in his arms. Kicking, she struggled to get free of his strong embrace. To no avail.

"No, Justin!" she wailed as he walked into the creek, boots, spurs, and all. He sank into the depths with her and the cool water swirled around them.

She struggled, gasping for air. Together, they burst out of the water, laughing. "Or maybe it was when I was washing your dirty shirts . . ." she said.

"Amberson!" he scolded and pushed her head under the water.

Sputtering, she staggered to the surface. She threw her arms around him and kissed him exuberantly. "I know!" she cried. "It was on that moonlit night, when you told me sweet words and did sweet things to my body . . ."

"God, Amberson," he said raggedly. "Can you ever forgive me? I should have waited . . ."

Her mouth on his stopped his words. At last she murmured, "Yes, you should have waited. I should have waited. *We* should have waited. But we made Gerald that night, Justin. And I don't regret Gerald, not one bit. I could never regret him!"

Justin kissed her. "I love you, Amberson."

"I love you too, Justin."

He lifted her in his arms and carried her wet, dripping body over to the grass. He dropped her to her feet, still holding her encircled in his arms. She nudged up against him willingly. This was the man she loved, she thought. Had always loved. This was the man she wanted to spend her life with. And, miracle of miracles, he wanted to spend his life with her!

There was nothing of pain between them now. The old hurts were gone, burned away by the love they had for one another.

"I never knew it was so powerful," she murmured.

"What is?" he asked, ripping off his shirt. She looked at him askance.

"Why, love," she answered, her eyes running over his broad shoulders, the black hair on his chest. And lower . . . She forced her gaze back to those emerald eyes. "Love, Justin. I didn't know how strong it could be, how wonderful to have a man of my own, to love. To love me!" She stepped out of his arms and held up her own, as though presenting him with the world. "This is what life is all about, Justin. The only thing that makes life worth living: love." She turned back to him. "Oh, Lord, Justin, I love you."

"Good," he grunted, pulling off his boots.

Her eyes widened. "Justin?" she squeaked. Why, he was undoing his pants. And sliding them off. Now he was kicking them aside!

"Justin?"

"Hmmm?" he answered nonchalantly, reaching for her. Seeing her stare at his pile of clothes, he rubbed his chin on her face and explained, "They're wet. Don't need them right now."

"Oh?" Her eyes narrowed. "Just what exactly do you have in mind?" But she thought she knew. In fact, it was hard not to know.

"Let's make love."

"But we're not married," she answered primly.

"We will be," he answered. "And I can't wait."

She put her hands on her hips, defiant, reveling in the fact that she was clothed, though dripping wet, while he was naked. She had the power now. "We'll wait until we're married. How do I know you won't seduce me and leave me?"

"Aha," he said. "I thought you might wonder about that." He was busy undoing the buttons on the back of her dress.

She felt him tugging away the sopping fabric. "Justin?"

"Won't leave you," he answered. He kissed the tip of her nose. "I love you. I came back to Montana for you. I stayed at that ranch, with Rowan and all his strange ways, waiting for you. I went through a rustler raid for you—" more tugging "—I went through a bank robbery for you, I even offered to give my ranch to Rowan for you."

"You didn't!" she squealed.

"Did," he confirmed. "And you think that now"—his hands were deftly peeling her dress down her sides. Where did the man learn how to do this?—"I'm going to taste you once and walk away?"

"Well . . ." she demurred.

"Forget it, Amberson," he said. He stepped back in triumph, wadded up her dress, and threw it on the ground.

He stood before her in all his naked splendor.

Excited now, she pulled her wet undershift over her head.

"Let me help you with these." He kneeled beside her, unrolling the last of her undergarments down to her ankles.

"Oh, Justin," she murmured, kicking them aside. "What if someone sees us?"

"No one around," he answered blithely. "And the baby's asleep." The next thing she knew, she was in his arms. And he was kissing her madly, hungrily, and she was kissing him back, all the pent-up love she had for him spilling over. "Oh, I love you so much," she whispered.

"Good," he grunted, and now he had her down on the ground, the grass cool on her back.

"You work fast, Justin," she complimented.

"When I have to," he agreed happily. His lips were on hers, his hands all over her as if he, too, had been holding back his desire for a long, long time.

"How ever did we manage to stay away from one another?" she purred.

"Your stubbornness," he explained before she could say any more.

She pushed at him, "It was not my stubbornness that kept us apart, Justin," she said firmly.

"Was," he said. How easily he had her down, flat on her back and him leaning over her. "Don't get stubborn with me now, Amberson." His green eyes pleaded with her. Even though he was much stronger than she, he was giving her a chance to say no, and she knew it.

"Love me," she whispered. "Please love me." She wrapped her arms around his neck and pulled him closer. He moved over her. "I couldn't bear for you to leave me now," she said softly, yielding to him.

When he entered her, she felt as if she was at last complete, whole and very, very loved.

"Ah, Justin." She sighed. "I do love you so."

He buried his face in her long hair at the same time as he buried himself in her body. She felt his strength and marveled that this man was hers.

They rocked together, and she felt the beautiful feeling coming on, hoping that it was like that for him too. Then suddenly, together, they exploded.

She gave a little cry and clutched him to her, wanting to prolong the moment . . . to prolong this time with him, these feelings, oh, Lord, if only, oh, forever and ever and ever. . . .

And then he was kissing her, slowly, gently, covering her face with kisses. "I love you, my Montana Angel."

She smiled and pulled his head down to her bosom, too exhausted and relaxed to say anything. She stretched, curling her toes, letting her happy sigh say it all for her.

REFERENCES

Bakken, Gordon Morris. "The Development of Law on the Rocky Mountain Frontier: Civil Law and Society, 1850-1912." *Contributions in Legal Studies,* #27, 1983.

Corpus Juris Secundum, 26A Deeds 179 to End. Brooklyn: The American Law Book Co., 1956.

Current, Richard Nelson. *Lincoln's Loyalists: Union Soldiers from the Confederacy.* Boston, MA: Northeastern University Press, 1992.

Folger Library General Readers' Shakespeare. New York: Washington Square Press, Inc., 1961.

Furdell, William J. and Elizabeth Lane Furdell. *Great Falls: A Pictorial History.* Norfolk, VA: The Donning Company/Publishers, 1984.

Hauptman, Laurence M. "Into the Abyss" in *Civil War Times Illustrated,* Vol. 35, No. 7 (February 1997): 46-59.

Madsen, Betty M. and Brigham D. *North to Montana! Jehus, Bullwhackers, and Mule Skinners on the Montana Trail.* Salt Lake City: University of Utah Press, 1980.

Malone, Michael P., Richard B. Roeder and William L. Lang. Montana: A History of Two Centuries, Revised edition. Seattle: University of Washington Press, 1991.

Martin, Cy. *Whiskey and Wild Women: An Amusing Account of the Saloons and Bawds of the Old West.* New York: Hart Publishing Co., Inc., 1974.

Silliman, Eugene Lee, Editor. *We Seized Our Rifles: Recollections of the Montana Frontier.* Missoula, MT: Mountain Press Publishing, 1982.

Thompson, Larry S. *Montana's Explorers: The Pioneer Naturalists 1805-1864.* Montana Geographic Series #9. Helena: Montana Magazine, Inc., 1985.

Captive Legacy

Theresa Scott

"Theresa Scott's captivating writing brings you to a wonderous time and shows you that love inself is timeless."
—*Affaire de Coeur*

Heading west to the Oregon Territory and an arranged marriage, Dorie Primfield never dreams that a virile stranger will kidnap her and claim her as his wife. Part Indian, part white, Dorie's abductor is everything she's ever desired in a man, yet she isn't about to submit to his white-hot passion without a fight. Then by a twist of fate, she has her captor naked and at gunpoint, and she finds herself torn between escaping into the wilderness—and turning a captive legacy into endless love.

_3880-3 $5.99 US/$7.99 CAN

Hunters of the Ice Age
Theresa Scott
Broken Promise

BESTSELLING AUTHOR OF *DARK RENEGADE*

Among the tribes warring at the dawn of time, the Jaguars are the mightiest, and the hunter called Falcon is feared like no other. Once headman of his clan, he has suffered a great loss that turns him against man and the Great Spirit. But in a world both deadly and treacherous, a mere woman will teach Falcon that he cannot live by brute strength alone.

Her people destroyed, her promised husband enslaved, Star finds herself at Falcon's mercy. And even though she is separated from everything she loves, the tall, proud Badger woman will not give up hope. With courage and cunning, the beautiful maiden will survive in a rugged new land, win the heart of her captor, and make a glorious future from the shell of a broken promise.

_3723-8 $4.99 US/$5.99 CAN

BRIDE OF DESIRE

THERESA SCOTT

"More than an Indian romance, more than a Viking tale, *Bride Of Desire* is a unique combination of both. Enjoyable and satisfying!"

—*Romantic Times*

To beautiful, ebony-haired Winsome, the tall blond stranger who has taken her captive seems an entirely different breed of male from the men of her tribe. Though Brand treats her gently, his ways are nothing like the customs of her people. She has been taught that a man and a maiden may not join together until elaborate courting rituals are performed, but when Brand crushes her against his hard-muscled body, it is only too clear that he has no intention of waiting for anything. Weak with wanting, Winsome longs to surrender, but she will insist on a wedding ceremony first. When Brand finally claims her innocence, she will be the bride of his heart, as well as a bride of desire.

_3610-X $4.99 US/$5.99 CAN

Bestselling Author Of *Yesterday's Dawn*

Talon has stalked the great beasts of the plains, but he has never faced prey more elusive than the woman he has stolen from his enemies. In her pale eyes, he beholds a challenge that will test beyond all endurance strengths he has thought indomitable.

As courageous as any man, yet as delicate as a tundra flower, Summer has longed for Talon's embrace; now, she will fight to the death before submitting to him. A terrible betrayal has turned Talon against her—only a bond stronger than love itself can subdue the captor and make him surrender to Summer's sweet, gentle fury.

_51952-6 $4.99 US/$5.99 CAN

DESPERADO
SANDRA HILL

Major Helen Prescott has always played by the rules. That's why Rafe Santiago nicknamed her "Prissy" at the military academy years before. Rafe's teasing made her life miserable back then, and with his irresistible good looks, he is the man responsible for her one momentary lapse in self control. When a routine skydive goes awry, the two parachute straight into the 1850 California Gold Rush. Mistaken for a notorious bandit and his infamously sensuous mistress, they find themselves on the wrong side of the law. In a time and place where rules have no meaning, Helen finds Rafe's hard, bronzed body strangely comforting, and his piercing blue eyes leave her all too willing to share his bedroll. Suddenly, his teasing remarks make her feel all woman, and she is ready to throw caution to the wind if she can spend every night in the arms of her very own desperado.

_52182-2 $5.99 US/$6.99 CAN